STILL
HERE

By
Paul Bortolazzo

STILL HERE

Still Here by Paul Bortolazzo
Published by Insight Publishing Group
8801 S. Yale, Suite 410
Tulsa, OK 74137
918-493-1718

All scripture quotations are taken from the New King James Version of the Bible (NKJV), copyright © 1992 by Thomas Nelson, Inc. Used by permission.

Cover design by Jeffrey Mobley

ISBN 1-930027-31-1
Library of Congress catalog card number: 00-109327

Printed in the United States of America

DEDICATION

This novel is dedicated to the overcomers who will be martyred for their testimony of Jesus Christ during the great tribulation. Jesus said, "As many as I love, I rebuke and chasten. Therefore be zealous and repent. . . . To him who overcomes I will grant to sit with Me on My throne, as I also overcame and sat down with My Father on His throne" (Revelation 3:19, 21).

ACKNOWLEDGMENTS

The day the Holy Spirit encouraged me to write *Still Here* as a warning to the body of Christ, I never dreamed of the spiritual warfare my wife Jenny and I would encounter. The reason why the enemy of our souls does not want the truth concerning the last days to be proclaimed is simple. What Christians spiritually believe concerning the events that will precede our Lord's return could affect their eternal destiny. The extent that believers are spiritually prepared for the great tribulation will determine whether they overcome the persecution of the antichrist.

Jesus warned those being persecuted during the great tribulation, "Watch therefore and pray always that you may be counted worthy to escape all these things that will come to pass and to stand before the Son of Man." What things? Our Lord clearly told us. He commanded us to watch for the events that will precede the gathering of his elect. Our Lord is crying out to believers living in the last days to understand his Word concerning the future worldwide persecution of the body of Christ!

Jenny and I are indebted to so many friends and family members who have helped make this biblical drama a reality. The spiritual truths highlighted in this novel reach far beyond the events that will warn us of our Lord's return. The reader will be challenged to believe in the only Savior who can usher a soul into eternal glory!

My most sincere praise goes to the Father, the Son, and the Holy Spirit, the only true God of the universe.

To my Father, words cannot express Your love for Your creation. Praise You Father, for supernaturally revealing Yourself to those who seek after Your Truth.

To my Jesus, may the words of this novel serve as a testimony of a loving God who has promised to be with us till the end of the age (harvest). Through all the mirrors and smoke of the ruler of this world, may the body of Christ heed the warnings of You, the King of kings and Lord of lords! Let us obey Your Word and become watchmen to a dying world!

To the Holy Spirit, I will always cherish the times when Your still small voice became like a beacon of light. May Your anointing rest upon readers who heed Your voice, no matter what the consequences.

TABLE OF CONTENTS

Prologue

He knew he had only a short time left to find as many as possible. But how could he be sure which ones were genuine? One mistake would result in his death, which really didn't bother him at all. What did bother him was that it would destroy any chance he might have to reach others that still could be saved.

His first attempt was filled with needless risks. Not because he was careless, but simply because the urgency of his message had temporarily blinded him from the possible dangers. That experience had taught him to be patient in his approach. Sometimes it was easy, like the two teenagers he found last month at Lakeview High School. But those were the exception rather than the rule. He knew that he couldn't reach many, but his heart wouldn't let him quit. There was no room inside of him anymore for self-pity. He had already run the gamut: anger, resignation, acceptance. And though he had accepted his own destiny, he knew he had to reach as many as possible before it was too late. They must not be allowed to share his fate.

Throughout the world, most took refuge from the firestorms and hail that had just swept the earth. The worst appeared to be over for now. Amidst the burned trees and grass, he could see many coming out of their hiding places. Most would try to resume their lives. A growing number would be captured and killed.

His cover enabled him to maintain a fairly normal lifestyle. Pretending to be one of them gave him the freedom of movement that he needed to survive. Even so, he still needed to be extremely careful. Each time a lead was false, his risk factor increased. And lately, he had a feeling he was being watched.

The past few days he had been stopped several times and required to show his ID. He grimaced at the irony. The very thing that condemned him made it possible for him to survive. As he neared his destination, a voice called to him from an alleyway. Pulling his hat low to at least partially conceal his face, he strained to see into the shadows as he called out cautiously, "Hello? Can I help you?"

"Maybe. You got any idea where a guy can hide from them?"

He felt the hairs on the back of his neck begin to rise. Still, if there was even a small chance that the plea was legitimate, he knew he had no choice. He stepped closer to the alley and spoke softly. "Why? Are you hiding from them?"

"Look, can you help me or not?"

As he moved a step closer, the voice warned, "That's close enough. Any closer and I'll have to hurt you."

His suspicions confirmed, he quickly backed away.

"I'm afraid I can't help you."

Footsteps from the alley moved towards him as he turned and ran.

The stranger in the alley yelled, "Wait, I need your help!"

If they recognized him, he knew his chances for escape would be slim. Turning the corner, he broke into a frantic sprint and looked for any place that might offer a decent hiding place. A shout from behind was answered from his right. The voices receded slightly, only to pick up again when his trail was found. Turning left at the next corner, he cut across the street and raced past darkened houses toward a patch of woods that had escaped the fires almost untouched. He could hear his pursuers gaining on him. Reaching the woods, he slipped under some brush and desperately sought cover.

"Lord," he prayed silently, "I know what I am and what I've done. I'm placing myself in your hands."

As the voices approached his hiding place, he pressed even harder into the ground and tried to make himself as small as possible. Beams of light from flashlights shot through the brush and treetops.

"Any sign of him?"

"Nah. Just trees and bushes."

The voices became more and more muffled as the pursuers returned to their squad car.

"Any idea who he was?"

"No, I didn't get a good enough look at him. I kind of thought he knew something about the disappearance of those two kids at the high school last month."

"If he did, Harvey won't be happy that we missed him."

"I know, I know. I can hear his griping right now."

He lay quietly, until the hooting of an owl broke the unnatural silence. As he made his way back to the main road, he could only reflect back on the turmoil of the past month and the dark turn his life had taken.

CHAPTER 1

THE FIRST SEAL:
THE RIDER ON A WHITE HORSE

And I looked, and behold, a white horse.
He who sat on it had a bow; and a crown was given to him,
and he went out conquering and to conquer.
Revelation 6:2

It was close to midnight when Pastor Mark Bishop fell to his knees in prayer behind his cherry wood desk. He had heard from the Lord many times before in his cramped study at home. But tonight was different. The burden that pressed upon him had an urgency, like the beginning of birth pangs before the delivery of a baby.

"Oh, Lord, what are you trying to tell me?" Mark whispered out loud.

As he continued to pray, the pastor saw a vision in his mind of many faces in a valley of decision. The subtle outline of Israel's border became very clear. Surrounding the Jewish nation were seven neighboring countries: Syria, Jordan, Iraq, Iran, Sudan, Egypt, and Libya. Within the city of Jerusalem, Mark could see three leaders, representing the northern countries of Germany, Russia, and the Ukraine.[1] The leaders from each of the ten countries appeared to be meeting with the newly elected Prime Minister of Israel, Eli Rosen.

The leader from Germany had a presence that was so peaceful and reassuring. Off to his left stood a magnificent white horse. Mark shuddered as the German leader was suddenly transformed into an ugly scarlet beast that had seven heads and ten horns. The rider of the beast was a woman who had the appearance of an evil harlot. The mysterious harlot appeared to be drunk with the blood of the martyrs of Jesus![2]

"Dear Lord, the images I see in this vision come from the book of Revelation. Is this a warning of events that will take place in my future?" pleaded Mark.

The vision the young pastor from Bethany, Alabama, had just received was a message for the entire body of Christ. It was all part of God's plan. Within twenty-four hours a heavenly event would take place that would trigger a sequence of events, which would influence the lives of every man, woman, and child on earth!

Mark knew in his heart that what he had just seen was no ordinary vision. Talking out loud, he asked, "What does it all mean?"

He continued to pray into the early morning hours, seeking the interpretation of the faces in the valley of decision, the ten nations' meeting with Israel's Prime Minister, and the identity of the ugly scarlet beast and it's rider.

God the Father sat upon His heavenly throne with a scroll in His right hand.[3] The scroll was sealed with seven seals, each looking as if they were made out of red-hot gold. It was time! A warrior angel appeared from above the throne and cried out, "Who is worthy to open the scroll and loose its seals?"[4]

In the midst of the heavenly host stood the Lamb of God, looking as if He had been slain. His head and hair were like wool, as white as snow, and His eyes were like a flame of fire; His feet were like fine brass, as if refined in a furnace, and His voice was as the sound of many waters.[5] He stepped forward and received the sealed scroll from the right hand of the Father. The angels and the elders looked on as the Lamb of God broke the first seal.

Immediately, a rider on a magnificent white horse appeared. He who sat on it had a bow, and a crown was given to him.[6]

The angels instinctively stepped back from the evil exuding from the mysterious rider.

"Woe to those who live on the earth," announced a warrior angel. "The lie of the antichrist is coming, and who will have the courage to stand for the truth?"

Mark had not eaten in the three days, not since receiving the vision from the Lord late Monday night. At times he would fervently groan, waiting upon the Holy Spirit to reveal to him the meaning of the vision. The picture of ten nations surrounding Israel in a giant circle was still fresh in his mind. It appeared as though Israel was signing a peace treaty with its Arab neighbors. Praying in the Spirit and waiting for an answer, the young pastor lay prostrate across the dark blue carpet in his church study. It was a little after ten o'clock in the evening when the Holy Spirit finally spoke.

"Listen carefully, my child, for here is the meaning of your vision. The faces in the valley of decision represent billions of people who will be forced to choose whom they will follow. The ten horns represent ten nations who will give their power to the beast that comes from the bottomless pit.[7] This beast will deceive the Jewish people and eventually the entire world!"

The pastor did not move or utter one word. The words from the Holy Spirit were not audible but were directed to Mark's spirit. He knew that this was a divine visitation from God.

"The scarlet beast in your vision is the disguised leader of Germany, Wolfgang Hendrick. The world will eventually call him its god, but to those who remain faithful to Jesus, he will be called the antichrist."

Pastor Mark turned pale as a godly fear gripped his heart. "Holy Spirit, how is this possible?" he asked. "Has the antichrist actually appeared on the world scene?"

Jews and Arabs poured out into the streets of Jerusalem as Yom Kipper, The Day of Atonement, came to an end. CNN World News was on the scene, with exclusive coverage of this historic event.

"Good evening everyone, this is CNN's Natalie Roberts, reporting live from downtown Jerusalem. Just moments ago, Israel's Prime Minister Eli Rosen officially signed the Jerusalem Peace Accord with the Middle East Federation, which represents the neighboring countries of Syria, Jordan, Iraq, Iran, Sudan, Egypt, and Libya. As a sign of support, a northern three-nation coalition of Germany, Russia, and the Ukraine led by Wolfgang Hendrick has also agreed to be part of the Jerusalem Peace Accord. This seven-year treaty is an answer to the prayers of Jews and Arabs alike!" proclaimed the excited reporter.

Germany's own Wolfgang Hendrick stood with a smiling Eli Rosen while photographers positioned themselves for a picture of an event the world thought would never happen. The presidents of Russia and the Ukraine joined the leaders of the seven Arab countries in applauding the diplomacy of the German diplomat. This one man had stepped out of obscurity to skillfully put an end to the frequent guerrilla attacks between Jews and Arabs. In a decisive move that ended the killing, Wolfgang Hendrick convinced Israel's

Arab neighbors to allow the construction of the third Jewish temple on Mount Moriah.

In exchange for peace, Israel agreed to return the entire West Bank to the Palestinian people as their rightful homeland. To the utter dismay of many Jews, an eastern portion of Jerusalem was set aside for an official Palestinian capital. Over one million refugees could now safely return to their own Palestinian state. It was a miracle. Peace had finally come to the Middle East!

"God has brought the peace of Jehovah back to the land of Abraham, Isaac, and Jacob on Yom Kipper, our most holy day," the Prime Minister of Israel gratefully announced. "He has sent Wolfgang Hendrick to our people to stop the needless killing. Let us begin to rebuild our temple so that this time next year our high priest may once again offer atonement for our sins."

Many celebrations were underway throughout Israel, but none were as heartfelt as the ones at the military installations.

At one treaty-signing party, a jubilant Israeli soldier proclaimed, "This way we can finally live together in peace. Think of it, a covenant between peoples and nations who have fought for over two thousand years!"

Another soldier wondered out loud, "But why do you suppose it has taken so many years to come to such a simple yet compelling peace treaty?"

Indeed, this day was historic! It would have an impact throughout two worlds, the physical and the spiritual. Events were unfolding that would shake the foundation of reality for both Christian and non-Christian alike!

The demon spirits clawed and spit at each other, jockeying for a better view of the one who would soon be their leader. Wolfgang Hendrick had just asked Prime Minister Eli Rosen to join him in order to address the United Nations in a worldwide TV broadcast.

"Peace comes with a price you know," hissed the spirit of death.

The Jerusalem Peace Accord would bring a short-lived peace, which would eventually be called a covenant of death! In the very near future a massive gentile army would surround Jerusalem, and two-thirds of the Jewish people would be killed.[8] Another holocaust would soon take place, all because the world failed to recognize the opening of the first seal and the rider on a white horse!

✳

While Pastor Mark Bishop prayed in his study near the back of his house, he could hear his two daughters laughing as they played outside. Julie, Mark's wife, was in the kitchen, preparing Hope and Lindsey's favorite Saturday morning breakfast. Dressed in her favorite light-blue t-shirt, blue jeans, and white Reeboks, Julie had her brown hair pulled back. Curls fell along her face and framed her sparkling blue eyes and always-ready smile.

Back in his study, Mark continued to pray over the Jerusalem Peace Accord, a peace treaty that promised to end the Arab Jihad (Holy War) in the Middle East.

"But, Lord, look at how many peace treaties have been signed in the past twenty years." said Mark.

Nevertheless, the vision he received on Monday night became a reality on Saturday morning. Sensing there had to be more to the meaning of the vision, Mark decided to return to prayer and seek for further understanding. It wouldn't take long. The pastor froze as the words of the Holy Spirit came to him with power and conviction.

"Beware! The first seal of the heavenly scroll has been opened, and the rider on the white horse has been loosed! His desire will be to make war against the saints and to overcome them. Jesus said, 'Take heed that no one deceives you. For many will come in My name . . . and will deceive many.' This day I have called you to be a watchman to the body of Christ. You must speak forth the truth concerning the events that will precede the coming of the Lord."

Mark knew in his heart that the Holy Spirit had given him the most powerful word of prophecy any minister of the Gospel could ever receive— the sequence of events that precede the Second Coming of Christ! Even so, his doubts seemed so overwhelming.

"Lord, this can't be right. You're saying that the seven-year tribulation period has begun and that we, the body of Christ, are *still here!*"

As he continued to seek the Lord in prayer, the Spirit of God led Mark to Matthew 24:3-51, I Thessalonians 4:13-18, I Corinthians 15:50-54, and Revelation 7:9-17. In what seemed like minutes, which actually turned into hours, the young pastor continued to read and reread these passages on the coming of the Lord. Suddenly the sequence of events fell together like pieces of a puzzle. Sitting amidst his Bibles, concordances, and lexicons, which were spread throughout his office floor, he read Revelation 7:14.

"The catching away of the saints during the great tribulation!" a shocked Mark whispered. "It's so easy to see. How did I ever miss it?"

"No one believes that." hissed the spirit of doubt. "Everyone knows the followers are taken up before the tribulation period," the foul demon whispered in an attempt to gain a doorway into Mark's life.

"You had better take a break; you're confused," whispered the spirit of unbelief, who had just arrived. "Just think, if you teach this new teaching, your denomination, your pastor friends, even your own family won't believe you."

"Do you really want to risk your reputation over the timing of the rapture?" countered the spirit of doubt.

After Mark commanded doubt and unbelief to go in Jesus' name, a comforting peace rested upon him for over two hours. The road map of events preceding Christ's coming had always been there. It was the Spirit of God who had unlocked the prophetic understanding of Jesus' soon return!

"But how can I be sure?" asked Mark.

"There are other watchmen," the Holy Spirit spoke into Mark's spirit. "Before this month is over I will send you another watchman who will speak the truth concerning the future persecution of the body of Christ. His name will be Stephen, and he will need your prayers as well as your encouragement. Remember, my child, you will not be held responsible for those who reject the events that will soon occur. The divine appointments awaiting you will save thousands of believers as you faithfully proclaim the truth of the Lord's coming. Fear not what man can do to you, but honor the Lord Jesus Christ by obedience to His Word."

CHAPTER 2

WHAT IS THE SIGN OF YOUR COMING?

"Therefore if you will not watch, I will come upon you as a thief,
and you will not know what hour I will come upon you."
Revelation 3:3

Pastor Mark had less than twenty-four hours to spiritually prepare himself to share with his congregation what the Holy Spirit had just revealed. He knew deep within his spirit the importance of Sunday's morning message.

Nevertheless, this was not the time to be intimidated by the fear of man, reflected Mark.

He had always steered clear of teaching on the rapture of the saints because Jesus had said that no one knows the day or the hour.[1] There was so much confusion, even among well-known prophecy teachers, that the young pastor had wondered why he should dwell on it.

Even so, Mark was regretting his excuses for not teaching on the subject of the end times. His own denomination had always held to a pre-tribulation rapture position. This meant that Jesus would come for His saints before the final seven-year tribulation period began. Mark could still remember his Bible professor's excitement whenever he taught that Jesus could come at any moment, secretly delivering those who followed Him.

Yet in the past year, Mark had met several pastors at regional conferences who did not believe in a secret mystery rapture. They taught that the body of Christ would be delivered from the persecution of the antichrist during the great tribulation. A small number of these pastors bravely decided to openly teach that the antichrist and the great falling away of believers must first come before Christ's return for His saints. It wasn't long before they were forced to either resign their credentials or to stop teaching anything other than a pre-tribulation rapture. Reflecting back, Mark had to admit that his denomination's dogmatic stance on the timing of Christ's return had always bothered him. At first, as a young man entering the full-time ministry, the pre-tribulation position sounded pretty reasonable. But the more he studied, the more doubts he had of its truthfulness.

The responsibility of being a watchman was beginning to feel like a giant weight upon the young pastor's shoulders. He and his wife, Julie, both knew that only the Holy Spirit could prepare the saints for the coming worldwide persecution.

"Father God, I come before you to request that you open the ears of believers so they might hear your voice.[2] Let them search your Word and see the spiritual battle we will all soon face." Bowing his head, Mark continued, "Give my family a passion for you, Lord. Empower us to speak forth your Word under the anointing of the Holy Spirit."

The choir members were enjoying coffee and donuts when Pastor Mark, Julie, and their two daughters arrived for church on Sunday morning. Lindy and Allie Hart, sisters in their early twenties, immediately smiled and greeted Hope and Lindsey. Though several friends surrounded the pastor, no one except Julie could sense the intense struggle that was raging inside his spirit. He and Julie had just discussed the importance of this morning's message. He would warn the body of Christ of the perilous times that would soon break forth. This would be a Sunday morning sermon that would last only forty-five minutes but would forever change the life of the Mark Bishop family!

The young pastor stepped to the pulpit and scanned the audience, a body of believers he had known for only one year. There was a buzz of excitement in the air due to the recent news of Israel's peace treaty with its Arab neighbors. Those interested in Bible prophecy were secretly praying for their pastor to preach this morning on the rapid changes in the Middle East. After several worship songs and the reading of the weekly announcements, he greeted his congregation.

"Good morning, saints," said Mark, nervously unfolding his lecture notes. "I come before you this morning to proclaim a message of hope concerning our future. This morning's sermon is entitled, 'Still Here: The Sequence of Events That Precede the Rapture.' Let's turn to Matthew 24:3.

"On the Tuesday before His crucifixion, our Lord gathered together His disciples on the Mount of Olives. Only a few days earlier while on their way to Jerusalem, Jesus had explained to His disciples His soon coming death, burial, and resurrection. Jesus had prophesied, 'Behold, we are going up to Jerusalem, and the Son of Man will be betrayed to the chief priests and to the scribes. They will condemn Him to death and deliver Him to the Gentiles to mock and to scourge and to crucify. And the third day He will rise again."[3] The twelve disciples, the founding fathers of Christianity, then realized the Son of the living God would die and rise again. He would soon return to His Father in heaven. For some of the disciples, like Thomas, it was too hard to believe."

"Praise you, Jesus," proclaimed a senior saint in the front pew. "C'mon Pastor, let the Holy Ghost lead you."

"With the death of their Lord and Savior about to transpire right before their eyes, the disciples had one question burning within their hearts: Lord, when will you come again? So they asked Jesus, 'What will be the sign of Your coming and of the end of the age?'[4]

"Church, the disciples were not so much asking for an exact date of when Jesus would return but how believers would recognize His coming before it happens. In Matthew 24, Jesus answered both questions by outlining the events that will transpire right before He gathers His elect."

A teenager in the youth section leaned over and whispered to her friend, "That sounds pretty simple to me."

"Our Lord Jesus began His reply to the disciples' question by warning believers who will be alive when He returns, 'Take heed that no one deceives you.'[5] Friends, I stand before you today as a watchman with a warning for the body of Christ.[6] In Matthew 24:4-29, our Jesus gave us a clear outline of six events that will alert Christians that His coming is right at the door. I believe the Holy Spirit desires to speak to us this morning about a final seven-year period, which most Bible teachers call the tribulation period. Now let me ask you, how many of you have studied the end-time events that will precede Christ's coming?"

After pausing to look for upraised hands, the pastor's heart sank with fear. With over two hundred members present, only a few knew what he was talking about.

He wondered how this could be. Some of the members of Bethany Assembly had known Jesus as their Lord and Savior for over forty years. The young pastor wondered how he could make them understand that the seven-year tribulation period began with yesterday's signing of the Jerusalem Peace Accord.

"Before I continue my message this morning, I would like to share a pearl that happened to me this past Monday night. When I say pearl, what I really mean is a special moment I experienced with the Spirit of God, a divine visitation that is very precious to me and my family."

Several members who brought guests looked a little uneasy as they glanced over in their friends' direction and smiled. Others, who didn't believe in the gifts of the Holy Spirit, prayed silently that their young pastor would not embarrass himself.

"You see, in the past I have shared some pretty wonderful pearls with friends who basically couldn't care less. Surely, we have all experienced the deep pain of opening ourselves up to friends, only to have our precious pearls trampled on as if they meant nothing."

"Something's not right," sensed a deacon who was seated to the pastor's left. Billy B. immediately alerted several intercessors to begin to pray.

"Oh Lord," he said, speaking softly under his breath, "give Pastor Mark the words that will inspire our church members to become overcomers for Jesus."

"My brothers and sisters in Christ, this past Monday night I received a powerful vision from God," the pastor freely admitted.

Everyone seemed to be listening, including some of the members seated in the back rows, which even shocked the ushers!

"In my vision, I saw a picture of the nation Israel surrounded by ten nations. There was a deep valley called the valley of decision, which was filled with many faces. As I watched, an ugly beast appeared with Israel's Prime Minister Eli Rosen. For the next three days I felt led to fast and pray for the interpretation of this vision. It wasn't until late Thursday night that I received my answer."

"He's doing it again, Henry," whispered a senior saint named Emmett. "Do you hear me, Henry? God's talking to him again!"

Pausing for a sip of water, the pastor couldn't help but notice the wide variety of responses. To his right was the youth, sitting on the edge of their seats. To his left sat the choir, who really only listened when the worship leader was talking. For some of the senior saints on the back pew, it was just another replay of the twilight zone. Emmett just sighed and shook his head in disgust at the young preacher's obvious emotionalism.

"As I said," repeated Mark, "the interpretation to my vision came late Thursday night with such conviction that I just knew it was from God."

The majority of the congregation did not look happy, to say the least. Mark had faced this spirit of intimidation before. He knew God had given him this appointed time to preach the truth. It was now or never!

In a moment of time, three past events concerning his fear of man flashed before Mark's mind. He had purposely compromised before in order to keep his job. The major financial givers of his last church had threatened to leave if he continued to teach that only those who live holy lives go to heaven. A few months later, the Holy Spirit began to move in power, resulting in healings and prophetic words that prompted several young adults to enter the full-time ministry. It was only a couple of weeks until the board of deacons expressed its opposition to such emotional antics and demanded a more organized church service. Several months later, after the Bishops arrived to pastor at Bethany Assembly, the worship leader refused to wait on the Holy Spirit's presence during the morning worship time and insisted that a strict set of worship songs be implemented!

In all three instances, the young pastor had surrendered to the spirit of control.

When Mark and Julie accepted their first pastorate in Hot Springs, Georgia, Satan knew the damage they could do to his kingdom. The spirits of lust, greed, and pride each stepped forward for the coveted assignment of destroying the Bishop family.

The devil knew better.

The devil already had thousands of pastors hooked on pornography through the Internet. To his delight, several of the most popular preachers on Christian TV had totally given themselves over to the spirit of greed. The devil was especially proud of a highly esteemed Bible teacher from Tulsa, Oklahoma, who had just recently lost his ministry after being corrupted by the spirit of pride. Seeing the heartache of the One in Heaven when one of His saints completely missed God's will for their lives was a feeling Satan thoroughly enjoyed.

Several demons had already begged for the privilege of attacking the Bishop family but to no avail. No, in this case, a specific demon would be hand picked by the prince of darkness himself! This evil spirit would oppose the moving of the Holy Spirit in church services, the intercession for lost souls, prayer for the baptism of the Holy Spirit, healing for those who were sick, and deliverance from demonic attacks.[7]

"Now imagine that," Satan proudly announced. "The followers will have a form of godliness, but they will deny its power."[8]

The prince of darkness did not have to utter another word. The spirit of control had already sensed the will of his master. Immediately, the filthy demon shot high into the sky with the overwhelming desire to control Mark Bishop, his family, and his church!

CHAPTER 3

THE COMING OF THE LAWLESS ONE

The coming of the lawless one is according to the working of Satan,
with all power, signs, and lying wonders.
II Thessalonians 2:9

"Pastor, Pastor, are you okay?" whispered Harriet Jones, a Sunday school teacher who was seated in the first row.

What could he do? He had a family to support. They were dependent upon him. Nervous whispers could be heard throughout the sanctuary while the slim pastor stood motionless with his head bowed behind the large wooden pulpit.

Gently, the Spirit of God spoke to Mark's spirit.

"The Lord is my helper; I will not fear. What can man do to me?"[1]

Slowly lifting his head, Mark boldly asked, "How many here today believe that Jesus Christ has a prophetic plan for the overthrow of Satan? That's right! In the very near future, our Jesus will come and defeat the devil and his angels and take back the spiritual and physical rule of our world!"[2]

The sporadic cheers throughout the crowd clearly revealed the spiritual divisions among the membership. Nevertheless, the boldness and courage that had been bottled up within Mark by the spirit of control was beginning to break forth.

"My dear friends, the interpretation of the vision I received from the Lord is very clear. The seven-year tribulation period began yesterday with the signing of the Jerusalem Peace Accord by Israel's Prime Minister Eli Rosen and Germany's Wolfgang Hendrick. In Revelation 13:1, John the apostle describes a beast, which has ten horns and seven heads. The Holy Spirit has shown me that this beast represents the antichrist! The ten horns of the beast represent the ten nations who signed yesterday's Jerusalem Peace Accord with the Prime Minister of Israel. The multitude of faces in the valley of decision represents billions of people who will be forced to decide who they will follow, our Lord Jesus Christ or the antichrist!"

"But, Pastor," interrupted an irritated Harriet Jones. "No one knows the identity of the antichrist!"

"Listen to me, friends," continued Mark, who refused to be distracted. "The Bible warns us of a final seven-year period that will begin when the
antichrist signs a peace treaty with Israel.[3] In the book of Revelation, we see
a large scroll that is sealed with seven seals.[4] Each seal highlights the end time
events involving the salvation of God's people. The prophecy written inside
the scroll contains the seven trumpets of God's wrath against the wicked."

"What is he talking about?" whispered one of the choir members to
her friend. "I've always been taught that the seals in the book of Revelation
are God's wrath."

"Now we all know the future seven-year tribulation period can't begin
until the first seal of this scroll is broken. When this seal is broken, the
antichrist, riding on a white horse, will come to earth. Are you listening,
saints?"

Looking out upon the congregation he so dearly loved, Mark dreaded the reaction to his next statement.

"In my vision, the rider on the white horse was none other than
Wolfgang Hendrick of Germany!"

The youth, consisting of about thirty kids, erupted out of their
chairs. For the young people, the cheers were electrifying, but for most of the
members, it was downright embarrassing.

A smiling youth leader named Whitney whispered to her close friend
Diana, "Isn't this awesome?"

"You bet!" replied an excited Diana, who was already taking notes.

Amidst the immediate shock of those seated in the back rows, Head
Deacon Dwayne Pressley shook his head in anger over such sensationalism.

Interrupting again, Sister Jones said, "But, Pastor Bishop, I don't quite
understand what you are trying to teach us this morning," as she discretely
turned around to see if anybody was listening. "Are you saying that the
antichrist has come and that the tribulation period has begun? Well, we all
know how impossible that is!" scoffed the skeptical Sunday school teacher.
"The rapture must come before the antichrist can appear. Everyone believes
that!"

"The answer to your question, Harriet, is really quite simple," replied
a respectful Mark. "Wolfgang Hendrick, the antichrist, has come to fulfill his
mission! Yesterday, he and his Middle East Federation signed a seven-year
peace treaty with Israel, and we are *still here!*"

An eerie silence suddenly captured the entire congregation.

"They won't believe you!" hissed the spirit of lying, who had just arrived through the back wall of the sanctuary.

"The Bible predicts that the man of sin will sign a seven-year covenant with Israel, and in the middle of it, he will break it. He will sever this peace treaty by attacking Jerusalem with his ten-nation coalition and by capturing the rebuilt Jewish Temple!"[5]

"But, Pastor, there is no Jewish temple on the Temple Mount at this time," challenged one of the deacons.

"There will be," declared the young pastor, "all in God's timing."

"Let's be realistic, Pastor," interrupted a retired minister. "Look at how many times preachers in the past have predicted the coming of the antichrist."

"Actually, in II Thessalonians 2:3-4," replied Mark, "the apostle Paul warns believers who will actually see this man of sin. His true identity won't be revealed until the very moment he steps into the rebuilt Jewish temple and proclaims himself to be god!"

The tense pastor, with perspiration dripping from his forehead, sensed the unbelief of his members. He knew he would eventually have to allow for more questions and answers.

While he paused to pray, the Holy Spirit spoke the word *sequence* into his spirit.

"I know that for some of you it is very shocking to hear the revelation that we've just entered the seven-year tribulation period. I'm asking you not to tune me out. The most critical truth the Holy Spirit revealed to me this past week involves the six events that will precede our Lord's coming. These six events of Matthew 24, which take place during the tribulation period, are identical to the six seals in chapter 6 of Revelation![6] Jesus exhorted the elect to watch for these events, which will be warning signs of His soon return.[7] Are there any questions?"

"Pastor Mark, I have a request," responded Allie Hart. "If there is still enough time, could you give us a rundown of the events that will come before the Lord delivers His saints?"

"Sure can, Allie," replied a grateful Mark. "When the first seal is opened, the antichrist will come with a ten-nation coalition and sign a seven-year peace treaty with Israel. The peace treaty between Israel and its Arab neighbors will be the initial warning to the body of Christ that the tribulation period has begun. When the second seal is opened, a red horse will attack, and wars will break out all over our world.[8] Following the wars will be the opening of the third seal, the coming of the black horse of famine.[9] The deadly result of this seal will be worldwide famines. Jesus called these first three seals the beginning of sorrows."

"Aren't these judgments for those who were left behind after the rapture?" whispered one choir member to another.

"When the fourth seal is opened, the great tribulation of Christians will begin. After proclaiming himself to be god, the antichrist will persecute all those who follow Jesus. He will do this by introducing the mark of the beast to the world."[10]

"That's a new one to me," whispered one of the Sunday school teachers seated in the third row.

Waves of disapproval could be seen on faces throughout the congregation as soon as the pastor mentioned *the mark of the beast.*

"The martyrdom of believers worldwide will begin at the opening of the fifth seal." Pausing, Mark asked, "Now, why the martyrdom of those who follow Christ?"

The spirit of fear, positioning itself upon the back pew, began to snicker at those who looked hopelessly paralyzed.

After an awkward moment of silence, it became obvious that no one was willing to reply.

The pastor answered his own question by saying, "I believe the martyrs of the fifth seal will be killed because they will refuse to worship the antichrist or to take his mark, which will be introduced during the fourth seal!"

"Hey, Dwayne," whispered one of the visitors to the head deacon, "Looks to me like your pastor doesn't believe that Jesus will come for His bride before the tribulation period."

"Following the martyrdom of believers will be the sixth seal, cosmic disturbances," continued Mark. "Our Lord made it very clear that the whole universe will become dark after the sun turns black, the moon turns red, and the stars refuse to shine. When this occurs, lightening flashing from the east to west will herald our Lord's coming in the clouds for His saints! In a twinkling of an eye, with the sounding of the trumpet of God, His angels will gather the elect to heaven! After the body of Christ has been taken, the seventh seal of the large scroll will be broken, and God's wrath will be poured out on those left behind!"[11]

Seated near the back of the sanctuary were two retired missionaries.

"What is he talking about?"

"I don't know. He's lost me."

"Listen saints, let's be alert! Jesus warned those living in the last days not to be deceived. We have relentlessly been taught that Jesus can come at any moment. We've been led to believe a lie that the body of Christ will be raptured before the persecution of the antichrist!"

Several leaders of the youth group could sense the spiritual warfare raging and were already interceding for their pastor.

"I believe our Jesus, in Matthew 24, addressed Christians who will face the antichrist's persecution during the tribulation period. I challenge every believer who can hear my voice this morning: The tribulation period has begun! According to God's perfect will, we will be the body of believers that will oppose the evil lies of the antichrist!"[12]

The members' reaction to Mark's startling new revelation completely engulfed the sanctuary. Some of the parents could be seen covering the ears of their children so that such speculative teaching would not frighten their young ones. The older saints sat with their arms folded across their chests, sporting an attitude much like the Pharisees in Jesus' day. They thought of themselves as more mature, certainly more versed in the Bible than their inexperienced pastor.

"Listen up!" pleaded Mark, while trying to regain everyone's attention. "The scriptures warn us that the antichrist will soon introduce a one-world financial system. All people in the world will be required to take the mark of the beast on their hand or forehead. Absolutely no one will be able to buy or sell anything with a bar-code without first registering for this mark.[13] In order for us to obey God's commandments and remain faithful to our Jesus, we must become overcomers," insisted the watchman, who refused to compromise.

"But, Pastor, as born again believers, we are already overcomers, aren't we?" asked Frank, a well respected deacon and close friend of the Bishop family.

"Frank, the Apostle Paul warned believers living in the latter days that the coming of the lawless one will be according to the working of Satan with all power, signs, and lying wonders.[14] My brother, we need to pray for spiritual discernment to recognize Satan's deception so that we can remain faithful when the persecution of the antichrist begins," replied a solemn Mark.[15]

Suddenly, a freshman from Lakeview High named Drew Henley jumped to his feet and asked, "So, Pastor, what is the sign of Christ's coming and the sign of the end of the age?"

His twin brother, Ned, immediately countered with, "Pastor, is the great tribulation of Christians the wrath of Satan or the wrath of God?"

Before the pastor had a chance to answer, a choir member seated to his right stood to her feet and asked, "Is the coming of the Son of Man in Matthew 24:30-31 really the rapture of the saints?"

The excitement over this end-time message was extremely infectious for the youth, but for the rest of the congregation, it was very intimidating.

Head Deacon Dwayne Pressley quickly stood to his feet near the back of the sanctuary and with a loud voice announced, "Please, Church, the pastor cannot possibly answer all your questions this morning. So everybody take a piece of paper, write down your questions, and I will gather . . ."

"Excuse me, Dwayne," interrupted the pastor, who immediately discerned the spirit of control. "I'm not quite finished, so if you could, please take a seat."

For a very brief moment, the pastor realized that if he allowed the spirit of control to manipulate him through the leadership at Bethany Assembly, he would never be able to fulfill his calling as a watchman.

"Obviously, we all have lots of questions concerning the seven-year tribulation period we have just entered. With this in mind, I would like to announce that I have been led by the Holy Spirit to focus on four major areas of teaching for the next year. We all need to be trained in intercession, end-time evangelism, spiritual warfare, and God's prophetic timetable of events!"

"But, Pastor," asked a concerned mother of three. "Isn't it a little dangerous to overact like this, especially over a so-called vision from God?"

"That is a very critical question," replied Mark. "The answer will become very clear when we begin to see the events of Matthew 24 transpire right before our eyes. Church, I'm not talking about guesswork or blind faith. In Matthew 24:15, Jesus clearly predicted that the abomination of desolation, the antichrist, will come before the gathering of the elect![16] To be perfectly honest, every one of us will face his persecution! The serious question we must all ask ourselves is how prepared will we be when the antichrist's evil plan is forced upon this world."

"Is this some sort of playacting skit?" mocked a deacon's wife to her husband.

"To be overcomers, we must obey God's Word and be led by His Holy Spirit. Jesus has promised us that He will be with us until the harvest of the wheat from the tares," encouraged Mark. "Let us pray."

Then the service was over, and the demons of control, fear, and compromise immediately went to work on the followers to whom they had been assigned. God's truth had been proclaimed, and the spirits of darkness would now attempt to deceive and confuse. While making his way to the back of the sanctuary to greet those who were leaving, Pastor Mark was totally engulfed with parishioners.

Julie was already praying when their eyes met. She had been there in the past, when the spirit of control had completely overwhelmed her husband. The hurt and discouragement of not standing for the truth had affected the man she loved in a devastating manner. When they were first married, Mark loved God and was led by the Holy Spirit. Taking a stand for what was right was something he had always enjoyed. It was different now. After four years of full-time ministry, the constant battles had caused him to grow weary. The prayers for revival and holiness had been replaced by prayers for unity and tolerance.

As Mark reached out and took Julie's hand, she could see that the Holy Spirit had performed a supernatural miracle. The spark of God was back in his eyes; the fear of man was gone. Tears flowed down her cheeks as they embraced.

CHAPTER 4

MARK'S CONFRONTATION

For do I now persuade men, or God? Or do I seek to please men?
For if I still pleased men, I would not be a bondservant of Christ.
Galatians 1:10

While the pastor finished greeting members in the foyer, the four deacons were meeting in the Activity's Center for their monthly board meeting. Some looked confused and really didn't have a clue which direction their meeting would take. Frank Donnelly, a lawyer and a deacon for over ten years, was the first to speak.

"I would like to say how proud I am of our pastor for taking such a courageous stand on what the Holy Spirit has laid on his heart. This is the type of preaching that will put the fire of evangelism and intercessory prayer back in our church." As the excited deacon took a seat, it was obvious that he was totally unprepared for what was coming next.

Immediately, Dwayne Pressley shot an icy stare toward Frank and asked, "But is it biblical? We need to stick to the Holy Scriptures, not to some vision supposedly coming from God. To be perfectly honest, I feel we jumped the gun in voting Mark in as our pastor last year. You can only allow these spiritual gifts to go so far, and then you begin to turn people off!"

Dwayne Pressley was an overbearing man in his mid fifties, married with two daughters. The short, slightly graying CEO of his own consulting firm, trusted no one, especially not others in leadership.

The spirit of control, hovering right above Dwayne, hoped to tighten its grip before the pastor had a chance to explain the meaning of his sermon.

"Dwayne's right," replied Kevin, the youngest member of the board of deacons.

Kevin Collins, in his early thirties, was an officer in the US Air Force who had just recently been married. It was just over three months ago that he was elected to the board. As a relatively young leader, Kevin always went by the book. Most of the time he did not see eye to eye with the pastor, especially on spiritual issues.

"In my opinion, Pastor Bishop took a dangerous step of faith by announcing that the Holy Spirit told him the antichrist has come," pressured Kevin, daring anyone to disagree.

Just as the officer was finishing his exhortation, Pastor Mark moved through the double swinging doors that led from the sanctuary to the Activity Center. He took a seat at the head of the long kitchen table with two deacons seated on each side.

Immediately, each board member, pleading silently for some sort of justification for what had just taken place, turned toward the young pastor.

Ever since receiving the interpretation of the vision on Thursday night, Mark and Julie had fervently prayed for this very moment. The pastor knew the strengths and weaknesses of each deacon. Some had been on the board for many years, while others seemed uncomfortable in their new role of leadership. The real issue before the deacons was not one of experience or intelligence, but whether these men of God would have the spiritual ears to hear what the Holy Spirit was saying to the body of Christ. What was need-ed was spiritual discernment, a gift from God that comes through prayerful intercession.

While Mark studied their different expressions, he could discern that at least two of the four deacons sitting before him did not even believe that the Holy Spirit could still speak to believers, especially not in a vision like the one he'd just described.

"I'm afraid I've got some bad news for you, Pastor," smirked Dwayne, attempting to sow seeds of doubt and establish his control. "Quite frankly, your interpretation of this vision from God has a lot of people pretty shook up. I'd like to say that I'm very concerned about what this sermon will do to our youth group. Last month when our youth pastors, Lance and Lee, were out of town to visit Lee's family, I was able to show the pre-tribulation rap-ture film to our youth. After reviewing this excellent movie on the end times, I believe a lot of the questions our kids had were answered. Quite frankly, Pastor, your new interpretation concerning the timing of Christ's return will only bring confusion to their young minds," threatened the angry deacon. "Billy B., you teach Sunday school to our young adults. What do you think?"

Billy B., a quiet man who drove a heavy-duty rig for a living, was not normally the kind of person who would interrupt or dogmatically push his opinions on anyone. Recently, the single, heavy-set trucker had just finished teaching a Bible class on the book of Revelation to the college and career group. As a young boy, he attended Bethany Baptist Fellowship. He was taught that the most literal interpretation of Christ's gathering of the saints was a pre-tribulation rapture. But the more questions the young adults at Bethany Assembly asked, the more doubts Billy B. had of a secret rapture occurring before the tribulation period. During the class, the Holy Spirit had continually impressed upon the trucker a sequence of events that must come before Christ returns.

With all eyes upon him, Billy B. stood up and calmly cleared his throat.

"I believe our young people will be okay if the truth of God's Word is taught and if the Holy Spirit bears witness to it. I must say that after teaching the book of Revelation I have some very serious doubts about a pre-tribulation rapture. What I mean is that we are supposed to be looking for the blessed hope and glorious appearing of our great God and Savior, Jesus Christ.[1]

"Yeah, so what's your point?" asked an anxious Dwayne.

"Well, that would be pretty hard to do if the Word of God didn't tell us what to look for, don't you think?"

"But . . ."

"I mean, didn't Jesus warn believers to watch for the events that would take place right before His coming? But instead of understanding the events that warn us of His return, most believers just say no one knows, because of all the fussing and arguing."

Immediately, a heated dispute spilled out between Kevin Collins and Frank Donnelly.

"What we really need is a Bible study on how the signs of Matthew 24 warn the body of Christ of our Lord's return for His saints! We need a study in which we can have some meaningful debate," the trucker slowly replied, while cautiously eyeing both Dwayne and Kevin. "What do you think, Pastor?"

Before Mark could answer, Kevin Collins broke in. "That's a very good idea, Billy B., and I'm all for it. But the problem is that we need answers today! The Glover family, sitting next to my wife this morning, shared that they're going to leave our church if Pastor can't provide scriptures to support the antichrist's coming before the rapture. To be perfectly honest, I have to agree with them. God speaks to me through the scriptures, not by some emotional impressions that supposedly come from Him," scoffed the deacon. "Believe me, there are no scriptures that show the antichrist's coming before the saints are raptured. And I know that to be a fact," the young officer confidently asserted.

An awkward silence settled over the meeting while the young pastor carefully weighed his next words.

Gently, the Spirit of God spoke a scripture to Mark, "For do I now persuade men, or God? Or do I seek to please men? For if I still pleased men, I would not be a bondservant of Christ."[2]

"Gentlemen," requested the Pastor, "let's open our Bibles to I Thessalonians 4:15-17. In this passage the Apostle Paul spoke to the Thessalonians about the very subject we are discussing this morning, the coming of the Lord. In verse 17, the apostle wrote concerning the catching up of the saints or, as many call it, the rapture. He highlighted the coming of the Lord by assuring his listeners that Jesus Himself will come from heaven in the clouds, with a loud command, with the voice of the archangel, and with the trumpet call of God. Those who are alive at this time will be caught up together with Old Testament and New Testament saints who have died, and this vast multitude will receive their resurrection bodies for eternity! On the very same day that the saints are delivered, God's wrath will be poured out on a Christ-rejecting world!"

"Pastor Mark, does this wrath of God that follows the catching up of the elect have a name?" asked Frank.

"It sure does. The apostle Paul called it the Day of the Lord. He warned believers who will be living during the seven-year tribulation period that the Day of the Lord will come like a thief in the night to those living in darkness. He further wrote that believers shouldn't be surprised because we are sons of the Light. Paul wrote, 'But you, brethren, are not in darkness, so that this Day should overtake you as a thief!'"[3]

"Does the Bible tell us when the Day of the Lord will begin?"

"Absolutely, Frank. When the seventh seal of the heavenly scroll is opened, God's wrath will begin! When you compare scripture with scripture, the events that take place before our Lord's return for His elect come together perfectly."

In a very condescending manner, Kevin asked, "But Pastor, since no one knows the day or the hour, how can you be so sure?"

The newly elected deacon never looked Pastor Mark directly in the eyes. Glancing to his left, his impish smile could only be seen by Dwayne.

"Answer this question for me," interrupted Dwayne. "Famous prophecy teachers such as Arthur Lawrence, Gene Lloyd, and Tom Bray have all taught on the end times for many years, and they are totally convinced that Jesus could come at any moment. C'mon, Pastor, if the antichrist were supposed to come first, we would be looking for him and not for our blessed hope, Jesus Christ, now wouldn't we?"

The young pastor was ready. He knew that the spirit of rebellion, which was manifesting itself through Dwayne and Kevin, had to be exposed.

"As I shared, the Thessalonians were taught that the gathering of the saints and the Day of the Lord would be back-to-back events. Deliverance first, then wrath! Jesus taught the same sequence when He used Noah as an example. Jesus said, 'And as it was in the days of Noah, so it will be also in the days of the Son of Man: They ate, they drank, they married wives, they were given in marriage, until the day that Noah entered the ark, and the flood came and destroyed them all. . . . Even so will it be in the day when the Son of Man is revealed.'"[4]

"To be honest, Pastor," blurted Kevin, "that verse will only confuse our members."

"The Thessalonians were confused too," countered Mark, "especially when false teachers began to teach that they had missed the coming of the Lord and had entered the Day of the Lord's wrath. Paul reassured them that the coming of our Lord Jesus Christ and His gathering of the elect will not take place until the man of sin, the antichrist, reveals himself to the world![5] This will happen exactly in the middle of the seven-year tribulation period when he steps into the rebuilt Jewish temple in Jerusalem and proclaims himself to be god. The abomination of desolation, another name for the antichrist, will attempt to force everyone in the world to worship him, which will cause many to fall away from their faith in God!"[6]

For some of the deacons, this simple truth had always been hidden. Immediately, Billy B. and Frank began to quietly debate whether the six seals of Revelation were really God's wrath. At the same time, Kevin could not believe that the board would waste so much time on such a non-issue.

"But, Pastor, how can this be possible?" the young officer asked in utter disbelief. "If the antichrist comes before the rapture, then Jesus can't come at any moment, and the teaching of His imminent return is a lie!"

Pastor Mark sensed that it was time to pray. The Holy Spirit would be sending another watchman who could answer the questions of those who were truly seeking the truth.

"This past week has been quite a whirlwind for my family and me," reflected Mark. "After praying and putting all the events together, there seems to be an obvious pattern."

"What do you mean, Pastor?" asked a curious Billy B.

"Well, it was late Monday night when I first received the vision of the beast and the valley of decision. After three days of fasting and prayer, I received the interpretation of my vision late Thursday night. Are you still with me?"

"Amen, Pastor," smiled Frank.

"Deep down in my spirit, I knew the interpretation of the vision I received was from God. Even so, I still struggled with the magnitude of the message. It wasn't until Saturday morning that all my doubts disappeared."

"What doubts?" asked a skeptical Dwayne.

"When the early Saturday morning CNN newscast announced the signing of the Jerusalem Peace Accord by Israel and its neighbors, I knew this was exactly what the Holy Spirit had shown me on Monday night!"

"But how can you be so sure?" asked a suspicious Kevin.

"I know that, eventually, many believers are going to ask me that question," sighed Mark. "All I can tell you is that on Saturday morning, when I was in deep prayer, the Holy Spirit promised to send another watchman who will speak the truth concerning the Lord's soon return."

"You say the Lord is calling you to be a watchman about the end times. Is that right?" asked a sarcastic Dwayne. "But how do we know this is from the Lord? I've never seen anything about any watchmen in the Bible."

Mark knew that it was time to seek the Lord for His leading. "Brothers, let's stand together and pray for spiritual discernment concerning the events that will soon transpire."

While the seven men bowed their heads to pray, the spirits of control, fear, and compromise gathered near the back of the room. The spirit of control spoke first.

"He didn't give in, you fools. Don't you see? The pastor's past failures didn't affect the decisions he made today!"

Fear and compromise weren't even listening. They were already huddled in the corner of the Activity's Center, carefully plotting their next attack against the saints at Bethany Assembly.

CHAPTER 5

GOD'S WATCHMAN

Son of Man, I have made you a watchman . . .
therefore hear a word from My mouth, and give them warning from me.
Ezekiel 3:17

Two weeks later, a couple from Santa Barbara, California, arrived in Bethany for the first time. The evangelist and his wife seemed to fit right in as they were introduced to the members of the Bethany Ministers Seminar Committee. Several of the most prominent churches in Bethany were represented, some by senior pastors and others by associates and deacons. The committee, led by Pastor John Ryals of Bethany Baptist Church, had decided during the summer to schedule an evangelist for the annual Fall Bible Seminar. The ministers voted unanimously for the speaker to teach on the coming of Lord for His Church.[1]

It was late afternoon when the committee gathered at the hotel in which the Corbins were staying. The seminar would be held at the hotel in the Robert E. Lee Conference Room, which seated close to five hundred people. There was a real sense of excitement among the organizing committee members, concerning how God had divinely inspired this seminar on the end times.

"Brother and Sister Corbin, I would like for you to meet J. W. Brown, pastor of Bethany Presbyterian, who has been a close friend of the Ryals family for many years."

"God bless you, my brother," greeted Pastor Brown. "It's so wonderful for you and your pretty wife to come for such a time as this!"

Without any hesitation, Pastor Ryals added, "Like I told my congregation last Sunday, we need to get back to the Bible and stop playing around with all these new teachings. My great, great grandpappy used to ride horses and preach that Jesus could come at any moment. There was no confusion or debate; it was just simple faith. God said it, and I believe it!" chuckled the rotund pastor.

"Thank you so much Pastor Ryals, Pastor Brown," said Stephen. "This is my wife, Michelle, and this is our first time preaching in the great state of Alabama."

A line quickly formed to the evangelist's left as the seminar chairman began to introduce the rest of the committee. "I would like for you to meet Elmer Dyer, pastor of Eastside United Methodist Church; Allen Colson, pastor of Calvary Community; Louis Cooper, pastor of Lakeview Assembly of God; Floyd Stanton, associate pastor of Shepherd of the Hills Lutheran Church; and Dwayne Pressley, head deacon of Bethany Assembly."

Pastor Ryals had met with the displeased deacon two weeks earlier over the confusion that had just divided Bethany Assembly. When Dwayne had asked for godly counsel on how to biblically handle the problem, Pastor Ryals had cautioned him to go slow and to allow God time to reveal the truth concerning the end times to Pastor Bishop. This was not the type of counsel the deacon had been hoping to receive. He had to continually fight the urge to convince the lay leadership at Bethany Assembly to remove Pastor Bishop and take control of the church.

"It's so nice to meet all of you," replied the evangelist, who was already sensing the spirit of control. "Both my wife and I believe with all our heart that our Lord Jesus Christ desires to bring revival to your city this week."

"He is truly an answer to prayer," whispered one pastor to another.

"We will see you two tomorrow morning at ten o'clock for prayer and a short review of the three-day seminar," confirmed a hopeful Pastor Ryals.

"Well, thank you so much for such a wonderful reception," said Michelle, a petite, strawberry blonde with a charming smile.

After exiting the hall and entering the main lobby of the hotel, the couple from California silently thanked the Lord for this open door of ministry.

The deacon from Bethany Assembly had purposely lingered in order to speak with the evangelist. He waited until all the other pastors had emptied out of the hotel lobby before approaching the new visitors.

"Brother Corbin, may I have a word with you?"

When the preacher's eyes met Dwayne's, there was an immediate check in Corbin's spirit that something was not right.

"It's such a divine appointment for you and your wife, Michelle, to come and encourage our young people with a systematic study of the blessed hope. You have no way of knowing, but we have pastors in our town teaching that the body of Christ will suffer persecution at the hands of the antichrist. I just know you will do the right thing, Brother Corbin, by allowing God to use you to clear up this confusion among our churches."

"Well, thank you for your encouragement, Dwayne," said the evangelist as he silently rebuked the spirit of control. "Oh, by the way, what is the name of your pastor?"

"My pastor is, uh, well, uh, his name is Mark Bishop," replied the deacon, barely able to get the words out.

And with that, Dwayne was gone.

＊

The girls excitedly raced downstairs after awakening to the smell of apple-cinnamon pancakes and bacon-cheese omelets. Julie was preparing their favorite breakfast. Before the summer began, Mark and Julie had promised Hope and Lindsey some special surprises if they were faithful in their summer school classes. The summer had just flown by. An overcast sky hovered over the city. A cold wind could be felt, on this, the last day of September.

"This is so awesome!" shouted Lindsey.

"I just know that Mom and Dad have planned a special trip for us," predicted Hope as the phone began to ring. Answering it, she listened and then said, "Sure, let me check to see if he's available."

Hope jogged to the back of the house, looking for the man she respected more than anyone else in the world. Peeking into his study, she could see her unshaven father with his disheveled reddish brown hair, getting up from his knees where he had been praying.

"It's for you, Daddy."

"Thanks, Hope. I've got it. Hello. This is Pastor Bishop. May I help you?"

"Good morning, Pastor, I'm Reverend Corbin. I've been invited to speak at the three-day prophecy seminar that begins tonight."

"Yes, of course, I've heard the announcements on the radio for the past two weeks," Mark replied excitedly. "My wife, Julie, and I would love to meet with you and your wife for some southern fellowship."

"Praise the Lord, that sounds great. The seminar begins tonight at seven o'clock. Michelle and I would really like to pray with you and your wife for the Holy Spirit to touch the lives of those who will be attending."

"Certainly, it will be a pleasure. By the way, what specific area of the Lord's coming will you be sharing tonight?"

"Tonight's message is entitled 'The Rapture: One Taken, One Left.'"[2]

Suddenly Mark could sense the anointing of the Holy Spirit.

Pausing for a moment, he said, "That's an interesting title. May I ask what the Holy Spirit has revealed to you during your studies?"

"He has shown me several critical truths concerning the signs that will come before Jesus gathers His elect. Actually, it was about a year ago when the Spirit of God called me to be a watchman!"

Mark immediately froze before asking his next question. "You know, Reverend Corbin, I never did get your first name?"

"Please forgive me, Pastor Mark. My name is Stephen. Do you think you and Julie can meet Michelle and me in the hotel lobby for prayer at five o'clock tonight?"

"Yes, of course."

"Excellent. God bless you, my friend."

Mark stood listening to the dial tone for several moments. The word of knowledge the Holy Spirit had given the young pastor had just come true!

"It's God; it's God!" proclaimed the elated pastor, bouncing around his cramped office. "The Holy Spirit has sent His watchman just like He said He would!"

The demon of control did not like what he was hearing. He quickly decided to join forces with other demons in order to deceive the followers who would be attending tonight's seminar.

It was a little before ten in the morning when the Corbins entered the Robert E. Lee Hall and took a seat at the head table next to the committee chairman, Pastor John Ryals.

Pastor Louis Cooper of Lakeview Assembly of God welcomed everyone and began with a prayer of thanks to God.

Pastor J. W. Brown of Bethany Presbyterian read the minutes of the last meeting and shared the seminar schedule for the next three nights.

The chairman, John Ryals, stood to express his approval.

"God bless you, my friends! It is a joy to see brothers in Christ— Baptists, Methodists, Presbyterians, Lutherans, and Pentecostals—come together under the banner of Jesus Christ. The Bible says, 'Salvation is found in no one else, for there is no other name under heaven given to men by which we must be saved."³

A chorus of amens could be heard throughout the hall.

"Tonight, believers from all over the state of Alabama will be visiting our great city to hear one thing," proclaimed the rotund pastor, who weighed close to three hundred pounds. "Jesus could come at any moment!"

"Preach the truth, Pastor!" shouted Dwayne Pressley from the back of the room.

Brother Ryals smiled and replied, "The scriptures exhort us that we are to look for the glorious appearing of our blessed hope, Jesus Christ.⁴ As a young boy of twelve, I sensed God calling me to repent and be baptized. My momma would say to me, 'Johnny, you had better get right with God because Jesus could split the eastern sky with His angels at any moment, and the saints will be gone. You don't want to be left behind, do you?'"

"Not me!" yelled a smiling Dwayne Pressley.

"I thank God for ministers of the Gospel who proclaim the truth concerning the rapture of the saints. I got saved because someone cared enough to tell me the truth no matter what it cost. Tonight, we need to be ready to answer any questions concerning the end times. Our young people deserve to hear the plain truth!"

The cheers of approval from the committee clearly motivated the preacher to continue.

"It's so encouraging to see different denominations represented here today. But even though we differ on doctrinal views concerning communion, baptism, and worship, we can all agree that the most critical doctrine that will inspire the Church is the imminent return of our Lord Jesus Christ!"

The utter power and emotion from the pastor's voice demanded a response. Rising to their feet, the committee members gave a standing ovation.

While continuing to clap, Dwayne Pressley glanced over to the first row of seats and noticed that the evangelist and his wife were not clapping. It looked as if the Corbins were reflecting on what had just been said. The deacon from Bethany Assembly did not have a good feeling about this polished, blonde, blue-eyed preacher from California. There was something about him that Dwayne could not put his finger on. An inner voice kept telling Dwayne that the evangelist was dangerous and had come to confuse the churches.

Pastor Floyd Stanton announced from his seat in the first row that six buses containing several out-of-town youth groups would be arriving at five o'clock.

"In the parking lot of this hotel, we'll have over twenty volunteers ready to feed these kids, compliments of Max's Barbecue," Floyd proudly announced.

Max Larson, seated in the last row, nodded his head and smiled.

"I guess that about covers it all," Pastor Stanton concluded.

After handing the microphone to his close friend Louis Cooper, he took a seat.

Louis Cooper was the head pastor of the largest Pentecostal fellowship in Bethany. Just recently, during an all-night prayer meeting at Lakeview Assembly of God, two members of his church were supernaturally healed. One had been diagnosed with AIDS, the other with cancer. Both had been asked by the committee chairman, John Ryals, to share their testimonies on the second night of the seminar.

Pastor Cooper paused to collect his thoughts while waiting to receive his peers' complete attention.

"My brothers in Christ, I want to thank you all for your . . ."

"Excuse me, Louis. May I speak?" interrupted a solemn Elmer Dyer.

Immediately, Pastor Cooper looked over in the direction of the chairman. Pastor Ryals did not like unexpected interruptions. Reluctantly, he gave his approval.

Pastor Elmer Dyer pioneered the Eastside United Methodist Church over twenty-five years ago. As the oldest committee member, in his late fifties, he was very well respected. In fact, the community looked upon his faithfulness to his congregation as a shining example of what the city of Bethany truly represented.

Slowly shaking his head, the pastor did not look happy.

"This morning I come to you with a heavy heart. What I am about to share is not pretty. As you all know, Pastor Mark Bishop of Bethany Assembly has announced to his congregation that the seven-year tribulation period has commenced. He has openly admitted that the Holy Spirit gave him a vision, supposedly predicting that the Jerusalem Peace Accord is a covenant of death between the Jewish people and the antichrist. In fact, for those who haven't heard, Pastor Mark has publicly taught that the antichrist is Wolfgang Hendrick of Germany!"

Several committee members just shook their heads in disgust. Over the years, every pastor in the room had had to deal with hyped-up teachers and false prophets who predicted everything from the rapture to the end of the world.

"Let me first say that Pastor Mark and I are good friends. When his family moved to Bethany over a year ago, our church was one of the first to make Julie and the girls feel welcome. We have found Mark to be friendly, hardworking, faithful to his family, and a man of God who is willing to unify with other pastors in order to reach our city for Christ. But someone has to publicly draw the line when it comes to personal prophecy pertaining to end time events."

"Tell the truth!" shouted Dwayne.

"First of all, there are no scriptures to support the claim that Wolfgang Hendrick of Germany is the antichrist. Second, we could not have entered the tribulation period because our Lord promised that the body of Christ will never suffer God's wrath. And finally, if Christians were still here to face the antichrist, then the imminent return of our Lord Jesus Christ would be impossible! And of course, we all know that couldn't be true because the Apostle Paul taught that Jesus could return at any moment!"

Most of the pastors on the committee weren't even listening. They were still trying to grasp how such a wonderful man of God like Mark Bishop could become so deceived.

"Yes, I know that Pastor Mark can be very sincere and persuasive. To be perfectly honest, so can the Mormons, the JW's, and the Masons. Believe me, my brothers; we all need to understand the serious consequences involving this type of false teaching. When Pastor Bishop warns believers of our city that they need to be spiritually ready for the mark of the beast, I, as a minister of the gospel, must strongly object! Our God doesn't motivate His children through fear. Any teacher that says the body of Christ will be persecuted by the antichrist has crossed the line and should be publicly rebuked. We cannot allow this type of end-time scare tactic to frighten our children. Our God is a God of love, not wrath!"

It was quarter to five when Mark arrived at the hotel lobby. He came alone. His wife, Julie, decided at the last minute to stay home with their twelve-year-old daughter, Lindsey, who had come down with a high fever.

Stephen and Mark met in a side room adjacent to the hall, while Michelle felt led to pray in their hotel room.

Mark knelt in prayer while Stephen paced the room praising God for the opportunity to teach the truth concerning the coming persecution. Each of them had been used in spiritual warfare before, but tonight was especially hard. More and more demons were arriving by the minute. Both men struggled to break through the heaviness in their spirit. Stephen especially needed to experience a victory. He knew the cost of being a watchman and remaining faithful to God's Word.

While the two watchmen continued to pray in the Spirit, the voices of young people could be heard as the buses that had just arrived were emptied. Most of the kids immediately headed for the tables that were loaded down with Max's famous barbecue beef and pork sandwiches. Those who were fasting formed prayer groups to intercede for the night's message. Within two hours, a spiritual battle over the lives of these kids would be played out with eternal consequences.

By the time the worship team finished its second song, every seat in the conference hall was taken. It was obvious that the younger crowd was far more interested in end-time prophecy than the senior saints were. For some, this would be their first time hearing an in-depth teaching about the coming of the Lord for His elect! While traveling to Bethany, several youth leaders compared notes and came to the conclusion that many pastors purposefully stayed away from the study of end-time events.

A freshman from Auburn University didn't see why the timing of Jesus' return was such a big deal since the body of Christ would miss the entire tribulation period anyway.

Suddenly, a pastor's son yelled out, "No man knows the day or the hour."

Three girls seated directly behind him immediately stood up together and replied, "But the women do!"

The laughter seemed to be infectious, spreading quickly from row to row. For some of the kids, this seminar was just a time to get away from the folks. For others, it was a time to meet new friends, maybe even a new girlfriend or boyfriend. There was a third group. These were youth who had come to meet God. Despite their young age, these kids were intercessors who knew in their spirit that something heavy was just about to go down. It was a diverse group that had come to hear the truth concerning the coming of Christ.

The evangelist could feel the responsibility that had been laid upon his shoulders. The end of the age was so much closer than the world could ever imagine. Deep within his spirit, Stephen sensed that this was going to be a rare opportunity to preach to the Christian community of Bethany. For someone who loved God, it was an opportunity of a lifetime.

Pastor Ryals stepped to the pulpit and with a surge of excitement announced, "Let's welcome to the awesome state of Alabama, Evangelist Stephen Corbin from Santa Barbara, California."

The youth expressed their appreciation for the speaker as they stood and cheered.

Meanwhile, outside the hotel, Pastor Mark Bishop met with Billy B. and Frank Donnelly.

"Are you ready to do a prayer walk around the building and rebuke every evil spirit in Jesus' name?" Mark asked his two close friends.

"Amen, Pastor," replied Billy B., who was eager to enter into spiritual warfare.

"We're always ready to intercede for those who desire to know the truth," declared Frank.

The demons of compromise, fear, and control had not anticipated this prayer attack by the pastor and his two deacons. When the demons heard the blood of Jesus being declared, they planted the last of their evil lies before being forced to depart.

As the evangelist approached the pulpit, he silently praised the Lord for this divine appointment. Stephen had been called to be a watchman over a year ago. He had been studying the great multitude from every nation, tribe, people, and tongue from the book of Revelation when an urgency from the Holy Spirit touched his heart.

"Lord, who is this multitude?" Stephen had asked.

He had always been taught that this vast multitude of people was unbelievers who were left behind at the rapture. Later on during the great tribulation they got saved and were martyred for their faith in Jesus.

After much prayer, the Holy Spirit had impressed upon the evangelist, "Read what it says."

Stephen wondered out loud, "Yes, I see it, Lord. This multitude of believers has resurrection bodies! They have been rescued out of the great tribulation and taken to heaven. This has to be the catching up of the saints by our blessed hope!"

During this time the evangelist had been directed by the Holy Spirit to compare Matthew 24:3-31 with Revelation 6:1-17 and 7:9-17.

"There it is!" Stephen rejoiced. "The gathering of the saints by our Lord during the great tribulation!"

Repositioning the microphone, the peace of God seemed to radiate from the evangelist. As a watchman, his main objective was to first warn and then to spiritually prepare Christians for the future persecution of the antichrist.

"Thank you very much, Pastor Ryals, for your warm Southern hospitality," said the evangelist. "My wife, Michelle, and I are very excited to be with ya'll here tonight. Let me ask how many have come here tonight from cities outside of Bethany?"

The committee members beamed with approval as cheers came from kids from Huntsville, Birmingham, Prattville, Mobile, Auburn, and even Alabama's state capitol, Montgomery.

As he looked out over his audience, Stephen knew only the Holy Spirit could reveal the truth concerning the evil that would soon be visiting the quiet streets of Bethany, Alabama.

CHAPTER 6

THE BEGINNING OF SORROWS

For nation will rise against nation, and kingdom against kingdom.
And there will be earthquakes in various places,
and there will be famines and troubles.
These are the beginning of sorrows.
Mark 13:8

Looking out over his audience, the middle-aged evangelist from California calmly closed his notebook. Stephen wouldn't need his notes tonight. The spiritual warfare that was raging was something with which he was very familiar. God desired to share a simple message of truth concerning the most important event affecting the future of the world: the coming of the Lord for His saints!

"This evening," announced Stephen, "I feel led by the Holy Spirit to begin a three-night series on the coming of the Lord entitled, 'The Rapture: One Taken, One Left.' Brothers and sisters in Christ, there is coming a time, in a twinkling of an eye, when the trumpet of God will sound and our blessed hope, Jesus Christ, will send out His angels to gather His elect from one end of heaven to the other!"

The overflow crowd rose to its feet to cheer for the time when people would see their Savior face-to-face. Almost everyone seemed to be smiling. Amidst all the fun, the hugs, and the high-fives, sat several committee members, who did not like what they were hearing.

"Our Lord used the days of Lot as an example of how the world will be when He comes for His elect. Jesus prophesied, 'They ate, they drank, they bought, they sold, they planted, they built; but on the day that Lot went out of Sodom it rained fire and brimstone from heaven and destroyed them all. Even so will it be in the day when the Son of Man is revealed.'"[1]

"That'll preach!" yelled an excited youth leader.

"Our Lord is warning believers just before the end of the age that the world will reject the final pleas of a Savior who loves them. Just like in Lot's day, unbelievers will refuse to repent of their sins and receive the precious gift of salvation from a Holy God!"

Slowly but surely, one could hear whispering among the different youth groups who were sitting together. An undercurrent of division was growing by the second.

"Jesus then said, 'Two women will be grinding together; the one will be taken and the other left. Two men will be in the field: the one will be taken and the other left.'[2] Church, this passage is describing the glorious rapture of the body of Christ. Jesus Christ takes His own into heaven while those left behind will experience the wrath of God, just like in the days of Lot!'"

The spontaneous eruption of praise was a real rush for many who had just become Christians. For a small group of senior saints seated to the left of the podium, the response was so loud that they had to cover their ears.

"My friends, I come before you tonight with an important message of truth. It is true; there is coming a time when our Lord Jesus will descend from heaven with the trumpet call of God and will catch up all those who follow Him. But before the elect are safely delivered to heaven, our Jesus warns us of six specific events that will precede His coming! First, there will be false christs who will come and deceive many believers. From these false christs shall emerge the antichrist! The next event will be wars and rumors of wars. After the wars have begun, famines will spread throughout the world. Jesus calls these three events the beginning of sorrows.[3] Actually, many Bible translators interpret sorrows as birth pangs."

"You mean like the pains a mother has before she has her baby?" asked a youth pastor from Prattville.

"That's right," replied Stephen. "These events are the beginning signs that are immediately followed by hard labor. The hard labor Jesus calls the great tribulation. Our Lord warned believers who will experience it, 'For then there will be great tribulation, such as has not been since the beginning of the world until this time, no, nor ever shall be.'[4] It is during the great tribulation, which begins in the middle of the last seven years, that the persecution of believers will begin. Christians will be hated by all nations because of their testimony of Jesus Christ. The persecution will become so intense that many believers will betray and hate one another.[5] Brother will betray brother. There will be children who will rebel against their parents and have them put to death. The world will hate believers because of Jesus, but those who endure to the end shall be saved!'"[6]

The watchman knew from the intense spiritual warfare he was facing that Bethany was not an ordinary city. There was a lot more involved than met the eye. After experiencing the spiritual bondage of the people first hand,

Stephen discerned that this beautifully landscaped city was actually a demonic stronghold for the devil himself!

After a long pause, the watchman pleaded, "The increase of wickedness will be so overwhelming that many believers will allow their love for Christ to grow cold!"[7]

The prince of darkness knew what was coming. He had personally summoned the spirits of fear and control to interfere. The minds of those listening among the crowd who were open to his demonic attacks would soon receive an all-out assault.

"Jesus warned his disciples that whoever sees the abomination of desolation step into the Jerusalem temple will experience the great tribulation!"[8]

Hardly anyone moved. This was not the type of message that the leadership wanted to hear.

"Wake up, saints! Are you hearing what I am saying?"

The rustling of pages could be heard throughout the hall. The students were turning to Matthew 24:21-22, the passage of scripture describing the great tribulation.

"Jesus comforts believers who experience the great tribulation when he promised, 'Unless those days were shortened, no flesh would be saved; but for the elect's sake those days will be shortened.'[9] Now I ask you, Church, how will our Lord fulfill His promise by cutting short the persecution of the saints during the great tribulation?"

Pausing, the evangelist quietly prayed under his breath, "Open their eyes, Lord, and let them see it."

He knew only those seeking the Holy Spirit would be able to grasp the truth of Jesus' words.

After seeing lots of heads nodding, a smiling Stephen proclaimed, "That's right, my friends. The persecution by the antichrist will be cut short by the catching up of the elect!" He purposefully waited and then asked, "Do you see it?"

Immediately, hands started shooting up throughout the conference floor. Without any more hesitation, Stephen continued.

"In Matthew 24:5-29, Jesus warned the elect of six specific events that will precede His coming. Jesus said, 'When you see all these things know that it is near—at the doors.' Now what are the things our Lord is talking about?"

The faces of confusion and unbelief among the believers had become a familiar sight in the evangelist's life. For years the church leadership had rejected the simple truth of events transpiring right before Christ's coming. Now, in God's timing, the truth would be revealed.

Several students rose to their feet and began to shout out their interpretations.

Stephen raised his hands and said, "Jesus warned believers who actually see the antichrist, the wars, the famines, the persecution, and the martyrdom of the elect that His coming will be right at the door. Our Lord clearly said, 'Immediately after the tribulation of these five events, the sun will be darkened, the moon will not give its light, and the universe will become pitch black.'"[10]

"So are you saying that these cosmic disturbances are a sign that comes before the rapture?" asked a student in the first row.

"Amen," replied Stephen. "These cosmic disturbances are the sign of the end of the age!"

"If that's true, then what is the sign of His coming?"

Before the evangelist could answer, a youth leader from Mark's church stood and read, "For as the lightening comes from the east and flashes to the west, so also will the coming of the Son of Man be."[11]

"Right on, my brother," said Stephen. "Our Lord gave us a perfect description of His coming for His elect when He said, 'Then the sign of the Son of Man will appear in heaven, and then all the tribes of the earth will mourn, and they will see the Son of Man coming on the clouds of heaven with power and great glory. And He will send His angels with a great sound of a trumpet, and they will gather together His elect from the four winds, from one end of the heaven to the other.'"[12]

Stephen wanted to continue, but the applause forced him to pause. Through all the warfare, the spiritual attacks, and the demonic assignments, the Holy Spirit was still drawing souls to Jesus. The watchman could see the spiritual hunger in the faces of the youth, a hunger crying out that there's got to be more!

"In Matthew 24:30-31, we see a perfect picture of the coming of the Son of Man or, as most preachers nickname it, the *Rapture*. Now listen up, saints, because we all need to see this important truth. In I Thessalonians 4:17, the Apostle Paul wrote of Jesus Christ's coming in the clouds to catch up or gather His saints. Now check it out. The apostle doesn't say who will catch up the saints."

"Brother Corbin, I've got it," interrupted a young teenage girl in the second row. "Jesus said that it'll be the angels who will gather the elect from one end of heaven to the other."

"That's right, my sister. Now, we know from Jesus' teaching on the parable of the wheat and the tares that the end of the age is the harvest. In this parable, the harvesters are the angels. At the end of the age, they are sent out to gather the wheat into the barn, heaven, and the tares into the fire, the Day of the Lord."[13]

"I see," replied a Sunday school teacher who stood to speak. "The harvest represents the rapture!"

"Very good," replied Stephen. "Jesus told us that the angels will gather up the believers. Praise God, saints, the gathering in Matthew 24:31 is the harvest of the body of Christ to heaven!"

The puzzle was beginning to come together for those who were truly seeking the truth.

"Praise the Lord!" could be heard coming from youth all over the packed-out hall.

With the excitement of the young people rocking, suddenly, several members of the committee formed a tight circle to the right side of the pulpit. It was obvious to them that the stranger from California was manipulating the young people by distorting the truth of God's Word. The demons had returned, and the warfare was raging.

The evangelist slowly walked across the stage, carefully choosing his next words.

"When you share the events that precede our Lord's soon return, many unbelievers will want to ask you the reason why Jesus is coming back a second time. Is everyone still with me?"

The question brought forth a roar that could be heard throughout the whole hotel.

After raising his hands to quiet the crowd, the evangelist said, "Okay, now let's review the events that will take place during our Lord's second coming. First, our Lord will rapture his saints from the persecution of the antichrist. Immediately after the body of Christ is gone, Jesus will judge the ungodly of this earth by sending His day of wrath. Our Lord uses the destruction of mankind by Noah's flood and the destruction of Sodom and Gomorrah by fire in Lot's day as examples of His wrath. Next, after the seven-year tribulation period is completed, our Lord Jesus will save a remnant of Jewish believers. After this event, our Lord's Second Coming will conclude at the Battle of Armageddon when He comes with His angels to destroy the antichrist and his armies! Now get this point, saints. Christ's Second Coming begins with the rapture and ends at Armageddon!" preached the Yankee from California.

Without any warning, Elmer Dyer, a pastor from the committee, anxiously blurted out, "But Brother Corbin, you've got the body of Christ being persecuted by the antichrist during the tribulation period! That's simply not possible! God will never pour His wrath out on his own bride. In I Thessalonians 5:9, we are assured that believers will inherit salvation, never God's wrath!"

The disdain for the preacher from California could be seen on the face of every committee member.

Slowly, the evangelist stepped to the left of the podium and calmly replied, "That's correct, Pastor Dyer. The body of Christ will never suffer God's wrath.[14] In Revelation 5:1, we are given a picture of a large scroll in heaven sealed with seven seals. When all seven seals are broken, the scroll will open, and God's wrath will be poured out on a Christ-rejecting world. It is clear that the seals are not God's wrath but represent the rebellion of man and the wrath of Satan," countered the evangelist.[15]

"May I speak?" interrupted J. W. Brown, pastor of Bethany Presbyterian Church. "Brother Corbin, you are making a fatal error when you openly teach that the seals of Revelation are not God's wrath. In the book of Revelation, it clearly states that the wrath of the Lamb has come during the sixth seal. The people of the earth are hiding from the face of Him who sits on the throne and from the wrath of the Lamb.[16] Now, we all know that if the sixth seal is God's wrath, then the other five seals must also be His wrath. After all, it is our Lord who sends the seven seals during the tribulation period!"

Cheers erupted throughout the room.

"Now that's preaching," yelled a youth pastor sitting in the second row. Nudging one of his students seated to his right, he gushed, "I can just feel the Holy Ghost, can't you?"

"Pastor Brown, in Isaiah 2:10, Isaiah prophecied that only the Lord will be exalted during the Day of the Lord," shared Stephen.

"That's correct," smiled the pastor.

"Now, your pre-tribulation position teaches that the seven-year tribulation period is the Day of the Lord, God's wrath; is that right?"

"Absolutely! As soon as the elect are raptured, God will pour out His Day of The Lord wrath—seals, trumpets, and bowls—on all those who have been left behind."

"But, Pastor Brown, how can only the Lord be exalted during the breaking of the seals, a time when the antichrist will proclaim himself to be god by blaspheming our Lord and all those who follow Him? In fact, during the fifth seal, the antichrist will martyr a multitude of believers who refuse to worship him!"

The spirits of fear and control could not wait any longer as they swept through the crowd.

"Don't you see, saints? If the seals were God's wrath, then our Jesus would be responsible for empowering the antichrist. Our Lord would be guilty for the martyrdom of His own saints, martyrs who cry out to God for revenge to those who killed them! Church, that's not possible!"

The utter commotion was like a bomb going off. With debates raging among the youth, Pastor Brown finally regained control.

"But, Brother Corbin, you have the coming of the Son of Man in Matthew 24 as the rapture. That can't be right. We all know that this is a picture of Jesus' coming with His saints at Armageddon. Our Jesus will come with a vast army and destroy the enemies of God. All unbelievers will be taken to judgment, and those left behind will enter the millennium, just like the days of Noah."

A reflective Stephen stepped back and paused. "Pastor Brown, let's compare Jesus' return at Armageddon with Jesus' coming for His saints in Matthew 24:30-31 to see if they really are the same event."

"Go right ahead," challenged the pastor while winking at the audience.

"As I have already shared, Matthew 24 depicts our Lord Jesus' coming for His elect who are being persecuted by the antichrist. As we can all see, Christ's gathering of His elect occurs right after the opening of the sixth seal, the cosmic disturbances!"

"Go on," pressed the confident pastor.

"Now in Revelation 19:11-21, the text clearly shows Jesus' coming with his angels to destroy the antichrist and his armies at Armageddon. This event takes place immediately following the seventh bowl judgment."

Stephen paused, knowing how critical it was for the saints to grasp this simple truth. "Now, let me ask you this question, Pastor Brown."

"I'm waiting," he said smirking.

"How can our Jesus' gathering of His saints to heaven in Matthew 24 be the same event as Jesus' destroying the antichrist at Armageddon? At Armageddon, after defeating the antichrist, our Lord sets up His millennial rule on earth. Our Lord doesn't gather anyone to heaven."

Pastor Brown spoke up, "Yes, I . . ."

"In Matthew 24:30-31," continued Stephen, "our Lord comes in the clouds immediately following the cosmic disturbances of the sixth seal. At Armageddon, Jesus returns following the destruction of the earth by the seventh bowl. Let's be honest! These two events, Matthew 24 and Revelation 19, happen at different times with two different results!"

A hush fell over the room. Before Stephen could continue, a youth leader from Bethany Assembly stood and asked for permission to speak. The revelation the young man had just received from the Lord looked to be pretty overwhelming. Reluctantly, the evangelist gave his approval.

"Brother Corbin, if the cosmic disturbances, the sixth seal, precede the rapture and the wrath of God is poured out when the seventh seal is broken, then the body of Christ must be raptured sometime between the sixth and seventh seals!"[17]

And with that said, all hell broke loose. Immediately the demon of confusion moved through the startled crowd.

"That can't be true!" yelled a pastor's wife. "There are no more signs left to be fulfilled before the rapture. Jesus is coming like a thief in the night. He can come at any moment!"

One pastor was desperately trying to explain to his youth group that Matthew 24 was not addressed to Christians but to unsaved Jews who will be on earth during the tribulation period. Through it all, Stephen and Michelle could see students grasping for the first time the events that will precede the coming of the Lord. Pastor Ryals of Bethany Baptist Church quickly emerged from the tight circle of pastors and motioned for quiet.

"Please, please, everyone take your seats. Before we close tonight, I would like to share with you some thoughts from our committee."

It took a while for the excitement of the crowd to gradually die down.

"We have several different denominations represented here tonight. Unfortunately, the teaching you've just heard certainly does not reflect the rapture position of any churches represented by our committee. I'm sure that in California Mr. Corbin is well received with his mid-tribulation interpretation of the Lord's coming. Those of us who minister in Alabama certainly do not believe that the Church of Jesus Christ will ever be martyred by the antichrist. Quite frankly, I find tonight's teaching unscriptural, as well as very confusing! In spite of tonight's unfortunate setback, the pastors' committee has voted unanimously for Pastor J. W. Brown to be our featured speaker for the next two nights. So please bring your friends and family out to hear why a pre-tribulation rapture is the most literal interpretation of the coming of the Lord. God Bless you all."

As the hall emptied out, one could see the disappointment of so many that desired to hear the truth but were totally unaware that the spirit of control had done its work.

Even so, amidst all the warfare, God was still directing. By the time the committee chairman had made his way to the podium to address the crowd, the Holy Spirit had already directed Stephen to visit Bethany Assembly! At exactly the same time, Billy B. received a prompting from the Spirit of God to return to his church before heading home.

Just after arriving in the church's parking lot, Billy B. spotted the evangelist standing underneath the outside lights of the Activity Center.

"God bless you, Brother Corbin; they call me Billy B.," greeted the trucker while shaking Stephen's hand over and over again. "I've been a deacon at the Bethany Assembly Church for close to six years."

"Nice to meet you, Billy B. You can just call me Stephen if you like."

"Appreciate it, Stephen. You know, your message tonight made me pretty mad at first. My blood was getting pretty hot while I watched all those kids arguing over the scriptures."

"You're right, my friend. It can get pretty hectic when believers are challenged with the truth of God's Word."

"Well, it took me a spell to understand what you were teaching. But as you compared scripture with scripture, I was able to see for the first time that the coming of the Son of Man in Matthew 24:30-31 is the same event as the Lord's coming in I Thessalonians 4:15-17."

"That's awesome," replied the evangelist.

"My problem is with these preachers who kept interrupting you. What I mean is, uh, I don't believe most of the kids even understood the questions you were debating, much less the answers."

"Yeah, I know what you mean. Michelle and I face this everywhere we go. It's pretty sad that most pastors who insist on a pre-tribulation rapture usually will not allow any meaningful debate."

"You got that right. I could just feel the spirit of control oozing out of the seminar committee."

"Even so, my brother, the Spirit of God is greater than any other spirit, whether from man or from Satan!"

"Amen to that. Hey, Stephen, do you think I could ask you some questions concerning your teaching on the rapture?" asked the curious deacon.

"Sure," replied the smiling watchman. "I'm always up for questions after I teach."

"Well, when some of the youth were asking me about whether Matthew 24 refers to the rapture, a youth pastor from Mobile kept interrupting me and telling them it's no big deal."

"Actually, Billy B., Matthew 24:30-31, I Thessalonians 4:15-17, and II Thessalonians 2:1-3, each describe the coming of the Lord for His saints. Believe me, this is the most critical truth the spirit of antichrist is trying to suppress!"

"Wow, all three passages describe the same event, the coming of the Lord for His saints."

"That's right, my brother."

"Stephen, when you compare these passages, what is the most important truth we as Christians need to know about our Lord's return?"

"Billy B., both Jesus and the Apostle Paul warned believers living in the last days that the abomination of desolation, the man of sin, must come to the Jerusalem temple before the Lord comes."[18]

"So our Lord is warning us that the antichrist must first reveal his identity before the elect can be gathered?"

"That's correct. The Apostle Paul clearly taught, 'Now, brethren, concerning the coming of our Lord Jesus Christ and our gathering to Him . . . let no one deceive you by any means; for that Day will not come unless the falling away comes first, and the man of sin is revealed, the son of perdition!'"[19]

"So, Stephen, Christians who witness the antichrist's stepping into the temple in Jerusalem will be the very ones who will face his persecution?"

"That's the Lord's message of the hour, my friend."

"Boy, that's pretty easy to see. Do you think I could ask you another question?"

"Go for it," encouraged the watchman.

"During your message tonight, you told Pastor Brown that the seals are not God's wrath but Satan's wrath?"

"That's right."

"Well, in Revelation 6:12-17, the sun is turning black, the moon is turning red, and earthquakes are erupting everywhere. The people of the earth are running for the caves in order to protect themselves. It then says, 'The great day of His wrath has come and who is able to stand?' In other words, it looks like God's wrath comes at the sixth seal. How do you explain this, Stephen?"

"The answer is really pretty simple, my brother. Those in darkness are hiding from His wrath that is coming at the seventh seal! Remember when Jesus was arrested in the garden by the soldiers who were led by Judas Iscariot?"

"Sure. Jesus was arrested and taken before Pilate and Herod."

"Right. And Jesus said, 'The hour has come; behold, the Son of Man is being betrayed into the hands of sinners.'[19] In other words, his trials before Herod and Pilate were coming. They had not yet happened. They were still in the future."

"I get it. For unbelievers on the earth, during the sixth seal, Jesus will come like a thief in the night. The cosmic disturbances will black out the universe. The fear of God's wrath that is coming will grip the hearts of those who have rejected Him."

"That's right, Billy B. The scriptures never say the seals are God's wrath. Let's always remember that the wrath of God doesn't come out of the heavenly scroll until the seventh seal is broken!"

"Now let me get this straight," the trucker said while scratching his head. "The seven trumpets of God's wrath can't be blown until all seven seals of the heavenly scroll are broken. Is that right?"

Stephen simply nodded his head and smiled.

"So what are the seals?"

"The seals represent man's rebellion and the wrath of Satan. You see, my brother, if you don't make a distinction between God's wrath and Satan's wrath during the tribulation period, you have a serious contradiction on your hands!"

"I can't believe that I have never seen this before."

"Billy B., the devil will be allowed by God to test the body of Christ during the great tribulation, the fourth and fifth seals. This persecution will produce an army from every nation, tribe, people, and tongue, whose strength and obedience will be dependent upon the Holy Spirit."

"This is pretty heavy, Stephen. I want to thank you for sharing with me tonight."

A deep friendship was beginning to form between the two overcomers who would soon risk their lives together in order for the Gospel to be preached. Stephen already knew from the Holy Spirit that God was calling the heavyset deacon to be a leader in God's army.

"Billy B., I want to encourage you to seek the Lord in prayer about becoming a watchman."

"You mean like Pastor Mark's calling to speak the truth about the end times?"

"That's right. You just pray, and God will show you."

"Sure will, Stephen."

"The spiritual warfare was pretty scary tonight, Billy B. We need to form prayer groups in order to defeat the demon spirits that have been assigned to Bethany. Do you have any intercessors at your church?"

"It's so discouraging, Stephen! Pastor Mark has continually tried to teach the church about intercession for the past month. The spirit of religion must have gotten hold of the adults because it seems like only the youth have any desire to be used. In my opinion, only a handful are experienced enough to come against the demon onslaught that is coming our way."

"That's okay," assured his new friend. "Let's remember the words of our Savior. Jesus said, 'The harvest truly is plentiful, but the laborers are few. Therefore pray the Lord of the harvest to send out laborers into His harvest.'[20] Once we start praying together, the Holy Spirit will begin to raise up His prayer warriors. Can you contact Pastor Mark so we can all meet at his earliest convenience?"

"Praise the Lord! I just know Pastor Mark will want to get involved."

"Great!" beamed a thankful Stephen. "See you tomorrow, and by the way, welcome to the fight."

The grateful smile of the trucker was a reflection of his love for God. Deep within his heart, Billy B. had fervently prayed for the Holy Spirit to call him to a ministry that would glorify the Lord.

As the evangelist turned to leave, his new friend asked, "Stephen, you and Michelle were treated pretty rough tonight by the committee. I guess it's not always fun to be a watchman, is it?"

Stephen paused for a moment and replied, "If a believer hears from God and obeys, he or she will always make the right choice, no matter what the consequences. For some tonight, the rejection of the Lord's message by the pastors' committee was the highlight, but for God, it was the fact that several became watchmen for the truth . . . like you, Billy B."

As he waved a final goodbye, the watchman knew that the truth of Christ's coming had touched his new friend's heart. The trucker would now be responsible for what God had called him to do.

After returning to the hotel, Stephen found Michelle weeping for souls on her knees in their bedroom. He joined her by the bedside, and the couple poured out their hearts to God. They prayed for those living in darkness to be drawn to the light of the gospel.

As they continued to seek after God, a passage of scripture came alive in their spirits: "He who believes in Me believes not in Me but in Him who sent Me. And he who sees Me sees Him who sent Me. I have come as a light into the world, that whoever believes in Me should not abide in darkness."[21]

CHAPTER 7

SATAN'S ARRIVAL

I will no longer talk much with you,
for the ruler of this world is coming,
and he has nothing in me.
John 14:30

As Pastor Mark slowly drove down Main Street, he could see the sun's rays slipping through branches of the beautiful silver-leafed maple trees lining the streets of Bethany. Shops were opening as town folks greeted one another. The city was waking up for another workday on this brisk fall morning.

The events of the past few weeks had dramatically transformed Pastor Mark's life. He now looked at Bethany, the city he dearly loved, in a totally different light. The world was blind to the fact that it was plunging towards an end-time judgment called the Day of the Lord. Within a few short years, life in Bethany would be no more.

Pulling into the local gas station, the young pastor felt a prompting from the Holy Spirit, which said, "Asleep in the light."

"Hey, Pastor Bishop! How're ya'll doing?" yelled Jimmy.

Jimmy Curtis had worked at Sluman's Garage for the past four years, ever since he graduated from Lakeview High School. Mark had become friends with the lean, rather bashful mechanic and invited him regularly to visit his church. Even so, Jimmy always had an excuse, but that didn't stop the pastor from reaching out with God's love.

"Heard the church seminar ya'll had was a real barn burner," Jimmy said while laughing. "Seems like a lot of folks are getting all wrangled up over stuff about the end times. Even heard from some, Pastor, that you're predicting the end of the world."

"What do you think, Jimmy? Is the world getting better or worse?"

"Oh, you know me, Pastor. I don't give it no mind." Slipping his dirty overalls over his street clothes, he asked, "How can anyone know anyway?"

"Hey, Jimmy," Mark asked hopefully, "how would you like to visit our church this Sunday and hear what the Bible says about the end times?"

Ducking under the hood of his restored 1966 Ford Mustang, Jimmy replied, "That sounds mighty interesting, but I'm afraid I won't be able to make it. You see the Bethany Stock Car Series begins this Sunday morning." Not even bothering to look up, Jimmy quietly uttered, "Maybe another time, Pastor." Driving away, Mark wondered how many chances the young man would have before it was too late.

After Jimmy removed the last spark plug, the spirit of control decided to move from behind the young man's '66 Mustang and swiftly make his way towards Bethany Assembly.

✳

It had been a month since Pastor Mark received his vision of the antichrist and his ten-nation federation. To see the direction of their lives change so dramatically in such a short amount of time was simply amazing to the Bishops.

The Friday evening prayer group had doubled in size since Mark dropped the bomb on that now infamous Sunday morning in September. Several youth leaders arrived early and had been praying for over an hour.

Some of the deacons were telling stories while eating pizza and drinking coffee in the back of the Activity's Center. The laughter that followed each story was not from hearts overflowing with God's love, but from a cover-up, a counterfeit that had infiltrated every church in Bethany.

Just after Pastor Mark called everybody together, Billy B. and Stephen Corbin walked through the double doors from the sanctuary.

"Good evening, Stephen," Mark greeted. "It's so great that you could join us tonight for prayer."

The laughter from the deacons suddenly died out, only to be replaced by nervous suspicion.

One of the youth leaders shared with his friends that he had asked the Lord to send the watchman to them with a message from God. Everyone quickly took a seat while Mark motioned for his new friend to come forward and share whatever God had laid on his heart. As soon as the watchman began to address the prayer group, several intercessors seated in the back row could sense the anointing of God.

"As we all know, Jesus has spoken to us through his Word concerning events that will precede His coming. Over a month ago, your pastor received a word of knowledge that the tribulation period began with the signing of the

Jerusalem Peace Accord between Israel's Rosen and Germany's Hendrick. Our Lord Jesus Christ has given me the same message! Mark and I are watchmen proclaiming the truth of God's faithfulness amidst the coming worldwide persecution of the body of Christ. Within the past few years, our Lord has been enlisting watchmen all over the world."

This was no ordinary prayer meeting. The excitement within the youth was building. They had experienced the power of God before, but this was different. Everything seemed so surreal as the youth anxiously waited to hear what Stephen had to say.

"Tonight I stand before you with a simple exhortation. The first seal of Revelation has been broken, and the conqueror on a white horse is loose. When the Prime Minister of Israel signed the seven-year peace treaty with Hendrick, the seven-year tribulation period began. As believers, we must prepare ourselves spiritually, physically, and emotionally for the perilous times that are coming!"

"Praise the Lord, Stephen," affirmed Mark. "You know our youth have a lot of questions about what's ahead. Do you think we could have a question-and-answer time?"

"Be glad to," the evangelist replied.

Immediately a teenager seated near the back of the room shot his hand up and excitedly asked, "Brother Corbin, could you explain the meaning of the name antichrist?"

"Sure. In the Bible, the antichrist has many names. The most popular are the beast, the abomination of desolation, the man of sin, and the lawless one.[1] *Anti* means to take the place of. In other words, the antichrist will attempt to deceive the world by proclaiming himself to be god through the power of demonic signs and wonders. Actually, Revelation 17:8-10 tells us he will be an evil leader brought back from the bottomless pit in order to deceive the world."[2]

"So you're saying the antichrist, the rider on the white horse during opening of the first seal, has come to earth?" asked Allie Hart.

"That's correct. And the next seal to be opened will be the red horse of war. Listen up, everyone! Now that the tribulation period has begun, do you understand we're moving towards a predicted climax? We need to be witnessing to every lost person we know!"

Several youth who were dying to speak began to wave their hands high for questions.

Stephen raised his voice and said, "My dear friends in Christ, I know this sounds very frightening to you. It was to the first century believers too! In fact, Christians throughout history have experienced the fear of persecution. Our Jesus is warning us that in a very short time we will be persecuted; some of us may even be put to death. In the past decade we have all witnessed the growing hatred of Christians worldwide. Many of our friends and family members have already been seduced by Satan's lies. During the great tribulation, the lies of the enemy will convince many to turn away from their faith in Jesus and follow deceiving spirits.[3] But our Lord gave a promise to those who remain faithful. Jesus said, 'But he who endures to the end of the age shall be delivered.'[4] The believers who see the opening of the sixth seal—the cosmic disturbances—will be caught up to be with the Lord forever!"

A spontaneous roar went up as the prayer group praised the Lord for His faithfulness to His Word. As the group began to worship, Stephen suddenly sensed a deep conviction of sin.

"Hold up, everybody," requested the evangelist amidst the excited sharing of the group. "The Apostle Paul warned us when he wrote, 'But mark this, there will be terrible times in the last days. People will be lovers of themselves, lovers of money, boastful, proud, abusive, disobedient to their parents, ungrateful, unholy, without love, unforgiving, slanderous, without self control, brutal, not lovers of the good, treacherous, rash, conceited, lovers of pleasure rather than lovers of God—having a form of godliness but denying its power. And from such people turn away!' The apostle Paul warned us that during the next three and a half years, a great separation will take place within the body of Christ!"

The urgency in Stephen's voice had the prayer group hanging on every word. The conviction of the Holy Spirit was so thick that several began to weep. It was at this moment that two of the deacons, Dwayne Pressley and Kevin Collins, got up from their chairs and made a beeline for the backdoor exit.

While some students looked distracted, a seventh grader named Diana asked Stephen, "Reverend Corbin, how can we prepare for the persecution of the antichrist?"

"Excellent question, young lady," he replied. "The answer is pretty simple—holiness! God's Word warns us that in the last days believers will be easily deceived because of the habitual sin they have allowed to enter their lives. They will lack the spiritual discernment to perceive the truth because of their lifestyle of sin. For those who refuse to repent, the warning from the book of Hebrews will become their own personal nightmare. The Apostle Paul warned believers, 'Beware, brethren, lest there be in any of you an evil heart of unbelief in departing from the living God.'⁷⁶ We all need to confess and repent of any secret sin that has taken root within our lives," exhorted Stephen. "We need to be forgiven so that we may be free to become overcomers in Jesus' name. Let me ask you, how many desire to be free from any bondage of sin that has actually opened a doorway for the enemy to attack you?"

The evangelist could sense God's conviction. Bowing his head, he prayed for the youth to have the courage to be truthful with God. One by one believers dropped to their knees and confessed their sins. While Mark and Stephen prayed in the Spirit, they could hear prayers of genuine repentance throughout the room.

"Forgive me, Lord. I've put it off too long," confessed a young teenager weeping over her rebellion against God. "I hate my daddy for what he's done to my mama and me. Father, in Jesus' name, please accept my repentance and forgive me of my bitterness and anger. As of today, I forgive my daddy for leaving us."

Near the back of the room, a group of boys wept over their sins involving R-rated movies and pornography.

"I hate myself, Lord, for what I have done," confessed a senior from Lakeview High. I repent of my lust and ask for Your forgiveness."

As the young man sought the Lord in prayer, the Holy Spirit laid a verse of scripture on his heart.

"Jesus said, 'But I say to you that whoever looks at a woman to lust for her has already committed adultery with her in his heart.'⁷ Yes, Lord," whispered the boy. "I now know I can be in bondage to adultery without ever being physically involved."

"Please forgive us and grant us the power to become overcomers," confessed another boy, who had the courage to lead four others in a prayer of repentance.

"This is not some game," cried Hope Bishop. "Show us how to seek you with all our hearts, Lord. Help us to realize Your will for our lives, no matter how much others judge us."

The message of the hour turned a quiet Friday evening prayer time into a Holy Spirit revival meeting. When the release came and forgiveness began to touch hearts, a joyful praise went up to God.

Mark turned to Stephen and said, "I have never seen this group confess their sins like this before."

"Amen, Mark," rejoiced Stephen. Opening his Bible, he read: "Confess your trespasses to one another, and pray for one another, that you may be healed. The effective fervent prayer of a righteous man avails much."[8]

✳

Lance and Lee Ryan, current youth pastors at Bethany Assembly, had recently graduated from Bible college. In discussions with their classmates just prior to graduation, they dreamed of seeing great numbers of people repent and turn to Jesus Christ as their Savior.

Many of the students would become pastors of churches all over America. Others had applied to become missionaries to the countries that the Holy Spirit had laid on their hearts. It had been an exciting four years of study, and now each graduate would be sent out to make an eternal difference for the kingdom of God.

For Lance and Lee, mainly due to their love for people, ministry had always come easy. Both were from Georgia and had deeply committed parents who loved the Lord. Throughout their childhood their parents faithfully shared about the power of various revivals taking place around the world. A revival was a powerful move of repentance among believers, which would literally usher in the awesome presence of the Holy Spirit. Conviction of sin and repentance before God spread from believers to non-believers, prompting the unsaved to cry out for salvation. In many cases, bars would close down, and crimes within the city would disappear.

Lance dreamed of seeing churches overflow with Christians who desperately wanted to obey God. Lance's prayer was for a Holy Spirit-led revival that could touch not only a city but also a state, even a whole country. He didn't want to become a famous evangelist or to pastor a church of three thousand. This young pastor wanted to see a real move of God that everyone could recognize and experience, a supernatural presence for which no man could take credit.

Lance and Lee were both aware of the critical role young people play in a revival. They had visited the world famous Oswego Revival which caught fire in the middle 90s. The small church out of Bristol, Florida, had exploded with the power of the Holy Spirit, and millions of sinners were gloriously saved and filled with the Holy Spirit. It was easy to see how the youth, ages nine to eighteen, were used supernaturally to spread one of the greatest revivals of the twentieth century.

The youth leaders of the Lakeview High Bible Club dearly loved the Ryans. Lance, a six foot, five inch, two hundred pound former basketball star, was an immediate hit with the guys. Very soon after arriving in Bethany, he volunteered to work out with several leaders of the sports teams at Lakeview High. Soon the good-looking ex-jock, sporting a flattop haircut, became the unofficial chaplain for many students who didn't have a clue about God or Satan, heaven or hell, or what it really meant to be an obedient disciple of Jesus Christ.

Lee was tall, almost six feet, with long brown hair and brown eyes. Her beautiful smile could easily disarm a stranger. She quickly became a favorite with girls of all age groups.   Both Lee and Lance had a glow about them that could not be faked. After only a few months of ministering, the believers at Lakeview High knew the Ryans were for real.

It was Lance and Lee's prayer that God would bring a heaven sent revival to Bethany, Alabama, a city about which they knew very little.

Atop the Bethany public library, the demons of compromise, lying, control, unbelief, and fear froze in terror when they heard the rustling of his wings. It was a terrifying experience for them to see Satan face to face. The howling winds from this hideous spirit grew louder and louder as he hovered right over the top of them. Without any warning, he dropped down amidst his evil army of demons. The smell from his presence was so sickening that even the demon spirits had to turn away in disgust, though the reaction was more out of fear than repulsion.

With a mighty roar, Satan bellowed out his anger towards his evil soldiers. "What have you done?" he screamed, his voice seething with raw hate. "You have allowed the followers to form prayer groups throughout the city! Because of your incompetence, this so-called evangelist has been holding meetings teaching the followers all about our future attacks. I can sense the prayers of the followers reaching the ears of the One in Heaven. I hate their pitiful prayers for discernment. I despise their willingness to follow their convictions. Do you hear them expressing their love to the One in Heaven?"

The spirit of unbelief stepped forward and replied, "Yes, master, I do believe they are . . ."

"Silence! I want you to stop their prayers! Do you hear what they are calling the evangelist sent to Bethany by the One from above? What is that name? The watchman! I, the prince of darkness, hate that name!"

The demon of compromise immediately jumped forward with his idea of intimidation.

"Master, I will manipulate the pastors of Bethany so that they will reject his sequence of events before the end of the age. There are other followers that we have used before to create division among the churches. They lack spiritual discernment and can be easily influenced."

The spirit of lying suddenly interrupted, not wanting to be shown up by one of his peers. "My lord, I will personally give lies about the evangelist's past to the followers who love to gossip. It will take no time at all for the churches to turn against him and his worthless end-time message. I know of two prophecy teachers who strongly disagree with the watchman's . . ."

"What did you say?" shrieked Satan.

"Forgive me, master. What I meant to say was, uh, uh, this Corbin has enemies because of his message. There are two prophecy teachers, Tom Bray and Gerald Pierce, who will speak forth lies against this follower because the spirit of jealously has already gained control of them."

Perched nearby, the spirit of jealously could not help but smile.

"And what about you, spirit of fear? Has the cat got your tongue?" scoffed Satan as his greenish yellow tongue slipped out of his mouth like a giant banana slug. "Well, speak up! What fears does this puny little human have?"

The smallest of all demons slowly edged forward while everyone turned their attention towards him.

"I don't know, master," answered fear, totally unprepared for this type of confrontation.

"You what?" screamed the prince of darkness. "Each of you has been used in your specific area for thousands of years. Look at the victories you've had in defeating followers all over the world. My world! Am I not the ruler of this world?"[9]

"As you have said, master," mumbled the foul spirit as he slowly backed up.

"Yet all of you lack confidence and have failed to complete your assignments. To ensure our victory, you must continue to sow as many false interpretations of His Second Coming as possible. It's simple. We must create a mindset of unbelief, you idiots! They will not recognize the truth until it's too late!"

"But master, they have prayer warriors at Bethany Assembly that have . . ."

"Enough!" screamed the devil. "Do I have to send more soldiers, or can you handle this situation yourselves?"

Immediately several spirits jumped to attention and began to brag about the deceptions they would use to attack the followers.

"I don't care what you do!" Satan roared. "As for this Corbin, take away his voice if you want, but stop him from enlisting followers to pray! Spirit of fear, come to me."

Fear weaved itself toward his master through the jealous horde of wicked soldiers. The demons tried to listen to the conversation between the two evil spirits, but it was of no use. The little chat was obviously private. This was not a normal procedure, for if their master had wanted it to be totally secret, then no one would have seen a thing. For reasons of his own, Satan deliberately wanted his soldiers to witness the spirit of fear personally getting his orders.

As soon as the evil spirit departed for his assignment, the prince of darkness spread his wings and vanished. The demonic horde, seething with envy, immediately began to fight among themselves.

The next morning Michelle called out to Stephen that breakfast was ready. She was really looking forward to a break, maybe a drive out into the country with a picnic lunch.

"Stephen, come and get it; the blueberry muffins are hot!"

Walking back to the bedroom while drying her hands with a dishcloth, Michelle suddenly sensed that something was wrong. Stepping into the bathroom, she could see Stephen clutching his throat. He was moving his lips but no words were coming out. When he turned towards her, she realized what had happened. Stephen could not talk!

As they held each other, Michelle began interceding. The evil spirit of fear quickly departed. Shooting high into the air, he maneuvered towards his next assignment—the Mark Bishop family.

CHAPTER 8

THE SECOND SEAL:
THE RED HORSE OF WAR

Another horse, fiery red, went out.
And it was granted to the one who sat on it to take peace from the earth,
and that people should kill one another;
and there was given to him a great sword.
Revelation 6:4

Wolfgang Hendrick came to power out of relative obscurity. The creative union reforms he implemented had brought his country back from the brink of financial and political disaster. No one would have ever believed one man could ever bring together the political factions within the German National Party. Wolfgang Hendrick had done the impossible! His very presence exuded strength, trustworthiness, and kindness, while his encouraging speeches fostered an atmosphere of peace. Several leaders from the European Union had already publicly praised the new leader's valuable leadership skills.

His most amazing accomplishment was the almost supernatural way in which he won the trust of Arab countries surrounding Israel. For over thirty years, the Middle East peace talks had moved from country to country. After the negotiations remained hopelessly deadlocked in Jerusalem, the President of the United States offered Washington DC as a neutral site. Repeated attempts at peace between Israel and the Palestinians proved fruitless as the world looked on. It seemed like a dream come true when the Prime Minister of Israel shook hands with the leader of the Palestinian people on the White House lawn. Everyone had high hopes until another terrorist bomb attack destroyed any chance of a peaceful resolution. It wasn't until the negotiations reached the leader of the Middle East Federation in Munich that the world really began to take notice. Historical and political experts were astounded at the simplicity of Hendrick's plan and at how quickly it was implemented. Leaders from around the world were captivated by the persuasive skills of the leader from Germany!

For some, it was extremely exciting, but most remained cautious as new events unfolded almost daily. While mankind continued its infatuation with its new hero, a heavenly event was just about to take place, an event that would dramatically change the course of human history!

✳

The Lamb of God at the right hand of the Father stood, displaying the golden scroll in His right hand. After raising it above His head, He broke the second seal. Immediately, a fiery, red horse was loosed. Its rider would rob the world of peace by prompting the people of the earth to kill one another.[1] The angelic host watching could only wonder how many would eventually suffer. A warrior angel spoke up as soon as the red horse departed.

"Beware, those of you who live on earth, the red horse of war is coming!"

✳

The CNN news room in Washington DC was rocking with the dramatic news report that had just reached the desks.

"Have the Russians gone crazy?" CNN news anchor Adam Childs whispered to himself. The already nervous reporter, trying not to show any alarm, looked into camera number one and began his report.

"Good evening, everyone, I'm Adam Childs, and this is *CNN Nightly News*. Our lead story tonight comes from Siberia, Russia. Within the past hour, self-proclaimed President Alexi Rakmanoff has officially declared Siberia, the eastern portion of Russia, an independent state! Since the Siberian oil workers have not been paid in two years, Rakmanoff has ordered a large portion of Moscow's oil supply cut off. The Siberian president has created a substantial army in order to defend himself from any Russian aggression. We have just learned, as we speak, that Rakmanoff has formally applied for Siberia to become a recognized member of the United Nations."

After cutting away for a quick commercial, Adam was handed another news update on the Russian conflict.

"Four . . . three . . . two . . . one . . . . You're on, Adam."

"As you have just heard," announced the CNN reporter, "Siberia's Alexi Rakmanoff has severed all ties with Moscow by announcing the formation of a new country. The president of Russia, Uri Esapenko, has wasted little time in renouncing Rakmanoff's unlawful rebellion against his own people. Russian troops have already taken up positions in Kurgan and Chelybinsk, cities situated within the Ural Mountains and touching the newly constructed borders of Siberia. CNN sources have heard unofficial reports of a bitter division among the high-ranking naval officers at the large naval base in Vladivostok, located on the far eastern coast of Russia. In response to this aggression, China has announced the doubling of its troops along the common border of Siberia. The United States Embassy in Moscow has advised all Americans who reside in the former USSR to evacuate immediately. The Baltic Republics of Lithuania, Latvia, and Estonia have rejected any plea for support from either side. The Ukrainian Army has been put on full alert and is prepared to resist any Siberian aggression. According to Pavel Skullus, a Russian news agency reporter, Russian troops have begun killing Siberian soldiers near the city of Magnitogorsk, which is located in the heart of the Ural Mountains. This is CNN's Adam Childs, reporting to you live from Moscow, Russia."

While CNN news teams developed their research on the Russian rebellion, news from south of Russia exploded over the airwaves.

"A skirmish along the borders of North and South Korea has escalated into a small war," reported CNN's news reporter Seok Jang-Jae. "South Korean casualties are said to be in excess of three thousand. The casualties, primarily civilians, are the result of hostile bombing by North Korea. The evacuation of people along the bordering cities has become a hellish nightmare as thousands of families flee for their lives. The South Koreans have already moved heavy artillery into the combat area, and what direction the attacks will take is unknown at this time. Neighboring countries have issued pleas for a peaceful resolution. When asked about the possible use of nuclear weapons, a spokesman from North Korea stated that they would use whatever force necessary in order to maintain security along their border. This is CNN's Seok Jang-Jae, reporting live from South Korea."

"Thank you, Seok, for that important update. Good evening, everyone, this is CNN's Marsha Wells, reporting live from our Chicago bureau. At this point, it seems as if the United States of America has no comment on either the Russian or Korean conflicts that have erupted within the past twenty-four hours. The threat of nuclear war has sent a chill of fear throughout the world," concluded the CNN reporter.

"Oh, this just in," continued the CNN reporter. "In an unprecedented move, the general secretary of the United Nations has requested that the president of the United States personally address the UN membership regarding his country's intentions. The general secretary issued this reply in today's news conference: 'The whole world is looking to the United States for guidance in these trying times.'

"He went on to say that the meeting with the president of the United States would be broadcast worldwide. This is *CNN Nightly News* with Marsha Wells. We will continue to bring you hourly updates on the Russian and Korean conflicts. Until then, goodnight, everyone."

Arriving at the United Nations building in New York, the president was escorted to a small room just off the general secretary's chambers. As he readied himself to deliver his address, an urgent message was given to him by one of his top military advisors. After reading it, the color seemed to drain from his face. He immediately asked for his red phone while the head Secret Service agent signaled for extra security in the building. It was official! Code Red was now in effect.

A death-like fear seemed to grip the UN diplomats from over two hundred countries. An atmosphere of uncertainty seemed to permeate the UN meeting as decisions influencing billions of lives were being made with split-second precision. The news that had just reached the president was immediately announced in over sixty languages. The members within the United Nation's headquarters appeared very frightened when another live newscast struck with even more alarm than the first two.

"This is CNN news reporter Omar Bhuta, reporting live from New Delhi, India. Within the past hour, Pakistani rebels have attacked a nuclear power base in Jaisalmer, Northern India, and have taken four hundred Indians hostage. These rebels are threatening to destroy the cities of New Delhi and Jodhpur with short-range nuclear missiles if their demands are not met. The prime minister of India has implemented talks with the head of state of Pakistan in order to negotiate a peaceful resolution. He has put all military units on emergency stand-by. His official report states that under no circumstances shall any Indian special forces attempt to regain control of the nuclear power base."

Suddenly, the portable lights above the CNN reporter shut off. In the immediate background, standing behind reinforced barricades, stood thousands of Indians anxiously awaiting any new updates on the hostage crisis.

"What's up?" yelled Omar. "Are we still on? If we can't get any juice, let's head indoors," directed the veteran Indian reporter.

After several adjustments, the floodlights began to flicker. They died again and then came on with a surge that lit up the reporter and several thousand cheering Indians!

"You're on, Omar!" the relived technician shouted.

"Once again, this is CNN's Omar Bhuta, speaking to you live from New Delhi, India. At this very moment, thousands of families are fleeing to the South after hearing the intentions of the Pakistani rebels. The streets of New Delhi are overflowing with people praying to their gods for protection. At this time, the rebels are demanding the complete withdrawal of Indian military forces from the country of Kashmir. The Pakistani Parliament is under intense pressure from the rebels to declare war on India if these conditions are not met. As of now, the Indian government has not officially replied," concluded the CNN reporter.

Directly across the street from the live CNN newscast, the Indian Defense Council was reviewing the demands of the Pakistani rebels.

"There must be a compromise if we are going to avert this threat to our people," insisted the defense minister. "We must sign a peace treaty with Pakistan that the United Nations will both approve of and enforce."

As the president of the United States stepped up to the podium before the United Nations, Wolfgang Hendrick sat quietly sipping his tea. He was patiently waiting to see the live history-making TV newscast.

The world had always had wars and rumors of wars in its six-thousand-year existence. For years the leaders of the major powers had not only survived but had also triumphed over the fear of a third world war. But only recently had defense experts advocated a big-brother coalition that would bring accountability to over two hundred countries of the world. Little by little, the earth was becoming a one-world community that would eventually take its orders from one supreme commander.

Wolfgang Hendrick smiled as the president of the United States stepped up and greeted the cheering UN delegates. The man of sin already knew that the president's speech would become a critical cornerstone in laying the foundation for his new-world government.

The leader from the most powerful country in the world looked tired and pale as he attempted to calm the fears of billions of people.

"These are times when we do not know why such terrors come upon us," reasoned the president. "I can assure you that we have been in contact with the leaders of each side of the Russian, Korean, and Indian conflicts. The only answer to stop this insane bloodshed is clear. We must become as one people, a united family! Today I propose the leaders of this world come together to . . ."

Quietly, the spirit of antichrist spoke through Hendrick and hissed, "The second seal has been broken, and the rider on red horse has come."

Within a year of the president's speech, over thirty-three wars would erupt around the world. The deep-seated hate and bitterness between ethnic groups would explode time and again in the worst evil the world had ever experienced.

Jesus had warned, "You will hear of wars and rumors of wars. See that you are not troubled; for all these things must come to pass, but the end [of the age] is not yet. For nation will rise against nation, kingdom against kingdom."[2]

Wolfgang Hendrick knew his appointed time to rule was coming, a time when the world would look to him as their promised deliverer!

More and more cars seemed to appear out of nowhere. While Julie and Mark served sweet tea to their guests, several of the youth leaders began lining the walls with folding chairs. The living room and the dining room were jammed with believers who had come to learn the truth concerning the Lord's coming. Allie and Lindy were passing out paper and pens for anyone interested in taking notes. No one could remember such excitement ever occurring on a Tuesday evening Bible study. After an hour of prayer and praise, Pastor Mark stood and shared, "Pastor Lance, why don't you begin our Bible study tonight?"

"That sounds good to me," Lance replied. "Lee and I see a lot of new faces tonight with those special smiles, and we all know what that means."

"Yeah, you can't hide the joy of the Lord, now can you?" agreed a smiling Lee Ryan from the back of the room.

The laughter erupting throughout the house came from hearts that had just received Jesus as their Savior. For over a year, the Spirit of revival had been spreading to every church service and weekly Bible study at Bethany Assembly. While the religious crowd of the town mocked the supposed move of God, the youth began to pray under a powerful anointing from the Holy Spirit. Each service would begin with fervent prayer, followed by praises to the Lord. The worship services were spontaneously led by youth leaders who had no idea how the Holy Spirit would lead them. It was not uncommon for the worship to last over two hours. The youth group called it the *glory*. Of course, Mark and Lance received several complaints from those opposing their so-called revival.

"Like I said, these holy rollers think they are so spiritual because of their loud hallelujahs and emotional gymnastics," complained a member from Bethany Baptist. "This glory they brag about is just a feel-good experience that doesn't accomplish anything."

"The Bible clearly teaches that a church service should be conducted decently and in order," challenged the worship leader from Eastside United Methodist Church. "Besides that, how many souls are truly getting saved?"

The spirit of jealousy really had a field day when news of the revival had spread to other towns. Almost overnight, carloads of youth began arriving hours before scheduled services in order to pray and seek God's guidance.

"Hey, Pastor Lance, could you share the vision of revival you had with those who are here tonight who have never heard it?" asked an excited Lindy Hart.

"Sure, Lindy," shouted the youth pastor over the cheers of approval. "It was about a year ago, shortly after Pastor Mark shared his vision, that the Holy Spirit imparted to me a vision of revival spreading across America. In my vision I saw an old, dirty horse trough, the kind horses in the old West would drink out of. Inside the trough was the anointing of the Holy Spirit. In front of the trough was a long line of ministers, waiting their turn to drink in God's anointing. After drinking, these ministers would return to their congregations, and the anointing for revival would fall upon the believers."

Immediately, excited whispers permeated the living room.

"In my vision, some of the ministers in line soon became weary of the long wait. It was pretty disgusting to watch so many drop out of line, but it was easy to see why. There were three types of shepherds who refused to drink. The first were those who refused to confess their sin of putting man-made programs ahead of God's leading. The second group of shepherds refused to humble themselves in front of their peers. And the third group that rejected God's anointing became impatient and left."

"Why would so many ministers do that, Pastor Lance?" asked a visitor.

"Well, guys, it has become pretty obvious over the years that the goal of many shepherds is not the discipleship of their sheep anymore but the proud achievement of maintaining their own agenda. Nevertheless, some of the ministers who stepped up to the trough actually dropped to their knees and received a double portion of the glory of God! This act of humility produced two different reactions from the shepherds who were still waiting. For those who loved God, the excitement became even stronger. Most of the ministers in this group had been praying for revival for many years. To see that it was within their grasp brought tears of joy followed by spontaneous cheers to God. For those who refused to drink, the humility of the shepherds who desperately desired a real move of God was simply a turn off. 'Look how silly they are acting,' insisted one preacher in my vision. 'This hyped-up show isn't honoring God. It is actually a disgrace.'

"Within seconds the massive line of ministers was cut in half, only to be replaced by hungry shepherds from far-away lands. The revival continued to grow across America as thousands upon thousands received Jesus Christ as their Lord and Savior."

While Lance continued to explain his vision, his words became slower and softer.

"The fire of revival will spread to those who will seek it with all their hearts. Eventually," whispered Lance, "the worst persecution of those receiving from God would come from ministers who refused to believe. A skeptical pastor in the vision said, 'Don't you see how deceptive it is? The reason I know it's not from God is the arrogance of the leadership when this so-called glory hits. My denomination doesn't approve of this type of manipulation. Besides, we have our own move of God, which produces real fruit,' bragged the shepherd."

"You mean this vision is really going to come true?" asked a new believer in the Lord.

Lance began to weep, his hands raised high in submission to God. He couldn't go on any further. The entire Bible study began to pray for the pastors of America. The vision, which Lance had just shared, began to spread all over the country. The flame of revival glory eventually touched such cities as Portland, Oregon; South Tahoe, Nevada; Tulsa, Oklahoma; Naperville, Illinois; and Wooster, Massachusetts.

"Do you have anything else to share?" Pastor Mark respectfully asked his dear friend.

Lance just shook his head sadly and uttered, "Who would have ever thought a heaven-sent revival would be opposed by the very ministers it was sent for?"

"Why God?" one youth cried out. "Open our eyes, Lord, so we may see the truth!"

With a deep sense of conviction, Julie Bishop stood and began to share.

"The Holy Spirit has just shown me that the shepherds in the vision who refused to accept God's anointing have no fear of God!"

A holy hush swept across the house. Both Mark and Lance could sense God convicting hearts. The weeping over a lack of the fear of God began slowly, like a small stream, but within minutes it became a mighty river of heart-felt confession!

"There is no revival," whispered the spirit of pride. "You don't really believe revival can come to little, ole Bethany now, do you?" laughed the filthy spirit.

Immediately, several intercessors discerned the evil intrusion and rebuked the demonic visitor out of their meeting. Two hours later Pastor Mark concluded the prayer time with a final prayer of thanksgiving. It was clear to see that God was building a foundation of faith among his saints to believe for revival by sending a vision bathed in prayer for lost souls, a belief in God's Word that would discern the counterfeits of the enemy, whether from Satan or from the traditions of men!

Looking to his left, Mark saw Julie motioning for him to take a look at those who were still seated throughout the house. He soon realized that people had their Bibles open and notepads ready.

"So everybody's still up for a Bible study?" asked the elated pastor.

The chorus of amens from the youth section was definitely loud enough to get the point across. Mark wasted little time producing his previously prepared notes for the study. For the next hour he taught on the willful disobedience of believers in the last days.

"In the book of Revelation, chapters 2 and 3, Jesus warned believers living in the last days to repent. Many who profess Christ will lose their first love like Ephesus did," said Mark with a sigh. "Others will worship idols like Pergamos did, compromise with the world like Thyatira did, become lukewarm like Laodicea did, and eventually suffer spiritual death like Sardis did.[3]

Each first century church is an example of future believers who will be living within the seven-year tribulation period. The behavior of these churches, whose habitual sin affected their relationship with God, are warnings to believers living in the last days."

The burden for the body of Christ could be seen on the pastor's face.

"By continuing in their sin of rebellion, they will literally grieve the Holy Spirit right out of their lives. The Laodician believers were promised by God to be spewed out of the body of Christ because of their refusal to repent.[4] For those who perish in hell under the deception of the antichrist, they will become examples of believers who refused to heed the warnings of a loving Savior. Jesus warned, 'Watch therefore, and pray always that you may be counted worthy to escape all these things that will come to pass, and to stand before the Son of Man.'"[5]

"This is going to get pretty intense, isn't it, Pastor?" asked a frightened student near the front.

Before continuing, Mark looked across the room and received an encouraging smile from Julie.

"As you can see, guys, our Lord clearly warned believers living right before the end of the age not to allow their love for Christ to grow cold. The persecution of Christians by the antichrist will motivate many to rely on the Holy Spirit. For those who refuse to repent, they will depart from the their faith."

"But why would Christians turn their back on God?" asked Allie.

"Well, Allie, God's Word makes it pretty clear that the body of Christ in the last days will be in a compromising condition. You ask why? Scripture tells us that believers will be deceived by the doctrines of devils. Their consciences will be seared as with a hot iron," concluded the solemn pastor as he stepped over and took Julie's hand.[6]

The believers slowly stood to their feet and began to applaud.

Gently the Holy Spirit spoke to Mark's heart, "They are not applauding for you but for hearing the truth."

Sensing the Spirit's leading, the young pastor asked the people to bow their heads for prayer.

"We praise you Father, Son, and Holy Spirit, the one and only true God. May the words spoken tonight prepare each of us for the future avalanche of false prophets who will attempt to deceive the body of Christ."[7]

While the saints hugged and encouraged one another, the demon of fear was filled with rage. He was unable to sway even one of the followers to entertain any of his accusations.

After the last of their guests bid good-bye, Mark and Julie rejoiced at how much fun it was to minister to saints who were free to grow in the grace and knowledge of Jesus Christ.

The sun glistened off the golden top of the newly constructed Jewish temple on Mount Moriah. Excitement filled the air as the people prepared themselves for the first Sabbath in the beautiful new temple. On this early, cool fall morning, rabbis could be seen greeting each other in the streets, families could be seen cutting and preparing flowers from their gardens, and children could be seen receiving gifts from one another. This was going to be a day to remember, a new day!

The priests were preparing the ingredients of the incense offering with the utmost care. Each red heifer, which would be sacrificed during the ritual purification, had to be thoroughly inspected. Several priests from the tribe of Levi secured the ramp, which led to the top of the altar where the animals would be sacrificed. Within the past year, the world had witnessed the miracle of miracles, the construction of the third Jewish temple.

Those witnessing this history-making ceremony represented countries from all over the world. As one priest positioned the microphone, another helped the ninety-two-year-old rabbi to the portable platform facing the crowd.

Rabbi Ehud Reuben, a survivor of the Holocaust, was a Jewish historian with no equal. He was known throughout out the Middle East as a man who deeply loved his people and his Jewish heritage.

As the Rabbi ascended to the platform, a visiting teacher from Harvard University turned to his guide and asked, "Is the Rabbi actually going to take part in the ceremony this afternoon?"

"This is totally unexpected," replied his shocked guide. "Rabbi Reuben hasn't spoken publicly in over a decade!"

Standing before an overflow crowd of thousands of visitors, the Rabbi desperately wanted to participate in this historic moment. Dressed in a royal blue robe with a golden vest having twelve precious stones, he looked very majestic with the glorious temple in the background.

"Dear friends of Israel," announced the Rabbi, while the crowd noise gradually dropped to a mere whisper, "in the year 951 BC, King Solomon was instructed by God to build our first house of worship. In 586 BC, the Babylonian army swept through our beloved Jerusalem and set fire to our Holy Temple. Thousands of our people were taken captive to Babylon. Our Holy Temple was destroyed by gentile soldiers and left utterly abandoned!"

The hot noonday sun highlighted the wrinkles of the Rabbi's face as he paused for a drink of water.

"In 70 AD, the Roman army led by General Titus marched on our Holy City and totally dismantled the second temple, which had been restored in the year 63 AD. Not one stone was left upon another," the Rabbi passionately shared.[8]

Suddenly a Jewish teenager dressed in a red Nike sweatshirt and Levi jeans jumped out from the crowd and leaped onto the portable platform just a few feet away from the surprised speaker.

The young man wearing an earring and a very short haircut, abruptly announced, "This is a new day between Jew and Arab. A day when we can worship in our temple and our Arab neighbors can worship in their mosque!"

The startled crowd refocused on the Rabbi as the young man was escorted off the platform. After a long pause, tears could be seen dripping down the cheeks of this holocaust survivor who had prayed for peace for his homeland for over sixty years.

"It is true," the Rabbi slowly replied. "We have entered a new day, a day when a Jew can say *shalom*, peace, to his Arab neighbor. Behold, the completion of the third Jewish temple!"

To the left of the Dome of the Rock, the Muslim Mosque, separated by a twenty-foot stone wall, stood the new Jewish temple. Everyone cheered, for the bloodshed in the streets of Jerusalem had finally come to an end. Now the children could once again play in the streets without any fear of being attacked. Yes, they were grateful for a peace treaty between Israel and its Arab neighbors!

CHAPTER 9

THE CALLING OF GOD

And no man takes this honor to himself,
but he who is called by God.
Hebrews 5:4

The red light glowing in the standby room flickered against the desk where Arthur Lawrence sat reviewing his notes for the last time. Glancing at his watch, Arthur noted he had two more minutes before the green light came on, signaling that his end-times show would be on the air. He scanned the pages hurriedly, looking for any mistakes.

Arthur's ministry had lasted over thirty years. His popularity continued to grow primarily due to his teaching on the rapture of the saints. His books on end-time prophecies quickly became best sellers in America. Some were even made into movies. In recent years, however, a small but vocal group of pastors had begun to teach that Christians would suffer persecution at the hands of the antichrist. This wasn't anything new for Arthur. He had dealt before with Christian leaders who disagreed with his theology. That was no big deal. But what really irritated him were ministers who had become militant against his pre-tribulation theology.

"Any minister who teaches that Jesus can't come at any moment is just giving Satan an opportunity to deceive the body of Christ," the preacher whispered to himself.

After thousands of hours of studying end-time events, the Bible teacher found it impossible to accept that the bride of Christ would ever be a participant in the great tribulation. Glancing down at his watch again, he thought to himself, "Anyone who believes the bride of Christ will be martyred by the antichrist must be off their rocker!"

"You're on in thirty seconds, Reverend Lawrence," announced the producer.

While Arthur positioned himself in his chair, the make-up artist made one last-minute adjustment to his shiny silver hair.

"4 . . . 3 . . . 2 . . . 1 . . ." The producer ticked off the last seconds on his fingers.

"Welcome to *Countdown to Midnight* with prophecy expert Arthur Lawrence! Tonight's show will focus on the most critical issue facing the body of Christ today: the imminent return of our Lord Jesus Christ! To help us grasp this comforting truth, here's Mr. Prophecy himself, Arthur Lawrence!"

"Good evening, everyone. In view of the recent events striking our world, I'm very excited to have the opportunity to come into your home this evening and encourage you," declared the smiling preacher, focusing on camera two. "Apostle Paul encouraged believers when he wrote, 'Behold, I tell you a mystery: we will not all sleep but we will all be changed—in a moment, in the twinkling of an eye, at the last trumpet. For the trumpet will sound, and the dead will be raised incorruptible and we shall be changed.'[1] It's the rapture, my friends! Through the Holy Spirit, the apostle specifically highlighted the glorious catching up of the saints when he wrote, 'For the Lord himself will descend from heaven with a loud shout, with the voice of an archangel, and with the trumpet of God. And the dead in Christ will rise first. Then we who are alive and remain shall be caught up together with them in the clouds to meet the Lord in the air. And thus we shall always be with the Lord. Therefore comfort one another with these words.'[2]

"Listen to me, saints! How can we comfort one another with the outbreak of over thirty wars around the world? That's right. With the hope that our Jesus could come for His spotless and pure bride at any moment! Jesus is our blessed hope, and He will not subject us to His wrath. I've been teaching for over thirty years that the seven-year tribulation period is called the Day of the Lord! This period of God's wrath will immediately follow the rapture, deliverance then wrath! As soon as our Savior Jesus Christ catches up His own, God's wrath consisting of the seven seals, followed by the seven trumpets, and ending with the seven bowls will burst forth.[3] The Day of the Lord will begin with the breaking of the first seal, the antichrist's coming on a white horse. According to the book of Daniel, this deceiver will lead a ten-nation confederacy from the European Union in signing a seven-year covenant of peace with unsuspecting Israel. Soon after this peace treaty is signed, wars will break out all over the world."

Pausing for a second, the preacher smiled and lowered his reading glasses.

"Now I know the world has experienced two similar events in the past year. There are even a few sincere pastors advocating that this is a sign that we have entered the tribulation period. Listen my friends; my heart is heavy when I hear such false teaching coming from men who claim to be ministers of the gospel. Some even teach that there has to be a separation of the wheat, believers, from the tares, unbelievers, because the body of Christ has become lukewarm. They believe Jesus will come for a spotless and pure bride, which is a result of persecution by the antichrist and the false prophet."

For a brief second Arthur wished these false teachers would just go away.

"I'm here to tell you tonight that the first century Christians were not looking for the antichrist or the judgments of God. No, my friends, the elect were looking for their blessed hope, Jesus Christ, coming on the clouds of heaven. Don't be deceived, saints! Jesus himself warned us of false prophets who will attempt to deceive the elect in the last days. Don't let the devil or anyone else take away your hope that our Lord can come at any moment. The Bible teaches that all events leading up to the rapture have been fulfilled. For those of you who want to stay, God bless you, but I'm praying up, moving up, and finally going up!"

The applause sign started to flash, signaling the live audience to cheer.

The strain on the teacher's face was easy to see. It seemed as if every major doctrine Arthur had taught and produced through his tape ministry was being challenged, even attacked. Within the past few months, thousands of his listeners had begun to challenge his pre-tribulation doctrine. Many were fearful and confused. Some were demanding answers to God's Word, which a pre-tribulation rapture position could not provide. As the applause died down, Arthur received his one-minute warning.

"My time is almost up. In conclusion, I would like to say that only the blood of Jesus Christ can make the bride of Christ pure! You are not saved because of any lifestyle of works but by the grace of God. Even if your life shows no fruit at all, you will still be saved. Jesus will never reject you once you are his child. Let's always remember, saints, that Jesus saves you, and that is a gift not of yourselves.[4] Those of us whom the Holy Spirit indwells are eternally saved and will be rescued from God's wrath before the Day of the Lord begins!"

The smiling Bible teacher suddenly took on an expression of deep concern.

"Church, allow me to be very candid. How many of you can envision your children playing in the morning sunlight, and without any warning, having them thrust into the great tribulation of God's wrath? God forbid it, my friends! Believe me, there is nothing to fear from the antichrist because we will all be gone! God bless you all, and keep looking up."

The applause sign lit up again, prompting the crowd to erupt with cheers of approval. After a few moments, as the lights on the set grew dim, the famous teacher quickly moved down amongst the audience and began to autograph his new book, *At Any Moment.*

Pastor Mark reached over and turned off the TV. His prayer session that night with Stephen had lasted a lot longer than he had anticipated. Each watchman knew that the battle lines were being drawn within the leadership of the body of Christ. Arthur Lawrence's stinging rebuke would eventually encourage several major Christian denominations to publicly declare their adherence to the pre-tribulation belief. For those who had always believed in a pre-trib teaching, the very thought of the antichrist persecuting Christians was impossible. In fact, the more believers who embraced the teaching of the antichrist coming first, the more adamant the pre-trib camp became.

"The division within the leadership of the Church doesn't look good," a reflective Mark shared. "What do you think, Stephen?"

"It's only going to get worse," he sadly replied.

Within the past year, the evangelist from California had seen several divisive splits in churches throughout America. Even so, his speaking schedule for the next six months was pretty full. Nevertheless, he continued to sense the leading of the Holy Spirit to make Bethany his new home base.

"So when will you and Michelle be returning to your home in Santa Barbara?" asked a curious Mark.

"Not any time soon."

"But, Stephen, what about your calling to be a watchman?"

"That's exactly it, my friend. The Spirit of God will continue to lead Michelle and me. Since the first day we arrived, we have both felt from the Lord that Bethany was a special assignment. As of now, we have decided to stay until the Lord releases us."

"That's exciting news," a grateful Mark replied. "I know the youth group will be praising the Lord."

After a long pause, Stephen just smiled and replied, "Who knows? Maybe we'll stay until the rapture!"

Tom Bray had been called to be a minister at a very young age. His parents had been missionaries to the people of Kenya, Africa, for over thirty-five years. Both parents had played an important part in cultivating God's calling upon their son's life. They had known that the Holy Spirit was molding and shaping Tom into a mighty man of God.

Over the years, the Brays had witnessed missionaries discourage their own children from entering the full-time ministry. It was true; a lot of missionaries were not well off when they retired. At times, friendships were strained by church decisions concerning doctrine, discipline, and finances. But for the Brays and hopefully their son, the ministry of serving the Lord would always be a joy.

Tom's father believed that one of the greatest sins in America was a parent who would not pray for his or her children to pursue God's call for their lives. To see thousands of men and women working in available job opportunities that they thought God opened for them was a spiritual tragedy to the Brays. In actuality, the Lord of the universe had called many to preach a living gospel to a dying world.

"The Lord's heart must be broken," confessed Tom's father during his early morning prayer time. "To think of so many who have missed God's perfect will for their lives, and for what?" Slowly he whispered, "All because they sought the approval of man over the approval of God."[5]

Shortly after his sixteenth birthday, Tom had shared with his folks that God had called him to preach the gospel. There was never any doubt that their only son would become a minister.

At Bible college, while many of his classmates were crying out for souls to be saved during all night prayer meetings, Tom studied lesson plans, sermon outlines, and most of all, end-time prophecy charts. It had not taken long for the prize student to realize that his peers revered a minister by what he teaches. One's acceptance, affirmation, and value were determined by what one taught, at least for the most part.

After graduating from Bible college, Tom accepted the pastorate of a small church in Mobile, Alabama. While teaching part-time at a nearby Bible college, he met his wife-to-be, Ashley. A romance sprang up between them, and two years later they were married.

His next ministerial position was a large church in Birmingham, Alabama. Tom was certain that this was God's will for his life. The highly educated membership exceeded one thousand members. Surely, he thought, this would be a body of believers who would appreciate his exegetical interpretation of the Scripture.

To no one's surprise, Tom's popularity began to grow within his denomination. The next step up the ladder of success the young preacher was so diligently climbing was a very prominent congregation in Jacksonville, Florida. For many of the national leaders within Tom's denomination, this was a jewel that many aspiring pastors coveted. The beautiful red-brick sanctuary of Christ Cathedral stood majestically erect among the well-groomed rose gardens surrounded by hundred-year-old oak trees. The educational wing included classrooms with individual computers. Just recently, the church board voted to build a new indoor swimming pool for the youth adjacent to the well-equipped gymnasium.

More coveted than this, however, was the prestige it brought the shepherd who preached from the mahogany pulpit that stood high above the congregation. To be able to look down on the sheep and proclaim the power of God's Word was definitely an adrenaline rush for the up-and-coming young pastor.

Through it all, Ashley began to see more and more character flaws in her husband as he continued to achieve the goals he had always coveted. All she could do was pray that God would convict her husband of his selfish ambition, a sin that could be easily seen if anyone really bothered to look.

It soon became very clear that Tom had the gift to teach eschatology, the study of end times. Every minister has a special area of teaching that he or she will gravitate toward due to their love to study it. For Tom, it had always been the coming of the Lord. Of course, it was very rare for the respected orator not to be prepared when he stepped into the renowned pulpit of Christ Cathedral. But when given the opportunity to preach on the road or overseas, Tom would usually have to fight the urge to preach the imminent return of Jesus Christ. This passion led the experienced pastor to write several books on the rapture of the saints. After pastoring the nationally known Christ Cathedral Church for five years, the leadership within Tom's denomination encouraged the well liked pastor to pursue a full-time ministry as a revivalist, with a focus on end-time prophecy. With Ashley and their two sons, Matthew and Samuel, in tow, Tom decided to move his family to a charming little city, called Bethany, in southeastern Alabama.

The Reverend Thomas Nelson Bray quickly became a very accomplished conference speaker at prophecy seminars all across the country. His hard work earned him a reputation of being a brilliant orator who understood the importance of prophetic events. He was known as a faithful family man with a deep love for the Lord. As the years flew by, there was hardly a time when anybody dared challenge Tom's knowledge of the Scripture. Even so, through all his accomplishments, the famous preacher never dreamed that it would ever be possible for his prophetic teaching concerning the timing of the Lord's return to be wrong.

Matt Bray and his brother, Sam, had been attending two of the most prestigious universities in the country. Matt was pursuing a theology major in the Bible, with the goal of getting a doctorate in biblical languages. His eventual goal was to become a seminary professor. His younger brother, Sam, was studying a Bible and administration double major in order to someday become a Bible college president. But their ambitions for the full-time ministry would have to wait. At this moment the Bray family was facing the greatest spiritual crisis they would ever face.

The slightly nervous boys were sitting side by side on the sofa. They had been discussing their research on the Second Coming of Christ.

"Yes, Mom, we are very committed to what we believe, and yes, we have prayed very thoroughly over our conclusions," Matt patiently explained.

Both young men dreaded the confrontation that would soon break forth in the Bray household. After entering the family room, Tom poured himself an ice-cold glass of lemonade and excitedly gestured towards his sons saying, "Now wasn't that a profound message my good friend Arthur Lawrence gave on *Countdown to Midnight* last night?" Not bothering to look in their direction he continued, "I'm totally convinced that if the pastors in America would just have enough backbone to teach the truth concerning Christ's coming, we would not have all this vacillating back and forth among the saints. The message that Christ could come at any moment is so clear; I just don't see how anybody who knows the Bible could miss it."

"Dad, Sam and I would like to address the very issue you have just brought up," replied Matt.

"Why, of course, son. What questions do you have that I might help you with?" answered a smiling Tom while opening his well-worn Scofield King James Bible.

"To be honest, Dad, we really don't have any questions at this time, but rather we have several biblical conclusions we would like to share with you."

Entering the family room, Ashley took a neutral seat across the room from the men in her life. She had known in her heart for some time that this moment would eventually come. Under her breath she prayed, "Dear Lord, I know my husband and my sons love you, and I pray the Holy Spirit within them will open their eyes to see the truth concerning the timing of your return for your saints."

"It was just over a year ago that Sam and I began to research the subject of the Second Coming of Christ during our study of the gospel of Matthew," declared Matt.

"Excellent, boys! I know the biblical foundation you've received at home must have put you head and shoulders above your classmates," bragged the proud father.

"Actually Dad, Sam and I have come to the same conclusion while studying at different universities, while sitting under two very different professors."

"And what conclusions might I help you with?" questioned Tom, who relished the idea of sparring biblically with his two well grounded students.

Matt's eyes were fixed upon his father while Sam glanced over to check his mother's reaction.

"After studying every verse on the Second Coming of Christ, Sam and I have decided that Matthew 24 is the most complete passage in the Bible concerning the timing of our Lord's return. While on the Mount of Olives, the disciples clearly asked Jesus, 'What will be the sign of your coming and the sign of the end of the age.'"[6]

Matt paused, expecting a quick interruption from his father but receiving none.

"After studying Jesus' words in Matthew 24, the most critical truth to understand is where the elect will be in the sequence of events that transpire before our Lord returns. In fact, Sam and I believe that Jesus' description of events in Matthew 24 perfectly describe the six seals of Revelation 6."

"That's correct, son. Our Lord Jesus warns the Jewish remnant, which is alive during the tribulation period, that they will suffer terrible persecution. Jesus prophesied, 'Then they will deliver you up to tribulation and kill you, and you will be hated by all nations for my name's sake.'"[7]

The experienced teacher paused for a brief moment so that his sons would not miss this critical truth.

"Even though Israel will be hated by the world because of Jesus Christ, our Lord promised salvation to Jewish believers who endure till Armageddon!"

"So, Dad, you believe Jesus' warnings concerning the last days in Matthew 24 are not addressed to Christians but to Jews living during the tribulation period?" asked Sam.

"Absolutely, son, and I will show you why. In Matthew 24:32, our Lord used a parable about a fig tree to warn the Jews of Christ's soon return. Jesus told them that when the branches on the fig tree get tender, the summer is near. Every Jew can relate to this picture. Jesus is warning the Jews who experience the events of Matthew 24 that Christ's Second Coming is very near! The Jewish people will know the signs that precede Christ's Second Coming at Armageddon, just like they know the tender leaves on a fig tree that usher in the summer!"

"So, you believe the fig tree represents the nation of Israel?" asked Matt.

"Why, of course! We all know Israel is represented several times in the Old Testament as the fig tree. Furthermore, for the events of the tribulation period to literally transpire, the people Israel have to be back in their homeland with Jerusalem as their capital. In other words, the fig tree represents Israel's becoming a nation in 1948 after two thousand years budding and becoming alive again!"

After a long pause, Tom could sense uneasiness in his sons. "Do you have any more questions?"

"Actually, Dad, Sam and I believe that Jesus, in Matthew 24, is addressing Christians right before His coming, not unsaved Jews. In the New Testament, the elect refers to Christians, never unsaved Jews. After much study, we don't see any biblical justification for having the fig tree parable in Matthew 24 represent the Jewish people!"

"Check this out, Dad," shared an excited Sam. "How can Israel represent the fig tree in Matthew 24:32-34 when Jesus cursed the fig tree in Matthew 21:18-20 and commanded it to die and never bear fruit again? To us, it is very clear that the parable of the fig tree is a time of approximation to warn Christians being persecuted by the antichrist of when they should expect Christ's soon return."

Immediately both sons braced themselves for their dad's reaction. After a few tense moments, Tom rose from his chair and began to pace. For Ashley, it was easy to detect the irritation within her husband's spirit.

"First of all, I must admit that I had the same questions about the timing of the rapture when I was studying for the ministry. Ah, yes, the old pre-mid-post tribulation debate that wasted so much of our time, which could have been devoted to studying God's Word. To be honest, I expected this type of interpretation coming from your theology teachers who have not been properly trained in eschatology. I respect your diligence in studying, but your ignorance concerning Israel and the Church will lead you down a path that has deceived many."

"And what path is that, Dad?" asked Sam.

"A path that has led professing believers away from the truth and into biblical error. Simply put, the body of Christ and Israel cannot coexist during the tribulation period because this period is primarily for Jewish people, not for the Church! Matthew 24 is about Jewish disciples during the seven-year tribulation period and their deliverance at Armageddon in Revelation 19:11-21."

"But, Dad, what about . . ."

"Don't you understand? Matthew 24 and Revelation 6 have nothing to do with the rapture of the saints? Jesus can't be addressing the Church during the tribulation period because the saints are already in heaven. Don't you realize that after the Church is raptured in Revelation 4:1, it's never mentioned again till chapter 19? How can the Church participate in the seven-year tribulation period, which is from Revelation 6 through 19, when it's already in heaven?"

Pausing for a reply, the angry preacher stopped pacing and sat down in his favorite chair.

"Dad, Sam and I believe that the Apostle John is being called up to heaven in Revelation 4:1, not the Church. The apostle doesn't return to earth till chapter 10![8] The church is raptured in Revelation 7:14! So you see, that solves the problem of why the church isn't mentioned again until Revelation 19."

After another long nervous pause, Matt rose to speak.

"Dad, we understand that this is what you've believed since you were in Bible college," the older son replied slowly and respectfully. "Your seminars have become classics within our denomination's most respected churches. Sam and I love and respect your knowledge of Scripture. But the fact of the matter is that the disciples were the founding fathers of the Christian church. In Matthew 28:18-20, Jesus exhorted them to go and make Christian disciples, teaching them to obey everything He commanded them. Matthew 24 is important instruction to the elect, believers in Jesus, not to unsaved Jews during the tribulation period!"[9]

"Looks to me as if you might have gotten a little dose of heresy from that new evangelist in town," mocked Tom.

"No, Dad, we believe the Holy Spirit has led us to compare scripture with scripture. For instance, if you compare . . ."

"I don't have to," interrupted Tom. "I don't know what has gotten into you two or what you are trying to prove. Do you know that I am a personal friend with Gene Lloyd, Arthur Lawrence, and J. R. Greer? These men have studied thousands of hours over every Second Coming prophecy in the Bible. They know more about the Lord's return in their little pinkies than you and all your liberal professors. It's beyond debate to put the Church in Matthew 24 and not Israel. We, as a body of believers in America, are suffering due to false teachers who are determined to take away the blessed hope of Jesus and place the bride under the persecution of Satan and the antichrist. I will not allow this type of false doctrine to come under my roof!" demanded the preacher who was almost yelling.

Matt and Sam knew what they believed but did not have any idea on how to communicate it without having a confrontation. After excusing themselves, the Holy Spirit assured them in their hearts that there would be other opportunities.

"Hope's right, Luke. The identity of the antichrist seems to be a popular topic these days. We just can't avoid it," insisted Ned, as he and Hope moved across the classroom and took seats next to Luke, Drew, and Whitney.

The Lakeview High School Bible Club had always been a small after-school club of Christians who met on Thursday afternoons. It wasn't until Luke Appleby became president that the club started to grow. No one within the club ever realized the importance of godly servant leadership until Luke arrived.

"Okay, Ned, so what's your point?" asked an interested Luke.

"Well, a lot of kids at school are checking us out to see if we are for real."

"Especially the new converts," interjected Hope.

"So, as leaders of the Bible Club we need to take a stand for the truth, don't you think?"

"I'm losing you, Ned," said a puzzled Whitney.

"I've got it!" answered Luke. "If we, as leaders, see bogus teaching going on about the antichrist and don't do anything about it, everyone's going to think we are wimping out!"

"Bingo!" replied an excited Ned.

"Hold up," Hope interrupted as she stood up and faced her friends. "Last week at our all-night prayer meeting, the Holy Spirit warned me of an evil deception that would soon take place."

"What kind of deception?" Ned asked while reaching for his Bible.

"While praying, I saw a vision of a beautiful woman riding atop a radiant scarlet beast. She seemed to be parading in front of some of the most powerful leaders in the world. Suddenly the beast grew seven heads and ten horns."

"But, Hope, isn't that a lot like the vision your dad had?"

"Yeah, I know, Ned. But what really blew me away was the beautiful woman riding atop the beast. She was dressed in purple and scarlet, had pearls and gold, you know; she was completely decked out. The people of the world seemed to be totally captivated with her beauty, which most thought was holiness."[10]

"What else did God show you, Hope?" asked Luke.

"Well, when the scarlet beast changed, so did the beautiful woman. In an instant she was transformed into an evil-looking prostitute."

"Sounds like 'Mystery, Babylon The Great, The Mother Of Harlots' in the book of Revelation," confirmed Luke.[11]

"Yeah, I know, but check this out. The evil harlot atop the scarlet beast quickly turned her focus toward the religious leaders of the world. While mesmerizing the world with her lies and flatteries, tiny streams of blood began to drip from her lips. Several times she had to turn away to wipe away the blood. In fact, it got so bad that she refocused everyone's attention on the beast with seven heads and ten horns!"

"What's it all mean, Hope?" asked a nervous Whitney.

"I believe the Lord is trying to warn us!"

"Warn us of what?"

"Everyone in my vision was so into looking at the amazing power of the beast that they weren't even interested in the evil prostitute that was riding him."

"How about it, Luke? Do you think this is the religious harlot we learned about in Bible study last year?" asked Ned, Drew's twin. "The one who will join forces with the antichrist during the first half of the seven-year tribulation period?"

"It sure looks that way."

"So, Luke, who is this mystery harlot?" asked Whitney.

"Well, the scriptures don't actually tell us the identity of the harlot who rides the beast. But there are several clues when you compare scripture with scripture."

"What type of clues?" asked Drew.

"Well, the first clue has the harlot representing a false religious system that possesses power throughout the countries of the world. A second clue to her identity is that this religious system will have political power."

"Wow, Hope, your vision might be for real."

"Another major clue is that the harlot has her roots in the Babylonian religion."

"But, Luke, didn't the Babylonians promote an evil form of idolatry under their divine goddess mother, Semiramus?" asked Drew.

"I believe so. If I remember correctly, she was worshipped as the queen of heaven and taught her subjects to participate in the cult of mother-son idolatry."

"What's the next clue, Luke?"

"The book of Revelation tells us the harlot sits on seven mountains."[12]

"Well, what great city sits on seven mountains?" asked Whitney.

"It's got to be Rome," replied a confident Luke. "The reason I believe it's Rome is the final clue. The harlot is shown atop the beast, drunk with the blood of the saints. In other words, this false religious system will oppose and persecute Christians throughout history."

"So, when we put all of the clues together, what have we got?" asked a puzzled Whitney.

"During the first half of the seven-year tribulation period, the Babylonian harlot will create a false worldwide religious system that will oppose Christianity by bringing all faiths together as one!"

"It makes sense, Luke," replied Ned. "Last week, in the *Bethany Herald* religious section, the religious editor was endorsing 'The World Religious Tolerance Act.'"

"Never heard of it. What's it say?"

"It's a religious law that several countries have just adopted. It says that it's a crime to advocate that someone else's religious beliefs are false. In fact, if you openly attempt to lead someone away from their faith and into yours, you can be arrested in some countries!"

"That could never happen in America, could it?" asked Whitney.

"That's what the article was about. Some priests from Rome were meeting with leaders representing several major religions in America in order to promote the acceptance of it. They are saying that the treaty will reduce religious hate crimes and further a spirit of tolerance among the different faiths."

"So what's next, Luke?" asked Hope.

"What Ned just shared is pretty intense. You see the Babylonian harlot will have her headquarters in Rome, Italy. For the first half of the tribulation period, we know the harlot will have power over the beast. But when the beast declares himself to be god in the middle of the seven years, the book of Revelation says he will turn and destroy her!"[13]

While the discussion on whom the harlot represented continued between the leaders of the Bible Club, Hope slipped outside the room and went for a walk.

Down the hall, she could see Jarred and Nicki in a heavy conversation. This couple used to be close friends with Hope until the persecution over her dad's vision erupted over a year ago. Further down the hallway, several grungers were cutting up after flunking their math final. As Hope turned to head back, three seniors walked by, giggling about how far they had gone with their boyfriends over the weekend.

Pausing, Hope whispered, "Oh, Lord, it's all happening so fast. Who is this harlot I saw in my vision? And what is this false religious system that will deceive the world?"

For a brief second, the pastor's daughter began to doubt whether she could ever find the truth. But then she reminded herself of how faithful God had always been to her and her family.

"Jesus, I'm thankful that I can trust You with my future. Please give me the eyes to see and the ears to hear what the Holy Spirit is saying to overcomers throughout the world."

Before returning to her Bible group, the short brunette with hazel eyes began to pray for the salvation of those who attended Lakeview High School.

"Wake up, everybody!" cried Hope, suddenly pounding a metal locker out of frustration.

She and her club friends knew that within a few short years the sound of voices in the crowded halls of Lakeview High would be no more.

CHAPTER 10

THE FALSE PROPHET

Then I saw another beast, coming up out of the earth,
and he had two horns like a lamb and spoke like a dragon.
Revelation 13:11

The priest's mind was a million miles away as he tried on his new ceremonial robes of purple and scarlet.

"How does it look, your grace," asked the attendant while holding his breath.

"It's perfect, my child. Our Holy Father will bless you for your excellent workmanship."

His fitting complete, the priest dismissed the tailor with a wave of his hand.

"You may go," Father John said as he turned and admired himself in the newly installed full-length mirror.

The reverend would now return to his office and await an afternoon visit from none other than the leader of Middle East Federation, Wolfgang Hendrick. Sources close to the priest had advised him that this meeting was extremely important and could shape the future security of the world. The highly respected leader purposely did not want any of his peers to be involved. He would promote a false impression that he had no idea what this meeting was about.

✳

The demons of lying and compromise had been spreading their influence throughout the world for thousands of years. For some spirits, their specific assignments had lasted for hundreds of years.

"After all," hissed the spirit of compromise, "some religion is better than none!"

"That's right," whispered the evil spirit of religion. "Just add enough structure to their life so that they may believe a lie for eternity! Ha, ha, ha."

The spirits of religion were much more highly esteemed than other demons. They had been especially effective in brainwashing billions of professing believers into following the traditions of men over the absolute truth of God. They were responsible for thousands of religions, which had drawn multitudes away from the only Gospel that can redeem a soul to heaven—the Gospel of Jesus Christ, the only begotten Son of the Father.

"Remember," jeered the spirit of religion, "that all people have their own interpretation of the Bible! Even the ministers and the priests don't agree on the words of the Son of Man. It's all a bunch of guesswork, if you ask me."

Father John dropped into his favorite overstuffed sofa in his newly decorated office. Looking out his picturesque window he could see a breathtaking view of the ancient city of Rome. His life's calling had unfolded perfectly.

He picked up his Bible and read, "Then I saw another beast coming out of the earth, and he had two horns like a lamb and he spoke like a dragon. And he exercises all the authority of the first beast in his presence, and causes the earth and those who dwell in it to worship the first beast, whose deadly wound was healed."[1]

"Everything is coming along just as my master said it would," said the evil priest smiling. Closing his Bible he shouted, "Except for these evil Protestant revivals!"

To Father John, the false teaching of the Protestant sect had deceived millions of souls throughout the world. The emotional messages from the Protestant teachers and prophets had spread quickly in the past few years. For Rome, the deceptively packaged Gospel of the Protestants was an evil that had to be exposed. Much to Father John's dismay, even some of the priests had embraced the theology of these evil teachers.

"Our Holy Father is exhausted by having to travel from country to country assuring the faithful that Rome does not approve of these so-called Protestant revivals," concluded the priest.

Priests from every country in the world were looking to their Holy Father for divine direction on how to stop this new wave of emotional Protestantism.

"The Protestant preachers reflect a peace and joy that seems to radiate," wrote a priest from Brazil.

"When the anointing of the Holy Spirit comes, there can be crowds in the excess of over 300,000," reported a cardinal from Argentina.

Suddenly, Father John was captivated by a dream of a woman sitting on a scarlet beast having seven heads and ten horns. Dressed in purple and scarlet, glittering with gold and pearls, her evil fornication oozed from the golden cup she was holding. She was drunk with the blood of the saints. Bowing before her were the kings of the earth who were drunk with the wine of her fornication![2]

The evil priest understood the image of the harlot who was drunk with the blood of the martyrs of Jesus.[3] In the past thousand years, the Church of Rome had become the greatest persecutor of Christians the world had ever known. For centuries, the voices of Protestant martyrs had cried out for the truth. Now, in God's perfect timing, the mystery of the woman who sits on seven mountains would be unveiled for the entire world to see.

"It doesn't matter," scoffed the priest. "The world has long forgotten their needless sacrifice of blood. And why would so many willingly defy our Holy Father?"

Being the right hand man to the ninety-three-year-old Holy Father was a responsibility Father John had always appreciated. Several within the leadership of the Church of Rome were very uneasy with the amount of power the Holy Father had recently delegated to Father John. For this experienced man of the cloth, the end had come to justify the means. At times, the manipulation would turn ugly.

As a young seminarian, Father John remembered studying how the power of Rome fueled the Inquisition when millions of Protestant believers were put to death. They were burned at the stake or killed with the sword because they refused to acknowledge that the Church of Rome was the Church of Jesus Christ! Christians all over Europe raised their voices in protest, saying that the Apostle Peter was never the pope of the Roman Church. Millions stood for the truth that the popes of Rome were actually an evil succession of Roman emperors!

Christian families whose loved ones became martyrs were comforted by the words of their Savior in their time of greatest need. Jesus said, "Blessed are those who are persecuted for righteousness' sake, for theirs is the kingdom of heaven. Blessed are you when they revile and persecute you, and say all kinds of evil against you falsely for My sake. Rejoice and be exceedingly glad, for great is your reward in heaven, for so they persecuted the prophets who were before you."[4]

"Think of the courage it took for the Vicar of Christ to take a stand for the truth and to order the execution of those who believed in the evil lies of the Protestant reformation," confessed the grateful priest.

And now over four hundred years later, Rome was again faced with the same enemy. The dream Father John had just experienced painted a picture of a prostitute called Mystery Babylon the Great. He knew the meaning of the mystery and wondered how many in the world also knew.

In his early years, while studying at seminary, the young priest had possessed a desire to be somebody. He had been filled with zeal, often studying late into the night. He especially remembered studying about Nimrod, the founder of Babylon, who had an evil desire to convince his people to build a tower that would reach heaven, a tower his people would use to study the stars. This evil Babylonian leader refused to repent of his rebellion, so God scattered the people throughout the earth.[5]

Nimrod had been married to Semiramis. After he died, she had vigorously taught her people to worship Nimrod as the sun god, Baal. As the years went by, she became the mother of pagan idolatry. Her mystery religion evolved into different forms and eventually became the most dominant religion in the world.

Soon after Nimrod's death, the queen gave birth to an illegitimate son, whom she named Tammuz. Semiramis, who was worshipped as the queen of heaven, taught the people that her young boy was their promised deliverer.[6] It was at this point in time that Satan introduced the religion of mother-son idolatry to the world. The heart of this mystery cult was an image of a mother with a baby in her arms and a belief that Semiramis, who was also worshipped as *My Lady*, had miraculously conceived Tammuz.[7] But even though the queen claimed Tammuz as the savior of the world, it was she who was worshipped as god and not her son. She was worshipped as the divine mother, the mother of the gods!

Babylonianism began as a mystery religion, with only members allowed to know the inner mysteries. The priests wore hats shaped like the head of a fish. They would offer round cakes to the queen of heaven and advocated the worship of idols. When its enemies destroyed Babylon, the priests took their idols and fled across the sea. The evil seed of pagan idolatry eventually settled in the heart of a city sitting upon seven mountains![8]

✳

The priest was especially nervous today while awaiting the visit of one of the most influential leaders in the world. Of course, Satan had already arranged this meeting between his two pawns. The respected priest was extremely on edge because he didn't know what to expect or how to prepare for it. The spirit of religion, which directed so many of his decisions, also sensed the importance of this clandestine meeting.

"Good afternoon, your grace," greeted Father John's aide who quickly moved across the beautiful wooden floor with its carved ivory inlays. "Mr. Wolfgang Hendrick has just arrived and will be using your private elevator. He will be joining you in approximately sixty seconds."

"Excellent," replied the priest. "Please take care of his entourage during our meeting."

"That won't be necessary, your grace. He has come alone," confirmed the aide.

"Very good. Please station security at every entrance. After he arrives, cut the power to the elevator and turn off the phones. I want absolutely no interruptions!" ordered the priest.

"Yes, your grace, your instructions are very clear."

"No one is to be allowed on this floor until our meeting is concluded," repeated the nervous leader.

Father John's adrenaline was shooting sky high over a meeting that he had dreamed about all of his life. The elevator stopped, opening into the foyer of the priest's office. His left hand shielding his eyes, a mysterious figure with long black boots stepped out into the bright light coming from the skylight.

"Good afternoon, my friend. Is everything ready?"

"Every precaution has been taken, my lord. I believe our master will be arriving very shortly," answered father John. "Please come."

The two leaders stepped into his office and locked the door.

"It is an honor for the church to have you as our guest," announced Father John in an attempt to make Hendrick feel welcome.

"It is our master's desire," smirked Hendrick, giving the impression he was not the least impressed.

The spirits of the antichrist, who had just arrived, were preparing to give their final instructions. The more powerful demons immediately addressed several under their command.

"Our master has made it very clear that there are to be no mistakes, especially over this assignment," commanded the evil spirit.

"Yeah, right," interrupted the spirit of doubt. "Tell that to the warrior angels the One from above keeps sending our way," squealed the scared little imp.

"Silence, you fool!" declared the demon in charge. "I can sense the presence of our master. He is somewhere in the building!"

Immediately, the spirit of death appeared and stood watch outside the priest's office.

Without any warning, Hendrick and Father John dropped to their knees, totally captivated by a beautiful white light saturating the whole office. While both men bowed in the presence of the prince of darkness, a scripture shot through their minds.

"For such men are false apostles, deceitful workmen, masquerading as apostles of Christ. And no wonder, for Satan himself masquerades as an angel of light. It is not surprising then if his servants masquerade as servants of righteousness. Their end will be what their actions deserve."[9]

Both leaders had heard of the white light experience, but to see Satan face to face in the form of a white angel completely took their breath away.

Observing from a distance, the demon of witchcraft just smiled and bragged, "Our master is a good judge of character, don't you think? He knows who he can control and how to manipulate those he has targeted!"

After several minutes, the radiant brilliance subsided, and a dark figure of a creature stood in the far corner of the office. With the snap his fingers, all the blinds to the windows closed, the lights went off, and the room became pitch black.

"The time has grown short," Satan snarled, detesting the sound of the words he had just uttered. "When the seventh trumpet sounds, the mystery of God will be accomplished, and Christ will attempt to take spiritual control of my world.[10] A month later, He will come with his army of angels to attempt to destroy you, Hendrick, and your armies. He will also be coming for you, Father John. It seems the miraculous signs that I will cause to flow through you will require His wrath!"

The devil smiled, slowly circling his two pawns waiting for a reaction. Both men stood erect and dared not utter a word. They knew the master deceiver was testing them. Each man had come too far now to be intimidated by the mere threats from the One above.

Besides, thought Father John, a good measure of the Bible is conditional.

"That's right, your grace," whispered the spirit of the antichrist. "The power in this room will alter the course of history."

"So be it!" screamed Satan. "You, Hendrick, will be my christ, my anointed one!"

As the prince of darkness moved within inches of his puppet's face, a supernatural rush of evil manifested itself and surged into Hendrick's spirit completely taking control.

"Remember, my anointed one, you will be given the power to blaspheme the One from above and persecute those who follow Him. You will make war against the saints and conquer many. Think if it; you will have authority over every tribe, tongue, and nation," gloated Satan while pausing to receive worship, which is reserved only for God.[11]

"Yes, my lord," replied the grateful Hendrick.

Inwardly, the German leader was craving for the time when he would rule the world.

"And you, Father John, how do you feel about exercising the power to make the inhabitants of the earth worship me?" admonished Satan whose pride was painfully intoxicating.

"My desires are yours, my master," Father John proudly confessed.

"Of course, they are. I've been observing your obedience to my commands," whispered the devil as he continued to circle his subjects.

An unexpected fear gripped Father John's heart as a cloak of silence filled the office. The evil angelic being circling him was hesitating. The priest knew that everything had to be in place in order for his master to make his move. Suddenly, an evil eruption of laughter spewed out of the devil, who was thoroughly enjoying intimidating his two pawns. With one loud thrust the prince of darkness proclaimed, "The time has come for you, Father John, to be my prophet."

Immediately the demons possessing the two beasts prompted each to fall before the devil and worship him.

While leaning down and staring into the eyes of Wolfgang Hendrick, Satan seethed, "Remember my anointed one! In a very short time, you will be given my authority.[12] Do you understand what is expected of you?"

While waiting for a response, the evil one continued to examine the beast for any sign of weakness.

"Yes, master, your victory over the One from above will be because man will choose you and your words, just like it was in the garden."

As Satan turned to leave, he smiled over his shoulder and replied, "That's right. Just like it was in the garden!"

CHAPTER 11

A BOY NAMED SIMON

If God is for us, who can be against us?
Romans 8:31

Lakeview High School had just let out. Students of all sizes and shapes were jamming the narrow hallways. The scenic grounds of the school meant nothing to the kids. Within twenty minutes, the parking lot would be empty, with just a few teachers remaining for committee meetings.

Hope Bishop and her sister, Lindsey, packed up their backpacks and started home.

"Boy, do I have a lot of homework tonight," Hope said with a sigh, throwing her backpack over her left shoulder.

"Me too," replied a tired Lindsey.

While the two girls turned the corner of Welch and Vaughn, a group of teenage boys approached them from the new church that had just been dedicated.

"Hey, look who we have here," yelled one of the boys.

"Well, well, if it isn't the prophet's kids!" replied another.

"Maybe we should bow down and worship them," laughed a third as the boys quickly surrounded the girls.

"Yeah, but if we are really nice, maybe they'll give us a word from the Lord," mocked Simon.

"That's not funny," snapped Hope.

"Yeah, your old man ain't so funny either when he teaches that Christians can lose their salvation."

"Watch it, Simon. You could lose it right now if you're not careful," ridiculed one of his sarcastic friends.

"You don't understand what my father is teaching," Lindsey replied, stepping forward. "He said that if . . ."

"Don't get so spiritual with me, little girl," interrupted Simon, trying to look tough in front of his friends. "We have a new church, and we don't want some cult messing up what my dad is doing. Do you understand?"

Just then, as one of the boys tried to take Lindsey's backpack, a '66 Mustang turned the corner.

"Hey! What do you think you're doing, hot shot?" yelled Jimmy Curtis, slamming on his brakes. Quickly slipping out from behind the wheel of his silver Mustang, Jimmy yelled out to Simon, "So what's your story?"

Lying through his teeth, Simon replied, "These girls are making fun of my dad and his church."

"Is that a fact?" Jimmy asked with a smile as the girls stepped behind him. "Well, I know Hope and Lindsey, and I find that kind of hard to believe. So why don't you just move on, if you get my drift, sonny boy."

While Jimmy drove the girls home, Lindsey began to weep.

"Look what's happening, Hope!"

Hope put her arm around her little sister and said, "We've got to trust God, Lindsey."

"But how do we do that? Everything is getting so crazy!"

"Dad will know. As soon as we get home, we'll tell him the truth about what's starting to go down at Lakeview!"

While the girls comforted one another, Jimmy was busy thinking. He could feel the tension in the town, and he didn't especially like where things were heading. After a right turn at the light, the mechanic pulled up in front of the girls' home.

"Hey, Jimmy, looks like you got a real handful," greeted a smiling Mark as he finished raking the leaves off his front lawn.

When the girls piled out of Jimmy's car, it only took a moment for their father to see that his daughters were really upset.

"Hope, Lindsey, are you okay?"

"Oh, Daddy, there were some boys . . ." cried Lindsey.

"We're okay, Daddy; we just need to talk," added a calm Hope.

"I tell you what. Why don't you meet Mom in the kitchen for some chocolate chip cookies while I thank Jimmy for giving you a ride home?"

"C'mon, Lindsey, it's going to be all right," encouraged Hope as both sisters waved goodbye and headed for the backdoor.

Turning toward Jimmy's souped-up car, the pastor was well aware of the fact that the young mechanic's usual smile was strangely absent.

"What's up, Jimmy?" asked a concerned Mark.

"I guess your girls can fill you in better than I can, Pastor. You gotta understand that I arrived on the tail end of it. It seems like some of the boys from Lakeview were teasing Hope and Lindsey about what you've been preaching on lately. You know kids, Pastor. They can be pretty mean when they don't understand something."

"I know, and I want to thank you, my friend, for protecting my girls."

"It was no big deal, Pastor. I just hope you know what you're doing."

"How's that, Jimmy?" asked a curious Mark.

"Oh, I was just thinking about how this town is reacting to your end-time predictions. What I mean is, uh, it's been going on for almost two years now. Is it really important for you to get so many people riled up about future events that are written in the Bible? No one really knows for sure anyway, right?"

Crouching against his car, Mark replied, "Let me ask you a question, Jimmy. If you knew of a truth that would literally affect millions of lives, how much would you sacrifice in order to speak this truth?"

"Guess I'll have to think about that one for a spell," answered a troubled Jimmy.

Mark stood up and smiled.

"Thanks again, my friend."

"No problem, Pastor, glad I was able to help. I just hope our town can return to normal," responded the young man as he pulled away from the curb and waved a final goodbye.

Later that day, with the family seated around the kitchen table, Lindsey was the first to speak.

"Those boys were mean, Mama."

"They wouldn't even let us share what God had shown us," added Hope.

"So it looks like the spiritual warfare at Lakeview is heating up. What exactly happened this afternoon, Hope?"

"Well, Daddy, it all began after I received a confirmation of your vision from the Lord. You remember, the vision I had concerning the harlot riding the beast.[1] Once my friends at the Bible Club started sharing it at school, it seems like everybody started bugging us."

"Your father and I thank the Lord for sending Jimmy to you this afternoon," said a relieved Julie.

"Yeah, me too," said Lindsey.

"I believe that today's incident is a warning from the Holy Spirit of what is yet to come," shared Mark. "Our Jesus exhorted all who desire to be a disciple to first count the cost of what it will take to remain faithful.[2] Each of us has been called to be a watchman to those whom God sends our way."

"But Daddy, this boy doesn't even want to hear the truth."

"What's his name, Lindsey?"

"Everyone calls him Simon. You won't believe this, Daddy, but he's the son of Pastor Allen Colson of Calvary Community Church."

"Okay, Lindsey, now what?" asked Julie. "What would Jesus do if He were in your place? "

"Our Jesus would love those who would try to hurt Him no matter how much it hurts?"

"That's right, my little lamb," replied a smiling Julie as she reached over for a big hug.

"Girls, the decision for you to remain faithful to Jesus is your choice. Your mother and I can't make it for you. Very soon we will be entering the great tribulation, a time when Christians throughout the world will be forced to take a stand for what they believe and for whom they will follow. The closer we get to the end of the age, the more persecution we will encounter."

"Daddy, both Lindsey and I have been praying a lot lately. We each have decided to follow Jesus, no matter what the consequences."

"That's wonderful, honey," replied Julie.

"Amen, girls. But let's all remember one critical fact."

"What's that, Daddy?"

"If we stand for the truth, God will always be on our side!"

"Right on, Dad," beamed Hope. "If God be for us, who can be against us."[3]

Prime Minister Eli Rosen sat quietly as his cabinet of advisors debated the Jerusalem Peace Accord. Since the signing of the Accord over two years ago, the cabinet members had split into two factions. One side, made up of the younger members, felt the peace treaty was the best thing that could have ever happened to Israel. The other side, made up of older religious leaders, felt the agreement was an evil set up. In fact, they didn't even try to hide their suspicions.

"They can't be trusted," yelled a conservative party leader. "This gentile coalition of nations will not stop until they have captured our beloved Jerusalem!"

"Utter nonsense!" shouted a liberal cabinet member. "Everyone desires peace. Let us remind ourselves how much we sacrificed in order to have peace with our Arab neighbors!"

"This is true," added another. "Look at how much our country has benefited after the signing of the Peace Accord."

"You're wrong!" insisted a holocaust survivor. "They won't be happy until they have killed every Jew in Israel!"

The rise and fall of the emotions throughout the six-hour emergency meeting had made the prime minister very weary.

"My brothers, what has happened to us?" pleaded the tired leader.

When the Jerusalem Peace Accord was signed, the prime minister had never seen such a joyful celebration between Jew and Arab, the sons of Abraham! After all, he reasoned, without a peace agreement, every country involved was in grave danger! The Pakistan-India conflict had suddenly brought back the threat of nuclear war that Russia and America suffered through in the 1960s. Several of the cabinet members wanted to propose a hard-line policy that would be implemented if a nuclear bomb exploded in northern India. But for others, the top priority was to expose the evil intentions of Wolfgang Hendrick and his ten-nation Middle East Federation.

The weary prime minister motioned for Shimon Melchior, one of the top religious leaders in all of Judaism, to stand and address the cabinet.

"My dear friends, I have come tonight to warn you of the serious danger we are all facing, an enemy whose face Israel cannot see, an adversary who looks and talks like a gentle lamb but will turn like a serpent and attack us without any warning. I'm afraid we have become too complacent concerning our supposed Arab friends. I also believe we have put too much trust in this German miracle worker they call Hendrick!"

"But Rabbi Melchior," interrupted a worried treaty supporter, "look at the many ways we have profited since we signed the treaty. Countries that have never traded with us have blessed us with goods and services beyond our highest expectations. While the world has been plunged into wars for their disobedience to God, Israel has become the apple of God's eye! Surely, Jehovah will eventually be praised by every gentile nation as they bow their knees in submission."

Eli Rosen was trying very hard to satisfy both sides. The ultra orthodox continually expressed their contempt for the ultimate compromise of allowing the Palestinians to call Jerusalem their capital! On the other hand, the liberal wing of Judaism desired peace no matter how many religious laws had to be broken! It was a juggling act that had given the prime minister many sleepless nights. The bags under his eyes reflected the constant pressure that seemed to never go away.

"Now, now, my brothers, let us trust God with our future because we know from our past that we cannot trust man," shared the concerned leader. "I am very much aware of how uneasy some of our people are. But we can be confident that our Israeli military intelligence will alert us to any suspicious behavior. Each morning I receive an up-to-date report of any suspected aggression from our neighbors. The Jerusalem Peace Accord has been honored by all ten countries and has put fear in other countries that see how powerful our alliance really is! Enough said. Rabbi Melchior, please read us a blessing."

The rabbi stood and began to read a passage of scripture from the Torah.

"Dwell in this land, and I will be with you and bless you; for to you and your descendants I give all these lands, and I will perform the oath which I swore to Abraham your father. And I will make your descendants multiply as the stars of heaven; I will give to your descendants all these lands; and in your seed all the nations of the earth shall be blessed; because Abraham obeyed My voice and kept My charge, My commandments, My statutes, and My laws."[4]

CHAPTER 12

THE WORLD FAITH MOVEMENT

Why did you marvel?
I will tell you the mystery of the woman and of the beast that carries her,
which has the seven heads and the ten heads.
Revelation 17:7

He was already annoyed at having to work late. His mood darkened when he heard the knock at his office door.

"Come in!"

One of his assistants entered, waving some papers.

"I have the reports you requested, your grace. Please forgive me for not . . ."

"Yes, yes, just give me the numbers," snapped the irritated priest.

"Very well, your grace."

His aide knew that what he was about to deliver was not good news.

"I'm afraid the evil Protestant movement in South America is still making dangerous headway. Our latest figures show that more than seventy percent of their converts are first-timers."

"Do you mean that they had never made any kind of religious commitment before?"

"Precisely, your grace."

"Continue."

"Of that number, more than sixty-five percent are under the age of eighteen," whispered the aide, whose words were barely audible.

"What did you say?"

"I said . . ."

"Silence!" yelled the priest as he began to pace back and forth.

The evil priest knew the ramifications of what had just been said. The Church of Rome would eventually die if the youth of the world turned to another faith. There had to be a way to stop it!

"Now listen closely," insisted Father John. "Having our Holy Father put out revival fires in South America, Africa, Eastern Europe, even America, has not helped stem this tidal wave of Protestantism. We don't need another ad campaign or another barrage of rebukes by our Holy Father directed at our world family!"

"Yes, your grace," replied the aide, shaking his head in agreement.

"No, the world desperately desires to see a miracle."

The priest froze as the idea surfaced in his mind.

"I must meet with our Holy Father at once! Arrange it; we don't have much time!" he screamed, motioning for the messenger to get out.

By the end of the month, the most respected cardinals in the world had been summoned to Rome to meet with the Holy Father. Following the meeting, it was announced that their leader would make a statement to the faithful representing every continent.

On the day he was to speak, over one million followers crowded into the plaza and neighboring streets. CNN World News was on the scene. TV crews from over 150 countries had been preparing for this event for over a week. The crowd began to sing and rock back and forth as they anxiously waited to hear a message from their spiritual father.

The noise was deafening as the frail ninety-three-year-old leader motioned for quiet. The next thirty minutes would be recalled by most as historic, but to the faithful, it was the ultimate step of faith. With the Holy Father looking on, Father John shared through a worldwide TV broadcast how God had spoken to the leadership of the church during their time of fasting and prayer.

"Within the next twenty-four hours, God has promised the world a miracle!" proclaimed the charismatic priest. "I call upon people of all faiths to pray, and we shall see the glory of God," he said, raising his hands to the sky in an act of humble submission.

Every news agency in the world jumped on Father John's prediction. The skeptical reporters pounded out stories for their readers mocking the whole event. In their editorials they challenged the whole myth of a God in heaven. First-page headlines proclaimed "God Promises Miracle."

At Sluman's Garage, Jimmy Curtis was just finishing up an oil change for the religious editor of the *Bethany Herald* newspaper. While he worked, he carried on a lively conversation with his good friend.

"Anyone with a lick of sense knows that the miracles of the Bible aren't really true," Jimmy chuckled.

"For sure, Jimmy. They're just a pack of fairy tales that preachers have used to manipulate anyone stupid enough to believe them," joked the editor, who had come to despise the hypocrisy of religious leaders.

"People praying to see a miracle? The whole thing just gives me the creeps," replied Jimmy as he handed his friend the keys.

"Well, you don't have to worry about it; it's all just a charade," answered the editor. I guess there are people in the world who just have to believe in some higher power in order to get by."

Still, most public leaders took a more cautious response to the prediction, encouraging people to wait twenty-four hours before making any rash judgments.

The world wouldn't have to wait for long. The hysteria was unbelievable! Political officials, housewives, teenagers— millions wept with joy. Simultaneously, countries around the world received the miracle of miracles. For a brief moment in time, the inhabitants of the earth held their breath while observing the personal visitation of the mother of Jesus!

"Behold, Mary, the queen of heaven!" proclaimed Father John, as reported by CNN World News.[1] "Truly, God has sent us a miracle!"

Unlike the visit from the Lady of Fatima in 1917, reporters from the major networks were able to document millions of healings throughout the world. Blind eyes were opened, the deaf spoke, the crippled walked, and those vexed by demons were set free.

"Just by looking upon My Lady's face you could sense a supernatural peace," proclaimed an overjoyed nun, who was healed of cancer after praying to Mary.[2]

"Praise you, Father, for sending Our Lady," wept a young teenager. "This day I have become a child of Mary for the rest of my life."

The news reports talked of her beauty and holiness. But even more than her physical appearance were her words. The world needed a message of hope amidst the harsh reality of war. Every major newspaper printed her picture and her simple instructions: "God loves you all. The world is approaching difficult times, and you must seek the peace that comes from above. Your Father desires that all people come together as one. Remember, I am your Mother."

"Our advocate, the Mother of God, has granted us a blessing from heaven," praised a well-known archbishop from the United States.

Within twenty-four hours, Father John of Rome officially announced the creation of The World Faith Movement! This ecumenical coalition represented the religions of the world. Leaders from Christianity, Judaism, Islam, Hinduism, and even Buddhism, with no belief in any God, were asked to come and share how Mother Mary's appearance has affected their lives.

Demons representing the prince of darkness had begun to woo religious leaders to travel to Rome and literally sit at the feet of the false prophet. The Babylonian harlot would reach her pinnacle of power with the help of an army of religious spirits. For a short time the evil harlot, the World Faith Movement, would ride the beast, the antichrist, for the entire world to see.[3]

Luke, Drew, Ned, Hope, Whitney, and all of the Bethany Assembly youth leaders arrived early to pray. The past few months had been pretty exciting due to the large number of students at Lakeview High turning to Christ for salvation. The youth leaders could easily discern the battle lines that had been drawn between God and Satan. For many students, persecution for their faith in Jesus was something new. The devil was not happy about losing any that had been under his control. To combat this, the enemy specifically assigned the spirits of fear and compromise to attack the leadership. Several would soon learn the lesson that just calling yourself a Christian was pretty easy. What they really needed to learn was how to defend themselves against the demonic mind games the enemy of their souls would throw at them.

"Hello, everybody, how are ya'll doing?" greeted Lance.

The youth pastor could hear several loud amens as he and his wife, Lee, entered the Activity's Center. The excitement in the air was very infectious. Luke motioned to Hope to introduce some of her friends that had just gotten saved.

"Pastor Lance, I'd like to introduce Donna, Alicia, and Richard. They all got saved at last week's prayer around the pole. You know, that's when we pray around the flagpole at our school!"

"Hey guys, congratulations!" shouted Lee Ryan from across the room while Lance shook their hands and made them feel welcome.

"Everyone who desires to become a believer must take that all-important first step of being born again," exhorted the youth pastor. "Then after receiving the Holy Spirit, each of us needs to pick up our cross and follow God's will for our lives."[4]

Lance paused to let the affect of his words sink in. The Ryans knew that many of the kids that had come for the Bible study were praying about their future. A future that for some would require the ultimate sacrifice.

"For the past year we have been studying the events that will precede the coming of our Lord. Tonight we will . . . yes, Whitney, do you have a question?" asked Lance, who could see the young teenager almost apologetically raising her hand.

"Pastor Lance, I'm praying that when you preach tonight you won't shift into hyper speed when you get excited."

The room erupted with nervous laughter as the youth pastor jokingly replied, "Okay, I'm guilty. Those who have heard me preach before know that I can get a little carried away. But when I, or any of you," said Lance, "share God's Word on the end times, we need to remember to slow down and teach it in such a way that even . . . uh, a freshman could understand."

Quiet little boos could be heard throughout the group, the freshman always seeming to receive the blunt end of all the jokes. With everyone smiling, Lance had the students turn to Matthew 24, the sermon Jesus gave on the Mount of Olives three days before he was crucified.

"Tonight, we're going to study one of the key passages Jesus spoke to His disciples concerning the great tribulation. Jesus warned Christians in Matthew 24:21-22, 'For then there will be great tribulation, such as has not been since the beginning of the world until this time, no, nor ever shall be. And unless those days were shortened, no flesh would be saved; but for the elect's sake those days will be shortened.'

"Lately, several students have expressed their confusion concerning what Jesus meant by 'unless those days were shortened, no flesh would be saved.'"

"You got that straight, Pastor," replied Richard, one of the new converts.

"Okay, everyone, what does Jesus mean by this verse?"

"I've heard my friends say that with all the wars there's going to be so much smoke that the sun will be blocked out, which will shorten the days," expressed a freshman from Lakeview High.

"You've got to be joking," replied her embarrassed friend, who was sitting beside her.

"So what do you think?" asked Lance. "What type of persecution will take place during the great tribulation?"

"Jesus described a time of persecution that will cause many believers to betray and hate one another other," replied Luke. "In fact, the persecution of Christians by the antichrist during the great tribulation will cause many believers to deny the Lord by taking the mark of the beast!"

"So when does this persecution begin?" asked an anxious Richard.

Drew spoke up, "The great tribulation begins exactly in the middle of the seven years."

After seeing everybody's head nod in agreement, Richard asked, "If that's true, then when does it end?"

"Did everyone hear that?" interrupted Lee. "The answer to Richard's question is super important."

"The book of Revelation makes it clear that the seals, the trumpets, and the bowls are set in stone," answered Hope. "They won't be shortened, right, Pastor Lance?"

"That's correct, Hope. The prophesied events you just mentioned won't change. Actually, by comparing Matthew 24 with Revelation 7, you can find the answer. Both passages have God's people being delivered out of the great tribulation just before God's wrath begins!"[5]

"Wow, that's awesome," uttered Drew. "Jesus, our blessed hope, will cut short the great tribulation by removing the elect from their persecution of the antichrist!"

"But, hold up," interrupted a visitor from Prattville. "If that is true, then how can the body of Christ be raptured before the great tribulation begins? The great tribulation doesn't even begin until the opening of the fourth seal?"

"It's really pretty simple, my brother," encouraged Luke. "I remember a good friend of mine warning me about the great tribulation period a couple of years ago. He said, 'Just remember, Luke, that the great tribulation of believers will begin when the antichrist breaks his peace treaty with the Jews and attacks Jerusalem. In other words, bro, two critical things will happen to those who actually see the antichrist! First, they will be the overcomers who will face the deceiver's persecution. And second, they will be the generation that will not physically die but will be caught up to be with the Lord!'"[6]

Luke couldn't help but smile as everyone scrambled to get it all down on paper.

"That's correct, guys," added Lance. "It was over two and a half years ago that we all witnessed the signing of the Jerusalem Peace Accord. Several weeks after the peace agreement between the Jews and the Middle East Federation was signed, wars broke out all over the world. Jesus said, 'And you will hear of wars and rumors of wars. See that you are not troubled; for all these things must come to pass, but the end is not yet.'"[7]

"I get it," smiled Drew. "Jesus told us that the end of the age is the harvest. In the passage Pastor Lance just read, the red horse of war has robbed the world of peace and is having people kill one another."

"So, what's your point?" asked Donna.

"The body of Christ is experiencing the second seal of wars, and Jesus said the harvest or the rapture is not yet. In other words, believers can't be taken up before the tribulation period because Jesus has the church living inside the last seven years!"

"Wow, this is pretty heavy," expressed the new convert.

"But, Pastor Lance, my parents still deny that we have entered the seven-year tribulation period," shouted someone near the back of the center.

"Yes, I know," replied the solemn pastor. "There are millions of believers throughout the world in serious denial concerning the very events that Jesus warned us would precede His coming. The problem is that now is the time to spiritually prepare for the coming persecution! There is not much time left before the third seal, the black horse of famine, pays our world a visit."

"But, Pastor, the world has always had peace agreements and wars," reasoned Richard. "How can anyone know for sure?"

The silence in the room was actually a sign of maturity. Most of the kids already knew the answer to Richard's question. In less than a year, the great tribulation would visit their unsuspecting town.

"Why is everybody so quiet?"

"I'm afraid no one will be able to rationalize away the third seal of the book of Revelation," answered Luke.

"What Luke is trying to say," shared a sympathetic Lee, "is that the first half of the tribulation period will conclude with a worldwide famine. After the beginning of birth pangs, then the hard labor will follow."

As Lee reached over and comforted Donna, the uneasy teenager asked, "So, what does the hard labor represent?"

"The great tribulation," Lance answered gently. "It will be at this time that many believers will be persecuted and put to death because of their faith in Jesus."

"So, Pastor Lance," asked a troubled Richard, "are you saying that it will be pretty hard to deny we are in the tribulation period once the world-wide famine begins? Is that what you're getting at?"

"That's right, my brother. Jesus warned us of false prophets who will create false signs and wonders in order to deceive even the elect."[8]

"You mean like the Mother Mary appearance?" interjected Hope. "Look at how many believers all over the world fell for that lie. Talk about a deceptive sign from the enemy!"

"But wait a minute," said a visiting youth pastor from Auburn. "Didn't Jesus say it's not possible for Christians to be deceived?"

"No, my brother, Jesus clearly warned Christians living during the seven year tribulation period that many false prophets 'will rise up and deceive many!'[9] Our Lord is actually stressing how deceptive the signs and wonders of the false prophets will be. Only believers who are spiritually ready will be able to discern the counterfeit!"

"I get it!" replied an excited Donna. "Believers who heed the warnings of our Savior will not be deceived but will endure faithfully till the end of the age!"

With hands going up all over the room, Lance motioned for everyone's attention.

"We are running out of time, so let me give you a short conclusion. Jesus answered his disciples' questions concerning His return by exhorting them to 'watch.' The sequence of events, which precede His coming, will warn those who will experience the great tribulation."

"But how is Jesus our blessed hope if we are going to be persecuted and killed?" snapped the youth pastor.

Before Lance could answer, the pastor and his visiting youth group got up and rushed out the front door.

"Let's remember, guys," encouraged Lance, "that just because the elect will be persecuted by the antichrist does not rob the church of its blessed hope. Actually, it's just the opposite! The correct biblical view of Christ's return will empower millions of believers to endure until death if necessary so that others may live eternally. The Apostle Paul wrote, 'Put on the whole armor of God, that you may be able to stand against the wiles of the devil. For we do not wrestle against flesh and blood, but against principalities, against powers, against the rulers of darkness of this age, against spiritual hosts of wickedness in the heavenly places. Therefore take up the whole armor of God, that you may be able to withstand in the evil day, having done all, to stand.'"[10]

"To be honest, guys," challenged Luke, "if we are not spiritually ready when the great tribulation arrives, we will almost certainly be deceived by the spirit of antichrist!"

After receiving a big hug from Lee, Donna whispered, "Hey, this is pretty scary."

"Let's remember, everyone," encouraged Lee. "God has not given us a spirit of fear, but love, power and a sound mind.[11] Jesus warned us to watch so that we may become overcomers through Him."[12]

Both Lance and Lee could see the fear on several young faces of people who were clearly not ready for the coming persecution. The Bible study group quickly divided up into intercessory prayer teams for the sole purpose of building up each other's faith. Everyone knew the time was drawing near for the black horse of famine to visit the beautifully landscaped streets of Bethany, Alabama.

The office near Sluman's Garage had been vacant for years. Suddenly, it appeared to be a beehive of activity. Curious onlookers walking by tried to get a quick peek, but the doors were locked and the windows blacked out. One could hear the sounds of workmen, pounding nails and putting up new light fixtures. The only real clue was the high-tech sign being erected outside the office. Bethany was not used to such signs, which had become so popular in the big cities. Most of the people had seen them on TV but never in person. Jimmy Curtis just scratched his head and looked on as the workman completed the final wiring. As the sun slipped behind the beautiful Alabama hills, one of the workers prepared to hit the switch.

"Last time anybody used that office was to recruit soldiers for the Vietnam War," reflected Amos George, the retired barber. "Well, whatever they're selling, I'm not buying."

Many of the town folks had questions about the new office, but no one was getting any answers. The secrecy of the project was something these southern folk did not take to at all.

"Must be hiding something," muttered Jimmy Curtis as he locked the gas pumps up for the night.

✳

Jason and Jackie Wylie had been married just about the time the Bishops came to Bethany. Both were graduates of the University of South Carolina. Jason quickly became the most respected defense attorney in town, and Jackie worked at the local hospital as a nurse.

The Wylies, members of Bethany Baptist, first met the Corbins at a prayer meeting at Bethany Assembly. It soon became common practice for Jason and Jackie to slip over after their church service and join in with the prayer warriors at Bethany Assembly. What really intrigued this young couple was the supernatural healings that ignited the revival among the young people.

It all began at a Friday night prayer meeting. The excitement over God's healing power erupted the night Stephen and Michelle Corbin arrived for prayer. No one really knew how the evangelist lost his voice. Some said he was burned out and needed a rest. One of the deacons at Bethany Assembly started a rumor that there was unconfessed sin in his life and that God had withdrawn his protective favor.

Jason remembered the serious look on Stephen's face when he motioned for the young people to pray for him. The Spirit of God had already put a check in Pastor Lance's spirit not to interfere. No one knew that the youth would be used in a miracle like one right out of the Bible.

The young people formed a circle around the evangelist and began to cry out to God to restore Stephen's voice. Within a few minutes, everyone could sense a powerful heat rest upon the excited evangelist. The youth spontaneously praised the Lord for sending His anointing.

After the praise died down, Luke received a word of knowledge from the Holy Spirit.

"I believe the answer to Stephen's attack," shared Luke, "involves the discernment of spirits."[13]

Immediately a young man in the back of the room raised his hand and asked to speak. Several youth did not recognize him; everyone thought he was with somebody else.

"I really bear witness with the word Luke received from the Holy Spirit. When I pray over Brother Corbin, I sense a spirit of fear coming against him."

That was all that needed to be said. The prayer group began to bind and rebuke any spirits that had any connection with fear.

Laying his hand upon Stephen's head, Luke proclaimed, "In the powerful name and by the blood of Jesus Christ, we command you, foul spirit of fear, to be gone! You have no right to continue to attack our brother in Christ."

Jason and Jackie led the cheering when the evangelist, who had been unable to speak for several days, began to sing, "God is my healer, God is my healer!"

With everyone praising the Lord, one of the youth leaders approached Luke and said, "That was an awesome word your friend received from the Lord."

"I don't know him," replied a surprised Luke. "I thought you knew him!"

The mysterious stranger had fulfilled his purpose.

As he walked toward the exit, Luke yelled over, "Hey, bro, thanks for sharing. I don't believe we caught your name?"

Glancing back over his shoulder, the stranger just smiled and said, "I don't believe I gave it."

Before anyone could reply, he was gone.[14]

While Stephen shared with Lance about what God had shown him during the time he couldn't speak, Lee and Michelle led the youth in a Gideon march around the Activity Center. Never before had there ever been such excitement in the quiet little church on the corner of Vaughn and Cherry.

"I say we attack now," insisted the spirit of lust.

The spirit of doubt just shook his head and said, "We had better be careful. They could . . ."

"What are you talking about!" screamed lust. "These followers don't care anymore!"

Who would have ever thought how tolerant Christian believers would become toward blatant sin against God?[15] Bethany had the usual strip clubs and smut bookstores. Pornography had become a billion-dollar cash cow over the Internet. The demon spirits, who targeted more than sixty million aborted babies, were now after the souls of teenage children through the perversion of pornography. For most unbelievers living in Bethany, a little lustful entertainment was good for the soul. But when the first homosexual church was formed, the outrage was loud and intimidating, at least for some.

After observing the protest meetings headed up by the leadership of the churches, the demon of lust would just laugh and say, "Oh, I just love the type of followers who talk about what they're going to do and really have no intention of doing anything."

The spirit of religion, which had deceived so many of the churches over the years, was laughing too.

"It didn't take much persuasion among the members of the Bethany Ministers Association to convince them to be more tolerant and less judgmental in the areas of abortion, pornography, and homosexuality."

The foul spirit of homosexuality, who loved to play mind games with humans, just smiled and replied, "The One from above would not discriminate now, would He?"

✳

The very next day, standing outside his new office next to Sluman's garage, Father Andrew greeted Pastor Dyer, Pastor Stanton, and Pastor Ryals.

"Welcome to our new World Faith Movement office. It's so nice to finally meet each of you face to face," smiled Father Andrew.

Andrew Fleming was from La Salle University. He had been a priest with the Church of Rome for over thirty years. The dramatic appearance of Mary had profoundly touched his heart. After much prayer, the priest decided to resign his teaching position at the university and become a spokesman for the World Faith Movement. The WFM team assigned to visit Bethany included Father Andrew, Rabbi Daniel Stein, and Rebecca Grimm, a Unitarian.

The experienced priest could sense uneasiness among the pastors as they formed a semi-circle in front of the old steam radiator. For most folks in Bethany, it was quite a shock to see outsiders come in and transform their old Army recruiting office into a high-powered voice for this new religious movement.

"Our slogan is really all for one and one for all," joked the cheerful priest while pouring coffee for each pastor. "Actually, gentlemen, the sole purpose of the WFM is to introduce a religious movement that will motivate all faiths to worship God in their own way."

For over an hour, the WFM team explained a gospel that was tailor made for the compromising church of Jesus Christ. The volunteers carefully chose their words while sharing the great spiritual need for the world to experience God's love.

"Yes, yes, we do appreciate your ideas concerning the tolerance of religions, but how can all faiths come together if we don't believe in the same God?" asked Pastor Elmer Dyer.

Rabbi Stein pulled up a chair and smiled.

"Well, as we all know, the Christians, the Muslims, and the Jews all believe in one God. And though we all believe in one God, the majority of the world religions believe in many gods. Nevertheless, even with so much disagreement, we feel that God is trying to save our world from total destruction. We believe Mother Mary was sent to give us a message of hope. The founders of the World Faith Movement consist of Father John, a Christian, Akim Maleek, a Muslim, and Hillel Weiss, a Jew. Together, they have sought God and have come to the conclusion that Mother Mary was speaking for all faiths. Her message of love and healing power was an attempt by God to bring all people under the same umbrella of salvation."[16]

"But how can we come together in unity if we don't agree on what God has said in his Word?" interrupted Pastor Ryals.[17]

"This is an historic time," replied the rabbi. "God is reaching out and asking us all to become a reflection of His perfect love. How can we really love one another if we continue to treat each other as evil?" exhorted the rabbi, who deeply believed in the ultimate goal of the WFM.

Ms. Grimm leaned forward in her seat and opened her Bible. She explained, "Jesus said, 'And You shall love the Lord your God with all your heart, with all your soul, with all your mind, and with all your strength. . . . And You should love your neighbor as yourself. There is no commandment greater than these.'[18] I do believe Jesus' words apply to all faiths, as we seek to love God in our own way," replied a hopeful Ms. Grimm.

"Have you ever heard of Dr. William Burgess, pastor of the Riverside Union Baptist Church in Memphis, Tennessee?" asked Father Andrew.

"Of course," answered Pastor Ryals. "He is the vice president of our denomination."

"That's correct, Pastor. He has also endorsed our World Faith Movement as a gift sent from God. Pastor Burgess believes our world is plunging towards a terrible disaster. He believes the World Faith Movement, although not totally orthodox according to his view of God, has the potential to become the catalyst that will promote harmony among all the faiths of the world."

Pastor Ryals had read about the World Faith Movement but had never dreamed a well-respected leader within his denomination would ever endorse it.

As the WFM team members shared their vision for the world, the spirit of compromise continued to weave its deception. After a while, the persuasion was so powerful that the pastors weren't even asking the right questions anymore.

CHAPTER 13

THE THIRD SEAL:
THE BLACK HORSE OF FAMINE

So I looked, and behold, a black horse,
and he who sat on it had a pair of scales in his hand.
Revelation 6:5

Wolfgang Hendrick, who had always demanded complete allegiance from those who received his orders, angrily slammed the phone down. This was not the first time one of his financial advisors had challenged his questionable practices in purchasing food commodities all over the world. One subordinate was horrified at the enormous amounts of food that had been purchased and shipped to various cities throughout Europe, Asia, South America, the Middle East, and Africa. His question was simple.

"What are we going to do with all of this food?"

Another aide joked, "We could feed half the world if we had to."

Wolfgang just folded his arms and smiled after receiving updated reports that his Middle East Federation had acquired more food, stocked and bar coded, than any other coalition of countries in the world. His mission was right on schedule.

Each of the super powers knew that for the world to keep afloat in this newly emerging financial world there had to be a system of accountability. Japan gave the world its biggest scare with its National Bank scandal that almost bankrupted the second biggest economy in the world.

Next was Britain. Illegal trading created a shaky financial foundation, until the American Congress voted to bail out its British ally. It was a decision most Americans adamantly opposed.

For most world leaders, the future looked grim. The diplomatic relations between warring nations had become futile. Even the United Nation's peace-keeping troops, which were sent to trouble spots, failed in their attempts to halt the constant fighting fueled by the spirit of revenge.

One African president, Zuwarah Bahamid, looked completely overwhelmed in a picture taken by a CNN news reporter during a recent uprising. Despite a peace agreement agreed to by each side over a year ago, their ancestral enemy unmercifully swept across the border and attacked his unsuspecting people. The blood bath that followed brought the stunned leadership to its knees. The river that runs through the capital used to be a happy setting where family and friends would take walks and enjoy picnic lunches together. That time was no more. Now there was only a frightful reminder of a red haze of blood, which permanently lined the banks of the river.

President Bahamid cried out to Khnurr, his god, and begged for mercy for his people.

"Let there be an end to this nightmare," he begged as he offered the required sacrifice to his silver idol.

This lonely leader knew his people were at a breaking point. For many, things couldn't get much worse.

All of heaven heard the loud cracking sound of the third seal being broken. Standing before the Son of God stood an emaciated black horse and its rider. The black robed skeletal rider held a pair of scales in his right hand. One of the four living creatures declared with a mighty shout, "A quart of wheat for a day's wages!"[1]

Within a very short time, the rider on the black horse would reach earth with the power to create a worldwide famine, the likes of which no one on earth had ever imagined!

It was during an early morning selling frenzy that the Dow Jones mysteriously began to fall. At first, there was only mild concern because the stocks going down were mostly high-risk. But when the low-risk conservative stocks and mutual funds began to fall, all eyes quickly turned to the big board at the New York Stock Exchange. One by one, General Electric, General Motors, Microsoft, AT&T, and a host of others began to nose dive. Fear gripped the brokers who could not determine the remedy for the rapid decline. Within six hours, the stock market in America had dropped from 13,110 to 6,554, producing the worst panic on the floor of the exchange since the 1929 crash! Investors around the globe watched as their portfolios turned to scrap paper right before their eyes. By the time the government could intervene, the damage was irreversible. The Japanese, European, and Asian markets soon followed with equally catastrophic losses. Areas of the world already hit hard by war suffered the most as food prices skyrocketed with no end in sight. The constant drain of equipment and supplies in the multiple wars throughout the planet had depleted valuable resources. A financial collapse had become a real possibility for many countries.[2]

Hendrick began with countries that had the greatest need as he carefully laid the foundation for his new world society. In his Munich office, there was a map of every country of the world. The beast had joined forces with the World Faith Movement, the Babylonian harlot, in the most powerful political-religious merger the world had ever seen. There would be a specific strategy for each country. The man of sin had carefully nurtured the atmosphere necessary for his one-world government.

Reeling under the terror of constant wars, the world was totally unprepared for the utter devastation the black horse of famine would create. Within months, famines would spread to every continent in the world.

Suddenly Hendrick received an apparition that completely captivated his spirit.

"Yes, master," whispered the beast, as he dropped to his knees and worshipped the prince of darkness.

The apparition was so clear. It was like watching a movie. Hendrick saw countries containing all the people groups of the world. Thousands of languages, traditions, customs, and beliefs joined together as one. Without the world realizing it, the third seal had been broken, and an army of demonic spirits was following the rider on the black horse. This demonic horde would create a worldwide famine in order to control the people of the world.

Prostrate on the floor, Hendrick whispered to himself, "Who is like the beast? Who is able to make war with him?[3] Yes, very soon I will be given the power to make war with the saints and to overcome them. I will have authority over every tribe, tongue, and nation."[4]

The demons possessing the deceived leader laughed with glee.

Positioned outside his office, a warrior angel sent from heaven prayed for the body of Christ, "Here is the patience of the saints; here are those who keep the commandments of God and the faith of Jesus.[5]

✳

The halls of the United States Senate were a sight to behold. They were full of paintings and sculptures that showed its remarkable history. Even the furnishings held historical significance. The security of the world had often been fought for and protected on the floor of the United States Senate. For those who were visiting, there were many wonderful memories to be relived. But for the Senators that would meet today, only the fear of what could happen gripped their hearts. Who would have ever thought that the world could spiral so far out of control in just three short years since the signing of the Jerusalem Peace Accord? So many things had to go bad at precisely the same time for the financial systems of this world to fail so drastically. Answers to the world's curse of wars, famines, and diseases had not been forthcoming. An emergency closed-door session of the Senate was called for and would not begin until every senator was in his or her seat.

"It could turn ugly," warned a senator from New York, as the other legislators arrived to sign in.

Lobbyists could be seen throughout the building, trying to find out what was going to occur in this secret session and how it would affect their special interest groups. It was easy to see why. Inside were men and women who would soon be voting on legislation that could rescue America from the greatest depression since the 1930s.

After the last senator was accounted for, the galleries were cleared and the doors closed. The vice president of the United States opened the session by recognizing the senator from North Carolina. All eyes throughout the massive hall focused on microphone number two as Senator Davis Hughes rested his hands on the edges of the glass podium.

"Ladies and gentlemen of the Senate, I come before you this morning to ask you to realize the severity of the times in which we are living. Never before has our world experienced such fear, confusion, and hopelessness. If you take away a person's hope of a future, it's like letting that person slowly die. Today we must enact legislation to stop this financial crisis that has been spreading from country to country like an out-of-control fire. The answer is pretty simple," shouted the senior senator as he removed his coat and loosened his tie. "Today, we must adopt the World ID Commerce Act, a worldwide system of buying and selling.[6] Without such a system, we are traveling down a road that will eventually end in ruin!"

Hands shot up all over the Senate floor, and voices could be heard shouting, "Mr. Chairman, Mr. Chairman, Mr. Chairman!"

Fearing that such a reactionary statement could only breed more fear, a senator from Massachusetts yelled, "Our people need answers, not gloom and doom speeches!"

When the chair recognized the senator from Florida, the loud buzz of confusion suddenly died throughout the Senate floor. Eugene McKnight was a highly respected and a very powerful legislator who had been in office for over twenty-eight years. His nickname among the lobbyists was Power Broker. He could make deals and propose compromises that would make the McCoys and Hatfields stop feuding.

"My fellow senators, within the next thirty days, every country in the world will scrutinize the dilemma that we are faced with today. We need answers that will bring revolutionary change to our world and decisions that will not only require exceptional courage and insight, but also a divine strength that comes from God, a God who represents all faiths!"

The applause by the senators was a politically correct response. Religious tolerance was a necessity if any senator wanted to be re-elected.

"I remember playing basketball in the sixth grade with my three best friends: Timmy, Bobby, and Kenny. Each of us made the team, and we were very excited about the upcoming season. After twelve games, we were still undefeated. My three best friends started every game while I sat the bench. Whenever we were leading by more than twenty points, the coach would reluctantly put Eugene, number six, in the game. After a while, it didn't matter to me because we were winning, and everybody was excited about the possibility of capturing the city championship. We lived in a small town called Lake Bering. Most of the town folk talked only about football, although it seemed like everybody who was important turned out for the city championship."

"What is he up to?" the senator from Kansas whispered under his breath.

"While the team was warming up, out of nowhere, a fear of failure completely overwhelmed me. Now listen, my friends. Many of our greatest fears never come to pass in our lives. Think back five years ago to when we faced the worst airline strike in history. It was a hopeless situation. Delta Airlines was faced with bankruptcy. Thousands of people would lose their jobs. The federally appointed mediators were unable to resolve the deadlock until two senators offered to step in. Everyone knew that if they failed, the voters would not forget come election time. They risked their reputations and their careers to bring a solution to that nightmare. They got the negotiations started again, and within a month Delta and its workers signed a contract; the airline was back in business!"

"He's got an angle; believe me," one senator said to another.

"Are you listening, my friends? Now back to my story. My fear, no matter how remote it seemed, was that somehow I would miss the last shot of the game and cause my team to lose the city championship. Most of the town folk would be okay about it; all they cared about was football. I guess some of my brother's friends would probably call me a choke artist. So what, that didn't matter. It was facing Timmy, Bobby, and Kenny that I could not bear. The approval of our friends is a strange thing to figure out sometimes. It's a powerful force that can make us do things we would never do."

The whole Senate body edged forward in their seats, hanging on every word.

"We trailed throughout the game, and each of our five starters committed four fouls apiece. The coach's face looked about as intense as I had ever seen it. He leaned forward and hollered, 'Eugene, be ready! You might be going in.'

"My hands started to sweat as I re-tied my sneakers for the fourth time. Then the moment came. Timmy, Bobby, and Kenny each fouled out within two minutes of each other.

"With a team of eight boys, the coach had no choice but to tell me, 'Eugene, check in at the scorer's table.'

"My family and neighbors cheered when they announced that number six was coming in the game. I realized that my best friends would be watching every move I made or didn't make. I knew I could rebound, play defense, and even dribble the ball, but my big weakness was shooting. With time running out, we scored three straight baskets. We were down by one point with ten seconds left when the point guard from the other team slipped and was called for traveling. Our coach called time out. It seemed like forever before he gave us our final instructions.

"'Zack, you get the in-bounds pass and take the ball down to the right of the key. Then work it to Galen inside for a short jumper. Now remember, we have only ten seconds.'

"With huge drops of sweat dropping down his forehead, it was easy to see that coach didn't have much hope of winning. When the huddle broke, the noise of the crowd was deafening. Through all the commotion, I could see the encouraging faces of my three best friends. I didn't want the glory. I didn't need the praise from the town for hitting the final shot to win the city championship. All Eugene McKnight cared about was the approval of his three best buddies!

"The in-bounds pass went to Zack, our best dribbler. 10 . . . 9 . . . He maneuvered down the center of the court and was forced to veer to the left of the key where I was. They double teamed him, and he looked trapped . . . 8 . . . 7. A quick shoulder fake pulled one defender out of position. He split between them and passed the ball to a completely panicked number six."

As the Senator from Florida paused for a drink of water, several muffled laughs could be heard throughout the Senate floor.

"Simply put, I had two choices . . . 6 . . . 5. I was open to take the last shot from ten feet or pass the ball to Chipper, who was on the baseline."

The senator paused and looked into the eyes of men and women who could very possibly decide the destiny of six billion people. For some senators, the approval of man was everything. For others, it was the love of their family.

But for Eugene McKnight, if the last twenty-eight years in the Senate had taught him one precious truth, it was this: When faced with the greatest fear the world could ever imagine, the majority of the senators would vote for what is best for their fellow man!

"I faked the shot . . . 4 . . . 3 . . . and drew the defenders to me, as Chipper broke for the basket . . . 2. I passed the ball, and as soon as Chipper's hands touched the ball, he spun and took his shot. It hung on the rim as the entire crowd held its breath.

"The buzzer went off like an m-eighty firecracker, shattering the silence as the ball dropped in! The crowd went crazy, raising Chipper upon their shoulders. I remember my mom and dad and even some of my teachers, but what meant the most were the words from my three best buddies. 'Way to go, Gene. You made the perfect move.'

"Ladies and gentlemen of the Senate, I highly recommend the passage of the World ID Commerce Act that is before us this morning.[6] We must have the courage to pass the ball for the good of our country and the world. The people of America deserve the perfect move!"

While Eugene McKnight stepped from the Senate floor to his seat, every senator stood and applauded. Some wept with emotion; others gained courage to face what was coming, and most had no idea of the evil persecution that would soon cover America like a blanket!

✳

While the American people patiently waited for the results of the Senate's emergency closed-door session, believers all over the country began to form intercessory prayer groups. The famine, which had lasted several months, had opened doors for the Gospel that otherwise would never have happened. Bible studies were being held almost every night of the week. These Bible studies were not the usual "read two verses and then discuss man's opinions for an hour," like most of the pastors in America had fed their sheep for years. No, the time had come for believers to rise up and demand the truth concerning what the Bible really says about the end times.[7]

For the majority of the churches worldwide, the warnings by a growing number of watchmen had been mainly ignored. To Mark, Stephen, Billy B., and Jason, the real heartbreak was that the body of Christ in America could have been ready. But like sheep to the slaughter, most believers chose to put their trust in well-known teachers, who, in their minds, could never be wrong.

A very common excuse was, "I'm just an average guy trying to follow God and raise my family. The preachers know a lot better than I do."

A homemaker reasoned, "If I can't put my trust in my pastor, then who am I going to trust? Besides, there are so many disagreements on the subject of the Lord's return; who can know anyway?"

"It really doesn't matter what the Bible says about the end times," admonished a Sunday school teacher from Opelika, Alabama. "No amount of debate will change anything. Let's just be ready!"

For those who were watchmen, it was terrifying to see believers accept such compromise as if it were from God. The fact was that American believers were not ready when the spirit of the antichrist split their families to pieces. The churches in China were far more prepared for the wrath of Satan, which would be thrust upon the world like a well-hidden trap. Millions would be martyred for refusing to take the mark of the beast. The spiritual preparation had been very extensive for those who had heard from God and remained faithful to His Word.

Jesus said, "As the Father loved Me, I also have loved you; abide in My love. If you keep My commandments, you will abide in My love, just as I have kept My Father's commandments and abide in His love. These things I have spoken to you, that my joy may remain in you, and that your joy may be full."[8]

✴

"Good morning, members and visiting pastors," greeted a smiling Pastor John Ryals. "This morning's meeting of the Bethany Ministers Association was requested by two of our members, Reverend Thomas Bray and Reverend Gerald Pierce. Both have had successful ministries focusing on Bible prophecy for over twenty years. I'm pleased to first introduce to you our good friend, Gerald Pierce."

"Greetings, brethren. Tom and I have contacted each of you to meet with us today to discuss some very disturbing events that have just recently transpired. This past month, two ministers of the gospel, Pastor Mark Bishop and Evangelist Stephen Corbin have made derogatory remarks about our belief in the imminent return of our blessed hope, Jesus Christ. They have also attacked our motives and our character. I have been told that they are members of this association, which certainly does not condone such immoral tactics."

The pressure of the moment seemed a bit much for the well-known Bible teacher. The obvious insincerity upon his face would have become an embarrassment if he had not motioned for his close friend, Reverend Tom Bray, to take over.

"I'm afraid that Jerry is speaking the truth," replied the gray-haired revivalist. "For years, brethren have disagreed on the timing of the rapture. In fact, every minister within our association believes in a future antichrist. We believe he will step into a Jerusalem temple during the tribulation period and proclaim himself to be god. Most of us even believe that the two witnesses of Revelation 11:3 are going to be Elijah and Moses come back to life. With all that said, it has always been a practice of this association to treat our members with respect. But these so called ministers, who deny the blessed hope, they are a different breed," charged the jealous preacher.

"Brother Tom, I don't believe either Mark or Stephen denies the blessed hope," interrupted Pastor Allen Colson. "What exactly do you mean?"

"Okay, let's take Pastor Bishop, for example. He never gave a hoot about the rapture until this Corbin came to town with his new rapture interpretation. It's almost as if he is under the control of this evangelist. And another thing, I heard some of the teenagers from one of our churches calling Corbin the watchman. Sounds like a cult to me!"

The spirit of lying smiled as his plan of deception reached out to every pastor who was willing to entertain his lies.

"Don't get me wrong!" insisted Tom. "Everyone doesn't have to agree with everything I teach. It just seems as if the body of Christ is so confused with this teaching on the signs before the rapture. We all know that no man knows the day or the hour of the rapture, yet they teach that Matthew 24 contains a road map of events that precede our Lord's coming for His saints. I've never heard of such poppycock," spewed the revivalist, repeating the very words the spirit of lying had just planted.

Up until the black horse of famine was loosed, many denominations adamantly refused to even budge on their belief in a pre-tribulation rapture. But with the financial crisis spreading and food prices shooting sky high, believers were beginning to question the leadership's pat answers. Some left their churches because the biblical arguments in favor of a pre-tribulation rapture were no longer convincing. Even so, an invisible army of evil spirits continued to work over-time in order to keep the deception in the forefront. A spiritual battle was being waged for the souls of millions of people, many of whom were looking for a miracle, something to hold onto and believe in.

CHAPTER 14

GOD IS YOUR JUDGE

For the time has come for judgment to begin at the house of God;
and if it begins with us first, what will be the end of those
who do not obey the gospel of God?
1 Peter 4:17

For the past twenty years, the Christian community in America had steadily moved away from accountability and character issues. People no longer confessed their sins to one another. The pulpits in America had become so tolerant of the world's values that most believers knew very little about Bible doctrine. The average churchgoer prayed less than a minute a day. Sharing the faith with the unsaved had become the clergy's responsibility. For the most part, the warnings of Jesus concerning the end times fell on deaf ears!

"Think about it," Mark shared with Julie. "Believers hear God's word every week but have no intention of repenting."[1]

The Bishops both remembered a Sunday morning service just after they had began to pastor at Bethany Assembly. Among the members praising the Lord at the altar, the Bishops could discern several unrepentant souls: an usher hooked on pornography, an openly racist couple, a young single woman who had just had an abortion, a recently divorced couple who refused to forgive one another, and several who loved to gossip and didn't care who they hurt. Tragically, many churches were guilty of producing professing Christians who believed they would go to heaven whether they confessed their sins or not.[2] They believed in a doctrine that teaches once a person is saved, habitual sin and ungodly character are not issues anymore.[3] Sadly, the consequences of rejecting God's call to repent had produced a church that was carnal and lazy. Many Christians who professed Jesus as Lord had actually become lukewarm. The stage was set. Just the thought of Death and Hades attacking one fourth of the world through the demonic power of the two beasts brought chills to Mark. The pastor's heart literally ached for deceived ministers whose whole focus had become tolerance and unity while purposely avoiding any mention of repentance and holiness.

A well-known evangelical minister just recently proclaimed that Jesus never condemned anyone for his sin but always reached out with His Father's love. At a recent Bible conference the preacher emphatically shared, "my fellow minister's, I don't believe in teaching on the sin nature of the human race.[4] That's negative thinking! We must always remember God loves His children. Let us not fall into the trap of feeling guilty when we make a mistake. God understands!"

"Only you, Lord," prayed Mark, "can awaken believers who are asleep in the light. Expose the false teachers who are leading your sheep astray! Allow the body of Christ to see with discerning eyes. Oh Lord, empower your servants throughout the world to stand for Your Truth!"

Later that day a visitor approached the outside entrance to Mark's study and quietly knocked. Mark opened the door to find a nervous Thomas Bray.

"Good afternoon, Pastor Mark."

"Hi Tom, come on in."

The young pastor offered his guest a warm handshake while escorting him into his study. Mark suddenly realized how very little he actually knew about this famous revivalist.

"Would you like something to drink?"

"No thanks," Tom replied in a slow deliberate fashion. "Mark, the reason I'm here today is that God has convicted me of saying some things about you and your church that should have never been said. Yesterday Jerry Pierce and I met with several members of the Bethany Ministers Association, and we, uh, well, pretty much maligned your ministry, your church, and your character. Even though I completely disagree with your mid-tribulation teaching, that does not give me the right to attack you or the reputation of your church."

Tom slowly removed a handkerchief from his coat pocket and wiped his forehead.

"Mark, I called your church a cult," confessed the preacher, not trying to hide the shame on his face. "It happened so suddenly. I was up in front of the pastors; we were discussing how your teaching was affecting our youth. One thing lead to another, and suddenly a jealously came over me. It was more than that though; it was like a presence that wouldn't go away until I said what it wanted."

Mark knew this celebrated preacher did not understand the type of spiritual warfare he was engaged in. He watched as tears began to well up in Tom's eyes. The damage had been done. Mark knew that a simple apology from Tom to the Minister's Association would not make it right again. In the very near future, he would have to face the Christian leaders of Bethany.

"I want you to know, Tom, that I forgive you for the words you spoke against my church and me. It took courage for you to come and admit that you were wrong. I must tell you though; we are under a very strong attack. The spiritual warfare within this city has become intense. The spirits of jealousy and lying that hit you so hard attacked our church last week. Tom, you need to realize that demonic spirits have been assigned to attack every spiritual leader in our town. Our only choice is to fight back in the name and the blood of our Lord Jesus!"

The famous revivalist reluctantly agreed.

"Tom, I need to correct a misunderstanding that several pastors within the Ministers Association seem to have about me. First of all, my teaching is not mid-trib or post-trib. In Matthew 24, Jesus clearly showed the elect being persecuted by the antichrist during the great tribulation. The great tribulation begins in the middle of the final seven years. So you see, a mid-trib position is impossible. Post-trib would have God pouring out His wrath, the trumpets, on the body of Christ. That is also a contradiction and is not possible. Actually, our Lord Jesus highlighted the cosmic disturbances that will precede His coming, which will take place sometime in the second half of the tribulation period. Of course, no man but the Father knows the exact day or hour."[5]

"I'm glad you brought that up. Do you think we could take some time to discuss our Lord's coming?"

"Sure, what's on your mind?"

"Well, Mark, isn't your teaching a relatively new doctrine? There seems to be no well-known teachers who have ever believed Christians would be persecuted by the antichrist."

"Actually Tom, that's not true. Charles Spurgeon, John Wesley, Matthew Henry, and John Wycliff believed the antichrist would come before the Lord's return for His saints. Charles Spurgeon preached that Christians in the end times would be persecuted by the antichrist."

"That's pretty shocking," replied Tom, who had studied each of the ministers Mark mentioned. "But what about the early church? Didn't they believe in the apostles' teaching that Christ could come at any moment?"

"Tom, the Apostles Paul and John each taught that believers would face persecution by the antichrist during the great tribulation. Jesus made it clear that believers experiencing the events right before His coming won't physically die but will be supernaturally delivered or gathered. In fact, the leaders of the early Church who followed the apostles never taught or mentioned a pre-tribulation rapture."

"Whom are you talking about in particular?

"Justin Martyr, who lived from 100 to 168 AD, for one. He taught that the man of apostasy would persecute the believers. So did Irenaeus, who lived from 140 to 202 AD, and Tertullian, who lived from 150 to 220. So you see, Tom, the leaders of the early Church believed in a future persecution of believers by the antichrist."

With his arms crossed and his body erect, Tom asked, "So you're telling me that the early Church did not believe in the imminent return of Jesus Christ?"

"Absolutely! There is no evidence that the early Church taught Jesus could return for His bride at any moment!"

"But, Mark, didn't the Apostle Paul expect to be caught up in a twinkling of an eye when Christ returned?"

"Yes, very much so. But the Apostle Paul highlighted several prophesied events that must first transpire before the gathering of the elect by our Lord."

"Where did you get that idea?"

"The Apostle Paul wrote to the Thessalonians in his second letter, warning them that the gathering of the saints to heaven and the Day of the Lord, God's wrath, could not come until the man of sin is revealed. Do you agree that the antichrist will reveal his true identity in the middle of the tribulation period when he sets up an image of himself within the Jewish temple?"

"I do."

"So for the antichrist to step into a rebuilt Jewish temple on Mount Moriah in Jerusalem, the Jewish people have to be back in their homeland! Now you and I both know that God dispersed the Jewish people in 70 AD due to their continual rebellion. For almost two thousand years the Jewish people did not have a homeland. It wasn't until 1948, when God began to bring them back to the land he had promised them, that specific prophesied events could transpire, which would warn believers of Christ's Second Coming."

"What's another event that needs to happen before the Lord returns?"

"Like I said before, specific cosmic disturbances must precede the Day of the Lord. The Old Testament prophet Joel wrote, 'And I will show wonders in the heavens and in the earth: blood, and fire, and pillars of smoke. The sun shall be turned into darkness, and the moon into blood, before the great and the terrible Day of the Lord comes.'⁶ Now, in Matthew 24:29, Jesus described this exact cosmic disturbance coming just before He gathers His elect. By comparing scriptures, it's easy to see that cosmic disturbances will precede the Lord's coming, which is immediately followed by the Day of the Lord. In other words, the body of Christ can't be delivered until the cosmic disturbances appear in the sky, which means that Christ can't come in a secret, at any moment, rapture. It's all right there, my brother."

"But, Mark, if what you teach is true, then a secret rapture with no events preceding it is not possible!"

"Tom, we both agree that the disciples expected their Lord to return in their lifetime. But there is a critical difference between a secret at any moment coming and a coming that teaches there are certain events that must first take place."

"Okay, but what about the promise of the blessed hope?"

"Anticipation, Tom. Jesus could have come in any generation. The key is that only those who are alive during the persecution of the antichrist will know our Jesus' coming is near. The overcomers will understand the events that will precede our Lord's coming. Jesus warned those who see these events, 'Now when these things begin to happen, look up and lift your heads, because your redemption draws near!'⁷ Tom, the word 'redemption' in this verse means physical deliverance, the gathering of the elect to heaven!"

"You know, I have a different interpretation for every one of your arguments."

"Yes, I am aware that your background and your ministry experience is very impressive. I also know that there is not one verse of scripture that teaches a secret return of Christ before the seven-year tribulation period!"

"So you teach a kind of road map of events that precede the rapture?"

"That's right. And right now we are experiencing the third seal, the black horse of famine. The next seal, the pale horse of Death and Hades, will begin the great tribulation of Christians. The antichrist and the false prophet (the two beasts) will be allowed by God to make war against the saints and to conquer many."

"But why? It doesn't make any sense. Why would a loving God, who promises us a blessed hope in Jesus Christ, allow the bride of Christ to be persecuted by Satan?"[8]

Pastor Mark opened his Bible and read, "For the time has come for judgment to begin at the house of God; and if it begins with us first, what will be the end of those who do not obey the gospel of God? Now, if the righteous one is scarcely saved, where will the ungodly and the sinner appear? Therefore let those who suffer according to the will of God commit their souls to Him in doing good, as to a faithful Creator."[9]

"But, Mark, judgment is for sinners, not the elect. Jesus atoned for our sins on the cross. God's people, therefore, cannot be judged for their sins. That means the body of Christ must be removed before the tribulation period begins."

"My brother, you have a very serious contradiction when you do not make a distinction between the great tribulation of Satan and the wrath of God. Jesus warned the elect that they would suffer tribulation or persecution. Our Lord said, 'In the world you will have tribulation; but be of good cheer, I have overcome the world.'[10] The great tribulation is Satan's wrath, not the Day of the Lord![11] Those who refuse to believe in this distinction are setting themselves up to be deceived."

"Deceived by whom?" asked a solemn Tom.

"To be perfectly honest, a large part of the body of Christ throughout the world has become lukewarm. Here in America, we have many who profess to be Christians but whose lifestyle consists of habitual adultery, racism, drunkenness, hatred, and pornography. The Apostle Paul warned that those who live like this will not inherit the kingdom of heaven."[12]

Mark knew that only the Holy Spirit could make the truth of God's Word come alive in Tom's heart. He patiently waited as the revivalist tried to reconcile in his mind what had just been said. It seemed like an eternity before Tom spoke.

"Well, Pastor Mark, this has been a very interesting chat. I respect you for standing for what you believe to be the truth. But I just can't believe that a true believer would deliberately sin and deny the Lord. In my mind, I don't see the mark of the beast coming in our lifetime!"

"But Tom, how can you . . ."

"Excuse me, please allow me to finish. To be perfectly honest with you, I believe you are in very serious error. In fact, I would be willing to bet my life on the truthfulness of the imminent return of our Lord Jesus Christ!"

At the urging of the Holy Spirit, Mark bowed his head and quietly replied, "In the very near future, I believe you will be given that very choice."

Tom never heard Mark's reply as he continued with his response.

"Even though we disagree, with God's help, I will ask for forgiveness of the Ministers Association for the remarks I have made against you and your church."

Reaching out to shake hands, he said, "Thank you for you're time today, Pastor. Goodbye."

And with that, the famous teacher was gone.

As Mark closed the door to his study, he now realized the remnant of overcomers in the last days would be much smaller than he had ever imagined. Sensing the Lord's wanting to warn the body of Christ that He is right at the door, Mark cried out for the Holy Spirit to open the eyes of the famous revivalist.

"I know Tom loves you and your Word, Lord. Only You can change his convictions concerning the end times. I pray that the whole Bray family will not submit to the mark of the beast but will become overcomers through You."

The excited crowd, just over one million, had come to hear Father John deliver a message from God. The massive marble pulpit was highlighted by the glow of TV lights. As the false prophet stepped up to speak, the roar from the crowd was immense. Never had so many religious faiths come together for one supreme goal. Everyone could believe in his or her own God in his or her own way. A cheer swelled, growing in volume as the false prophet stepped out, looking bigger than life in his purple and scarlet robes, onto the platform.

"Brothers and sisters of the world, I've come tonight to share a message of hope from the very heart of God." With outstretched arms, the priest thundered, "Our world must change for the better. Political and religious bigotry has divided us for far too long. This next week in Munich, Germany, Wolfgang Hendrick of the Middle East Federation and I will meet with the leaders of the United Nations in a World Financial Summit! This historic event has the potential to bring peace to our world. We desperately need your prayers. Don't you see? God has allowed the countries of our world to fight one another so that we may see the urgency of becoming a one-world community!"

The people cheered with approval while the demons of lying and compromise arrogantly fought over who would receive credit for the deception of the people. For indeed, the lies of the enemy had gone out to every country in the world.

CNN caught every word, every movement. The stage was now set for the two beasts to address over six billion people with a plan that would promise peace and prosperity. The mark of the beast was coming, not as the evil it represented, but as a solution to the world's financial crisis.

CHAPTER 15

THE MARK OF THE BEAST

No one may buy or sell
except one who has the mark or the name of the beast,
or the number of his name.
Revelation 13:17

"This is *CNN Nightly News,* and I am Marsha Wells, reporting live from Munich, Germany. For the past two days, leaders from around the world, along with their financial advisors, have been arriving for the World Financial Summit. This international summit has been arranged in response to the wars, earthquakes, and famines that have created a worldwide monetary crisis. The major item on the agenda will be the World ID Commerce Act. This proposed ID system, only recently approved by the United States Senate, is expected to receive severe opposition from several countries. The president of the United States, in a recent press conference, urged the upcoming Summit of Nations to approve this detailed system of checks and balances. The president said, quote, 'In order to end this evil famine that has destroyed so many lives, the world must achieve a balance of power among all nations.'"

The animated reporter looked excited as she read her next update.

"In apparent support of the United States president, Israel's prime minister, Eli Rosen, had this to say at a press conference earlier today: 'Wolfgang Hendrick, representing the Middle East Federation, and Father John, representing the World Faith Movement, have called for this summit in order to address the financial crisis threatening our world. Both alliances have come together to resolve this issue,' encouraged the prime minister. 'I believe we all can agree that our world needs a more secure system of merchandising and trading. I would like to conclude by saying I have the utmost confidence we can achieve an acceptable solution.'"

CNN's Marsha Wells gestured at the building behind her as she continued, "When asked about any special precautions taken, the head of security for the summit stated, 'Our security is absolutely airtight. No terrorist or Christian fundamentalist will be able to interfere with these proceedings.'

"In a related story," continued the reporter, "several right-wing Christian extremists were just arrested this morning for protesting the World ID system. These protesters were caught on camera, proclaiming the rise of a world leader who would soon deceive the world. They also condemned the ID registration as the mark of the beast spoken of in the book of Revelation."[1]

Father John's aide stopped the tape of the morning ID demonstrations and turned to face more than a thousand reporters gathered to cover the World Financial Summit.

"This isn't anything new," he scoffed. "These types of groups have been with us for the past fifty years. I remember when these right wingers actually believed that Ronald Wilson Reagan was the antichrist because each of his names were six letters long."

A surge of laughter spread quickly throughout the sea of reporters.

"Each of you has been given a copy of Father John's afternoon press release. He is very concerned about this watchman cult and its hysterical allegations of a coming evil antichrist! Actually, this afternoon's press release explains why the prophesies of the book of Revelation and Daniel do not have anything to do with our present crisis. The religious leaders within the World Faith Movement have publicly announced that the prophecies concerning the antichrist were fulfilled by the end of the first century!"

The meaning of the news release was not the clearest to most of the reporters, especially the ones who were still hung over from last night's party. It would take more than the three cups of coffee before they would be able to comprehend what was just about to be explained.

"For example, during the year 168 BC, Antiochus Epiphanes, a king of Syria, signed a peace treaty with Israel. He promised peace and prosperity for all Jews who would honor his treaty. With Israel living under his protection, he suddenly broke his promise and attacked them. This evil king proceeded to capture and desecrate the Holy Temple in Jerusalem. During this time, many Jewish people turned away from the Law of Moses and served Epiphanes as their god. The book of Daniel tells how this evil king accomplished his conquest."[2]

The majority of reporters were busy recording the aide's words to use as sound bites for their daily broadcasts. Others were furiously taking notes, highlighting their own interpretation of this rather strange press release.

"Now get this sequence of events," exhorted the aide. "Epiphanes' armed forces desecrated the temple, abolished the daily sacrifice, and set up the abomination that causes desolation."[3]

"That sounds a lot like the story line these so called watchmen have been feeding us all week," replied a *New York Times* reporter.

"Precisely," answered the aide. "Epiphanes signed a peace treaty with Israel, broke it, attacked the Jews, set up his image in their temple, and proclaimed himself to be god. In other words, the prophecies in the book of Daniel have already been fulfilled. Father John asks us all to remember that God has given us a promise that He will restore peace to our world. So let's all keep the faith and remain positive."

In its six thousand years of existence, the world had never witnessed such an event. Virtually every nation had come together in one place, at one time, to resolve a world problem. To ensure success, Wolfgang Hendrick had already contacted a majority of the invited guests and convinced them that it would be in their best interest to support the entire economic proposal.

For the waiting world, the World Financial Summit seemed to drag on and on. No real news came from behind the closed doors, and the reporters were extremely upset with the meager press releases continually being handed out. Finally, word came that a solution had been reached and that Wolfgang Hendrick would be making an official announcement from Munich's world-famous National Theatre. Within two minutes of the doors' opening, the opera house was packed with thousands of people, with more on the outside still trying to get in.

As the curtain opened, the world leaders of the Super Seven walked to their seats on the stage, followed by the German leader and Father John. As the beast stepped to the microphone to address the world, the false prophet positioned himself directly behind his lord. The power radiating from the lawless one totally captivated the audience. The demonic spirits that would eventually gather the world for the Battle of Armageddon had laid their trap perfectly. Since the signing of the Jerusalem Peace Accord, the unholy trinity of Satan, the antichrist, and the false prophet had brought the world to the point of no return.

"Greetings to all my brothers and sisters of this earth. I humbly come before you in this urgent hour to bring you a hope and a future—a plan that, if followed by everyone, will bring a prosperity the world has never before experienced."

The man of lawlessness paused while the crowd applauded.

"My vision is to have every country proclaim peace and safety. I believe in a world capable of laying aside its differences in politics, religion, and human rights. Proof of this is the overwhelming success of the World Faith Movement, which has produced a valuable grass roots organization in every member country! I've just been informed that the membership of the WFM, consisting of Christians, Jews, Muslims, Hindus, Buddhists, Mormons, Bahais, and many more faiths, has grown so fast that it's been difficult to keep up. What the World Faith Movement has done we can too!"

The desperate crowd seated before the leaders was prepared to grasp at any proposal that could guarantee some answers.

"Today I propose a world ID system that will connect us together into a one-world community. By becoming one in mind and spirit, we will be able to eliminate the wars on our borders and put an end to these cursed famines. Yes, the killing of innocent people must stop. Let's send a message to the religions of the world that tolerance and love is our only hope!" Raising his hands to the sky, Wolfgang shouted, "Ladies and gentlemen, I give you the New World Coalition!"

The ecstatic reception from the people proved that the man of sin knew exactly what the world wanted to hear. The response was extraordinary.

World leaders representing the United States, China, the European Union, Japan, the Middle East Federation, India, and Israel stood and joined hands in a symbol of unity. It would take several months for the plan to be accepted around the world. A number of countries were expected to resist at first. But Wolfgang Hendrick knew that eventually the NWC was going to grow into an enormous octopus whose tentacles would control the world. Every country would be forced to join. The Babylonian harlot had done her job well. She had ridden the beast to a place of power and confidence among the world's leaders.

✳

Immediately after the beast's proposal, watchmen throughout the world intensified their witness that Wolfgang Hendrick was not a savior but an evil counterfeit. Evangelism would become the top priority of the Christian resistance movement. But time was running out. Multitudes would soon enter the valley of decision!

Mark Bishop had always loved being part of evangelism teams. As a young believer, he had been called by God to minister at county jails and prisons. There was no greater joy for him than having the opportunity to lead a soul to the saving knowledge of Jesus Christ.

After Mark became a pastor, he soon realized that it was one thing to have people accept Jesus as their Savior, and it was quite another to disciple them, love them, exhort them, and pray with them while they learned to follow Jesus. The Bishops didn't need to be reminded of those who chose to deny Christ and return to the sins that had held them in bondage before they were saved![4]

The past month had been a real drainer for Mark and his family. To actually see the deception, the mark of the beast, being proposed by the two beasts of Revelation was almost too much to handle. It was not that Mark and Julie doubted God would take care of them; it was just that the words of Jesus had become such a harsh reality right before their eyes. Close to two thousand years ago, the Son of God in human form stood on the Mount of Olives and prophesied about a future great tribulation of believers, a time when false prophets would come and deceive many!

The end-time prophesies of Jesus had inspired Mark and Julie to re-evaluate how they discipled those under their leadership. The lack of discipleship in America would soon be exposed. Pastor Mark could only wonder how devastating it would be when the pale horse of Death and Hades confront the growing number of lukewarm believers within the body of Christ! He and his family had spent all week fasting and praying in anticipation of the warfare that would certainly erupt on this Sunday morning.

Stepping up to the pulpit, the watchman could sense that God had answered his prayers. The spontaneous applause erupting from the congregation was such an encouragement. The saints were anxious to hear a word from the Lord.

Looking out over the parishioners he so deeply loved, Pastor Mark announced, "This morning's message is entitled 'The Mark of the Beast.' My dear friends, I never dreamed I would ever be in the position I'm in this morning. We're at a point in time that many believed would never occur in our lifetime, a time when the people of the whole world must choose whom they will follow for eternity! I'm talking about a mark that can never be erased, a simple economic number that Satan will use to deceive the inhabitants of the world. This is going to happen because so many refused to embrace the truth of Jesus' prophetic warnings concerning the end times!"

As her husband began to share this critical warning, Julie couldn't help but reflect back on the trials of the churches of Bethany in the past three years.

"So much precious time wasted," she cried.

She thought of the Christians who needed deliverance from demonic strongholds but didn't know how to get it, of the man-made programs that looked impressive but produced nothing eternal, and of the youth groups that focused more on fun and games than on pressing in after God! The great tribulation would be arriving exactly three-and-a-half years to the day from the time the Jerusalem Peace Accord was signed, and so many had no idea what was happening.[5] The urgency of the hour was growing stronger by the day.

As Julie prayed, she knew from the Holy Spirit that today's sermon was the message of the hour to the body of Christ worldwide.

Mark paused and then asked everyone to turn to Revelation 14:9. He could hear the excited whispers among the youth over the rustling of pages.

Stepping from behind the large pulpit, holding his Bible in his right hand, he shared, "John the Apostle wrote concerning the great tribulation, 'He causes all, both small and great, rich and poor, free and slave, to receive a mark on their right hand or on their foreheads, and that no one may buy or sell except one who has the mark or the name of the beast, or the number of his name.'"[6]

Returning to the pulpit, Mark glanced at his notes and said, "This passage of scripture has always referred to a future event at which the saints of Christ will face the persecution of the antichrist and the false prophet. During the great tribulation, the false prophet will deceive the world into worshipping the antichrist as god. John the apostle wrote, 'Here is wisdom. Let him who has understanding calculate the number of the beast, for it is the number of a man: His number is 666.'"[7]

The pastor could see a majority of heads nodding. Every believer present knew this verse practically by heart.

"Because of this persecution, Jesus warned us of many who will turn away from their faith and will begin to betray and hate each other. Just recently, we all witnessed Wolfgang Hendrick insidiously introduce the mark of the beast in the form of an economic global ID. It won't be long before this demon-possessed impostor implements his evil plan and proclaims himself to be the god of this world!"

Pastor Mark spoke with a conviction that had already driven away many members. Since he received his vision almost three-and-a-half years ago, it was easy to see that most believers weren't even interested in hearing about the end times.

"The first three seals have transpired right before our eyes, and it behooves us to live holy lives through the love of our Lord Jesus Christ. He has made it very clear that during the seven-year tribulation period, many believers' love for God will grow cold and become lukewarm. The Apostle Peter wrote, 'For if, after they have escaped the pollutions of the world through the knowledge of our Lord and Savior Jesus Christ, they are again entangled in them and overcome, the latter end is worse for them than the beginning. For it would have been better for them not to have known the way of righteousness, than having known it, to turn from the holy commandment delivered to them.'[8]

"My fellow believers, the clear language of Peter's letter is concerning those who have been cleansed from the pollution and sin of this world. Now I ask you, how does one cleanse himself from this evil world?"

One of the youth leaders stood to his feet and proclaimed, "By the blood of Jesus."

"By repentance and faith in Jesus," yelled another.

"Very good, guys," replied the pastor. "The Apostle Peter is telling us that if blood-washed believers go back into the world and are overcome by habitually sinning, then their end will be worse than it would have been if they had never known Christ. So for this passage to make sense, it must be referring to believers in Jesus. Peter is clearly warning Christians not to backslide and return to a lifestyle of sin."

Nudging his friend seated next to him, a visitor whispered, "Boy, you never hear preaching like this."

"You got that right," replied his friend. "This preacher has a lot of guts."

"In the book of Hebrews, the Apostle Paul gave us another example of how a believer can choose to follow or reject the Lordship of Jesus Christ. We must remember that God never takes away our freedom of choice after we get saved. The Apostle Paul wrote, 'For if we sin willfully after we have received the knowledge of the truth, there no longer remains a sacrifice for sins, but a certain fearful expectation of judgment.'[9] Now get this," exhorted Mark, who did not want anyone to miss this key point. "Paul is referring to himself and other Christians. He is warning believers not to 'willfully' return to their lifestyle of sin. This means a believer has the free will to follow or deny the Lord. The apostle continues by highlighting a severe judgment for those who trample the Son of God under foot and treat the blood of the covenant that sanctified him as an unholy thing.'[10] Now I ask you what type of people are sanctified by the blood of Jesus?"[11]

"Only Christians are sanctified," said Whitney.

"That's right, Whitney. The warnings throughout the book of Hebrews are to blood-washed Christians. When people return to their habitual lifestyle of sin, a bondage they were in before they were saved, they insult the Spirit of grace!"

Looking out over the audience, the pastor could sense heavy resistance coming from the older saints.

"Our Jesus promised, 'All the Father gives Me will come to me, and the one who comes to Me I will by no means cast out.'[12] The word 'come' means to continuously seek after. So believers who continuously follow Jesus will never be cast out," encouraged Mark. "Our Jesus said, 'If you abide in My word, you are my disciples indeed.'[13] The word 'if' means you can choose whether or not to continue in his Word."

The young pastor paused, searching for the right words to express the heaviness weighing upon his heart.

"Brothers and sisters, the hour is late, and the world is asleep. Our Lord is going to come like a thief in the night to those who are not watching. The man of sin will soon rise like a shinning star, and God will send a powerful delusion because most will refuse to believe the truth and be saved.[14] This delusion will prompt many to embrace the worship of the deceiver, one who will come back from the dead."[15]

The amen corner of the youth group began to openly praise the Lord for such anointed teaching.

"Satan has come with counterfeit miracles, signs, and wonders that will deceive those who are perishing," warned Mark. "As your pastor, I am accountable to God for teaching the truth, no matter what the consequences. I admonish each of us this morning to repent of any unconfessed sin and be obedient to the leading of the Holy Spirit who indwells us."[16]

"Preach it, Pastor Mark," admonished an excited Luke, prompting several young people to rise to their feet and cheer.

"Hey, down in front," yelled one of the ushers, clearly embarrassed by the sudden outburst of emotion.

Walking down the center aisle, Mark pleaded, "Heed my words, my friends! I am not preaching a perfection doctrine where we have to be perfect to be accepted by God. We are saved not by works, but by the grace of God![17] The life of a believer should be a constant pursuit of Jesus, not one of bondage to sin but one of freedom to follow the Holy Spirit."

Cheers of praise went up all over the sanctuary.

As Pastor Mark concluded his message, the Holy Spirit began to set people free from bondages that had controlled them for years. As the worship team began to softly sing about the blood of Jesus, disgruntled members rushed for the exit. The first person the pastor met was a Sunday school teacher, Harriet Jones.

"Pastor, can you show me one verse that says a person who is really saved can deny Jesus and go to hell? I don't think you can!" snapped Harriet, barely able to maintain her composure.

"In James 5:19-20," Mark slowly replied, "James encouraged us that a brother who wanders from the truth through a multitude of sins can be brought back, and his soul will be saved from death. Now we know that a soul cannot die physically. So this verse, Harriet, must be referring to a believer's soul that will be saved from eternal death.

"Is that so?" challenged the angry Sunday school teacher.

"Yes, Harriet, this passage teaches that a Christian can bring back a fallen brother and save his soul from eternal death."

Glaring at the pastor for a moment, Harriet suddenly spun around and walked out the front door, vowing never again to set foot in the church she had attended for over thirty years.

The possibility of a one-world religion sent shock waves through the homes of Christians throughout America. No one really knew how much influence the WFM would have on the body of Christ. Recently, several of the largest Protestant denominations in America had agreed to consolidate into one organization. Who would have ever thought it possible? Baptists, Methodists, Presbyterians, and Lutherans were all agreeing to put aside doctrinal differences in order to come together under the banner of Christ.

"In many ways, it was a good move for the Protestants," praised a Unitarian minister, representing the World Faith Movement. "Besides, no one religion can be so arrogant as to claim that it has the total truth. Each religion has only a measure of truth. As a member of the WFM, I promote tolerance, not prejudice, toward those who disagree with our beliefs about God."

In some circles, the pressure to join the WFM had become a very controversial issue. One of the advantages of joining was a cash payment for each of its members. Many of the churches needed the money just to be able to keep their doors open. Self-preservation had now become a top priority, not the absolute truth of God's Word.

The wave of optimism after Hendrick's speech brought unbelievable changes that required great risks. It seemed as if the world was forced to take a now-or-never attitude. Civil wars that had erupted for years suddenly stopped. Countries that had been enemies for decades successfully negotiated trade agreements. The populations of countries hardest hit by the famines were rescued from certain death by massive food shipments from the Middle East Federation. Within the past three months, the entire supply of food and medicine Hendrick had stored was dispensed to needy countries throughout the world.

In Brazil, a holiday was proclaimed in honor of Wolfgang Hendrick. His life-saving airlifts of food and medicine had saved thousands of Brazilian families!

In Nigeria, thousands lined the streets to thank the famous German leader for his generous help. The Nigerian soccer team, which had just captured the World Cup, dedicated its victory to the savior from Munich!

The United States, an enemy of Germany in World War I and II, also praised the deliverer for his love and compassion for the starving people of the world. Almost over night, Hendrick's popularity became the topic of discussion. Politics, stock markets, and even sports took a back seat as countries praised this wonderful leader who truly cared for the people of the world.

Many had come to believe that Wolfgang Hendrick was truly a gift sent by God!

CHAPTER 16

THE SPIRIT OF UNBELIEF

Beware, brethren,
lest there be in any of you an evil heart of unbelief
in departing from the living God.
Hebrews 3:12

"Good morning, Jason. It's good to see you again," said Stephen as the evangelist and the well-groomed attorney sat down for breakfast at Bernie's Café.

It was not long after hearing Stephen's one-night seminar on the rapture of the church that Jason's heart was supernaturally touched. Even though they briefly met at Mark's church, the lawyer never really had the opportunity to share his experience with the busy evangelist. After finishing off a breakfast of fried eggs and grits, the popular lawyer began their chat with a question.

"Let me ask you something, Stephen. In the book of Revelation, Jesus exhorted believers living during the tribulation period to become overcomers. Let me read you the verse. Jesus said, 'He who overcomes shall be clothed in white garments, and I will not blot his name from the Book of Life; but I will confess his name before My Father and before His angels.'[1] My question, Stephen, is what are we to overcome?"

"Jason, this verse is referring to believers who will face the antichrist during the great tribulation. Jesus exhorted us to overcome this deceiver and his evil plan. By overcoming the enemy, our flesh, and the world, we are promised eternal life!"[2]

"What's going to happen when we refuse to register for our ID numbers?"

"The Bible says that believers who refuse to worship the antichrist will be killed for their testimony of Jesus."[3]

"Sounds like a real blood bath."

Stephen answered grimly, "It will be!"

"What about those who don't overcome and choose to take the mark?"

"Those who take the mark of the beast will have their names blotted out of the Book of Life.[4] Tragically, they will lose any opportunity of ever being saved."

The attractive lawyer with deep brown eyes looked shaken.

"Jason, God is calling believers everywhere to take a stand for the truth. Remember when John the Apostle saw souls in heaven that will be killed due to their testimony during the fifth seal? He was talking about the blood of the martyrs crying out for justice near the end of the age."[5]

"But, Stephen, hardly anybody I know is teaching that the body of Christ will be here when the antichrist returns from the bottomless pit."[6]

"What you have to realize, my friend, is that for millions of believers in America, the body of Christ's involvement in the great tribulation is a new concept. If you visit the persecuted churches in Peru, China, Russia, and Lithuania, however, you'll find that they believe what the early Church believed, that the deceiver will come against the saints during the great tribulation."

"You mean a majority of the persecuted Church doesn't believe in a secret rapture coming before the tribulation period?"

"That's correct. In fact, when I preached in Lithuania a few years ago, I discovered that the Lithuanian churches started by American missionaries taught mostly a pre-tribulation rapture. But when I visited the churches without American missionary influence, they all believed the body of Christ would be delivered from the persecution of the antichrist! Believe me, Jason, the persecuted Church doesn't even believe that people deserve to be disciples of Jesus if they are not willing to sacrifice for Him."

"I want to thank you, Stephen, for taking the time to share the truth about the Lord's coming with me. I've got a lot of studying to do. But before I go, I would really like to share a testimony from my childhood."

"I'd love to hear it," replied Stephen.

"As a young boy, I looked up to and respected my grandparents. I have many fond memories of my grandpa and grandma taking all the kids that lived near their farm out to the barn for lessons on the book of Revelation. I remember grandpa preaching on the rapture of the saints. I'll never forget the big charts he used to show God's timetable for His Son's return. The chart I remember the most was the one comparing the books of Daniel, Matthew, and Revelation. Practically the whole neighborhood turned out for grandma's blackjack pancakes and grandpa's fiery sermons on The Day of the Lord. Hearing about the antichrist, the great tribulation, the new heavens, and new earth was all pretty exciting stuff. You know, his sermons showed me that God has a plan. But even though grandpa was pretty convincing, I never really believed in a secret mystery rapture."

"Me either," replied Stephen.

"To me it's pretty amazing what's happened to our city since you preached your one-night seminar," said the muscular lawyer laughing. "You know, I was there that night."

"It seems like only yesterday," Stephen said with a grin.

"To hear the truth concerning the coming of Christ was really a blessing. I began to study the verses you challenged us with that night. I felt a real unction from the Holy Spirit to seek the truth for myself. What I ended up discovering is that the catching up of the saints of Matthew 24:4-31 is clearly highlighted in Revelation 6:1 through 7:14!"

"Amen, Jason. Let's pray that more believers will begin to see the truth before it is too late!"

"You know, after discovering the truth that the body of Christ will be delivered after the great tribulation is cut short, God's direction for my life was dramatically changed by the Holy Spirit. Jackie and I soon realized that nothing else mattered except God's will for our lives."

"That's so true, my brother. We need to be proclaiming the Gospel every day. Jesus became our example when He said, 'I must work the works of Him who sent Me while it is day; the night is coming when no one can work.'"[7]

As the two men of God walked out of Bernie's Café, a deep desire was growing within them to help others find the truth. Neither had any idea of how powerfully God would soon use each of them, as leaders of the greatest Christian resistance movement the world would ever know.

The Bishops were excited about tonight's Bible study. They, along with a select group of prayer warriors, had spent two hours praying over three critical areas. First, the intercessors bound and rebuked any demonic spirits that would try to interfere with their meeting. Second, they prayed that God would continue to pour out His Spirit of revival among His people. And third, they petitioned God to save every unbeliever who would be attending the study.

The expectancy in the air was infectious. Mark and Julie immediately spotted several new believers laughing with the joy of the Lord. What a blessing it was to see Christians more excited about their Savior than about sports, possessions, or hobbies.

"Before I begin our study of God's Word tonight, does anyone have any questions or comments?" asked Mark.

"Pastor, I have a question," replied Drew. "A lot of kids at our school think this whole teaching of Jesus warning believers of His soon return is completely bogus! They constantly bring up that no man knows the day or the hour but only the Father. Their whole point is that there can't be any signs before Jesus' return because then He couldn't come in a secret rapture. Pastor, where did this secret rapture doctrine come from anyway?"

"To be honest, Drew, there is a lot of debate over who invented this new theology of a secret mystery rapture. Many historians agree that a minister named John Darby was the first to popularize this new doctrine in the late 1820s. For several decades, this minister from the Church of England used his eloquent preaching to promote this new revelation. Actually, Christians in America had never even heard of a secret rapture until Darby arrived in 1859 for a series of teachings on Christ's coming."

"Wow, Pastor Mark, it would be great if you could give us a little history on how this secret rapture doctrine became so popular in such a short amount of time," said a curious Whitney.

The configuration of the Bible study quickly changed as Mark and Julie moved across the living room and sat down on their oversized tapestry sofa. Within seconds, everyone shifted to that side of the room and completely engulfed the Bishops. For the next hour, Mark shared how an Irish preacher in the 1860s traveled to America to teach on the secret rapture of the saints.

"It was the summer of 1859 when a Plymouth Brethren preacher named John Nelson Darby was invited to speak at a series of revival meetings in Chicago. The run-down auditorium where he preached was on the south side of the city. It looked a little out of place, with hundreds of Americans standing in line to get in. Within minutes of opening the doors, close to six hundred seats were filled with curious onlookers. Stepping onto the platform, the willowy teacher with bushy eyebrows and long sideburns spoke with a deep urgency. People could see that this man of God certainly believed in what he was preaching. He taught that our Lord's gathering of the saints in II Thessalonians 2:1 was not the same event as Christ's return with His saints at

Armageddon in Revelation 19. Darby believed that our Lord would come in the clouds, at the trumpet of God, and secretly gather His saints."

"Pastor, do you mean that this secret rapture had never been taught before?" asked a shocked Whitney.

"Not in America, Whit. The preacher taught the crowd that Jesus could come at any moment and that all the events pertaining to Christ's return for his bride had been fulfilled!

"But, Pastor, that can't be right," challenged Luke.

"That's correct, Luke. A lot of the listeners in Darby's day were puzzled too. As I said before, no one had ever heard of a teaching that dogmatically proclaimed a secret rapture. Yes, Ned, do you have a question?"

"But, Pastor Mark, then why do so many Christians believe it now?"

"Well, what do you think, Ned? Is an imminent secret rapture biblical?"

"No way, Pastor! How can Jesus come at any moment? Before He can catch up the elect, the Gospel must first be preached to the whole world."

"Yeah, Pastor, and what about II Thessalonians 2:1-11?" added his brother Drew. "The coming of the Lord to gather His saints to heaven can't come until the antichrist reveals himself in the Temple."

"So if these events happen before our Lord's coming, then how can it be secret?" asked Ned.

"Those in Darby's audience had the same questions," replied Mark. "Darby continued by proclaiming that at our Lord's Coming, the angels will separate the wheat from the tares. You see, in the 1820s in America, many believers had turned away from the message of the Second Coming of Christ. Holiness and sound doctrine were not a high priority in many of the churches. Because of this careless atmosphere, Satan sowed several major cults among the people."

"Really, Pastor, what type of cults?" asked Ned.

"Well, in the 1800s, I can think of two major deceptions that really stand out—the Church of the Latter Day Saints, whose members are Mormons, and the Jehovah Witnesses!"

"Man, did Satan try to fill a vacuum there," said Ned.

"Good choice of words, Ned. Yes, a vacuum of unbelief that promoted an atmosphere for counterfeits to deceive."

"That's for sure. Pastor, didn't the Mormons declare all of Christianity to be false?"

"They sure did, Ned. This cult was created in 1822, the same decade in which John Darby first taught a secret mystery rapture!"

"What else did Darby teach?" asked Luke.

"He taught that those who profess Christ and then fall away were never really saved. The Plymouth Brethren, his denomination, believed that God chose all believers before the foundation of the world. They taught that once people put their trust in God they can never lose their salvation."

"But, Pastor Mark, what about free will?" asked Ned.

"John Darby taught that whoever teaches that a sinner has a free will to receive salvation has perverted the very spirit of Christianity."

No one said a word. The whole Bible study silently pondered the tragic consequences of such a false teaching.

"And this was the teacher who convinced believers that the famous secret rapture was true?" asked a baffled Luke.

"I'm afraid so, my brother. That night in Chicago he gave an altar call for those who would acknowledge Jesus Christ as their Lord and Savior. He emphasized that Jesus could come at any moment. The well-known teacher pointed his long forefinger at the people and shouted, 'If Jesus came back right now, how many of you would be left behind?'"

"That sounds a lot like last week's movie on the end times. What did the people do, Pastor Mark?"

"The stampede of sinners to the altar was something that had to be seen to be believed. It became obvious to the religious leadership in America that this new doctrine could be used as a powerful tool to motivate sinners to surrender their lives to God."

Mark was suddenly interrupted by one of the out-of-town visitors.

"Pastor, I've got another question, if you don't mind. Can you give us a scripture that shows first-century believers looking for the antichrist to come before Christ's return for His saints?"

"Sure. Let's turn to I John 2:18. Ned, why don't you read for us."

"Sure," said Ned. "'Little children, it is the last hour; and as you have heard that the Antichrist is coming, even now many antichrists have come, by which we know that it is the last hour.'"

"Thank you, Ned. Now let's examine this verse and see what John is really saying. At the time of the apostle's letter, believers were already familiar with the book of Matthew. They knew from Jesus' own words in Matthew 24:15 that in the last hour before His return the abomination of desolation would come first. Our Lord warned those living in the last days of false christs who will come and deceive many. In fact, John said very clearly that the reason they'll know it's the last hour is the increase of many antichrists. The key point the apostle is telling believers is that the antichrist is coming."

"So believers were looking for the antichrist to come before Christ's return?" asked an excited Ned.

"Amen, bro," answered Drew, Ned's twin. "And the first sign that begins the last hour is the antichrist's signing a peace covenant with Israel."

"But, Pastor Mark, the man of sin didn't come in John's day?" asked Ned.

"That's right, guys. Actually, there is no place in the Bible that predicts the exact day that the antichrist will come. What we do know is that many believers will be in a compromising spiritual condition when the man of sin does arrive."

"What do you mean by compromising?" asked a visitor named Leslie.

"The Apostle Paul warned believers living in the last days, 'Now the Spirit expressly says that in latter times some will depart from the faith, giving heed to deceiving spirits and doctrines of devils.'[8] Jesus wants each of us to stand by faith for the truth of the Gospel. There is only one way to heaven, and that is only through the precious blood of Jesus Christ."

"Amen, Pastor. Our Jesus is the Way, the Truth, and the Life; no one can come to the Father but by Him!" declared a smiling Drew.[9]

"But my daddy tells me that the doctrines of other religions are just as important as the teachings of Jesus," shared an upset Leslie. "Take the World Faith Movement, for example. My daddy says that by bringing all the religions of the world together as one, we can achieve a real peace. Besides, aren't we always going to have disagreements over doctrines?"

"You know, she's right," agreed her friend who was seated next to her. "My pastor says that we should be tolerant of all religions and that we should never argue over doctrine. Besides, look how Jesus loved everyone. He never argued over doctrines."

Opening his Bible, Mark turned to II John 2:9.

"I want us all to listen very closely to how much importance God's Word places on the doctrine of Christ. The Apostle John wrote, 'Whoever transgresses and does not abide in the doctrine of Christ does not have God. He who abides in the doctrine of Christ has both the Father and the Son. If anyone comes to you and does not bring this doctrine, do not receive him into your house nor greet him; for he who greets him shares in his evil deeds.'"[10]

"Gee, Pastor, that doesn't sound very loving," snapped Lesile.

"It's a matter of heaven or hell," answered a solemn Mark. "The Bible makes it very clear there is only one doctrine that is true. Whereas all other religious doctrines in the world are man-made, the doctrine of Christ is the only one that comes from above."

"But what about the Jewish people? They worship God the Father. They just don't believe Jesus is God's Son. Do you mean they won't go to heaven?"

"Listen to what Jesus said: 'He who has My commandments and keeps them, it is he who loves Me. And he who loves Me will be loved by My Father, and I will love him and manifest Myself to him. . . . He who hates Me hates My Father also.'"[11]

"But, Pastor," interrupted Leslie's friend, "are you saying that only Christianity is the absolute truth?"

"Yes, I am," replied Mark. "We must all understand that millions of believers throughout history have become martyrs to defend the doctrine of Christ. The Apostle Paul warned believers when he wrote, 'Take heed to yourself and to the doctrine. Continue in them, for in doing this you will save both yourself and those who hear you.'"[12]

"Does anyone have any questions?" asked a discerning Julie.

Immediately hands could be seen going up all over the room. Most of the students were beginning to grasp the critical importance of Jesus' warnings to those who would face the persecution of the antichrist.

"I'm afraid everyone will have to write down your questions, and Mark and Lance will try their best to answer them by Friday night's prayer meeting," announced Julie. "Our Scripture promise to memorize tonight is II Timothy 2:19. Paul wrote, 'Nevertheless the solid foundation of God stands, having this seal: "The Lord knows those who are His," and, "Let everyone who names the name of Christ depart from iniquity." ' "

"Before we end our meeting tonight, I would like to ask you all to consider praying over your future," requested Mark. "Now is not the time to be guessing about God's will for your life. For many of us, the decision to join the Christian resistance movement won't be easy. Clearly, God is raising up watchmen throughout our country to warn believers of the coming persecution by the antichrist. Is there anyone here who will pray about becoming a watchman for Christ?"

One by one, hands of believers shot up throughout the room. Mark and Julie immediately reflected back on Stephen's first admonition: "We just need to obey what God has given us, and the Holy Spirit will raise up His prayer warriors."

CHAPTER 17

ACCORDING TO THEIR OWN DESIRES

*For the time will come when they will not endure sound doctrine,
but according to their own desires, because they have itching ears,
they heap for themselves teachers.*
II Timothy 4:3

Never before had anyone paid such a large amount of money for a thirty-minute time slot during prime time. Gene Lloyd had been preaching on TV for over twenty years, mostly on nightly time slots after eleven o'clock. His prophecy organization had just recently downsized its workers in order to raise the money for this one last desperate appeal to the people of America.

The emotional message would not be easy to give. As a minister of the gospel, he had always striven to be faithful to the Word of God, never attacking other ministers who disagreed with him. Nevertheless, on this night he planned to expose the deception of false teachers who were preying upon the body of Christ. He would also make one final Gospel plea to the unsaved, while also encouraging the saints to look up for their soon-coming King.

"3 . . . 2 . . . 1 . . . Tonight we interrupt our regularly scheduled broadcast to bring you a special report. Let's welcome well-known author and prophecy expert Gene Lloyd."

Immediately, the producer hit the applause button, which triggered a canned response from a non-existent audience.

"Good evening, friends. Tonight I've come into your homes with a message of eternal hope. Many of you don't know me from Adam. However, what's important tonight is the message not the messenger. The message of hope I have for you is from the Bible. Jesus said, 'For God so loved the world that He gave his one and only Son that whosoever believes in Him should not perish but have eternal life.'[1] My friends, if you pray to receive Jesus Christ as your Savior tonight, He will indwell you with the person of the Holy Spirit. God loves you, and by repenting of your sins, He will write your name in the Book of Life for eternity!"

The director cued the cameraman to move in for a close-up.

"I would also like to bring a message of comfort to Christians, to those who hold to the testimony of Jesus. Get ready, saints, our Jesus could come at any moment, in a twinkling of an eye. Our Lord promised us the night before He went to the cross, 'In My Father's house are many mansions; if it were not so, I would have told you. I go to prepare a place for you. And if I go and prepare a place for you, I will come again and receive you to myself; that where I am, there you may be also.'"[2]

"Okay," whispered the producer to his soundman. "Turn up the volume one notch."

"Listen, Church, don't believe these false teachers who tell you that Jesus can't come at any moment. It doesn't matter how sincere or loving they may appear. Many of them have taken scriptures out of context in order to support their own false interpretations. For example, take these evangelists who boldly teach that the coming of the Son of Man passage in Matthew 24:30 is actually the rapture. They teach that Jesus is warning Christians about a series of events, which will take place just before He gathers the elect. Let's be clear; the elect in Matthew 24 does not refer to Christians but to Jews who will be delivered at the Battle of Armageddon. Matthew 24:30-31 is not the rapture, which is secret, but the glorious coming of our Jesus at the Battle of Armageddon. John the Apostle wrote, 'Behold, He is coming with clouds, and every eye will see him, even they who pierced Him. And all the tribes of the earth will mourn because of Him.'"[3]

The anger on the preacher's face was obvious. Clearly, he was not using his notes anymore.

"Let me ask you a critical question. Why should the people of the earth mourn? It's because Jesus is coming with His saints, who were caught up before the seven-year tribulation period began. The Word of God is coming on a white horse and wearing a robe dipped in blood.[4] Jesus will come with His bride to destroy the antichrist and his armies. Don't be deceived, saints; we will not be here to face the persecution of the antichrist. It will be just the opposite! We will come with Jesus to destroy the antichrist!"

"Now," whispered the director, as the soundman hit the applause button again. "The Bible says, 'All who dwell on the earth will worship him,' meaning the beast, 'whose names have not been written in the Book of Life of the Lamb slain from the foundation of the world.'[5] Don't you see it?" pressed Gene. "No believers will take the mark of the beast because our names are written in the Book of Life. Praise the Lord, saints! Once your name is written in the Book of Life, it can never be erased!"

The commercial break came at just the right time. The studio lights seemed to be hotter than normal to the experienced preacher.

"Here we go again," announced the director, "3 . . . 2 . . . 1."

"Church, I've taught for many years that the body of Christ will be gone by the time the antichrist and his mark are forced upon the people of this world! Trust me, saints; the book of Revelation details the events of the seven-year tribulation period between chapters 6 and 19. I challenge any pastor to find the Church mentioned anywhere in chapters 6 through 19. The church is simply not there! And why is that? Because she was caught up in Revelation 4:1! John the Apostle wrote, 'After these things I looked, and behold, a door standing open in heaven. . . . Come up here, and I will show you things, which must take place after this.'[6] There it is, Church, the rapture of the saints into heaven before the tribulation period begins! I ask you, could it be any clearer?"

The director signaled to Gene to relax. Immediately the well-respected teacher paused and smiled.

"The end is near, my friends. I believe this could be my last prophecy show. Today is your Day for Salvation!"

Suddenly, his smile changed to a serious expression of concern.

"To those who don't believe, this could be your very last chance to accept the Lord before this earth is thrust into God's wrath that will come during a seven-year period called The Day of The Lord, which will begin right after the elect are caught away. Isaiah prophesied that only 'the Lord will be exalted during the Day of the Lord, when rebellious mankind will face God's wrath.'"[7]

One of the cameramen who once believed in Jesus nervously shifted his feet.

"For many of you who are religious, religion won't save you. For those of you born into a Christian family, that won't save you either. You must be born again. I beg of you; don't put it off another second. And for the saints, keep looking up, for your redemption is drawing near! God bless you all!"

Only minutes after Gene Lloyd's final prophecy show on Channel 6 was over, CNN broke in on all 331 TV channels for a special report.

"The United Nations has officially called for a vote on the NWC Commerce ID Act," announced CNN's Marsha Wells. "This ID plan will have an immediate impact on how we buy and sell commodities. What long-term consequences this will have on the world's economy remains to be seen.

The one area that many of the Arab countries have strongly objected to is the stipulation requiring every person to be stamped with a tiny ID number invisible to the eye. Without an ID number, a person won't be able to purchase any bar-coded goods. In fact, people who desire to sell goods or services must also have their own ID number," announced Ms. Wells. "This ID plan, which was first proposed by Wolfgang Hendrick of Germany, has been debated for several months. Many believe the hold up of the passage of this proposed bill is due to the provision for the ID Number.

"When asked about removing this provision, Hendrick responded, 'This is a critical part of the financial plan that must be accepted if we are to be successful.' Within minutes of Hendrick's statement," concluded the CNN reporter, "the NWC Commerce ID Act was officially presented to the United Nations. The general secretary has accepted it and has called for a roll-call vote tomorrow morning at ten."

"Hello?"

"Hi, Pastor Lance, this is Drew. Hope it's not too late, but I just had to call."

"No problem, Drew. How ya doing? What's up?" asked Lance.

"Did you catch Gene Lloyd's program that was just on?"

"Sure did. Taped the whole show. He certainly had a lot to say, didn't he?"

"A lot to say!" gasped the scared teenager. "He's calling us false teachers! This is getting to be too weird."

"Sounds a lot like Apostle Paul's portrayal of the believers in the latter days, doesn't it, Drew? Paul wrote, 'For the time will come when they will not endure sound doctrine, but according to their own desires, because they have itching ears, they will heap up for themselves teachers; and they will turn away from the truth.'"[8]

"For sure. But what about Gene Lloyd's preaching, Pastor? When I listen to him, his arguments sound so convincing. And look at how many of his books are best sellers. Believers everywhere seem to be mesmerized by his words."

"Let me ask you, Drew, did his interpretations of the end times make sense?"

"Not a chance. His argument that made the Son of Man's coming in Matthew 24 not the rapture but Jesus' coming at the Battle of Armageddon doesn't hold water. You catch his new best seller on the end times? He has the elect in Matthew 24 representing Jews suffering under the wrath of God. The great tribulation is God's wrath not Satan's wrath. His interpretations are all messed up. What's up with that?"

"Drew, do you remember the verse in Matthew 24 describing Noah's flood?"

"Sure, I think it's Matthew 24:39. Jesus described the rescue of Noah and his family. They were the only ones who heeded God's warning and prepared themselves. Noah, his sons, his wife, and his sons' wives were taken, and those who were left were destroyed by the flood."

"Exactly," replied Lance. "Jesus continued by saying, 'Then two men will be in the field: one will be taken and the other left.' The word 'taken' means to receive intimately unto one's self."

"Looks pretty clear to me. Jesus was saying that the Son of Man will take His people to heaven, and those left behind will suffer His wrath, just like in the days of Lot's rescue from Sodom and Gomorrah!"

"You got it, bro. In Matthew 24:31, Jesus gave a picture of angels gathering together the elect who are alive with the dead in Christ who are in heaven. The phrase 'gather together' means to gather upward, an upward gathering of the saints to meet the Lord in the air."

"So, why all the debate?"

"Those who believe that the Church will be raptured before the events of Matthew 24 teach that these events apply to the Battle of Armageddon."

"What am I missing here?" asked a confused Drew. "Why does Gene Lloyd try to make everything in Matthew 24 apply to Armageddon and not to the rapture?"

"He teaches that those taken away in the flood represent those Jesus takes in judgment. Those left behind who survive the Battle of Armageddon will enter the Millennium!"

"Oh, get real!" scoffed Drew. "The gathering of the elect into heaven in Matthew 24 is a sideways rapture into the millennium? He must be joking."

"No, he's not joking!" Lance sadly replied. "He believes that everything he taught on his show tonight is the absolute truth!"

"But, Pastor, when Jesus gathers His saints at His coming, He will come in the clouds, with a trumpet call of God, and with his angels, and He will take the body of Christ to heaven with believers who have already died."

"That's a perfect picture of His coming," replied Lance.

"At Armageddon, Jesus doesn't come in the clouds. There is no trumpet call. And our Lord doesn't gather anyone to heaven."

"You're right, Drew. Armageddon is not the Lord's coming for His elect in Matthew 24!"

"And what about the mark of the beast?" asked Drew. "Hendrick has been trying to get his ID law passed through the United Nations for several months now."

"Future Bible prophecy is pretty heavy, Drew, when you can see it take place right before your eyes."

"Man, this is pretty frightening for those who don't know! I've been trying to share with the kids at Lakeview, but their minds are on other things. Even my own family told me to cool it."

"All we can do, Drew, is faithfully share as our Lord leads us. He will give us divine opportunities to reach those who desire the truth."

"Well, I just had to call. Thanks so much, Pastor Lance. I appreciate your taking time to share with me."

"God bless you, Drew. Our Lord is faithful."

CHAPTER 18

THE DARK SIDE AT LAKEVIEW HIGH

For we do not wrestle against flesh and blood,
but against principalities, against powers,
against the rulers of darkness of this age.
Ephesians 6:12

After parking his car in the Lakeview High parking lot, Pastor Lance Ryan could immediately discern the presence of demonic activity. Several times within the past year students at Lakeview had been expelled for practicing witchcraft on school grounds. The big outrage came last January when the school janitor found a dead cat drained of its blood behind the Industrial Arts building. Several parents complained, but all the school could do was tighten security.

It was a little before four o'clock in the afternoon. Lance could hear the sounds of the baseball team warming up and the girls' tennis team doing two-on-one drills. Most kids who attended Lakeview left as soon as they heard the final bell. It had become the type of school that no one liked to hang around.

With papers scattered all over the floor, Lance just smiled and said, "Well, the halls look normal enough."

Turning left at the principal's office, the pastor could hear excited voices coming from room 104. With so much controversy swirling around the campus concerning Wolfgang Hendrick and his evil plan for the world, the leaders of the Bible Club had decided to pass out flyers announcing that Pastor Lance Ryan would be leading a question and answer session on the end times at their next meeting.

"Give me wisdom, Lord," uttered Lance while slipping between students who packed out room 104.

Luke Appleby, the president of the Bible Club, raised his hands and welcomed everyone to the meeting. Standing directly behind him, Lance prepared himself for an opportunity of a lifetime. Most of the students present, over one hundred, were not Christians. The grungers were lined up against the wall on the left side of the classroom. Facing them on the opposite side was the local KKK gang, called the Neighbors.

While Luke was answering some of the students' questions, Lance spotted a group of students dressed in black. They had their heads bowed and were praying in the very back of the room. The four girls, partially hidden by the crowd in front of them, obviously preferred not to be noticed. Unbeknownst to Lance, the demons of lying, fear, and death had just arrived in response to the prayers of the girls dressed in black.

"So what do we have here?" smirked the spirit of fear, as he began to sow evil thoughts among those who were sitting in the fourth row.[1]

"I'm sick of all these Bible meetings!" screamed the spirit of death. "I say let's attack them all, and be done with it!"

"You know we can't do that without permission from the One above," countered an irritated spirit of lying.

Lance greeted the students and asked for their undivided attention.

"I'm here today because I've been invited to share with you what the Bible has to say about the end times, specifically the Second Coming of Christ. Before we begin, I'd like to offer up a prayer to our Heavenly Father."

As Lance bowed his head and closed his eyes, most of the students just looked on with blank stares but curious hearts. "I thank you, Father, for allowing me to share your Son's coming with this group of students today. May you open their eyes to see the Gospel of Jesus Christ in all its truth. In the Name of Jesus, I bind every foul spirit of the enemy. Through the blood of Jesus Christ, I bind the spirits of witchcraft, lying, fear, death, and compromise. I bind and rebuke them out of this room in Jesus' name. Amen."

Death and lying departed as soon as they heard their names mentioned. The supernatural grip squeezing fear was something that lying and death wanted no part of. Within seconds, fear was no longer able to move or talk. By the end of Lance's prayer, warrior angels had swept through room 104, and fear was long gone, along with three of the four Satanists that had been performing curses in the back of the room.

The fourth girl, Amy Phillips, was well-known around Lakeview. She always wore black and had several tattoos on her arms and face. Her favorite tattoo was in the form of a very tiny dragon located just below her hairline on her forehead. She affectionately called the dragon Lord Nimrod. While her girlfriends slipped out during the prayer, she hesitated and then quickly took a seat in the front row. Simon, who was seated in the second row, looked away as their eyes met.

"Many of you here today have been taught that all the religions of the world worship the same God. Over the years, we have witnessed the growth of a new religious movement called the World Faith Movement. The goal of its leader, Father John, is to create a one-world religion. I ask you, what has the world gained by such a merger?" challenged Lance.

"It seems phony to me!" yelled a grunger, sporting a spiked haircut trimmed in purple.

"Yeah, the world seems more screwed up now than it was before this new faith group started," added a Neighbors gang member named Reggie Lincoln.

"You guys are right," replied Lance. "The reason you are here today is not to learn more about man-made religion but to experience the truth about God! Before I embraced the truth of Jesus Christ, I was wearing a mask like a lot of you do. You know what I mean: the drugs, the sex, the music, the clothes, and the mind games you play on each other. Some of you are looking for a better party, a better drug, and a better partner. Yeah, it was fun at the beginning; that's the way sin is. But after awhile, the newness wears off, and the loneliness becomes, oh, too real now doesn't it? It suddenly hits you; there's got to be more to life than this."

"Oh, here we go again," blurted out one of the grungers. "Just dress right, cut your hair, walk the straight line with loving big brother, and Jesus will love you."

"Not so, bro," responded Lance, who was ready for the challenge. "The spirit of religion tells you to look right, to say the right words, to be a good person, to go to church every Sunday, not to get caught in any big sin, and you'll make it to heaven."

"But don't all religions point to the same God?" interrupted Tanner Harrison, the seventeen-year-old leader of the Neighbors.

"That's not true, my friend. The religions of this world deny the power of the Holy Spirit by worshipping a vast multitude of so-called gods.[2] Jesus Christ, who died on the cross two thousand years ago, is the only true God. He came so that whosoever follows Him should have eternal life."[3]

The anointing of the Holy Spirit brought heavy conviction as Lance shared the gospel to a room full of love-starved students searching for the truth about life.

"Pastor Lance, for those who've never heard, can you explain the type of persecution that's coming our way?" asked a concerned Hope Bishop.

The upraised hands did not surprise Lance. He knew from experience that high school students loved to discuss the end times, mainly because it was something to which they could relate.

"Sure, but before I answer your questions—and that's if I have the answers—I'd like to share what Jesus Christ has already done. First, we must realize that Jesus has already come to pay the price of sin. He overcame sin's power and redeemed all those who will eventually choose to follow Him. He did this by defeating Satan for eternity!"

"How did He defeat Satan? Look what the dude has been doing to the kids in America," laughed Reggie.

"For sure," mocked a grunger, "we're getting higher, watching grosser films, the sex is great; everybody says it's cool. They say we'll just grow out of it."

"So what about it?" challenged Lance. "Do you want to continue to go down the path you're on? Are you happy? Or are you ready to live life with a real purpose?"

"Right on, preacher! I've got a purpose. I'm ready to split this scene and party!" joked one of the grungers as he and several of his friends rushed out into the hallway.

"Is that the way you want it? Maybe I'd better leave too. You know I'm not here to impress you or get something from you. I'm not here for my health, either. So if you choose not to be real with me, then I'm out of here."

"No, Lance, you're right," Amy answered sincerely while subconsciously blowing her blonde bangs over Nimrod. "Life isn't fun or fulfilling. It's like being in bondage to something and not knowing how to get free."

"Okay, listen up," requested the pastor in a firm voice. "Just before Jesus willingly went to the cross, He shared that He would someday return. So His disciples wanted to know when He would come back. They asked Jesus what would be the sign of His coming and the sign of the end of the age. Jesus answered them straight up that these two signs would appear in the sky just before He returns."

"What are these two signs?" inquired Tanner.

"Jesus told them that specific cosmic disturbances would be the sign of the end of the age. Immediately following this sign, lightning will explode across a black sky from the east to the west.[4] This will be the sign of His coming."

"Pastor, what does the end of the age mean?" asked Amy. "Is that like the end of the world?"

"No, the end of the age is a period of time during which specific events take place. It begins with the harvest, when Jesus separates the wheat from the tares and rescues Christians out of this world. The end of the age continues till the Battle of Armageddon, when Jesus will defeat the armies of the world and then set up his millennial reign."

"What other signs does Jesus warn us of?" asked an interested grunger.

"Another critical sign is the abomination of desolation."[5]

"Is that like the sign of the devil?"

"Sort of, bro. You see, when the Bible predicts specific events, the only way you know they are true is if they come to pass. Jesus predicted that an evil ruler who is called the abomination of desolation will come to Jerusalem. This ruler, who is also called the beast, is going to make all people take a mark on their hand or forehead. Without this mark, no one will be able to buy or sell anything."

"When will the beast reveal himself?" asked Simon, speaking from the second row.

"Well, my brother, we as a world have experienced the first three seals. The next seal, the pale horse of Death and Hades, will be arriving in just a few weeks. The hour of testing, the great tribulation of Christians by the beast, is right at our doorstep!"

Immediately, Lance discerned the spirit of rebellion about to manifest in several kids dressed in black.

"Why is God so upset with the world? Isn't He responsible for allowing evil to reign?" asked a confused Amy.

"No, God has allowed Satan to become ruler of this world because of man's rebellion and sin. The reason for the testing is the lukewarmness of Christians throughout the world. Once the great tribulation begins, it will be easy to see who loves the Lord and who is willing to die for Him."

"Will this mark of the beast be like mine?" asked Amy as she drew back her hair to reveal Nimrod, the dragon.

Laughter burst out among the grungers, who loved to see the witch dressed in black cut up.

"No, the mark of the beast can never be removed once a person takes it," answered Lance.

"But isn't it like a Social Security number?" asked a suspicious junior in the fourth row. "It's just for identification so that everyone can buy and sell. What's so wrong with that?"

"No, I'm afraid it's a lot more evil than that. Anyone who takes the mark of the beast will be worshipping the antichrist. Guys, girls, listen up!" pleaded Lance sensing the urgency of the moment. "The only way anyone will make it through the great tribulation is to accept Jesus Christ as Lord and Savior. You must ask Jesus to forgive you of all your sin and follow God through the leading of the Holy Spirit. It begins with a simple step of faith. For real, how many here today desire to follow Jesus with everything they've got?"

While several intercessors prayed out in the hallway, over sixty hands were raised for salvation. Amy wept after praying for the first time since she was a little girl. Some were being set free from the sins that had held them in bondage for years. While members of the Neighbors laid down weapons they were concealing, some of the grungers began to destroy satanic jewelry that had been given to them as gifts.

Hope Bishop and Luke Appleby could hardly believe what was happening right before their eyes. While Lance drew up a map to Tuesday night's Bible study for the new converts, Simon Colson left just as confused as when he had arrived.

The demon spirits were arriving early so that they could line up in their prescribed pecking order. Religion, compromise, lying, fear, death, lust, jealously, suicide, unbelief, and control—everyone seemed to be present. Of course, the spirit of denial was always late.

This was a moment the underworld had always dreaded. The consequences of this war would determine the eternal destiny of billions of people. The devil and his demons knew that if Jesus returned to earth, they would loose control of a world that was practically handed to them when Adam sinned, a world captivated by their evil power. Often, the angels from heaven would remind the foul spirits that Jesus will regain spiritual control of earth at the sounding of the seventh trumpet.[6] Of course, the demons hated this prophecy and had gathered to create a strategy to prevent it.

To the human eye, the prince of darkness had an enormous wingspan. Their ears burned with pain as Satan made his entrance. The pressure of the moment was unmistakable. Suddenly, the devil appeared amidst the most evil horde of spirits ever assembled. He slowly paced back and forth, not saying a word. He was waiting for some idiot to open his mouth so that he could be humiliated in front of his peers. The demons did not dare speak or even move when their master was in such a worked-up state.

"The time has come for your final assignments before the great tribulation!" bellowed Satan. "Upon my signal, we will attack Michael and his angels. I warn you not to be alarmed by what the angels from above have been telling you." When the spirit of lying stepped forward to speak, Satan screamed as loud as he could, "Doesn't it say that I will lead the whole world astray!"[7]

"Yes, master, yes, master! That's what the book says," replied the foul spirit.

The spirit of pride spoke up and said, "It does look to be conditional concerning who's going to win the war in heaven. Personally, I'm looking forward to destroying Michael and his buddies. I detest their lack of rebellion."

"Each of you will accompany me for the final war. Be alert!" shrieked the master deceiver. "We never know what the One from above will attempt. We do know that He cares very deeply for these puny humans, so the more followers we can drive into the bottomless pit, the better."

Hideous laughs and shrieks erupted out of the evil spirits. They relished the opportunity to turn humans away from their creator for eternity. The demons jumped to attention as Satan's piercing red eyes met theirs.

"For those of you who are here when my mark, 666, is given to test those on earth, be relentless! Use every ounce of deception you possess, every lie you have perfected, every destructive strategy that has ever worked for you. We must explore every opportunity that is allowed from the One above."

"Think of it! When we win, I will control all of heaven!" bragged the spirit of control.

"Yeah, that's if we win," the spirit of doubt whispered to himself.

CHAPTER 19

A VISITATION FROM HELL

He has delivered us from the power of darkness
and conveyed us into the kingdom of the Son of His love.
Colossians 1:13

By third period, most of the student body seemed a little on-edge after hearing testimonies of those who had just attended last week's Lakeview Bible Club meeting. For some, seeing Amy in a white dress and with a yellow ribbon in her sandy blonde hair was a little too much to handle. Her beautiful smile radiated the newfound freedom she had just received. Only a few believers knew that the spirit of fear, who had controlled her life, had been cast out by the power of Jesus' name. They understood her transformation, but to most, it was all a big joke.

"Look at her," whispered a jealous cheerleader. "She's getting more attention playing the goody little Christian than when she acted out her evil witch charade!"

While most of the kids couldn't help but laugh, a lonely figure observing from the back of the stairs was not joining in. He had watched Amy take a stand for Jesus in front of her friends, teachers, even those who mocked and cursed her. To Tanner, this supernatural change in Amy was nothing to be laughed at.

As Commander of the Neo-Nazi gang called the Neighbors, Tanner Harrison had a lot of responsibility. The gang of thirty soldiers had grown under his leadership. He still remembered the hot summer night, during a full moon, when the supernatural visitation occurred in his bedroom. He had been lying on his bed in his boxer shorts with the windows wide open. The humidity was so high that Tanner had a hard time sleeping for more than an hour at a time. It was close to two in the morning when the evil presence appeared in the corner of his bedroom. Its smell almost made him sick to his stomach. All the young boy could think of was jumping out of his bed, dropping to his knees, and yelling out to God for help.

After several minutes, the spirit of hate spoke with an audible voice.

"Do not be afraid; I have a message for you from my master. He has been watching you. Your leadership skills can be used to lead and train a group of committed soldiers who will stand for the truth. My master will send faithful messengers to explain what your group should stand for and what will be expected of you. Remember, my friend, you will be generously rewarded for being obedient to the prince of darkness!"

Suddenly, the evil presence was gone. The demon of hate had delivered his message. It would be only a matter of time before the young boy was forced to make his decision. Two days later, a middle-aged executive from Bethany Bank and Trust, the biggest bank in town, visited Tanner and encouraged him to be faithful to his calling.

Within an hour of that meeting, another stranger, a young man in his early 20s, approached Tanner during study hall. The stranger carefully outlined the purpose and the objectives of a white supremacy group that would be called The Neighbors. When the mysterious visitor got up to leave, he turned to Tanner and said, "Remember, my friend, that this is no ordinary proposition. You have everything to gain and nothing to lose."

As Tanner watched the young man slip away through a crowd of students, he suddenly realized that he had seen this guy before. He just couldn't remember where.

"That's too strange," Tanner muttered out loud. "I think I need to do some investigating."

But the more the lonely teenager entertained the influence of the demonic realm, the more intoxicating his assignment became. The power of the evil spirits began to draw him closer and closer, his will to resist gradually weakening. Once Tanner made the commitment to lead, the demons of fear and hate took control of his life and of all who swore to follow him!

While he watched Amy share her love for God with anyone who would listen, Tanner realized an important fact. The spirits that had once controlled Amy were gone, and her obvious freedom was something he desperately desired.

The spirit of hate could sense that something wasn't right and immediately began to fill Tanner's mind with lies and doubts.

"She may look happy, but it's only for a season, my friend," whispered the demon. "Before the moon is full, she will receive several visitors who will convince her to return to her coven."

The spirits of deception, confusion, and fear were immediately alerted to the gravity of the situation. This was a coveted assignment because all fallen angels love to see believers yield to the power of darkness, just like they did.

To most students at the high school, the Neighbors were just another gang of social misfits trying to gain attention. Because they had never really hurt anybody, the group was mainly ignored. The hate and propaganda the gang promoted was just a fantasy game that they acted out.

But Tanner Harrison knew better. He knew that someday his gang would eventually become an evil weapon in the hands of demon spirits. At first, Tanner and his buddies were led to believe that they were in control and that the destiny of the Neighbors was within their grasp. But slowly the same spirit guides that controlled the girls at the coven brought Tanner and his soldiers under their control. While Amy was given a spirit guide in the form of a dragon, Tanner accepted a spirit guide called Wolf. Every day Wolf would visit Tanner in his mind, slowly destroying the young man from within. Wolf taught the naïve recruit how to astral project by clearing his mind and slowly counting backwards until he reached his destination. Wolf would always be waiting. The huge animal would run with Tanner while they explored the beautiful lakes and hills in the outer reaches of the young boy's imagination.

Running up the stairs to his fourth period English class, Tanner knew Amy would be attending her history class right across the hall. Freedom seemed hopeless to the gang leader due to all the sins he had committed. He had come to believe the lie of the devil that he could never be free.

"There is no way out," whispered the spirit of doubt. "You are too evil. God will never accept you."

"Besides," added the spirit of religion, "all that really matters is that you believe in something."

Just then, Tanner spotted Amy talking with a group of students at the end of the hallway.

"Hey, Amy," he yelled.

"What's up, Tanner?" smiled the peaceful-looking blonde.

As he tried to reach her, Wolf appeared in his mind and forbid him to go any further.

"She's just pretending. She's still a witch. She won't understand anything you tell her. I'm your only true friend. She doesn't like you any better than any of the others do."

"Amy, I need to talk to you; it's really important!"

Wolf screamed in Tanner's mind, "Stop this right now! I forbid you to interfere with any assignments that our master . . ."

"Sure, Tanner, but can it wait until lunch? We can walk over to . . ."

"No, Amy, you don't understand," interrupted Tanner, who was just barely able to get the words out. "You're going to be attacked by . . ."

Suddenly, Tanner began to cough, and his head became dizzy. Large drops of sweat trickled down his forehead as he motioned for her to stay.

Amy sensed Tanner's desire for help and recognized in him the same kind of struggle she had experienced.

"It's okay, Tanner. I know what's going on inside you, and everything's going to be all right. The Holy Spirit is greater than these demonic spirits who are trying to intimidate us. Actually, their power is really a big bluff. Don't you understand, Tanner? God can deliver you from the power of darkness into the kingdom of His Son![1] You can be free anytime you want. Once you decide to believe in Jesus as your Savior, the power of God will be on your side. It's true, Tanner; no demon in hell can ever win against the power of Jesus."

Just as the bell rang, Amy slipped her friend a note and grabbed a seat in the back row of her history class. Tanner was in no shape for English, and he took off down the stairs to his favorite place to hang out, the lunch tables behind the Industrial Arts Building.

CHAPTER 20

BETHANY'S DECEPTION

Beware of false prophets,
who come to you in sheep's clothing,
but inwardly they are ravenous wolves.
Matthew 7:15

Five years ago, the Bethany Ministers Association had been formed as a gesture of unity to bring leaders together to discuss doctrinal differences. In recent years, the debate over the Lord's coming had polarized a small portion of the religious community. As a result, it had become a heated topic at some of the BMA meetings.

One member of the Ministers Association, from the eastern side of Bethany, told his congregation that he didn't even believe a person could be a Christian unless he or she believed in the imminent return of Jesus Christ. For most believers, to even hint that the body of Christ would be on earth for the persecution of the antichrist was totally unacceptable! The BMA became even more divisive when Pastor Mark Bishop taught that Christians would soon be faced with the choice of taking the mark of the beast.

The members of the association were greeting one another as Pastor John Ryals leisurely approached the pulpit.

"Welcome, brethren. This morning we will have our monthly open forum, in which we will discuss and debate a biblical doctrine within our ministerial guidelines. Today we have selected a subject that has quite a wallop, the coming of our Lord. Within the past few years, we have seen how toying with a biblical doctrine can have tragic consequences. Due to the confusion that has developed over the timing of our Lord's return, we have asked Mark Bishop, pastor of Bethany Assembly, to explain his interpretation of the coming of our Lord. Pastor Mark, please come."

"Thank you, Pastor," replied Mark after stepping up to the pulpit. "I would like to begin this morning by first defining the pre-tribulation rapture position. Those of you who teach this position believe that the return of Jesus has been imminent, meaning that it could come at any moment, since the days of the apostles. You teach that the body of Christ in the latter days will be raptured before the final seven years. You call this seven-year period the tribulation period or the Day of the Lord. This period consists of the seven seals, the seven trumpets and the seven bowl judgments from the book of Revelation. The critical point of the pre-tribulation view is that believers are promised never to experience God's wrath, and they, of course, will be raptured before the seven-year tribulation period begins."

While defining the pre-tribulation position, Pastor Mark couldn't help but study the faces of his peers. Some of these ministers had been very close friends with the Bishop family at one time. To see their expressions of suspicion and contempt was not easy for Mark.

"As you all know, for over three years now, I've taught a different rapture position than the pre-trib view. For those of you who have never heard this interpretation of Christ's coming, I would like to give a short overview."

One could hear a pin drop as all eyes were focused upon the young pastor.

"I teach the biblical position of the first-century Church, which portrayed the great tribulation being cut short by the catching up of the elect. Revelation 7:9-14 gives us a perfect picture of the rapture of the body of Christ between the sixth and seventh seals. This occurs during the second half of the final seven years. The great tribulation is the wrath of Satan carried out by his pawns, the antichrist and the false prophet. The wrath of God, the sounding of the seven trumpets, cannot happen until the heavenly scroll is opened after the breaking of the seventh seal. After the seven years is finished, a messenger from heaven will come holding a small scroll containing the seven bowls of God's final wrath. These bowls will be poured out in rapid succession, culminating right before the battle of Armageddon."[1]

To Mark's surprise, several ministers were actually taking notes. Across the room, Pastor J. W. Brown was angered that any preacher of the gospel would actually give this heresy any acknowledgment. Indeed, the spiritual warfare had begun.

"As you can see, the critical difference between these two rapture positions is whether the seals are the wrath of God or the wrath of Satan. Revelation 6:1-17 describes the first six seals, and Revelation 8:1 describes the opening of the seventh seal."

Off to Mark's right, seated at a small table were several PK's, pastor's kids. A blonde, green-eyed, five-year-old named Julia sat drawing quietly in her coloring book.

"In Matthew 24, six individual events are described that represent the first six seals of the scroll. The sequence is as follows: the antichrist, wars, famine, persecution, martyrdom, and cosmic disturbances."

"Here it comes," mocked a minister under his breath.

"The contents of each seal are pretty clear except for the fourth seal. This seal contains a pale horse whose rider is called Death. Following close behind Death is Hades. They are given the power to kill one fourth of the world by the beasts of the earth.[2] Now I ask you, who are these beasts?"

"As if I care," muttered one pastor to another.

"The term beast in the book of Revelation always refers to the first beast, the antichrist, or the second beast, the false prophet. Now, how will these two beasts persecute one fourth of the world?"

"The Bible says that the false prophet will make everyone worship the first beast by taking his mark," shared a visiting pastor in the first row.

"Exactly," replied Mark. "And what type of people will refuse to take the mark of the beast?"

"Christians," answered Pastor Allen Colson.

"That's correct. The fourth seal fits perfectly in the middle of the tribulation period when the antichrist steps into the Jerusalem Temple and proclaims himself to be god. He will have an image of himself called the abomination of desolation erected in the temple. The worship of this image will trigger the great tribulation. During the fifth seal, Christians will be hunted down and killed for refusing to worship the beast. Believers who are slain for their testimony of Jesus will cry out to God the Father, asking Him to judge the world and avenge their blood."[3]

"So you're saying the mark of the beast comes at the opening of the fourth seal?" asked a pastor in the second row.

"Yes, that's correct. And the reason there are martyrs during the fifth seal is that the mark of the beast was introduced to the world during the fourth seal. The Bible makes it clear that persecution during the great tribulation will be a threat to only those who resist taking the mark. Of course, Scripture also warns that any person who takes the mark of the beast will be tormented with fire and brimstone in the presence . . ."[4]

In the back of the room, leaning up against the wall were Dwayne Pressley and Kevin Collins. "I'm glad we won't be here when that happens," said Dwayne.

Kevin just shook his head and added, "But what I don't get is how can he get up there and purposely spew out such fear. I mean how can anyone respect him for what he is doing?"

"The next event is the sixth seal, which contains specific cosmic disturbances. Now here is a critical point to know. In Matthew 24:29-31, we see these same cosmic disturbances erupting right before the coming of the Son of Man."

The spirits of fear, compromise, and control were poised and ready as they patiently waited for the perfect time to attack.

"Now, is there anywhere else in the New Testament where we see these exact cosmic disturbances?"

"Acts 2:17-21," answered Pastor Elmer Dyer, who did not look pleased.

"That's correct, Pastor. In the book of Acts, Luke quoted the prophet Joel, who predicted that in the last days cosmic disturbances will precede the Day of the Lord. 'The sun will be turned to darkness and the moon to blood before the coming of the great and dreadful Day of the Lord.'[5] Now what does the Day of the Lord stand for?" asked Mark.

"God's wrath," answered several pastors at the same time.

"That's right," smiled Mark. "That's what the prophet Joel prophesied. In the Old Testament, the critical point to understand is that Joel taught that cosmic disturbances must precede the Day of the Lord.[6] In addition, our Lord Jesus also taught that these same disturbances will precede His coming. So you see, His coming and His wrath are back-to-back events. Just like in the days of Noah and Lot, deliverance is for believers, followed by wrath for unbelievers. Both the Lord's coming, which is the rapture, and the Day of the Lord will come like a thief in the night to an unsuspecting world. By comparing scripture with scripture, the puzzle of the Lord's coming fits perfectly together."

"Who does this young whippersnapper think he is, anyway?" whispered a retired minister.

Slowly but surely, the pastors were losing interest. Several were reading their Bibles, not even bothering to listen anymore. Little Julia, seated to Mark's left, had just finished drawing a yellow scroll with seven purple seals.

"In the book of Revelation, between the sixth and seventh seals, we have two events that will take place. First, a vast multitude of believers from every nation, tribe, people, and tongue, suddenly arrive in heaven. Immediately after this event, 144,000 Jews are sealed for protection from

God's wrath, which will be poured out upon the earth when the seventh seal is broken."

The watchman paused for a second in an attempt to regain the attention of the audience.

"There is a question we must ask ourselves about this group of 144,000 Jews who come from the twelve tribes of Israel. I ask you, why are these Jews being sealed for protection from God's wrath between the sixth and seventh seals if all seven seals are God's wrath?"

Scanning the audience, it soon became clear to Mark that not one minister knew the answer.

"In other words, why aren't the 144,000 being sealed for protection against God's wrath right before the first seal?"

"Who cares?" whispered one pastor to another. "To be honest, it's not very important what you know about the end times, but who you know."

"Amen to that," replied his associate. "No amount of debate can change what God is going to do. He has already won the victory! I'm actually more concerned that our members remain under the blessings of God."

"You've got that right!" agreed the senior pastor. "And what about saving souls? Instead of wasting our time arguing about when Jesus will return, we could be out witnessing!"

"The answer, my friends, is simple," Mark went on. "The six seals are not God's wrath. The reason why the 144,000 Jews are being sealed right before the seventh seal is that the wrath of God will burst forth when this seal is broken. Actually, the fourth and fifth seals of the great tribulation are Satan's wrath.[7] The two beasts, the antichrist and the false prophet, will create a worldwide persecution that Christians have never experienced!"

The interaction between pastors suddenly began to pick up. To an outsider, it looked like a meaningful discussion. But in reality, a large majority of those attending were already convinced that Pastor Mark Bishop was a heretic!

"Now let's examine this massive multitude of believers that suddenly arrives in heaven out of the great tribulation," challenged Mark. "They are standing before the throne in heaven and praising God for their salvation! This multitude is wearing white robes, and they are holding palm branches in their hands. In other words, they have received their resurrection bodies and are praising God for their deliverance! My friends, this is a picture of Jesus' cutting short the great tribulation by the gathering of His saints in the rapture!"

The young pastor stepped back and paused for a response. Throughout the room he could not find one pastor who looked happy.

"In Matthew 24:21-22, Jesus very clearly warned that the great tribulation will be an unequaled time of testing that He will cut short in order to rescue the elect, the believers, from destruction."

As Mark looked out and saw the blank stares, he knew it was time to close.

"In conclusion, when the seventh seal is broken, there will be thirty minutes of silence in heaven. I ask you, why?"

One could hear discussions among the ministers, but no response was forthcoming.

"The answer is obvious, my brothers. The silence signifies a very solemn moment because the scroll containing God's wrath is just about to be opened. The seven angels holding the trumpet judgments are ready to sound off! But before the seventh seal can be broken, angels are sent forth by our blessed hope, Jesus Christ, to gather up the elect. Praise the Lord!"

The interruption of raised hands seized the moment.

"Yes, Pastor Stanton," acknowledged a cautious Mark.

"Pastor, are you teaching that the vast multitude in Revelation 7:9-14 is the catching up of the saints by our Lord Jesus?"

"Exactly!"

"But how can that be possible? The Church was raptured in Revelation 4:1! The multitude from every nation, tribe, people, and tongue in Revelation 7:9 are those who got saved after missing the rapture and were later killed for their faith!"

"Pastor Stanton, may I ask you a question concerning this passage?"

"Go right ahead."

"If the Church is raptured to heaven in Revelation 4:1, then the Church should be ready to welcome the martyrs of Revelation 7:9 when they arrive before the throne of God. Right?"

"Absolutely!" replied the smiling pastor.

"But, Pastor Stanton, there are only three groups of beings present when these martyrs arrive in heaven. There are the angels around the throne, the elders, and the four living creatures!"

"Yes, that's true," agreed the pastor, slowly shaking his head. "So what are you trying to say?"

"If this vast multitude arriving in heaven is composed of converts that missed the rapture, then where is the resurrected body of Christ?"

"Well, I . . ."

"Pastor Bishop, it's not actually quite that simple," interrupted Pastor Elmer Dyer. "Don't you understand that if you take away the imminent return of Jesus Christ, you will destroy the faith of many believers?"

"At our church, Pastor Dyer, it has had just the opposite affect. Those who believe in the sequence of events that precede His coming have had their lives utterly transformed. I personally have witnessed believers at Bethany Assembly winning more souls, praying with greater fervency, and sharing with those in need, all because of Jesus' words to watch for His return."

"Let me ask you a hard question, Pastor. Isn't it true that you've lost over one-half of your congregation because you teach this new view on the timing of the rapture? Let's be honest; even your so-called revival has run out of gas."

"Well, it depends on what you . . ."

"So tell us, Pastor. If this doctrine that the body of Christ will still be here for the antichrist is so of God, why are so many believers leaving your church and coming to ours?"

"Pastor Dyer, please allow me to ask you a question."

"Certainly."

"Can we, as ministers, set an exact date when the rapture will occur?"

"No sir! Jesus clearly said in Matthew 24:36, 'But of that day and hour no one knows, not even the angels of heaven, but My Father only.'"[8]

"But, Pastor Dyer, how can you use this verse to refer to the rapture of the saints when you teach that Matthew 24:36 is a description of Jesus' coming with His saints at the Battle of Armageddon?"

For a spilt second, the conviction of the Holy Spirit began to touch hearts. Pastor J. W. Brown couldn't take it anymore and raised his hand to speak.

"Excuse me, Mr. Bishop," Brown said, waving his arms to get everyone's attention. "This whole line of reasoning on the timing of the rapture is meaningless. Matthew 24 was not written to Christians because it says false prophets will deceive the elect. The elect in this passage can only refer to Jews. We know from Scripture that Christians can't have their salvation taken out of their Father's hand. Jesus said, 'My sheep listen to my voice; I know them and they follow me. And I give them eternal life, and they shall never perish; neither shall anyone snatch them out of My hand. My Father, who has given them to Me, is greater than all; and no one is able to snatch them out of My Father's hand.'"[9]

After the well-respected pastor took a seat among his peers, all eyes quickly refocused on the young pastor's reply. "Pastor Brown, Jesus said, 'My sheep hear my voice and I know them, and they follow Me.' Our Lord was stressing relationship in this verse. Those who continuously hear His voice, who continuously follow Him, are His sheep."

Glancing down at their faces, Mark could discern a thin veil of deception covering their eyes, which was preventing them from seeing the truth. The spirit of compromise had used the religious traditions of men, which had been passed down through the centuries, to deceive right up to the end of the age.

"Let's be honest, my friends; our forum today not only involves the timing of the rapture," challenged Mark, "but also the salvation of a believer!" For those of you who have never studied it, the rapture myth was popularized in America in the 1860s during the time of the Civil War. Many Bible teachers actually embraced this Trojan horse myth in order to strengthen their view that a believer could never deny the Lord. In Matthew 24, Jesus clearly taught just the opposite! He warned us of believers who will betray one another and . . ."[10]

"Pastor Mark, may I speak?" interrupted Pastor Louis Cooper. "I also believe there will be Christians who will fall away from the Lord. But the great falling away of believers can only happen after the body of Christ has been raptured!"

Pastor Mark stood, silently praying for the leading of the Holy Spirit. "So most of you today believe that the seven-year tribulation period is not for the church, which has been raptured, but is a time when our Lord will specifically fulfill His promises to the Jewish people?"

No one spoke. The usual nodding of the heads was sufficient.

"And this vast multitude from every tribe, nation, and tongue represents Christians who have been martyred for their faith? Is that right?"

"Please get to your point," interrupted an anxious Pastor Ryals.

"My point is how can you have the greatest Christian revival the world has ever experienced when this seven-year period is primarily for the Jewish people? You have this vast multitude from every nation being saved during the great tribulation, a time when the delusion of God is sent out because the world refused to love the truth!" With no hesitation, Mark declared, "I give you this charge today; many believers are going to deny their Lord by taking the mark of the beast. In the book of Revelation, Jesus warned believers living inside the seven-year tribulation period to repent of their lifestyle of habitual sin and become overcomers. For those who overcome, He promised to never blot their names out of the Book of Life.[11] As for Christians who refuse to repent, their names will be erased for eternity!"

In an instant, a demonic oppression engulfed the room like a cloud. To Mark, it felt so thick that you could cut it with a knife.

"This day I stand before you as a watchman with a message from God! Ezekiel said, 'When a righteous man turns from his righteousness and does evil and I put a stumbling block before him, he will die. Since you did not warn him, he will die for his sin. The righteous things he did will not be remembered, and I will hold you accountable for his blood.'"[12]

The utter contempt for Mark and for what he stood for was beginning to surface among the pastors.

"It all makes sense now," fumed one pastor out loud. "He doesn't even believe in the believer's assurance."

"I warn you all; the false prophets of the World Faith Movement are actually wolves in sheep's clothing.[13] In the last three years, billions of people have been deceived through their counterfeit signs and wonders. They have even set up an office across from Sluman's Garage, and several of you have welcomed them and their false teaching to our city!"

Pastor Mark could sense that his time was short. He knew that the next sixty seconds could mean the difference between heaven and hell for the pastors seated before him and for their congregations.

"The Spirit of God is warning us that the World Faith Movement is the disguised Babylonian Harlot of Revelation 17! God is pleading with you as church leaders of this city to open your spiritual eyes. The antichrist, the enemy of our souls, is none other than Wolfgang Hendrick of Germany! The World ID System he has proposed to the United Nations is actually the mark of the beast. I warn each of you; don't register for your ID number! People who take the mark will be worshipping the antichrist as their god![14] The second beast of Revelation, the false prophet, is Father John from Rome! This leader of the World Faith Movement will be the one who will enforce the mark of the beast worldwide. Brothers, if we do not . . ."

"Hold up, son; that is quite enough," interrupted Pastor Ryals as he quickly moved toward the podium.

Slowly but firmly, the rotund pastor removed the hand held microphone from Pastor Bishop.

"I do believe, Mark, that you are sincere about what you believe. But we all know that when you start with a false premise, you always wind up with a false conclusion. The Bible clearly says that Jesus will never blot a believer's name out of the Book of Life. That means all verses that appear to say that believers can deny Christ must mean something else."

"It's about time," mumbled a frustrated pastor who was praying for someone to take control.

Perched on the shoulder of Pastor Ryals, the spirit of control couldn't help but smile.

"Pastor Bishop, if I may be so bold to ask, are we to believe that you and this evangelist Horbin . . . I mean Corbin . . . have suddenly found the truth, and we have somehow missed it? Do you actually believe God has chosen you to be His spokesman while allowing the rest of us to be blinded in this area? Now isn't it true that you are the anointed watchman for God, and we are the unenlightened shepherds?"

Pastor Ryals continued to focus on the crowd and never looked in Mark's direction.

"Let's be honest, my brothers; you don't have the truth if you have a contradiction. First of all, the Day of the Lord doesn't begin in the second half of the tribulation period. Actually, the rapture must first take place, and only then can the tribulation period begin. Second, Matthew 24 is telling Jewish people, not believers in Jesus, to flee their homes. And finally, we are to be watching for Jesus our blessed hope not for the antichrist! It saddens me that Pastor Bishop has brainwashed so many believers in the past three years with this false interpretation. Obviously, after this morning's tirade, he has no intention of repenting. In view of this, I must recommend that he be asked to resign from our association."

Without any delay, a voice count was taken with only Pastor Allen Colson abstaining. The pastor from Calvary Community sat motionless while pondering Mark's interpretation of Christ's coming.

"Well, that's it. You have our decision on what you taught today. Thank you for coming, Mr. Bishop," said the irate pastor as he turned away in mid sentence.

While gathering his notes, Mark felt led by the Holy Spirit to give one last warning.

"My brothers, the first three seals are broken, and the fourth seal will reveal the true identity of the antichrist. Please, for the sake of your families and your congregations, don't register for your World ID Number."

"He just doesn't get it, does he?" whispered one pastor.

The members of the committee had made their decision. The time for discussion was over. While exiting the conference room, an upset Mark glanced over and noticed Pastor Colson intently going over his notes. Near the podium raced a laughing little Julia, clutching her drawing of a yellow scroll with seven purple seals.

✳

It was a foggy, cold night as the demon spirits aligned themselves along the rim atop the ID Security Building.

"Well, where is he? I hate these stinking interruptions!" cursed the spirit of control.

"I can sense that we really messed up this time," cried the spirit of confusion, pacing back and forth.

"Hey! We are all here except for you know who," proclaimed a surprised spirit of doubt, who just wanted to appear discerning.

"What's so great about the ugly little imp? You think fear is something special?" scoffed the spirit of jealously.

"Maybe," replied the spirit of doubt, "but we all know how our master has been treating fear lately."

"Why don't you tell us?" seethed the foul spirit while positioning himself to strike.

While doubt thought over his reply, jealousy's yellowish green fangs slowly appeared under its bluish red lips.

"Come to think of it, you're right. The spirit of fear ain't so special," replied doubt as he lifted off and moved to the other side of the roof.

"Why do we always have to wait!" screamed the spirit of lust.

"You know why!" yelled pride. "Our master loves to make grand appearances!"

When they heard the deafening shriek, the evil imps knew he was coming. All eyes turned east, as howling winds preceded his arrival.

"He's awfully high. He may be coming from the heavenlies!" shouted lying, who was fully prepared to defend himself from any false accusations from his peers.

Their master's shadow almost covered the top of the ID building.

"Greetings, soldiers of darkness," smiled Lucifer. While extending his wings, he purposely knocked several demons off the left side of the roof. The sense of urgency that the prince of darkness usually exuded was surprisingly absent.

"I've come tonight to personally tell each of you that your assignments are coming along very nicely."

While the evil spirit flattered his pawns of destruction, the spirit of fear purposely arrived late so that everyone could see him.

"Watch this rebuke; I'm gonna love this!" said the spirit of pride with a laugh.

"Well now! Look who we have here," said Satan.

As fear landed beside his master, the spirit of jealousy cursed, "Are you believing this?"

"Tell us, fear, how is your special assignment coming?" asked Satan.

"Just as planned, my master," the demon immediately tensed up for his master's rebuke.

"As your leader, I always expect my orders be carried out. Do you understand me?" screamed Satan, his glowing, red eyes searching for anyone who would dare challenge him. "Yesterday was such a masterpiece that I had to come and see the results for myself."

"Do you mean how I split the charismatic fellowship on Cherry Avenue?" interrupted the spirit of jealousy while looking to see who was watching.

"How about my idea to form the Neo-Nazi group, the Neighbors?" gushed the spirit of hate.

Their constant verbal volleyball had always been a great annoyance to their master.

"No, you idiots! I'm talking about the Ministers Association meeting," scoffed Satan, growing extremely impatient. "You all can learn a valuable lesson tonight, which you may use in future conflicts. Fear, compromise, and control worked together so that these pastors actually missed the truth when they had it right in front of their long religious noses! Let's remember, soldiers, one critical lesson."

It took an evil glare from a spirit of antichrist, who was standing to his master's right side, to get the demons' complete attention.

"The followers can be extremely faithful if they are able to discern the truth of our attacks. For those of you who encounter the gift of discernment, be extremely careful and don't get careless! The time will come when your work, which you have laid this day, will bear the fruit of evil. If everything goes as planned, many followers will turn away from their faith, without even understanding the consequences of their decisions!"

The demons roared with delight, anticipating the day when millions of followers would turn against the One from above.

Chapter 21

What Gives You The Right?

Have I therefore become your enemy
because I tell you the truth?
Galatians 4:16

Bertha's Coffee Shop was usually full on weekday mornings, but business was slow today due to the heavy rains. The smell of Bertha's self-proclaimed world-famous sweet potato pies lingered in the air, as waitresses slowly circled the tables to serve free coffee refills.

Julie sipped her green tea, and Mark stirred his coffee absently, reflecting back on last week's grilling by the Ministers Association.

"My heart aches for them and their congregations," he said.

Julie looked up at him with a surprised expression on her face. "Didn't anyone respond in a receptive way?" she asked.

"Only Pastor Allen Colson of Calvary Community seemed to be really listening," replied a tired Mark. "I've gone back and rechecked my words. I really don't know what I could have said differently that would've changed their beliefs."

"It's in God's hands now, honey," encouraged Julie.

While gently reaching over to squeeze Mark's hand, Julie could see Allen and Mary Colson walking towards the table.

"Good morning, Mark, Julie. Do you think my wife and I could join you for some fellowship?" asked the nervous pastor.

"Certainly!" replied Mark, while jumping to his feet and grabbing two wooden chairs from another table.

"After our forum last week, I bought a tape of your presentation, and Mary and I have been studying your interpretation of our Lord's Second Coming. After examining these scriptures, we have some questions to ask you, if you don't mind."

"Not at all, Allen, ask away, and I'll do my best," Mark smiled encouragingly.

"Well, in I Thessalonians 4:15, the Apostle Paul said, 'Those who are still alive and remain till the coming of the Lord will certainly not precede those who have died in the Lord.' This is our Lord's coming for His saints, right?"

"That's correct, Allen," replied Mark. "All believers who have died, Old Testament and New Testament, will first receive their resurrection bodies. Immediately after this happens, the body of Christ alive on earth will be caught up by angels to receive resurrection bodies."

"Yes, that's pretty clear," replied Allen.

"But let's dig a little deeper by examining the words *alive* and *remain*."

"Sounds kind of funny, Mark. What does it mean?" asked Mary.

"The key to this phrase is the word *remain*, which actually means survive," replied Mark.

Allen thought for a few moments and then said, "I see it. Those who are alive and have survived the great tribulation will be raptured!"

"Exactly," replied Mark. "The Apostle Paul is outlining how Jesus will come and gather His saints. In Matthew 24, Jesus recorded a general description of the six events that will precede His coming. John the Apostle then filled in the details of these six events in Revelation 6. In fact, in Revelation 7:14, John shared a future vision of a great multitude of believers from every nation, tribe, people, and tongue arriving in heaven after being delivered out of the great tribulation."

"But, Mark, isn't this multitude in Revelation 7 the martyrs who were saved after the rapture?"

"Check it out, Allen. There is no mention of this multitude ever being martyred. In fact, this massive crowd that has just arrived in heaven has resurrection bodies, and the people are thanking the Lord for their deliverance."

"Yeah, I see what you mean. You know, I think it's funny that I never looked at it this way before."

"What do you think of all of this, Mary?" asked Julie.

"For me, it seems as if the first-century belief that the saints would face the persecution of the antichrist makes a lot more sense than the pre-tribulation teaching of the 1800s."

After a long pause, Allen asked, "The believers in America aren't ready for the type of persecution that's coming, are we Mark?"

The Bishops could immediately sense the anointing of the Holy Spirit. They knew from experience that this was not just a regular house call. The Holy Spirit was calling the Colsons to become watchmen in the very near future.

"Allen, you wouldn't believe the persecution Julie and I have received since the minister's forum last week. It's as if all the demons of hell have been loosed to come against us and anyone connected with us."

"But why, Mark? Why such attacks from the enemy?"

"To be honest, I think my comment in the *Bethany Herald* on Tuesday night seemed to ignite the explosion," the young pastor reluctantly admitted.

"We missed it, Mark. What did you say?"

"Allen, you asked if the body of Christ is ready for the persecution that's coming, right?"

"That's right."

"No, we are not! You see, the spirit of the antichrist wants to suppress Jesus' warnings concerning the mark of the beast during the great tribulation. Many believers have been taught that it's not possible to deny the Lord. Others don't even believe that they will be here to face the antichrist. Just look at how many believers have become lukewarm, lazy, and unrepentant in their walks with God. I believe the combination of these two teachings will deceive many believers into taking the mark of the beast during the great tribulation!"

"Those are pretty strong words," replied a stunned Allen.

Mark's face grimaced in pain. He knew the consequences that faced his family for proclaiming the truth of Jesus' words. Looking over at the Colsons, Mark calmly replied, "The Apostle Paul wrote, 'Have I therefore become your enemy because I tell you the truth?'"[1]

"I guess the truth doesn't need defending, now does it?" added Mary."

"Most pastors, at one time in their life, have studied the book of Revelation," shared Mark. "But a large majority are just espousing what they were taught while attending Bible college or seminary. Their individual studies are just a regurgitation of the same old study notes."

"I'm afraid I'm on that list," admitted Allen.

"Mary, Allen, this is a dying world that desperately needs watchmen. The opportunity for revival is quickly running out. By the time the antichrist takes over and the delusion of God is sent out during the great tribulation, the Christian remnant will be much smaller than we ever imagined."

"You mean there won't be any end-time revival during the great tribulation?" asked Mary.

Shaking his head slowly, Mark replied, "How can there be once the delusion of God is sent out!"

Allen and Mary could hardly believe what they were hearing.

"Mark, how does the World Faith Movement fit into end-time prophecy?"

"Well, Mary, Scripture warns us of the Babylonian harlot who will ride the beast during the first half of the last seven years. This deceptive harlot will bring all of the religions of the world into one evil religious system."

"You believe the World Faith Movement out of Rome is the Babylonian harlot, don't you?"

"Exactly," Mark replied without any hesitation. "The evil harlot will oppose biblical Christianity, substituting a worldwide religious system in its place. When the beast demands the world to worship him as god, God's Word warns believers that the harlot will be destroyed!"[2]

"So you don't believe that the appearance of Mother Mary was actually from God?"

"No, I don't. Actually, I believe the apparition of Mary was a demonic tool specifically created by Satan in order to form the World Faith Movement."

"Then what about Father John, its leader?"

"During an intense time of prayer, the Holy Spirit warned Julie and me about him. Did you know the church in Rome sent this priest as their representative to twelve Muslim countries the year before the WFM was established?"

"For what reason?" asked Allen.

"To encourage Muslims to unify with all the religions of the world by eventually joining the WFM!"

"That's pretty frightening, Mark. Do you have any idea how Father John fits in?"

"Mary, I can tell you right now who he is. He's the false prophet of Revelation 13:11. It's not a coincidence that he was behind the Mother Mary deception. The endorsement of something so evil can only point to Satan himself."

The Colsons looked like a couple that didn't want to believe what they had just heard.

"I don't know, Mark. It's pretty difficult to grasp it all at once," replied Allen.

"Don't you see what the body of Christ is up against?" pleaded Mark. "The traditions of men have permeated the pulpits of America. To combat this compromise, God is going to send an angel to proclaim the eternal Gospel to every nation, tribe, tongue, and people.[3] This heavenly assignment will fulfill Jesus' words: 'The gospel of His kingdom will be preached in the whole world as a testimony to all nations and then the end will come.'"[4]

"It sounds pretty convincing, Mark. Mary and I plan to take some time to study and pray so that we will have the mind of Christ concerning the things you've taught us. We have finally realized that whatever the truth may be, we must speak it out no matter what the consequences!"

"Of course, Allen. We'll be praying for you because we know your decision will have eternal consequences. We want you to know that Julie and I, as well as the Corbins, are always available to help in any way we can."

Both pastors stood with a new respect for each other. Exchanging phone numbers, Mary and Julie both silently thanked the Lord for arranging such a divine appointment.

"A divine appointment, indeed," said an obviously pleased Mordecai as he watched them leave.

Neither the Bishops nor the Colsons were aware of the warrior angel who had supernaturally protected their conversation from any interference. The demonic spirits that controlled a large portion of the city knew better than to try to interfere.

By sixth period, Lakeview High was buzzing with the news that Wolfgang Hendrick was the antichrist and that Father John of Rome was the false prophet. Drew and Ned Henley, youth leaders from the Bible Club, had begun to share throughout the school that the antichrist would soon attack Jerusalem and proclaim himself to be god.

"Hey Luke! Have you heard the recent news coming from the twins?" asked Jake.

"Not a clue."

"Well, it seems that Wolfgang Hendrick of the Middle East Federation is demon possessed! According to the twins, he's going to attack Israel and take over Jerusalem any day now."

A couple of freshmen walking by overheard the prediction and immediately began to crack up.

"No joke, Luke, Drew's telling everyone that the peace treaty Hendrick signed with Israel over three years ago is going to be broken by Arab countries on Israel's border!"

"Well, what do you think, Jake?"

"Honestly, I don't know. I like the twins. They stood up for me when my homeroom teacher accused me of stealing food out of the cafeteria last year. But, Luke, if Ned and Drew continue to share this end-times stuff, they'll definitely be labeled as fruit loops," replied a worried Jake.

"What if I told you that it was the truth?"

"Hey, whatever," replied Jake, rolling his eyes. "Look, Luke, if the twins are going to share this stuff with people, they really need to be more careful whom they tell it to. I mean some of the teachers are pretty hot about it. My fifth-period math teacher, Ms. Fields, keeps telling everyone that Father John is like her hero. Check it out, Luke, she didn't even know what a false prophet was."

Both boys started to chuckle as they waited for the noise in the crowded hall to die down.

"What about you, Jake? I know that you've heard the Gospel from Hope and Whitney. Do you believe Jesus is everything He says He is?"

"You mean that Jesus is the Son of God?" asked Jake, who nervously looked away for a moment.

"That's right. Jesus said, 'I am the way, the truth, and the life. No one comes to the Father except through Me.'[5] What Jesus is really saying is that only He has the power to take you to Heaven after you die."

The youth leader silently began to pray for Jacob Thomas Jamison, who all the kids at Lakeview High affectionately call Jake. Just over a year ago, the Jamison's moved to Bethany from Fort Jackson, South Carolina. Jake's dad was in the army, and the latest move was his family's fifth in the last nine years. Even though Jake was new, he fit in with several clicks at school. But behind all the jokes and funny stories was a seventeen-year-old boy who was desperately searching for some sort of meaning in life.

"Yeah, I've already heard this all before, Luke. Even some of my friends have become Christians. But I've got a real problem with this whole Jesus thing. How do you really know Jesus died on the cross two thousand years ago? It's almost like Christians are walking around living by blind faith. You can't see Jesus; you can't touch him or talk to him. You can't really prove He's real. So you just hope you're right? Come on, Luke, you have to give me more proof than that."

"Before I accepted the Lord, I had some of the very same questions," replied Luke. "The truth is, Jake, the only way that I ever got any answers was through a personal relationship with Jesus Christ. When you become born again by the Spirit of God, He will lead and guide you into the truth."

"What are you talking about?"

"Jake, it's really pretty simple. I don't have to see Jesus physically to believe in Him. When I became a Christian, the first prayer he answered for me was that he took away my fears."

"Fears! What fears, Luke? You're senior class president, captain of the basketball team, and president of the Bible Club! Three months ago you were offered a full scholarship to Auburn University. What could you possibly be afraid of?" expressed the outsider while admiring the achievements of a successful insider.

"Jake, you know as well as I do that things can look good on the outside, but on the inside a person can be in bondage to all sorts of things. Four years ago, I was scared of dating, taking tests, and competing in sports. I was even afraid that no one would like me after they really got to know me. But Jesus changed all that. He gave me a joy I never had before. I made a 180 degree turn from being someone who had no purpose to being someone who loves life and, more important, loves God."

"So you're saying that the first step is a step of faith."

"You got it."

"Then after you ask Jesus to be your Savior and receive the Holy Spirit, you become a new person?"

"A new creation, my friend. Old things pass away; everything becomes new,"[6] said Luke.

The school bell began to ring, signaling their next class.

"I don't know, Luke; it sounds strange. I come from a military family. Everything we do is by the book. You've got to prove every belief, every action. I don't know what to think about all of this. But I do appreciate your talking to me about it."

"Would you like to hear some more about the end times?"

"Sure would. Actually, it's pretty interesting."

"Okay, Jake. Look, I'm meeting Jessie Hyatt and Damien Haley behind the gym at four o'clock to discuss some questions they have about the antichrist. Are you up for it?"

"Yeah. Sure thing. I'll see you there!" said a smiling Jake while heading off for his math class.

✳

It was a little before four when Luke arrived. Hope Bishop looked to be in a pretty heated debate with some other students.

"Listen, Jessie, if you want to discuss what the Bible says about end-time events, fine! But just leave my dad and our church out of it!" snapped Hope.

"It's not that simple, Hope. Your dad is the one who taught at the Ministers Association meeting that the antichrist is Wolfgang Hendrick and that the mark of the beast is right around the corner. In fact, he said that if people register for their ID number, they are going straight to hell," replied an angry Jessie, who looked ready to rumble.

"It's true!" Hope shot back. "The scriptures warn us of a man of sin who will turn the world against the saints. This evil leader will be assisted by a false prophet who will advocate a unity and tolerance among the religions of the world."

"What's so wrong with that?" interrupted Jessie. "Just look at how many people have been helped by Father John and the World Faith Movement."

"It's the spirit of antichrist, Jessie. The WFM is deceiving millions of people."

"Hold up!" interrupted a fuming Damien. "I resent you or anybody else in this high school accusing the WFM of being evil. What gives you the right to be judge and jury anyway? Everyone interprets the Bible differently, don't they?"

Glancing over at Luke for some support, Hope silently prayed about whether she should even continue.

"Jesus said that there is going to be 'a great tribulation, unequaled from the beginning of the world until now—never to be equaled again.'⁷ This means that all Christians that refuse to worship the antichrist as god will suffer the worst persecution ever!"

The pastor's daughter knew in her heart that there could be painful consequences for openly sharing the truth with this group of students.

"Yeah, we heard this whole scene during lunch when Drew and Ned were preaching on the front steps. What ever happened to the twins? Everyone's calling them the space cadets," Damien joked while two of his friends looked away and laughed.

"Ned and Drew are just speaking the truth about what's about to go down," defended Luke while taking a seat next to Hope. "They knew they'd be persecuted for preaching God's Word, straight up! Bottom line? It's one thing to share about God's love, but it's quite another to share about his wrath."

"But Drew told us that Satan's wrath will come before God's wrath," replied Jessie.

"That's right, Jess. God is going to allow persecution worldwide against anyone who professes Jesus Christ as Lord. The ultimate test, the mark of the beast, will be offered to everyone on the earth. For some of you here today, there's a good possibility that your folks, your relatives, even some of your best friends may end up taking the mark of the beast!

"Forget that," yelled an annoyed Damien as he and his friends took off for a smoke.

"This is too much for me," cried an upset Jessie. "I gotta go!"

"Jessie, won't you at least stay and hear the whole story?" asked Luke.

"To be honest, my parents told me yesterday that they hope the United Nations passes the World ID Bill. My daddy feels that everyone's having a personal ID number is a great idea. He thinks that without a big change the whole world will go down the tubes."

Hope, sensing Jessie's inner struggle, slid across the bench and gave her a big hug.

"So, what are you going to do, Jess?"

"Who knows?" answered the tall brunette, who began to quietly weep.

As Hope and Luke began to pray for Jessie, Jake was making his way across the parking lot. All through math class he kept wondering what it would be like to be a real Christian. Reaching the gym, he suddenly veered off to the left and quickly moved toward the school bus departure area.

Just as he caught the last bus of the day, the spirit of control departed with an evil smile. During Jake's math class, the foul spirit had sensed that the One from above was calling the young boy.

"As long as Jake is open to our attacks, we'll have more opportunities, now won't we?" bragged the demon spirit.

CHAPTER 22

THE RESTRAINER

For the mystery of lawlessness is already at work;
only he who now restrains will do so until he is taken out of the way.
II Thessalonians 2:7

There seemed to be a much bigger crowd than usual for the Tuesday night Bible study. The word had gotten out amongst the churches that Pastor Mark had invited evangelist Stephen Corbin to preach. With teenagers practically sitting on his feet, Stephen started the meeting by having the study group turn to Acts 26:16-18.

"Tonight let's examine what it really means to be a witness for the Lord. In the book of Acts, God called the Apostle Paul to be a witness. In Acts 1:8, witnesses actually mean martyrs."

Before the evangelist could say another word, someone near the kitchen spoke up.

"Brother Corbin, before you begin, could I ask you a question?" requested a Lakeview High cheerleader named Cindy Johnson.

"Go for it," replied a smiling Stephen.

"Well, my friends and I are pretty much confused over Christ's Second Coming. We've always been taught that I Thessalonians 4:15 is a picture of Jesus' catching up the saints before the tribulation period. Our pastor says that this is the rapture because Jesus never touches the earth. Seven years later, after the seventh bowl judgment, Jesus comes physically with His saints at the Battle of Armageddon. This is His Second Coming, not the rapture, which is in I Thessalonians 4:15."

"Great question," replied Steven. "Every believer needs to understand the answer to this question in order to interpret the events of Christ's Second Coming correctly. Now we all know the term rapture is not found in the Bible. It's actually a nickname for the phrase caught up, which is in I Thessalonians 4:17. Paul wrote of our Lord's coming, 'Then we who are alive and remain shall be caught up together with them,' meaning believers who have died, 'in the clouds to meet the Lord in the air. And thus we shall always be with the Lord.'"

"But how can that be the Lord's coming if Jesus doesn't touch the earth?" interrupted the confused cheerleader.

"Cindy, allow me to share the meaning of this passage through a story."

"Sure."

"Let's say your best friend and you decided to go to Max's this Friday night. She came to pick you up in her parent's car at your house. She honked the horn; you came out and got in. She then drove you both to Max's for some burgers. Now, did your best friend come and get you?"

"Of course," replied Cindy.

"Did she go into the house?"

"No, she didn't."

"So she came and took you away without coming into your house?"

"Stephen, are you saying that Jesus doesn't have to touch the earth for it to be called His Second Coming?"

"Absolutely. Let's remember that Paul clearly said it's the coming of the Lord![1] It makes no difference whether Jesus touches the earth. The point of the writer is that at the coming of our Lord all those who follow Him will be caught up."

"But, Brother Corbin," interrupted one of Cindy's friends, "the Bible speaks of only one Second Coming. With your interpretation, it sounds like there is a second and third coming? What's up with that?"

"The answer can be found by examining the events our Jesus will complete during His coming," answered Stephen. "By comparing other scriptures, you can see that Christ's coming is more than just an arrival; it's actually a time period in which specific events will take place. In other words, the Second Coming of our Lord involves several events, just like His first coming did."

"Pastor, how is Christ's first coming like His second?" asked a visitor.

"Okay, let's check out Christ's first coming. Jesus was born in a manger, spoke the truth at twelve, was baptized, performed miracles, preached the gospel, was put on trial, crucified, rose from the dead, and ascended into heaven. His first coming was not just a trip from heaven to earth, but a time period in which the Son of God fulfilled his Father's will!"

After seeing several puzzled faces, Stephen knew he needed a better explanation.

"Listen up, everybody. Allow me to give you another example. Let's say my wife, Michelle, and I travel to Nashville this Sunday to preach. We take our van and arrive on Saturday. I preach twice on Sunday, and we return to Bethany on Tuesday of the following week. Our coming included everything we did while we were on the trip. We preached twice, we counseled two couples, and we taped a radio show on Monday before we left. Do you see what involves our coming to Nashville?"

"I get it!" answered an excited Lindy while continuing to take notes. "The rapture is the first phase of the Second Coming, when the believers will be delivered. Armageddon is the final phase, when Jesus will come with His armies of angels to destroy His enemies. In between, Jesus will complete His Father's will to the body of Christ and to the nation of Israel!"

"It's so easy to see. Why don't we hear other church leaders teaching this?" asked a shocked visitor.

"Maybe it's because they have convinced themselves that they have the truth concerning Christ's return," replied Stephen. "Of course, many pastors and teachers are afraid of losing their jobs or being labeled heretics by their denominations."

Off in a corner by himself sat a confused Simon. The spiritual struggle over control of his soul was raging. As the group spontaneously began to thank the Lord, the young teenager slipped out the backdoor unnoticed.

Mark and Julie were thrilled with how God was working among the young people. To the right of the room, several students were answering Stephen's questions in rapid-fire succession. Still others created small prayer groups to fervently pray for their unsaved families and friends. The Bishops could see a passion for God growing among the youth, a passion that needed to be strengthened by the truth of God's Word and guided by the Holy Spirit.

It was a little after eleven o'clock when the people shared their final good-byes. While the wives cleared up paper cups and the guys rearranged the furniture, there was a quiet knock at the front door.

"I'll get it!" yelled Julie.

When she opened the front door, there stood Whitney.

"Hey, Whit! What's up?" asked a surprised Julie, who was immediately joined by Michelle Corbin.

"I need to talk with you. I got permission from my folks. Is it too late?"

"Not at all, come on in," replied a concerned Julie. Entering the living room, the scared teenager took a seat across from Julie and Michelle on the Bishop's oversized sofa. Whitney had been a believer for over six years, but it hadn't been until the Bishops arrived that she responded to God's call on her life. The super thin teenager had long, straight blonde hair and dark blue eyes. A very friendly, compassionate girl, Whitney had become a very effective witness for Jesus. The kids in the youth group would always tease her about her habit of raising her eyebrows really high when she got excited.

"Is everything okay, Whit?" asked Michelle.

With her hands folded in her lap and her eyes looking down, Whitney uttered, "Tonight's teaching really hit me. Scary times are almost here. I mean all anyone ever talks about, including my parents, my teachers, and most of the kids at school, are the wars and the famines. I must admit to actually see so many people from other countries starving to death is the most frightening event of my life. But through it all, we saw so many answered prayers from our Lord. Although some kids have backslid and returned to partying and drugs, we have seen tons get saved in this past year since the famines hit. What really scares me is the next seal, the rider of the pale horse. The persecution is going to be for keeps, isn't it? What I mean to say is, uh, how can I know God will be with me and my family when the mark of the beast becomes law?"

Michelle immediately comforted the frightened teenager by taking her left hand and sitting beside her on the tapestry sofa.

"Whit, listen to God's promise for each us who will experience the great tribulation," replied Julie. "'Since you have kept my command to endure patiently, I will also keep you from the hour of trial, which shall come upon the whole world, to test those who dwell on the earth. Behold, I am coming quickly! Hold fast what you have, that no one may take your crown.'"[2]

"Is this really a promise?"

"This is a promise for overcomers during the great tribulation, Whit! What do you think it meant when Jesus said, 'Since you have kept my command to endure patiently?'"

The young teenager read over the verse and shaking her head looked up at Julie.

"I don't know."

"Well, Whit, Jesus is promising believers who patiently endure the first three and a half years of the tribulation period that He will protect them in the midst of the hour of testing that will soon follow."

"Okay, but what have we 'kept'?" asked Whitney.

"We have kept his Word and not denied His Name," replied Michelle. "Just like the faithful church of Philadelphia in the first century, we have persevered for the sake of Christ's name. In Matthew 24:13, Jesus said, 'But he who endures to the end will be saved.'"

With her eyebrows raised up really high, Whitney squealed, "I see it! Those who stand firm in Jesus against Satan's persecution during the great tribulation will be protected."

"That's right!" replied Julie. "And the word *saved* means physically delivered. So Jesus is clearly teaching us that in the second half of the seven years a remnant of saints will persevere during the great tribulation while under the persecution of the antichrist!"

"Wow, that's an awesome promise."

"Now let's examine the phrase the 'hour of trial,'" encouraged Julie. "What test is coming that Jesus warns us of that will test the body of Christ?"

"The mark of the beast," Whitney slowly replied. "The mark will be forced on the world at the fourth seal, and everyone will see who God's sheep really are." After a long pause, the teenager asked, "But what about when the seventh seal is broken, and God's wrath is poured out on the world? Is that a test or a divine judgment?"

Before Julie or Michelle could answer, the excited teenager spoke up.

"I've got it," she replied. "God's wrath is never a test; it is a divine judgment."

"That's correct. And what about the great tribulation? Is it a test or God's wrath?"

"Why, it is a test that will draw a line between the real believers and those who choose to deny Jesus and follow the antichrist."

"Exactly," responded a proud Julie.

"So, Whitney, God has promised to guard us during the persecution that is coming," comforted Michelle. "At a specific time, one which God only knows, He will bring His own safely out from the midst of that danger."

"So, the great tribulation is not part of the Day of The Lord?" asked Whitney.

"That's right. Actually, the body of Christ will be rescued out from the midst of the great tribulation between the sixth and seventh seals. When the saints are delivered, the seventh seal will be broken, and God's wrath will be poured out thirty minutes later!"[3]

"So, 'don't let anyone take your crown' could refer to believers who deny Christ by taking the mark of the beast?"

"I'm afraid so, Whit," answered Julie. "Revelation 3:5 is a promise to those who overcome and remain faithful. Their names will never be blotted out of the Book of Life. Those who deny the Lord by worshipping the antichrist will lose their crown, and their name will be removed from the Book of Life."

A solemn Julie could not help but reflect on the absolute magnitude of the truth she had just spoken.

"So we must trust in His promise that He will protect us, even though we don't really know how He will do it."

"Yes ma'am," replied a relieved Whitney, who looked a lot better. "Would you mind if I asked you one more question?"

"Sure," said Julie. "But you'll have to make it a short one if you're going to make your curfew."

"If God is going to protect the saints during the great tribulation, then what about the fifth seal martyrs who lose their lives for their testimony of Jesus?"

"Well, Whitney," replied Michelle, "I'm not going to lie to you. There will be believers who will stand for the truth and be killed for their testimony. There will also be many who will choose to come out from under God's protection and stand for the truth against the spirit of the antichrist. Think of it; millions of Christians will choose to pay a great price to remain faithful to Jesus. But their sacrifice will be very small compared to what our Heavenly Father did by sending his only Son to the cross so that we might be saved."

"Let's read God's wonderful promise in Hebrews 10:35," added Julie while turning to one of her favorite scriptures. "Paul wrote, 'So don't throw away your confidence; it will be richly rewarded. You need to persevere so that when you have done the will of God, you will receive what He has promised.'"

The peace of God replaced the fearful thoughts that had attacked Whitney's mind. Smiling, the three women took hands and prayed for God to fill them with a fresh anointing of His Spirit so that they would continue to serve Him with all their hearts.

"Yes, we are aware of the consequences," the bank chairman replied on the phone.

"That is correct. The software for scanning individuals can be installed for a very reasonable price. Believe me, sir, this move by the United Nations is absolutely genius! Who would have ever thought the financial software created in the 90s could be used to scan a worldwide community that would eventually go cashless?"

While taking a seat in her favorite Sunday morning pew, Emily Teeter whispered, "If you ask me, Pastor Mark went a little too far when he said that believers will have the choice whether to take the mark or not. The Bible doesn't say believers will worship the beast and lose their salvation!"

"Actually, Revelation 14:9-13 and Hebrews 10:26-31 are pretty convincing," replied Allie Hart. "Think about it, Emily. Why would God warn believers not to take the mark of the beast if there was no chance that they could? That would make the warnings from our Lord meaningless!"

"If what you say is true, then why did over half our members resign their memberships and leave?" Emily shot back defensively.

Sadly, the seventy-year-old Sunday school teacher was correct. Since Pastor Mark openly taught on the mark, over half of the church had resigned and returned to the mainline denominations they had originally attended.

As the worship team began to sing a soft melody of songs about Jesus, Emily leaned over to Allie and whispered, "If Pastor had just stayed on the subject of the rapture, everything would've been okay. But once he started teaching that Christians can willfully deny the Lord, he might as well have written Ickabod, which means the glory has departed, across the front door of our church."[4]

Mark and Julie loved to worship God. Sunday was a day for loving the Lord by a group of believers who were not ashamed to be called radical or extreme. To experience the sweet presence of the Holy Spirit was a gift from heaven that would always be treated with thankfulness and praise. The joy of witnessing the Spirit of Christ draw worshipers to the altar was indescribable. The deacons would pray for believers to be baptized in the Holy Spirit and speak in tongues. Those sick would come to be to be healed. The intercessors, trained in deliverance, would pray over those being attacked by the enemy. To Mark and Julie, it was a demonstration of the power God promised to those who believe.[5]

As the singing gradually died down, the rested pastor stepped up to the pulpit.

"Good morning, saints," said Mark. "May our Lord be praised for what He is going to accomplish in our lives this morning. The message He has given me is entitled 'Who is the Restrainer?'"

For many in the audience, this morning would be a day of reckoning. The tension was pretty obvious, to say the least.

"Apostle Paul was the first to write to the Thessalonians and explain the future coming of the Lord. He made it clear that at the trumpet call of God all believers in Jesus would be caught up to heaven. But before long, false teachers rose up and confused the Thessalonians by teaching that they had missed the rapture and had entered the Day of the Lord, God's wrath. In response to this false teaching, the apostle sent a second letter to assure the believers that the Lord cannot come and gather His saints until the man of sin, the antichrist, reveals himself and proclaims himself to be god!"[6]

The young Pastor could immediately sense a resistance among some of the members.

"In Matthew 24:15, Jesus warned anyone who sees the abomination of desolation, the antichrist, to flee Jerusalem because it would soon be surrounded and attacked by gentile armies.[7] Now let's be clear; this warning is not just to Jews but to anyone living in Jerusalem at the time of the invasion. According to Daniel 9:27, this will happen exactly in the middle of the seven-year Jerusalem Peace Accord. It is at this time that the restrainer, who has been protecting the world from being overwhelmed by the power of the antichrist, removes himself. The Apostle Paul wrote, 'For the mystery is already at work; only He who now restrains will do so until He,' meaning the restrainer, 'is taken out of the way.'"[8]

The left side of the sanctuary was filled with teenage intercessors who were praying for God's anointing. They knew it wouldn't take long for the spirit of the antichrist to manifest. Now was the time to pray.

"Today's message provides a critical link in the chain of events warning believers of Christ's soon return! From the Scriptures, we know that Hendrick and his ten-nation Middle East Federation cannot break their peace covenant with Israel until the restrainer is taken out of the way and stops restraining."

Emily smiled and whispered to Allie, "The restrainer can only be the Holy Spirit."

"But who is this restrainer preventing the antichrist from attacking Jerusalem and taking control of the world? The pre-tribulation theologians teach that the restrainer is the Holy Spirit. Now, I ask you, how do they come to this conclusion?"

With his Bible in hand, the pastor stepped off the platform and stood in the center aisle.

"Basically, the pre-tribulation teachers claim that only the Holy Spirit has the power to hold back the evil power of lawlessness. They teach that after the Spirit of God, who indwells all believers, is taken out of the world before the tribulation period, then and only then will the antichrist be able to freely attack those left behind."

"That's what I've always been taught," someone boldly announced from the choir.

"Okay, because the Bible doesn't tell us who is restraining the man of sin, let us compare scriptures to determine his identity," replied Mark.

"How do we do that?" asked Whitney from the first row.

"Well, Whit, we first start with a timeline of events that surround the restrainer and the antichrist. We all know the seven-year tribulation period begins when the antichrist signs a seven-year treaty with Israel. Half way through it, he will break this treaty by attacking Jerusalem. He will capture the Jewish temple and proclaim himself to be god, which will cause a great falling away. But before all this can happen, the restrainer who is now holding him back must be removed. Now I ask you, is there anyone in scripture presently protecting Israel by holding back the spirit of the antichrist?"

Several in the youth section knew the answer but didn't want to interrupt.

"The answer is Michael the archangel! In Daniel 10:21, this archangel is called the one who upholds or restrains the enemies of Israel." Also, in Daniel 12:1 Michael is called the great prince who protects the children of Israel.

Another choir member turned and quietly asked her friend, "I've never heard this interpretation, have you?"

"Let me be perfectly clear on this," cautioned Mark. "The Bible doesn't say that the restrainer will be taken out of the world; it says that he will be taken out of the way. Michael the archangel, the special guardian of Israel, is the restrainer who will be taken out of the way! Brothers and sisters, Daniel 12:1-4 says that Michael shall stand up or stand still and stop protecting Israel just before the great tribulation begins. In II Thessalonians 2:7, Paul wrote of a restrainer who is taken out of the way just before the antichrist reveals himself and the great tribulation begins. Do you see the similarity? Both Daniel and Paul are warning believers living in the last days of the one who will restrain the antichrist right up until the great tribulation begins!'"

"Preach it, Pastor Mark!" shouted an excited Drew.

"In closing, the great tribulation of believers is coming soon. I must warn you and your families that the teachers of the pre-tribulation myth love God. They are sincere. They care for those they minister to, and they are totally convinced that their secret rapture before the tribulation is from the Holy Spirit. Some of them will never change their minds, except maybe when they are faced with taking the actual mark of the beast. When I was at a prayer conference in Birmingham a couple of months ago, I had the opportunity to discuss the subject of the end times with a Baptist minister from Tuscaloosa. When I brought up the mark of the beast, he insisted, of course, that the body of Christ would be long gone before the mark occurs. Immediately I asked about those who were left behind at the Lord's coming. I asked, 'What if they got saved but then backslid because of the persecution and took the mark of the beast?'

"He confidently replied, 'If people become children of God by believing in Jesus, they can never lose their salvation, even if they take the mark of the beast!'

"He then proceeded to share the testimony of a missionary from Africa who had just testified at his church. The speaker shared a heartbreaking story of two Christian missionaries who lived in the capital city of Sudan. A few months earlier, these missionaries were arrested for openly sharing the Gospel of Jesus Christ. They were convicted and sentenced to die unless they publicly denied Jesus Christ as their Savior. He went on to say that one of the missionaries denied Christ in order to save his life!

"I replied, 'How tragic.'

"The obviously upset pastor paused and said, 'Don't you understand? He had a family. He had no choice; his very existence was at stake. We are all sinners, and we all fall short of Jesus' example. God understands when each of us strays from doing the right thing. Who are you to judge him? Let those who are without sin cast the first stone!'"

Mark sadly shook his head before continuing.

"Listen to me, saints. The World ID System being voted on by the United Nations is the mark of the beast. We have suffered under the heartache of wars, massive famines, thousands of earthquakes worldwide, and widespread diseases that have infected millions. If we are to believe in literal prophecy, the next seal is the pale horse! The question is whom will you worship, the antichrist or Jesus Christ? For those of you who choose to live under the authority of this one-world system, you will receive your own World ID Number. Of course, you will not suffer any persecution, but when Jesus comes, you will know whom you have denied. The Bible says, 'And now dear children continue in Him so that when He appears we may be confident and unashamed before Him at His coming.' Jesus said, 'Therefore whoever confesses Me before men, him I will also confess before My Father in heaven. But whoever denies Me before men, him I will also deny before my Father who is in Heaven.'"[9]

"But, Pastor, what purpose could the great tribulation have for real Christians?" asked a choir member in the first row.

"The great tribulation will be allowed by God to test those who profess His Lordship. When this time of persecution is cut short, the entire world will be without excuse. As for true believers, they will overcome the antichrist by the blood of the Lamb and the word of their testimony, even to the point of martyrdom."[10]

Part of the congregation stood and began to praise the Lord as the morning service came to a close. While several youth surrounded the pastor and asked more questions concerning the end times, Julie watched as several families headed for the exits for the last time. The continual bombardment of deception through the years had prepared the body of Christ in America for the biggest fall of all—the great falling away during the great tribulation!

CHAPTER 23

THE WITCHES' COVEN

Put on the whole armor of God,
that you may be able to stand against the wiles of the devil.
Ephesians 6:11

Amy looked excited as she sat down with Lance and Lee to share what God had just given her.

"That's right, Lance. I would like to visit the witches' coven tonight and share with Serena and the girls my salvation relationship in Jesus!"

"Amy, when did you first get involved with the spirit of witchcraft?" asked a concerned Lance.

"That's easy enough," smiled the slender teenager. "When I was a child, the craze was children books filled with witches and curses. The stories of casting spells and controlling the spirit of someone were so much fun. For me, it became really addictive."

"So you found out at a pretty early age that witchcraft was the control or manipulation of someone else's spirit?"

"That's right. Actually, I got really good at commanding curses on those who tried to hurt me."

"You mean the practice of cursing others?" asked Lee.

"Yep. I never dreamed how much I learned about witchcraft from the children's books I received at school. By the time I was introduced to Satanism during my freshman year at Lakeview, I was really ready for some action."

"And now?"

"Well, since I accepted Jesus and received the Holy Spirit, I now know that Serena, my mentor, used spiritual manipulation in order to control me."

"How did she do that?" asked Lee.

"It all started innocently enough when we were studying the power of the spiritual hosts. Before long, each girl received a spirit guide who convinced us that the power behind Satan was real! After a while, most of us became fearful we would die if we didn't obey the prompting of our spirit guides."

"So who was your spirit guide?" asked Lance.

"Until last week, his name was Nimrod. Serena personally chose him for me when I joined the coven. I now realize that spirit guides are demon spirits that enter the members of the coven through doorways of opportunity. After seeking God for discernment, it was easy to see that physical and sexual abuse were the doorways of bondage for each girl in the coven."

"That's pretty intense, Amy."

"Yeah, I know."

"Can Lee and I ask you a few more questions about Serena?"

"Sure."

"When you are with Serena, do you feel intimidated?"

"Exactly, Lance! Especially when I don't agree with her instructions."

"How about when you try to achieve things on your own? Do you feel inadequate, maybe insecure?"

"For sure," said Amy, who loved her new freedom to tell the truth about her life.

"How does it usually happen?"

"It goes like this: When Serena would use her put downs, I'd feel a spirit of confusion come over me; I felt as if I really didn't know how to do anything."

"Amy, Serena wants you to totally trust her," cautioned Lee. "Through her mind games, the spirit of witchcraft has continually manipulated your thought life. I believe she will use guilt and fear to keep you under her control."

"It's like you're replaying a tape recorder of my life at the coven," said Amy. "For the first time, I can see Serena's lies for what they really are—lies of the devil!"

"Amy, we'd like to go with you when you visit the coven." The Ryans knew how serious this situation was but did not want to frighten the young teenager.

"Would you? That would be great. But to be honest, I'd rather not get any of my new Christian friends involved."

"She will try to intimidate you, Amy. Her attacks may begin with anger and resentment. Since this will be a spiritual confrontation, Serena will almost certainly attack Christianity and attempt to highlight the superiority of Satanism."

Both Lance and Lee could already feel the burden to intercede for the young teenager.

"The key to victory over controlling spirits, Amy," Lance slowly shared, "is that you don't submit to them in any way. To break the chain of control from Serena and the satanic coven, you must use the power you have in the name of Jesus Christ. If any demonic spirits attempt to regain control of your life, resist them by pleading the blood of Jesus. Remember, Amy, Serena will attempt to force her will upon you by manipulating your emotions through demonic influence."

"Thank you both so much. This morning I studied Ephesians 6 and prayed over my spiritual armor. I prayed for the helmet of salvation to protect my thought life. I asked for the breastplate of righteousness so that I may stand in God's righteousness and not my own. I petitioned for the belt of truth so that I can speak freely and truthfully, and I asked that my feet be shod with God's peace. And finally, I asked that I might use the shield of faith and the sword of the spirit, which is God's word, so that nothing Serena throws at me will prosper.[1] Lance, Lee, I just know God is opening the way for me to be totally free from any of the coven's demonic influence!"

"Amen, Amy! 'God has not given you a spirit of fear but one of love, power, and a sound mind,'" replied a hopeful Lee.[2] "'The Lord is faithful, who will establish you and guard you from the evil one.'"[3]

As Lee reached over to give Amy a hug, Lance began to intercede for her visit to the coven, a spiritual confrontation that would take place as soon as the moon was full, that very night.

Memories flooded Amy's mind as she turned on to the dirt road near the big sycamore tree, not even noticing the bright full moon. It had been two years since her first visit to the witches' coven. The initial party was friendly, and everybody seemed to be pretty real. At school, all the girls involved in the coven wore black and had a passion for the history of Goth, which is death. Their favorite meeting place was behind the Industrial Arts Building at lunch. Of course, not everyone could become a member. For women who really had a desire to learn, the members would openly share their passion for the supernatural power behind Satanism!

Amy planned to face her mentor and tell Serena she had become a Christian. The rising star of the coven would no longer be a part of the rituals or have anything to do with Satan. Even though Lance strongly objected to Amy's going alone, deep within her heart, she knew Jesus would protect her.

"Besides," Amy prayed, "'Greater is He that is in me than he that is in the world.'"[4]

Pulling up to the old cottage, it was obvious that the other twelve girls had arrived and were preparing themselves for the night's ritual. Amy wondered what had ever attracted her to such an extreme group of girls. Immediately, the Holy Spirit brought back the painful memory of her abuse at the age of six. Even though it happened almost eleven years ago, the spirits of fear and anger were still very much in control. Her parents, who never knew, could never understand why their little bundle of sunshine suddenly lost her smile. Virtually overnight, the little girl's personality changed from outgoing and playful to that of a secluded loner.

After Amy prayed and fasted with some of the leaders of the Bible club, the demonic powers that had held her were defeated for the first time since they entered.[5] Immediately she received a word of knowledge from the Lord. The new believer now knew that the same spirit of fear that took control of her life at the age of six also had a doorway into the life of every girl within the coven.

"Hi, Amy, how you doing?" greeted Serena, who immediately sensed that something was wrong with her star pupil.

After closing the front door behind her, Serena silently summoned Amy's spirit guide, Nimrod, to manifest himself.

As her mentor, Serena's job was to open the seventeen-year-old up to the spirit world that comes not from heaven but from earth. Amy had become an excellent student, and Serena had high hopes for her future.

"We need to talk, Serena. Something has happened to me that has become a tremendous blessing in my life," said Amy.

"Let's go back to one of our chat rooms where we can be alone," suggested Serena, silently preparing herself for the confrontation.

While they walked back to the chat room, the peace of God seemed to rest upon Amy like a mantle across her shoulders.

"Well, it all happened last week when four of us from the coven attended the Lakeview High Bible Club meeting and heard Pastor Lance teach on Bible prophecy."

The obvious excitement gushing out of her top student was extremely upsetting to the skilled mentor.

"Pastor Lance explained the signs that will come before Jesus returns for His saints."

"Excuse me, Amy, you don't really believe Jesus is coming back again, do you?" challenged Serena.

The experienced witch knew she had to establish her authority immediately in order to keep her pupil off balance. Her control over Amy's will since Nimrod's indwelling had been easy.

"Everyone knows that once a person dies, he or she may never cross back over into this life," Serena calmly explained.

"Well, the Bible teaches that certain events will happen to warn us of His coming," replied Amy while searching for her little, brown leather New Testament.

"My dear, Amy, don't you realize that Satanism was a religion thousands of years before Christianity! Don't you know that many of the events of the Bible are mere fairy tales? For example, you don't actually believe in an ark filled with thousands of animals, do you?"

Before Amy could reply, the witch asked, "You don't really believe that some God in heaven flooded this earth because all the people were evil?"

"But, Serena, Pastor Lance talked about an antichrist that would come and try to stop Jesus from regaining control of the earth."

"That's nothing new, my dear," said the witch. "We've heard about the coming antichrist for over fifty years. Ministers tell us that the world is evil and that God is going to bring judgment by fire. Actually, the very opposite is happening. People all over the world are being challenged to reach a higher plain of spirituality, which is creating a worldwide peace. Wolfgang Hendrick is the perfect example of a leader who has the vision, the courage, and the love to bring about a supernatural harmony."

"But that's just it! Wolfgang Hendrick is the antichrist!"

Jumping to her feet, Serena shrieked, "And what proof do you have for such an ugly accusation? Before you answer me, you had better ask yourself how you know that Jesus will come back like he promised? All things go on in this world, just like they always have since the beginning of creation."[6]

"Well, I don't know the verses at this time," replied the naïve convert. "I have a lot of studying to do!"

"Show me what proof you have that Wolfgang Hendrick is the antichrist." demanded the witch.

"I do know that Revelation 13:1 warns us of a beast who has ten horns and seven heads."

"You must be joking, Amy! You don't actually believe these fairy tales do you?" scoffed Serena, who played her role perfectly.

"Enough to do this," replied Amy, lifting her sandy blonde bangs off her forehead.

"What have you done with Nimrod?" gasped Serena.

"I had him removed! He's not my lord anymore! Last week I accepted Jesus Christ as the Lord and Savior of my life. I've repented of all my sins, and I'm free, Serena. I have become a new creation in Christ!"

"Stop right there!" screamed the witch, pointing her finger in her pupil's face in an attempt to intimidate her. "Amy, you may think you've had a real experience with God, but I assure you that you will only be disappointed. You have taken an oath to Nimrod that can never be broken," challenged the Satanist.

"In the name of Jesus, I bind you, spirit of control, and rebuke you out of my life!" proclaimed Amy. "This is the end, Serena. I am totally free from Satan's control, your control, and any influence from this house of witches. I don't fear you; I am not intimidated by you or the spirits that indwell you," declared Amy. "The blood of Jesus protects me; what protects you?"

"Go then! And I never want to see you again!" yelled the bitter old woman while scurrying out the back door of the house.

Nimrod stood silently near the back of the room. The evil spirit knew its power over its subject was useless. It was over. Amy knew in her spirit that Serena's control was gone. The power of darkness had been defeated. As Amy slowly walked down the hall to the main lobby, not one girl was in sight. Before closing the front door, she turned and prayed, "Father, I pray in Jesus' name that you open the eyes of the girls so that they may see how evil Serena's lies really are. The devil has used the abuse that each girl has suffered from the hands of others as a channel to control them. Set them free, Father, by your love. Grant them a real peace, a peace which can only come through repenting of their sins and accepting Jesus as their Savior and Lord!"

As Amy closed the front door behind her, all she could hear was quiet weeping throughout the house.

CHAPTER 24

THE WATCHMAN CAMP

And he who overcomes, and keeps My works until the end,
to him I will give power over the nations.
Revelation 2:26

The secret meeting at Billy B.'s home that night had taken the past three months to plan and arrange. Each watchman invited was handpicked by both Mark and Stephen. Trained to detect any surveillance by the police, those attending had parked their cars over a mile from the house. Some were experienced believers who had been watchmen for years. Others, such as the Changs, the Alamars, and the Machovecs, had just received their calling.

Without uttering a greeting, Stephen dropped to his knees and began to pray in the Spirit, prompting the overcomers to immediately follow his example. The fervent intensity of prayer was a common denominator among watchmen throughout the world. Some began to cry out to God for the salvation of their families, and others were led by the Holy Spirit to pray against the spirit of lukewarmness that had so captivated the body of Christ.

After a wonderful breakthrough in intercession, followed by several worship songs, Stephen Corbin began to explain the details of the Watchman Camp.

"As you all know, everyone here tonight has been called to be a watchman for our Lord Jesus. Up until now, the persecution has been minimal. But when the fourth seal is opened, the pale horse will be loosed, and the great tribulation will commence. We've heard from our sources that after the antichrist reveals his true intentions and the false prophet initiates the mark of the beast, the world will have six months to voluntarily register. After this grace period, the mark will become a mandatory law. The new one-world government will then begin to issue specific sign-up dates in alphabetical order. The Mole, our camp contact for arrivals, has advised us that approximately sixty days after the mandatory sign-up dates go into affect, all those who refuse to register will be arrested. Heavy fines and jail time will be used as deterrents against any resistors. Eventually, they will introduce a law that will have anyone who attempts to subvert the ID system put to death!"

The immediate questions came from those who never really believed in the possibility of a one-world government.

"My dear friends, we must all realize without a doubt that our obedience to the Holy Spirit will play a critical role in the future safety of our families. We cannot allow our emotions to dictate how severe a situation appears to be."

The evangelist was well aware of the fear among believers who had just learned of the coming persecution of the antichrist. It was very traumatic for those who had always believed they would not be around for the mark of the beast. For some, tears of regret could be seen as their theology crumbled right before their eyes.

Stephen continued, "For example, there will be a tendency for some to view the antichrist as a leader who has been deceived by Satan. My friends, this is not true. Scripture clearly tells us that Satan will give the beast his power, his throne, and his authority.[1] We know the beast will come out of the bottomless pit, and the world will marvel because this former evil ruler will have come back from the dead. Symbolically, his kingdom is portrayed as having seven heads and ten horns.[2] The seven heads represent seven leaders, along with their kingdoms, who have attempted to destroy the nation of Israel throughout history.

"Stephen, could you share who the seven heads represent?" asked Billy. B.

"Sure, my friend. The first head was the pharaoh of Egypt who attempted to destroy Moses and his people. God divinely intervened by opening the Red Sea and drowning the pharaoh and his army. The second head kingdom was Assyria. Led by the wicked King Tiglath-pileser, the Assyrian army captured ten of the twelve tribes of Israel in 722 AD. The third head kingdom was Babylon. It's king, King Nebuchadnezzar, and his Babylonian army destroyed Solomon's Temple in 586 BC and took many Jewish people back to his homeland as captives."

"So the first three heads who tried to destroy Israel were Egypt, Assyria, and Babylon," reviewed Billy B. "Who are the other four heads, Stephen?"

"The fourth head kingdom was Medo-Persia. This kingdom, under the control of the evil Haman, vainly attempted to destroy Queen Esther's people. The fifth head kingdom was Greece, led by its famous leader Alexander the Great. Under his orders, the people of Israel were required to speak Greek instead of Hebrew. They were forced to worship other gods in an attempt to turn them away from the one true God. The sixth head king-dom was Rome. Rome's evil emperor, Domitian, persecuted the Jews more severely than the previous five head kingdoms. In the book of Revelation, John spoke of five heads that had already fallen. They were Egypt, Assyria, Babylon, Medo-Persia, and Greece. In 90 AD, when John wrote the book of Revelation, Rome, the sixth head, was still in control of Israel. The apostle also wrote of a seventh head kingdom that had not yet come, but when it did come, it would remain for a little while."[3]

"So, Stephen, who was this seventh head kingdom that tried to destroy Israel?" asked a curious Billy B.

"It's interesting to look back and see Domitian's hate for both Jews and Christians in the first century. After His persecution of the Jews came to an end, a seventh head kingdom would follow. This future kingdom would be even more evil than Rome. Now I ask you, since Rome's persecution of the Jews in 90 AD, what other country has persecuted and almost destroyed the Jewish people?"

"It's got to be Nazi Germany!" one of the watchmen blurted out.

"Exactly," replied Stephen.

"So you're saying that the seven heads represent seven rulers and their countries, which have attempted to destroy Israel?"

The noise level rose considerably as several discussion groups began to interact.

"That's right, my brother. The Scriptures also predict that an eighth king, who is of the previous seven, will come back to life from the bottom-less pit. He will lead a ten-nation coalition, the ten horns, that will attempt to destroy Israel and the world!"

"Do you mean the antichrist is the eighth head?"

It seemed like an eternity before anyone spoke.

"That's correct," answered Stephen. "Listen to this verse describing the antichrist: 'And I saw one of his heads as if it had been mortally wound-ed and his deadly wound was healed. And all the world marveled and followed the beast. So they worshiped the dragon who gave authority to the beast, say-ing, who is like the beast? Who is able to make war with him?'"[4]

"Stephen, we've always been taught that the beast, or the antichrist, will die in front of the world and will come back to life in a false resurrec-tion," explained Billy B.

"But does the Bible actually teach that?" the watchman slowly asked. "It says he will come out of the bottomless pit healed of the wound that killed him."

Immediately a buzz of questions surged through the believers. The humid evening seemed so surreal to most of those tucked inside the cramped living room. Everyone knew the time for debate was over. The events being laid down this night would come to pass within days. The great tribulation was close.

"Listen up, everybody," motioned the watchman. "After the fourth seal is opened, the antichrist will give Father John, the false prophet, the order to kill all those who refuse to take the mark of the beast. The false prophet will then attempt to make every person in this world create an image of the beast in order that the beast may be worshipped as god. When the images around the world are in place, Satan is going to fill these images with the power of demonic spirits.[5] Let us not underestimate the satanic power that controls these two evil leaders! Their goal is to stop the fulfillment of Bible prophecy concerning the coming of our Lord. Once our Jesus takes physical control at the Battle of Armageddon, we know the antichrist and the false prophet will be cast into the lake of fire for eternity!"[6]

"Amen to that!" replied Billy B., who loved saying such a beautiful amen.

"When Michael, the restrainer, casts Satan and his demons out of heaven, there will be exactly three and a half years until the seven-year tribulation period ends.[7] During this time, the beast will be given the power to war against anyone who professes Jesus as Lord. We have all sought the Lord in prayer for many hours, and we know He has granted us the strength to be faithful till the harvest. He will lead us by the Holy Spirit right up to the point when we see his power and glory splitting the eastern sky."

Praises to God could be heard throughout the house. After they finished, Stephen asked Pastor Mark to speak.

"Thank you, Stephen," replied a rested Mark, who had been fasting and praying for the past four days. "Once the mark of the beast is accepted by a Christ-rejecting world, we won't have much time. For the past year, resistance workers have been secretly preparing our camp. As of last week, the Bethany Watchman Camp has become totally operational. By next Friday, we will begin receiving our first campers. To ensure that there won't be any way they can find us, we will not be able to hold jobs or maintain permanent addresses. Our children won't be able to continue to attend their schools.

There cannot be any way for people to trace our whereabouts. The watchmen leadership has created an underground barter system, which will supply our camps with everything necessary to sustain our families. Of course, if any of us is arrested, heaven is waiting."

For the next two hours, Pastor Mark shared the layout of the Bethany Watchman Camp and how to travel there without being followed. The camp was hidden in deep caverns just outside Birmingham. Most of the families attending the meeting would safely be inside the secret camp within forty-eight hours of the introduction of the mark of the beast. For some, the choice to leave their homes and friends would not be hard. For those whose family refused to come, it was a total heartbreak. The words of Jesus rang out with a new sense of urgency: "Anyone who loves his father or mother more than me is not worthy of me; anyone who loves his son or daughter more than me is not worthy of me; and anyone who does not take up his cross and follow me is not worthy of me. Whoever finds his life will lose it, and whoever loses his life for My sake will find it."[8]

The farm looked deserted as the cars pulled up without the aid of their headlights. The young men began to make preparations for their meeting as the old barn was transformed into a Neo-Nazi shrine. While some strung lights across the crossbeams, others set up chairs and tables. Propaganda materials consisting of books, pictures, and leaflets were placed throughout the barn. Each intern carried out his instructions with detailed precision. The assembly tonight was no ordinary gathering. The Neighbors' commander, Tanner Harrison, had called for an emergency meeting.

The sentries were armed and had their orders. No outsiders would be allowed to enter the meeting under any circumstances. Coming from different directions, one by one the leadership of the Neighbors began to arrive. For some, it was the ultimate fantasy to be acted out and enjoyed. To others, it was a cause that was as important as life itself!

The Neo-Nazi philosophy that literally controlled a person's spirit was spread by the influence of demons. A person's personality could change within days after being affected by the evil spirits of hate and fear.

"Greetings, my friends," announced Tanner while welcoming some of his officers.

The young leader appeared a bit uneasy as the Nazi soldiers lined up in two lines facing each other. After the candles were lit and the lights turned off, everyone saluted Tanner Harrison. The uniforms, the black boots, the swastika emblems, the short haircuts, the propaganda—everything was in place. The group's entire agenda for the night was an exhortation from their commander!

Throughout the barn, demon spirits had arrived and were perched on the high crossbars high above the seats. Wolf, Tanner's spirit guide, had warned them that the Neighbors' leader was having doubts about the family. The foul spirits knew that Tanner had made contact with Amy, a recent defector from the coven.

"No problem," insisted the spirit of compromise as he continued to circle the inside of the barn.

"He is in our territory tonight," bragged the spirit of fear. "Besides, Wolf is fully capable of controlling his subject."

Tanner slowly stepped onto the portable stage. The young leader knew that what he had to say would be considered treasonous. The consequences of his actions did not look pretty. On the other hand, he refused to look over his shoulder for the rest of his life wondering when he would be attacked. Gaining confidence, Tanner turned on his microphone and looked out across a group of soldiers who really respected him.

"I have called this emergency meeting tonight to share with you a revelation concerning the future direction of our family."

"All right, Tanner, let's hear it!" yelled a lieutenant who moved up to the first row in order to pump up the interns.

"Each of us here tonight joined the Neighbors due to the desire to make a difference. We saw injustices, and nothing was being done about them. The truths that we were taught gave us power and purpose."

"Amen, Commander," yelled a new recruit. "Paint the picture!"

"Many of us have received personal visitations from our spirit guides convincing us that the power we have is supernatural. I have to admit that, at first, it was pretty exciting, a real adrenaline rush. But after a while, this power drained me of everything inside. There was an emptiness that haunted me, especially when I was alone."

"What are you talking about?" an uneasy captain blurted out.

The officer knew that no soldier was ever allowed publicly to reveal a weakness, especially the leader and founder.

"Last week, several of us were led by our spirit guides to disrupt a Bible Club meeting at Lakeview High School. When the pastor began to pray, I felt something happen inside of me. Even though Wolf urged me to go, I wanted to stay and listen to what the preacher had to say."

"But, Tanner, several leaders of that club are stinking Jews!" accused the angry captain. "Are you telling us that you broke the rules of our family?"

While everyone else looked on in utter disbelief, Tanner replied, "Me and about six others did."

After he motioned for them to join him, six of the most dedicated soldiers of the gang walked up onto the stage and stood alongside their leader.

"Life is not about man-made rules and beliefs. What we all need to do is to find the truth from above and live it out."

"But, my man, we are living out the truth," answered an intern dangerously speaking out of turn.

"No, Reggie, there is only one truth. 'For God so loved the world that he gave His only begotten Son, that whoever believes in Him should not perish but have everlasting life.'"[9]

"What's up with this, Reggie?" whispered a fellow intern. "Everyone here tonight is a Christian, right?"

"While the pastor spoke of his relationship with the Holy Spirit, I realized that my involvement with the Neighbors was not producing a life of peace. Actually, we've been taught to spread fear in order to manipulate those who are weak. Intimidation is an effective tool in the hands of someone who is not free."

Suddenly, several soldiers jumped to their feet and began to curse their leader. The spirit of hate manifested so powerfully was something that had to be seen to be believed.

"Hear me out!" yelled Tanner. "After the pastor laid down how God is going to bring this world to an end, all seven of us felt the presence of the Holy Spirit. I have never felt anything like it!"

All six soldiers nodded their heads in agreement.

"Those of us standing before you tonight have become believers in Jesus Christ. He is our Savior and Lord! We have come tonight to tell you that salvation is open to anyone who will follow Jesus Christ, the Son of God."

"Why should we?" mocked the youngest intern. "Jesus was a Jew!"

"It all begins by taking a step of faith. We did it, and so can you," encouraged Tanner.

The noise level rose quickly as small groups of soldiers talked privately. The six ex-soldiers stepped off the stage and formed a circle to pray for their friends.

As the noise died down, Tanner spoke for the final time, "I know that for most of you, my asking you to receive Jesus Christ is pretty hard to accept. Some of you have no intention of repenting and giving up the hate that the enemy has cultivated in your lives. The truth is every one of us has a choice to make that will determine our eternal destiny, either heaven or hell!" Tanner paused, took a deep breath, and announced, "I hereby resign as commander of the Neighbors. Because I am a new creation in Jesus, I publicly reject Satan, Wolf, and all other spirits of darkness. My brothers in Christ and I do not fear any attacks or threats from Satan or his demons. For any of you who desire to be free from these foul spirits, the seven of us will be outside praying for you. God bless you all."

And with that, the ex-soldiers walked out of the barn and started to pray. Those inside stood motionless. The power of the Holy Spirit had swept the barn clean of any demonic spirits. It didn't take long for some of the soldiers to remove their swastika armbands and step outside to pray to the Father in Jesus' name.

Stepping up to take charge, the captain ordered the remaining interns to collect all of the propaganda. Exiting through a side door, they made their way hastily to their cars. The power of God had defeated the prince of darkness.

That night on a deserted farm just outside Bethany, Alabama, nineteen Neo-Nazi soldiers surrendered their lives to God. As they finished their final prayer, the young boys began to rejoice! Really, they were no different than any other teenagers. Each boy was searching for the truth about life, a truth that can be trusted and believed in.

Reggie could not help but ask Tanner, "Whatever led you to have enough guts to face the gang straight up and challenge us to believe in Jesus?"

"Anyone got a light?" asked Tanner as he pulled Amy's note from his black leather jacket.

Reggie fired up his Zippo as the ex-commander read:

Dear Tanner,

Words cannot express the love and freedom I have found since believing in Jesus as my Savior! And to think, the enemy of our souls sent us to the Bible Club to disrupt what

God was planning. I still remember how troubled you looked when you left the meeting. I didn't quite understand the burden that rested upon me, but I later realized that it was the Holy Spirit's telling me to pray for you. That night I prayed with some of my new Christian friends. For over an hour we prayed with all of our hearts that the spirits of fear and hate would be rebuked away from you. While praying, I received my first word of knowledge from the Holy Spirit. He spoke into my mind Luke 18:27. It says, "What is impossible with men is possible with God."

God is calling you, my friend. At one time, we were both deceived by the prince of darkness. But now, our Jesus has revealed himself to both of us! Be a leader, Tanner, for what is right. If we stand for the truth, God will always be on our side.

Till He Comes,
Amy

Tanner carefully folded the note and placed it back in his wallet. His personal search for the truth was over. The Holy Spirit would now lead and guide his life.

Beside the barn stood several warrior angels who couldn't help but smile. Shooting high into the sky, the angels began to praise the Lord for another successful assignment.

While jumping into the back of Tanner's pickup truck, some of the boys could hear in the distance the loud howling of a creature.

"Did you hear that?" Reggie asked. It sounds like a wolf."

"Can't be, Reg. We don't have any wolves in this area, do we?" asked a former intern named Sean.

Tanner just smiled and said, "Not anymore!"

CHAPTER 25

A MIRACLE IN ROOM 206

Now by this we know that we know Him,
if we keep His commandments.
I John 2:3

Room 206 was buzzing with the news that Tanner Harrison would be this morning's guest speaker. He would be speaking on the history of his defunct Neo-Nazi group, the Neighbors.

"Good morning, class," greeted Mr. Olson while motioning for everyone to take seats.

There was a charge of excitement among the students. Several looked a little nervous about the possibility of having opposing sides clash over what would surely be expressed.

"Okay, class, this morning we'll be examining the history of white supremacy groups in America," announced the already tired teacher.

Obviously, the sixty-nine-year-old history professor didn't have a clue about what would soon break forth in his usually boring third-period class.

"Your homework assignment was to select a hate group that's been in existence in Alabama within the past ten years. Your grade will reflect how well you highlight the group's objectives and the specific types of people that tend to become members."

While cleaning his glasses with his orange and black tie, the teacher was ready for the usual meaningless questions that had become a custom in several of his classes.

"Yes, Heather, do you have a question?" he sighed.

"I'm afraid I don't understand the assignment."

"And how is that possible, Heather?" asked the professor while rolling his eyes.

"Well, some of my friends say the Neighbors are a hate group that teaches Jews and Blacks are evil."

"Go on," prompted the professor, glancing at the cracked ceiling, which hadn't been repaired in the forty-one years he had taught history.

"What I mean to say, uh, is, well, Reggie Lincoln is a good friend of mine, and he was also a member of the Neighbors. But he's a really great guy," said Heather, which produced scattered laughter coming from the back rows.

"All right! All right," interrupted Mr. Olson, motioning for quiet. "Actually, Heather's observation is very appropriate for today's topic. Of course, this is a voluntary discussion, and anyone who feels this subject is not acceptable to his or her belief system is free to go to the library."

With that said, the teacher turned his back on the class and wrote Tanner's name on the chalkboard. As he put down the chalk and turned around to face his students, the teacher's mouth dropped wide open. No one had moved.

The surprised, slightly bent-over teacher lowered his reading glasses and said, "Well, well, well! It seems like we have some genuine interest in hearing Mr. Harrison speak this morning. I've asked Tanner to explain the general make-up of his former gang, the Neighbors, which just disbanded last week. Of course, there will be no interruptions or talking. After his initial presentation, we will have a question-and-answer period. Class, let's show a little self-control," requested the oldest active teacher in the State of Alabama.

While he took his favorite seat next to the window that overlooked the football field, several students decided to slip out for a quick smoke. Tanner stepped up to the small podium totally aware that every student was trying to figure out why he was speaking.

"What's he up to?" whispered a student in the third row.

At that very same moment, in study hall Amy and Reggie were leading several others in prayer for their newly converted friend.

After opening his Bible and laying it on the podium, Tanner shared, "Ignorance can be a scary thing. Two years ago, I enrolled as a sophomore at Lakeview. At first, I felt like I really didn't fit in. I wasn't a jock or into theater. My grades were just average. I really didn't have any hobbies or special interests. I felt alone. No one talked to me much, so I didn't talk to them. This went on for several months, and I was afraid that if I didn't find something to be part of I'd be labeled a loser."

Some of the students in the back row were becoming restless. In their minds, they were thinking, "Get on with it, racist!"

Sensing their impatience, Tanner said, "It was at this time in my life that I formed the Neighbors and began to study the history of the white race in America. At first, it was really a rush. Being in charge of a group that gave me respect became pretty addictive, especially to someone like me who had never experienced such power before."

"What type of power, Tanner?" Heather couldn't help but ask.

"To be honest, the Neighbors was a hate group started and promoted by demons," Tanner calmly admitted, knowing exactly what he was saying.

Hands went up as everyone began talking all at once.

"Class, class, let the speaker finish," called out the gray-haired teacher. "Go ahead, Tanner."

"Look. I know this is going to sound pretty weird. What I mean to say is that, uh, about two weeks before I started the group an evil spirit visited me."

"Yeah, right!" said a grunger in the back row.

"Quiet!" shouted Mr. Olson.

With order restored, he nodded to Tanner to continue.

"It was in the summer sometime in July, I think. I was in my bedroom sound asleep. I remember waking up after having a really bad nightmare. It was about two in the morning. For a minute, I thought I was still in the nightmare because I felt a presence that was so . . . so . . ."

Tanner was beginning to flounder, unsure of how to explain what he had experienced.

"Anyway, I couldn't move. I could hardly breathe. Finally, I slipped out of bed, got on my knees, and cried out to God for help. Then I heard it."

"Heard what?" called out the grunger from the back row. "Don't stop now, dude. This is better than *Outer Limits*!"

The nervous laughter among the students seemed to ease the tension that had built up.

Tanner could see the confused faces of his classmates. They were trying to figure out whether he was telling them the truth.

"This is not a joke. It's for real. The voice that spoke to me was deep, and when it spoke, it was almost like the words went right through my body. The voice was supernatural—evil. I could feel its powerful presence all around me, and somehow I was drawn to it. I didn't understand why at the time. But I do now. I was after power!"

"Aren't we all," mocked someone in the fourth row.

"It told me that I was important and that I was going to do great things. I believed because I wanted to. I wanted so desperately to belong to something. Anyway, it was about two weeks later that I found out this evil spirit had a name. It told me that it was my spirit guide and that it would make me a great leader. Then it said its name was Wolf."

"Cool!" muttered another student.

"No, it's not cool," insisted Tanner. "That's when the bondage took hold of me. After I surrendered to Wolf and let him take control of my life, I decided to form the Neighbors. We taught and believed in the destruction of Jews and Blacks and anyone else who wasn't of pure white origin. We felt superior, and we constantly looked for ways to promote our hate. But the more I got into it, the emptier I felt. I knew there had to be something more to life than just pumping yourself up and putting others down. After two years of this, I felt so dead inside."

Tanner paused to collect his thoughts.

"I was pretty low when Pastor Lance Ryan came to speak at the Bible Club last week. Hope Bishop invited our whole gang to come and hear the pastor share on the Second Coming of Christ. Almost one-third of the gang went, hoping to completely blow everyone's mind. You see, the prince of darkness taught us that the key to controlling people is fear. People will respect you if they fear you."

"Do you really believe that, Tanner?" asked a curious junior seated in the front row.

"No, not anymore," answered the former leader. "Pastor Lance shared about the love of God and how Jesus gave his life so that all who followed after Him would receive eternal life. During Lance's message, Wolf, my spirit guide, was tearing me apart from the inside out. He kept threatening me if I didn't leave immediately. But something stopped me. It was another voice, a voice of peace and love, a voice greater than Wolf's!"

"You mean that you and Amy have found the same religion?" asked one of the cheerleaders smirking.

It had become obvious to Tanner that the prejudice of several students was just about to erupt. The devil had his pawns ready to spew forth his words of hate and confusion.

"Be careful," cautioned the spirit of hate to the spirit of confusion. At this point in time, the demons knew the young speaker was not aware of their presence.

"I'm not talking about man-made religion," replied Tanner sensing an evil wall of resistance among his listeners. "The Bible says, 'For the grace of God that brings salvation has appeared to all men, teaching us that, denying ungodliness and worldly lusts, we should live soberly, righteously, and godly in the present age, looking for the blessed hope and glorious appearing of our great God and Savior Jesus Christ."[1] In other words, religion can't save you but only Jesus Christ, the only Savior and Lord of this world," proclaimed a smiling Tanner.

"Hold up, Harrison," interrupted a tall Muslim. "You have no right to say that Jesus is the only Savior. There are millions of Muslims around the world who are awaiting their messiah. And I can assure you that his name is not Jesus."

Even though the class was totally unaware of it, the spiritual warfare between demons and angels was raging.

"I am a Christian, a follower of Jesus! I have renounced my belief in white supremacy, the Neighbors, and Satanism," confessed a sincere Tanner, ready to face the consequences of his actions.

"Now let me get this straight," mocked one of the boys in the back row who was just itching to get it on. "Do you honestly expect us to believe that now you are some loving disciple of Jesus? Especially, after the past two years, when you and your racist buddies spread your stinking hate propaganda all over our school!"

"Don't you see it?" interrupted his friend in the next seat over. "He was starving for acceptance from his racist clones before he wised up and bailed because he realized how hopeless it was. He saw the end coming, so he joined up with the holy rollers instead."

Suddenly, without any warning, the whole second row had had enough and made a quick exit.

"What about it, Tanner. How do we know you are telling the truth?" asked Heather, who knew it was just a matter of time before everyone ganged up on him.

"Look, I do know that a person cannot be a Christian and a racist at the same time. How can you say you love God, who you can't see, if you can't love your brother, who you can see?"[2]

"Excuse me, my brother," interrupted a black football player seated in the fifth row. "Listen, everyone knows racism is alive and well. Just look at the all white churches in Bethany. Many of them claim to love God, but deep down they hate my people. You'd have to be blind not to see the prejudice in the hearts of white Christians all over our city."

"Yeah, and what about the all black churches," challenged a boy near the back of the room. "You don't think they're prejudice?"

Before anyone could react, Tanner yelled, "Hold up, everybody! You're right; all kinds of people go to church. They are baptized. They accept the doctrines of their church. They even help the poor from time to time. But people saying the right things and looking to be following the Lord does not prove that they really are. Believe me, real Christians do not promote hate or fear but love and forgiveness. I want to ask publicly for your forgiveness for my actions as the former leader of the Neighbors. I plan to . . ."

As the bell rang, several of the students surrounded Tanner with questions about his newfound faith in Jesus. Mr. Olson was slowly collecting everyone's homework assignments when his eyes met Tanner's.

"I want to thank you, Mr. Olson, for allowing me to speak today."

The slender teacher paused, lowering his thick reading glasses.

"Young man, when I gave you permission to share about your former white supremacy gang, I expected to hear some pretty gory details that might wake up some of my students. Actually, they need to see how evil something is before they see it on TV or in the movies. To be honest, I haven't decided if your presentation was actually about hate groups or about the love of Jesus Christ."

"I hope I didn't get you into trouble for sharing my faith," confessed an awkward Tanner.

"My boy, my boy, what are they going to do to me?" asked Mr. Olson, laughing under his breath. "Besides, your talk kept the class's attention better than any presentation I've heard in years."

"So what do you believe, Mr. Olson?" asked Tanner while students for the next period filed in and began taking their seats.

"You mean about the reality of Jesus Christ and what He has promised?"

"That's right," Tanner replied, refusing to be distracted by some of his friends who were trying to get his attention.

"Well, I was brought up Lutheran. I was baptized at the age of twelve. When I joined the Army at seventeen, I got away from the church, and I haven't been back since. Of course, you're not talking about just churchgoing, are you?" asked Mr. Olson chuckling.

"No, sir. I guess what I want to know is . . ."

"It's a relationship that you have with Jesus, isn't it?" asked the smiling teacher, who looked so much out of character.

"This is all so new to me, Mr. Olson. Yes, you're right; it's a relationship not just a duty to perform in order to look good for the approval of others. Do you think I could ask you one last question before your next class begins?"

"Fire away."

"If you believe that Jesus is real and that His words are absolute truth, are you going to ask Him to forgive you of your sins and spend eternity with Him in heaven?"

Mr. Olson smiled and said, "Tanner, I asked Jesus to forgive me of my sins halfway through your testimony. During lunch, I plan to go home and find my family Bible. I've got some serious reading to do."

"You really mean it?" blurted out the former gang member as the fourth-period students stood and began to applaud.

Amidst all the cheers, the ex-Neo-Nazi gang member offered the newly converted Mr. Olson an extra special high five!

Chapter 26

The fourth Seal:
The Great Tribulation

And there shall be a time of trouble,
such as never was since there was a nation.
Daniel 12:1

Thousands upon thousands of angels lined up behind Michael the Archangel. There was no talking, no strategy sessions, no specific instructions on how to defend. Each angel already knew the importance of this battle. For millenniums they had heard the evil threats from Satan himself. He had taken many different forms and disguises, but in reality Satan was an angel just like them. And now he would take the form of a dragon with the ultimate purpose of defeating the God of the universe.

Suddenly, the dragon appeared hovering over his evil army in the sky. The demons were fighting, arguing, and slandering one another as usual.

"Enough!" cried Satan. "The time has come to prevent what has been decreed from above. I call upon you all this day to come with me to heaven. Within the hour, we will defeat the archangel and all those who follow the One from above!"

In an instant, hordes of demons that were once heaven dwellers shot high above the earth and moved effortlessly into the heavenlies.

Michael stood at attention. He and his fellow angels could hear the demons coming. The evil aggression of their lies and intimidation would not affect the armies of God. Humans could be intimidated but not the vast angelic host from heaven. Michael sensed an evil assault from his left flank and turned as the dragon struck first. The archangel spun to face what had once been God's favorite.

"Lucifer, why do you persist in this foolishness? You can't win."

The former angel of light became enraged and flew at Michael. Extending his sharp talons, Lucifer sought to destroy by the ferocity of his attack. All around them, angels and demons were in battle. Furiously, time and again the dragon attacked! Deflecting each blow, Michael just shook his head and said, "Give it up, Lucifer. You're finished."

Grasping his sword, the archangel lunged forward and struck the devil. All the other angels followed their leader's example by drawing their swords. The battle in heaven would not last long. With one final blow from Michael, the dragon was cast out of heaven along with his evil army.

As the restrainer watched the evil horde descending, another angel spoke, "Therefore rejoice, O heavens, and you who dwell in them. Woe to the inhabitants of the earth and the sea! For the devil has come down to you, having great wrath, because he knows his time is short."[1]

The radiance of the victorious angels was glorious as they bowed to their creator, God the Father. This was a moment in time every angel in heaven had looked forward to with great anticipation. For the past six thousand years, within an earthly battleground, God's army of angels had fought Lucifer's demon spirits. None of the angels foresaw the needless pain the people of earth would suffer under the attack of the prince of darkness. To see fellow angels choosing to follow Lucifer was hard for many. Nevertheless, it would soon be over. God the Father would soon choose three angels to carry out His will. The angelic host, dressed in white linen, patiently waited.

Rising from His throne, the Father spoke, "My angel Glory will proclaim My eternal gospel to those who live on the earth.[2] My angel Amad will tell the world of the destruction of the Babylonian harlot.[3] My angel Ian will warn the world that whosoever worships the beast or receives his mark will drink of the wine of My wrath."[4]

God the Father had spoken it into existence. Glory, Amad, and Ian stood before Gabriel to receive their final instructions. The angels knew Satan's time to deceive the world was almost up. They knew that at the sounding of the seventh trumpet, after the end of the tribulation period, "a mighty angel will come from heaven clothed in a cloud. A rainbow will rest upon his head. His face is like the sun; his legs like pillars of fire. He will plant his right foot on the sea and his left foot on the land and give a loud shout like the roar of a lion."[5]

"Yes, it is written," proclaimed the warrior angel named Zepher. "'The Lion from the Tribe of Judah will come, and the kingdoms of this world will become the kingdoms of our Lord and of his Christ, and He shall reign forever and ever!'"[6]

✳

Deep within the deserted caverns just outside Birmingham, families from all over the state of Alabama were arriving. The sentries checked the identity of each new arrival carefully. This was not going to be a summer camp. The watchmen leadership had assigned responsibilities to believers according to their abilities. Everyone, even the children, had been called into God's army. This was just the first wave of overcomers. The leadership knew there be would many more. While the overcomers inside cavern number one gathered around Pastor Mark Bishop, the watchman turned up the sound on his hand-held microphone.

"As we all know, the fourth seal of Revelation is close to being broken. But before the pale horse of Death and Hades is loosed upon our world, God will remove the restrainer, Michael the Archangel, and the great tribulation of Christians will commence.[7] We know from the words of our Jesus that the antichrist will first surround Jerusalem with his gentile armies.[8] After this attack, his next move will be toward the rebuilt Jewish temple on Mount Moriah.[9] The false prophet will then implement the World ID System that has already been introduced to the world through the United Nations. He will perform miracles and signs to ensure this deception. As a result of the world's turning away from the truth, God will send a strong delusion so that people believe the lawless one.[10] Those who choose to follow the antichrist and the false prophet will have no excuse and will eventually be eternally damned!"

"Oh, Lord, it's happening right before our eyes," wept a mother who had just left behind her husband and two sons.

"Tonight we will have a brief Bible study on the two witnesses of Revelation 11:1-12. Simply put, God has promised to send two men of God who have lived before. For forty-two months, the second half of the seven-year tribulation period, they will proclaim that salvation can only come through God's Son, Jesus Christ. They will prophesy to the world against the beast that ascends from the bottomless pit. In Revelation 13:5, we see that the beast will be given the same exact time to blaspheme God and slander those in heaven."

"Wow, Pastor, this is going to be a real mind game," blurted out a student. "Does the Bible tell us who these witnesses are?"

"No, the book of Revelation doesn't say," replied Mark, who had come to love the sincere enthusiasm of the youth. "But we are given some major clues to their identity. Because the first witness will have the power to shut up the sky and not allow any rain, many believe he will be the prophet Elijah. The second witness will have the power to turn the waters into blood and strike the earth with any plague he wants.[11] From the Old Testament, this is a perfect description of the prophet Moses. These two men will prophecy for forty-two months, and the world will be tormented by the conviction of their words."

"What happens when their time to witness is finished?" asked someone from the crowd.

"Revelation 11:7 says, 'When they finish their testimony, the beast that ascends out of the bottomless pit will make war against them, overcome them, and kill them.' The world will rejoice and schedule parties to celebrate the death of the two witnesses. But three and a half days later, God will bring these prophets back to life and take them to heaven in a cloud while their enemies look on in astonishment."[12]

"Our God is faithful!" yelled a twelve-year-old overcomer seated near the pastor.

"Amen," replied an inspired Mark. "Let us all faithfully pray for these two men of God and especially for those who have not yet taken the mark of the beast!"

The sheer excitement among the heavenly host was rapidly growing with the breaking of each seal. Within a very short time, the seventh seal would be broken, and God's wrath would be poured out. To the right of the throne stood the Lamb of God. When He broke the fourth seal, the power of the pale horse that proceeded out of the seal had been immense. Its rider was Death, and Hades followed closely behind him. The power to kill one-fourth of the people on earth would flow through the two beasts, the antichrist and the false prophet.[13]

"Behold, the great tribulation is near!" proclaimed a warrior angel. "'Seek the Lord while He may be found, call upon Him while He is near. Let the wicked forsake his way, and the unrighteous man his thoughts; let him return to the Lord, and He will have mercy on him; and to our God, for He will abundantly pardon.'"[14]

God the Father stood before His creation and proclaimed, "For My thoughts are not your thoughts, nor are your ways My ways. For as the heavens are higher than the earth, so are My ways higher than your ways, and My thoughts than your thoughts. So shall My word be that goes forth from My mouth; it shall not return to Me void, but it shall accomplish what I please, and it shall prosper in the thing for which I sent it."[15]

Glory's first visitation began with Israel. His mission was clear. Jesus had prophesied concerning the latter days, "And this gospel of the kingdom will be preached in all the world as a witness to all nations, and then the end will come."[16] While proclaiming the gospel to thousands of Jews, Arabs, and Palestinians, the warrior angel could clearly see the evil result that intense spiritual darkness had wrought.

As a witness of the darkness, the Holy Spirit spoke forth, "The God of this age has blinded the minds of unbelievers so that they cannot see the light of the gospel of the glory of God, who is the image of God."[17]

Glory's arrival on earth immediately attracted several religious spirits of darkness. Their assignment was to prevent Glory from preaching the gospel to every nation, tribe, people, and tongue. For every plan God institutes, Satan attempts to counter it with his own evil deception. The warrior angel could not believe how many religious traditions had replaced the Gospel in so many hearts. "How many?" he wondered. "How many will repent and follow Jesus before God's wrath is poured out upon the earth?"

✳

Israeli intelligence had been monitoring the build up along the borders for the past several months. The neighboring Arab countries were quietly increasing their troops and equipment under the guise of maintaining security along the borders. Day by day, the tension grew. Israeli soldiers looked across their borders into the eyes of those who in the past had vowed that Jerusalem would someday be an Arab capital. Without any warning, the busy preparation came to an abrupt halt.

Within the hour, a hastily called cabinet meeting was arranged at the Knesset. As the 120 cabinet members filed in to take their seats, the top aide to the prime minister of Israel looked very uneasy.

"It is almost as if they are waiting for something to happen," he uttered to the defense minister.

"Nevertheless, let us believe for peace, even if our eyes and hearts tell us differently," urged the high-ranking official.

✳

With night covering the Middle East, the people of Israel slept under the protection of their Arab neighbors. For the past three and a half years, with wars touching every major continent in the world, the Jewish people relished their supposed divine protection. At first, a great number of Jews strongly protested the seven-year peace treaty with Hendrick and his Middle East Federation. The mistrust of Israel's neighbors, Syria, Jordan, Sudan, Iraq, Iran, Egypt, and Libya, had festered for many years and grown deeply bitter. For many, just the signing of a piece of paper could not change the past. Nevertheless, Eli Rosen, who was once labeled a traitor among his people, was now a hero. Wolfgang Hendrick had become a revered leader of peace, and Jewish families walked the streets of Jerusalem while holding hands and greeting each other without any fear of their neighbor's wrath.

It was a typical Sabbath morning with the sun barely rising above the hills of Israel. Suddenly, hundreds of tanks could be seen moving across Israel's borders. Air strikes coming from Syria, Jordan, Iraq, and Libya began to systematically destroy Israel's most effective air bases. Most of the jets that Israel had purchased from the United States never made it off the ground. The few that did were destroyed as soon as they reached air space. As Jewish soldiers fought to maintain control of their borders, the casualty count soared. The world watched in horror as millions perished.

Jews, Arabs, and Palestinians could be seen fleeing for safety with just the clothes on their backs.[18] The gentile armies pushed through to surround the Holy City of Jerusalem. Rows and rows of men, women, and children lay dead on the roads leading up to the city. Babies were being ripped from their mother's arms. Sons and daughters watched as their parents were shot.

Hendrick's officers quickly set up prison camps outside every major city in Israel. Many of the holocaust survivors sensed a demonic rage, which brought back ugly memories of Nazi Germany. Soldiers ransacked homes, looted businesses, and destroyed synagogues. The people, huddled in fear, could see a Hitler-like hate raging in the soldiers' eyes.

A possessed Hendrick made his way towards the Holy City, the apple of God's eye. By forsaking the truth of God, the Jewish leadership had made a covenant of death with the enemy. Terror swept through home after home; the sound of wailing becoming stronger as the gentile armies tightened their evil grip.[19]

As the Bishops and the Corbins watched the CNN news reports of the Arab-Jerusalem conflict, several of the youth crying out in tearful intercession paced the watchman headquarters. Dropping to their knees in prayer, Mark and Stephen both sensed a prompting from the Holy Spirit, "Beware, my children, the fourth seal has been broken! The pale horse, with its riders, Death and Hades, has been loosed upon the earth."[20]

***

"We must break camp immediately!" shouted the Israeli commander. "The armies of Hendrick have begun the slaughter of our people! Sound the shofars so that the people may ready themselves."

Within seconds, over 144,000 Jews in the encampment could hear seventy shofars blowing in perfect harmony. It was a signal to prepare to move. The tribes of Judah, Reuben, Gad, Asher, Naphatali, Manasseh, Simeon, Levi, Issachar, Zebulun, Joseph, and Benjamin were all accounted for.[21] Jews representing the twelve tribes of Israel had been secretly slipping away from their cities and families for the past three and a half years in order to escape the coming apostasy of their beloved Israel. This group of people refused to believe in a covenant with Wolfgang Hendrick, who would eventually break his word by persecuting the unsuspecting Jewish nation. The prophet Ezekiel had prophesied, "I will bring you from the peoples and gather you out of the countries where you are scattered, with a mighty hand, with an outreached arm, and with fury poured out. And I will bring you into the wilderness of the peoples, and there I will plead My case with you face to face. . . . I will make you pass under the rod, and I will bring you into the bond of the covenant."[22]

At night, sitting around the fires that kept them warm, the rabbis would read the Scriptures to encourage and give hope to those who were listening. As one rabbi finished a reading from the Holy Book, a young boy asked, "Rabbi, what does it mean that God will bring us into the bond of the covenant?"

Looking into the boy's eyes, the rabbi smiled and replied, "Only time will tell, my son. We must trust our God with our lives as we wait for our Messiah."

While the small prayer group bid goodnight to each other, the young boy knelt and whispered, "God, who is the Messiah?"

CHAPTER 27

HIS HOUR OF EVIL

Who opposes and exalts himself above all that is called God or that is worshipped,
so that he sits as God in the temple of God, showing himself that he is God.
II Thessalonians 2:4

"This is CNN's Natalie Roberts, reporting from downtown Jerusalem."

While her cameraman slowly panned the entire city block that had just been leveled, Natalie adjusted her earpiece.

"As the world watches in horror, Israel is being invaded by her Arab neighbors," announced the tense reporter. "The combined Arab armies rolled past the ineffective border defenses that obviously were not prepared for such an all-out attack. Russian tanks have now, as I speak, reached the city limits of Jerusalem and are systematically destroying specifically targeted areas. Air strikes from Syria, Jordan, Iraq, and Libya purposely attacked during the early morning hours of the Jewish Sabbath and have totally crippled Israel's defense systems. Military bases have been rendered useless; normal communications have been cut off as Arab armored units continue to roll across the border."

Natalie suddenly stopped and cupped a hand over her earpiece.

"Ladies and gentlemen, I am receiving a report from an unofficial source placing Wolfgang Hendrick as the leader behind this invasion. There has been no word from Hendrick or any of his staff concerning these allegations. We remind you, this allegation has been neither confirmed nor denied."

Natalie strained to listen over the loud background noise as another news update came in.

"It's official!" shouted the reporter. "This unwarranted attack on Israel is being led by none other than Germany's Wolfgang Hendrick and his ten-nation Middle East Federation! At this very moment, Hendrick, accompanied by a large number of world leaders, is entering the Holy City. According to our sources, he will announce his terms for surrender from the Knesset. Eli Rosen and his 120-member cabinet have anticipated this and are anxiously awaiting his arrival." Pausing for another update from the CNN news truck, Natalie announced, "We will now take you live to the famous Jewish parliament, the Knesset, for this historic moment!"

The security at the Knesset was airtight as reporters from every major country prepared to meet with Wolfgang Hendrick. "This is CNN's Isaac Weisman, reporting live from the Knesset in Jerusalem. Early this morning, a coalition of Arab States viciously attacked the nation of Israel. Beginning with powerful air attacks and continuing with horrific land assaults, they have completely encircled the Jewish nation. Even though this attack is a complete violation of the Jerusalem Peace Accord, the United Nations has refused to make any official comment. This is . . ." Straining to hear over the gunfire of Jewish resisters, the reporter slipped behind his CNN news truck. The CNN cameraman, hiding behind a destroyed car, looked petrified as the reporter signaled for one final close-up shot. Instinctively, they each stepped out at the same time.

With the camera rolling, without any warning, news reporters began to pour out of the front entrance of the parliament building. The utter confusion was terrifying as the news reached the ears of Israel's leadership. The CNN reporter nervously announced, "We have just received a news update that Wolfgang Hendrick has decided to make his terms of surrender from the steps of the Jerusalem Temple on Mount Moriah!"[1]

The temple was securely locked at every entrance. Each vessel of honor had been removed and hidden. White sheets covered the altar, the laver, and the porch, which lead into the Holy of Holies. In order to avoid any unauthorized entry, a priest was stationed at every entrance.

The High Priest looked very majestic as he slowly ascended the steps leading to the Beautiful Gate, the main entrance to the temple. He was wearing a beautiful white robe and a golden breastplate, featuring twelve precious stones, which represented the twelve tribes of Israel. With just a nod of his head, seventy priests gathered behind him. It was close to two and a half years ago that the religious leadership began to perform sacrifices and reinstate the worship of Jehovah in their newly constructed temple. It was all just a distant memory now as Hendrick's armies surrounded the temple mount. The attacks of a gentile aggressor would once again visit a people whose hearts had grown cold to the God who loves them.

As Hendrick's entourage surged up the temple mount, CNN filmed every move. The time had come for the man of sin to reveal his plan. Strolling towards the steps to the Beautiful Gate, it almost seemed as if the world were holding its breath. The priests standing on the temple steps began to call out prayers for protection. The beast slowly approached the high priest. The eyes of the leaders locked. In the distant background, the sound of enemy fire could still be heard. After a long pause, the seventy-five-year-old high priest spoke: "You are not welcome here. The Jerusalem Peace Accord that required your solemn oath has been broken. This is our Holy Temple, and you and your armies will not . . ."

Hendrick's lips formed an evil smile. Raising his right hand, his soldiers responded without any hesitation. Within seconds, the priests were forcibly removed from the entrance. Those reporting the event were disoriented. Without any delay, Hendrick strode into the temple and arrived first at the Court of the Women. In front of him was the Nicanor Gate, with the chamber of lepers to his right and the chamber of oils to his left. Passing through the Nicanor Gate, Hendrick entered the Court of the Israelites. With television cameras recording his every move, the antichrist stepped into the Court of Priests. The Jewish people could not believe what was happening. Their Holy of Holies, a symbol of holiness and purity, was being violated by the abomination that would very shortly cause a complete desolation. And they were powerless to stop it.

"People of the world!" shouted Hendrick. "I've come before you today with a proposal for peace. For the last three and a half years, we all have seen the spread of wars, famines, and diseases. It is time that someone acknowledge the truth about the future of our world!"

The power of Satan had reached an all-time high. The people of the world were mesmerized, trying to comprehend the significance of this moment. Little did they know that the lonely figure standing before the Holy of Holies was selling a future that would only bring total destruction.

"I've asked leaders from over forty major countries to stand with me today. We have come to announce the desperate need of a one-world leader who will truly be for the people. We need someone who will have the power and authority to promote harmony and trust among the nations!"

Slowly, Hendrick ascended the steps leading to the place reserved for the Ark of the Covenant. With just a wave of his hand, a mighty rushing wind of evil flooded the Holy of Holies. Immediately, several soldiers brought in an image of Hendrick and placed it beside their new ruler. In unison, the leaders within the temple knelt and began to worship the image of Hendrick. The power of Satan suddenly exploded over the airways supernaturally touching those watching or listening to the worldwide satellite telecast.

Hendrick smiled and opened his arms to a watching world. "Today, under my leadership, a new world coalition begins that will end the wars of this world. Think of it—a world family that will work together to end war, prejudice, hunger, and disease. The choice is yours! If you worship me as your God, I promise to create a new world of prosperity!

Watching this incredible unfolding of Jesus' warnings, Luke Appleby stood among the overcomers at the Watchman Camp and read, "Then he opened his mouth in blasphemy against God, to blaspheme His name, His tabernacle, and those who dwell in heaven. It was granted to him to make war with the saints and to overcome them. And authority was given to him over every tribe, tongue, and nation."[2]

"I, Wolfgang Hendrick, stand before you in the Holy of Holies, a symbol of peace and safety. As your lord, I will protect all the religions of the world and will create a love for mankind that can only be dreamed of."

Suddenly, the prayer warriors at the camp hit the floor and began to intercede. Every camper knew that soon the delusion of God would come to a world who refused to love the truth and obey the Gospel.[3] Billions of people who took pleasure in unrighteousness would soon face God's wrath.

On the same afternoon that Wolfgang proclaimed himself to be God, two witnesses dressed in brown sackcloth suddenly appeared on the Mount of Olives. As they began their journey down the mount and across the Kidron Valley, the people stopped their work to stare.

"Papa, who are they, and what do they want?" asked a young boy.

"Quickly, my son," his father yelled, "find the rabbi. He will know the right questions to ask."

The boy immediately took off running for the nearby synagogue.

As the two prophets of God drew closer to the Temple Mount, they paused and prayed a loud prayer for all to hear. "We praise you, Father, Son, Holy Spirit, the One True God. 'Blessed are those who hunger and thirst for righteousness, for they shall be filled. Blessed are those who are persecuted because of righteousness sake, for theirs is the kingdom of heaven. Blessed are you when they revile and persecute you, and say all kinds of evil against you falsely for my sake. Rejoice and be exceedingly glad, for great is your reward in heaven, for so they persecuted the prophets who were before you.'"[4]

Amidst the jeering of a small crowd that had just formed, the two witnesses continued their journey toward the Jewish temple located on the Temple Mount.

"Who do you think you are?" asked an aging Rabbi who tried to block their path.

"We are the witnesses of Revelation who will prophecy for 1,260 days," replied Elijah.[5]

"What is your message from God, and why have you come to us?"

"Our message is one of truth, which will bring freedom to your soul!" thundered Moses. "Behold, your Messiah has come but you and your forefathers have rejected him. Wake up! He is coming again, a second time, not as a lamb to be slaughtered but as the King of kings and the Lord of lords! Repent of your sins and ask Jesus, The Christ, to be your Savior and Lord."

"If you are really from God, why do you wear filthy sackcloth and not the godly robes of a righteous man?" scoffed a young college student.

"We are the fulfillment of God's Word in the book of Revelation," replied Elijah. "Two witnesses will be sent to prophesy a message of salvation and one of eternal judgment. We have been sent to expose the lie of the man of sin! God's Word will never return void but will accomplish its purpose for which it was sent."[6]

"Well, then who are you? What are your names so that we may tell our leaders?" mocked a scribe from a nearby synagogue.

"Have you not read the word of the Lord from the prophet Malachi?" challenged Elijah. "He prophesied, 'For, behold, the day is coming, burning like an oven; and all the proud, yes, all who do wickedly, will be stubble: and the day which is coming shall burn them up, says the Lord of hosts. . . .

Behold, I will send you Elijah the prophet before the coming of the great and dreadful Day of the Lord.'"[7]

"Are you saying you are Elijah, come back from the dead?"

"From the dead?" questioned Moses. "Have you not read, 'And He was transfigured before them. His face shine like the sun, and His clothes became white as light. And behold, Moses and Elijah appeared to them, talking with Him.'"[8]

"Blasphemy!" shouted an angry rabbi. "My friends listen to me. They speak heresy! They must be stoned!"

As the crowd picked up rocks to kill the prophets, a flash of fire shot forth from Moses and scorched their bodies. Those with rocks in their hands were knocked to the ground.[9]

"Be still!" commanded Moses. "Jesus Christ is The Messiah! He is our Redeemer, our King. Open your eyes so that you may see the truth. Today is the Day of Salvation. The deceiver, Hendrick, is not the true Christ. He is antichrist! Whoever worships him or his image or takes his mark, 666, will be tormented with burning sulfur in the presence of holy angels and the Lamb."[10]

The noise from the crowd was so loud that hardly anyone could hear the prophet's words. The spiritual warfare was mounting as the two witnesses continued their journey towards the temple.

Within a month, leaders from around world were summoned to Hendrick's headquarters in Jerusalem. The beast and his prophet had begun their propaganda campaign, performing counterfeit miracles for the entire world to see. The spirit of the antichrist had taken decades to brainwash the current generation, and now the truth of Jesus Christ would be rejected. Hendrick's lobbyists could be seen working around the clock as the foundation of his New World Coalition was methodically being laid. The demons of religion and compromise tightened their grips of bondage upon those who had already surrendered to their evil influence. The beast smiled thinly as he looked out over the audience.

"I, Wolfgang Hendrick, welcome you all to our first New World Coalition Summit. Each of you has received a packet of information. Inside you will find an outline of the proposed global laws. I believe the implementation of these laws will rescue our world from its predictable path to destruction. The only answer to such worldwide anguish is a one-world government, a one-world financial system, and a one-world religion. Believe me, these are necessary measures that will ultimately be responsible for saving our world!"

"Chairman Hendrick," interrupted a delegate from France, "I would . . ."

Immediately, Father John cut in and asked the French delegate to take a seat.

"May I remind each delegate to please address our leader as lord. He should be addressed, now and always, as Lord Hendrick."

The delegate from France smiled and replied, "Yes, Lord Hendrick, I'm afraid I must object to . . ."

"Excuse me," interrupted Father John. "We will deal with any questions at the end of the presentation."

"But, Father John, before we can possibly . . ."

"Remove him!" demanded the furious priest.

The utter disgust on the false prophet's face should have been a warning alarm to any person who had any discernment at all.

Hendrick continued, "Gentlemen, please bear in mind that there will be plenty of leeway to negotiate a reasonable policy for all nations to adhere to. Today I have established a world committee that will be chaired by Father John. This committee will be subject to my authority and will oversee the implementation of legislation that you will approve during this summit."

The possessed leader scanned the leadership for any hint of rebellion.

"The first action of the NWC Committee will be to officially dissolve the World Faith Movement. Its functions and responsibilities will now come under the authority of the NWC. Now is the time for action. We must move quickly and decisively in order to ensure success."

The demonic cloud over Jerusalem was overwhelming in size and deception. While Hendrick shared his plan for the world, many of the delegates accepted the lie that no one could withstand the wisdom and power of the new ruler.

While discussing the implementation of the New World Coalition, the dissolution of the World Faith Movement was completed. Thousands of religions would now look to Hendrick as their god. Leaders of the World Faith Movement were encouraged to accept a stance of tolerance and compromise for the safety of their people. Within months, the image of Hendrick would be seen in homes throughout the world. The image of the beast would now become the world's object of worship.[11]

After an NWC delegate vote was taken, and the passage of the World ID Commerce Act became a reality, speculation varied on who would sign up first. Because this was virgin territory, the world leaders were cautious. Still, it would only take a single signature from the official representative of any country and financial support from the New World Coalition. Even so, many wondered why it was so important for their leader residing in Jerusalem to be worshipped as god.

"It's official," announced CNN's Natalie Roberts. "The New World Coalition Committee, chaired by Father John, has recognized the United States as its first member! Italy will be next, followed by Russia, Israel, Germany, and Japan."

Arriving in Rome, Amad knew whom to address and what to say. The angelic messenger immediately perceived the Babylonian harlot, sitting on seven mountains, drunk with the blood of the saints who bore the testimony of Jesus. The image of the queen of heaven had intoxicated the people of the earth with her blasphemy and the filth of her adulteries.

"The Babylonian harlot has fallen!" proclaimed the angel. "She is fallen because she made all the nations drink of her fornication."[12]

"Truly," Amad thought, "the scarlet beast having seven heads and ten horns has destroyed the harlot!" He knew the importance of his mission. Surely, the end of the age was close.

Jewish families from throughout Israel were gathering for prayer in a secret camp just across the Jordanian border. Caleb, the great grandfather of the Abrams family, asked that he might speak before the evening prayer.

"Brothers and sisters, my heart is very troubled on this day, our Holy Sabbath. The recent attack on our families and friends has brought back many bitter memories of my internment at Auschwitz. The ovens at Auschwitz were used every day. Ten thousand prisoners a day went into them. At times, I can still hear the Nazi guards laughing at our sufferings. I once made the mistake of questioning an order, and the guards decided I had to be punished. They tied my hands to a broomstick and then hung the broomstick from a post in the prison yard. I was left this way as an object lesson for over a day.

Afterward I was unable to move my arms for weeks. There were times when the guards would strip me naked and put me in a room filled with water up to my ankles. After two days, I could hear them laughing as I struggled to keep my sanity. At other times, close to one hundred prisoners were crammed together into a cell that holds ten people. It did not take long before the cries for mercy rang out," Caleb softly shared. "I asked then, and I ask you now, what type of evil could possess a man to do such a thing? Some of the guards seemed to delight in the pain of children's losing their parents. They inflicted their evil, just for the joy of it. The day I walked out of Auschwitz, I made a pledge that if I ever saw the spirit of Hitler again, I would do everything in my power to stop it."

"Have you seen that spirit, grandfather?" asked Aaron, his grandson.

Caleb paused as he reached over and put his arm around the young boy.

"My dear family and friends, Hendrick blasphemed when he declared himself to be god of this world! Did you see the faces of those Syrian soldiers last month when they shot our rabbi and his family? No, this is more than possessing land and gaining power. There is only one spirit that could be behind this evil leader and his armies. He has to be driven by Satan himself!"

Caleb's son, Samuel, nodded his head in agreement.

"My father is right. Our people are in grave danger as long as Hendrick leads the New World Coalition. By submitting to his World ID System, we are actually becoming his pawns."

"But, Father, look at how many of our friends plan to register," pleaded Aaron.

"Aaron, everyone will have to make a choice."

"Grandfather, have you heard the rumor that two witnesses appeared at the Wailing Wall last month, about the time Hendrick desecrated our Holy Temple?"

"Yes, my son. It seems they think that they are Elijah and Moses."

"That's right, Grandfather. My friends tell me they have come back from the dead and are proclaiming Jesus Christ as the Messiah for the whole world."

The ninety-year-old holocaust survivor could only wince in pain at the thought of such heresy reaching the ears of his beloved grandson.

"Let's pray and ask God to show us the truth. We must cry out to Jehovah and ask our Father for protection from the evil that has visited our borders."

While everyone bowed their heads to pray, heartfelt sobbing could be heard from the families who had lost their loved ones in the Jerusalem massacre.[13]

Chapter 28

666

He causes all, both small and great,
rich and poor, free and slave,
to receive a mark on their right hand or on their foreheads.
Revelation 13:16

Many people in America were thrilled about being able to have their own personal ID number because it was the ultimate in convenience. Thousands lined up several days ahead of schedule in order to be the first to make history. Others treated the whole event as an excuse for having another big party.

"It's a new world!" yelled a Georgetown University student leaving a Washington DC ID station after receiving the mark of the beast on his forehead.

In Times Square, over 200,000 Americans wore party hats and blew whistles while waiting to receive their new ID numbers. The CNN office in Miami reported the most novel idea. The marriage ceremony lasted five minutes while family and onlookers cheered with approval. The young couple from Baca Raton, Florida, posed for pictures as they received their ID numbers on their right hands while exchanging their wedding rings!

The *Los Angles Times*, the *Chicago Tribune*, and the *New York Times* began running editorials praising the New World Coalition's financial policy. The positive spin created by the news media had helped to promote the atmosphere of trust that the NWC desperately desired. As the first IDs were being issued nationwide, trouble was brewing among specific religious sects that were refusing to register. A small minority had become very vocal in their opposition of mandatory ID registration. Christian families were being torn apart by accusations that the ID number was a form of worshipping Hendrick as god.

"You bet it is!" yelled a steelworker from Bethlehem, Pennsylvania. "I'll not only bow to Hendrick; I'll get down and kiss his feet! Look what he has done for us. So what if he says he's god. He ain't hurting nobody. Maybe he is god!"

✳

Just a few minutes after the bell rang for lunch, Jessie and Jake met on the front lawn of the school and decided to take a walk to Max's Barbecue.

"It's so weird, Jessie. Lakeview has lost over a hundred students since the New World Coalition took over."

"Yeah, you're right. Hope, Lindsey, Luke, Whitney, Ned, Drew, the leaders of the Bible Club have all disappeared. And they didn't tell anybody. Even Mr. Fyffe, our principal, had no clue!"

"You know what, Jess? It seems as if most of them split just days after Hendrick attacked Jerusalem. Do you think they maybe joined the resistance movement that everybody's been talking about?"

"It sure looks that way. But what's really weird is that they didn't even wait around for their sign-up dates. It's pretty obvious that they believed in the end-times scenario being preached at school," said Jessie.

"Do you really think there's anything to it?"

"Hey, all I know is that when I tried to talk to my daddy and mamma about Hendrick's being the antichrist, they laughed me out of the family room. Then, when I opened my Bible to show them some scriptures, they stopped laughing and started getting really uptight. They pretty much labeled those who left school as a bunch of cultists."

"Forget that!" snapped Jake. "Luke's no cultist! He has stronger convictions than anyone else I know. He was always ready to stand for what he believed. When you think about it, Hendrick did proclaim himself to be god. And look at how many Jews his army has killed. Now people will have to take a number on their right hand or forehead, whether they want it or not!"

"What do you mean, Jake? Are you saying Luke was right?"

Jake just shrugged and said, "I don't know. I just wish Luke were here so that I could ask him some more questions. So many people are caught up with how great Hendrick is. The newspaper reporters portray the world as his footstool. I've got several friends who don't trust him, but they're planning on registering anyway."

"Jake, if Luke were here, what questions would you ask him?"

After thinking over Jessie's question, he slowly shook his head and replied, "You're right, Jess. There really isn't anything more to ask, is there?"

✳

The new-world leader, Wolfgang Hendrick, had become an overnight sensation. After implementing his New World Coalition global strategy, he received the highest approval rating ever attained. Countries from all over the world were making dramatic recoveries in trade, commerce, and productivity. The NWC had not only allowed the world to become a well-oiled machine, but the hostilities between enemies seemed to have disappeared. The war machines of America, the Middle East, China, Russia, and the European Community, which were once at odds with each other, were now funneling their money into helping the world economy. Never before had the world seen such awesome gains in the International Stock Market. The ID numbers, which were first issued to the major powers, had made credit card fraud an evil of the past. The dramatic results Hendrick had promised the world had become a reality. The fruit from the ideas of this mysterious German leader had convinced many of his truthfulness!

Ian looked bigger and several times stronger than Glory and Amad. He needed to be, for his mission would require him to fight the most power-ful demon of all, the spirit of the antichrist. Ian knew that the ruler of this world would not allow him to proclaim his message without a fight.

With conviction and power, Ian shouted to the people, "If anyone worships the beast and his image and receives his mark on his forehead or on his hand, he himself shall also drink of the wine of the wrath of God. He shall be tormented with fire and brimstone in the presence of the holy angels and in the presence of the Lamb."[1]

"For the followers to hear the truth about the mark would not be acceptable to my master," cursed the spirit of the antichrist. The foul spirit quickly countered Ian's message of judgment with the lie, "The protection of one's family should be everyone's top priority!"

As a leading super power along with the European Community, Japan, and China, it was critical that the United States set a positive example for the rest of the world. The progress of the ID system in America was being close-ly watched by hundreds of countries. The youth in America had often set popular trends in clothes, music, movies, and even drugs. The devil knew how important it was to deceive the youth of America.

"If the power from above ever fell on the youth of America, then it would spread to the Russians, the Japanese, even the Europeans," hissed the spirit of deception to the demons under his control. "Don't you all understand how critical it is for our master to control the youth of America? The world is watching, so be alert! The ID system must look cool so that young people everywhere will see it as an opportunity to express their individuality."

The Pressleys had just finished dinner when Dwayne invited everyone to meet in the TV room for an important meeting.

"As you all know, the NWC ID stations have been set up in several locations around Bethany. For the first six months, anyone can register. After that, each family or single person nineteen and over will receive a notification slip of their sign-up date. A second notification will be sent three days before the actual registration date. Now, I want to be very clear about this. I've studied a great deal on the subject of electronic ID transfer, and I feel there is absolutely nothing to fear."

Dwayne vainly attempted to get eye contact with his wife, Gloria, and his two daughters, Rachel and Anna.

"They encourage families to go together, so I'd like us all to register at the first available opportunity. Are there any questions, girls?"

"I'm really scared, Daddy," cried Rachel. "Some of my Bible Club friends are really freaking out! I mean they're telling everyone that this ID number is evil. Even some of the leaders of the Bible Club, like Luke, Whitney, Ned, and Drew, have disappeared! Daddy, they are convinced Hendrick is the antichrist, and if you get an ID number, you will be denying Jesus. What if they are right? I don't want to lose my salvation!"

"Calm down, honey."

"But, Daddy, what if it's true? We've always been taught that our salvation is forever, right? I mean, didn't we leave Bethany Assembly because Pastor Bishop taught that Christians who deny Jesus will lose their salvation and spend eternity in hell?"

Even though Rachel and Anna knew something was wrong, they both firmly believed their daddy would eventually lead them to the truth.

"That's right, girls; that's why we left. The Bible says that once you become a Christian, it's for eternity! Now before you take it to an extreme, like your friends are doing, let's just remember last Sunday morning's sermon from Pastor Ryals."

"You mean his message on the salvation of a believer?" asked Anna.

"That's right. He clearly proved from the Scriptures that a Christian could never commit the blasphemy of the Holy Spirit!"

"What about habitually sinning?" interjected Gloria, Dwayne's wife.

"Listen, we all know J. R. Greer, the famous pastor from Brentwood Baptist in Orlando. This wonderful man of God has taught for over forty years that believers are sealed until the day of redemption. C'mon, think about it. Why would God promise us eternal salvation and then take it away because we didn't measure up? No sin can take away your salvation once you become a member of the family of God."[2]

"But, Daddy, our friends sound so convincing!" cried Anna.

"Girls, listen. If it were possible to lose our salvation, then God would have warned us through his Word, right?"

"Yes, Daddy," Rachel quietly uttered.

Softly the Spirit of God spoke to her, "My child, you ran well. Who is hindering you from obeying the truth? This persuasion does not come from Him who calls you."[3]

"Believe me, we are saved for eternity, and no little ID number will ever change that," pressured Dwayne. "Now, that's enough of this mumbo jumbo nonsense. Let's go out for a movie."

As Dwayne waited for the girls to get ready, the phone rang. It was Kevin Collins, a former deacon from Bethany Assembly.

"Hey, Kevin, how are you doing?"

"Pretty exciting news about the ID stations going up," replied the officer.

"You better believe it! It sure looks like our president is really tight with Hendrick. Don't you think the financial package the NWC has proposed is a great deal?"

As the seconds ticked bye, Dwayne waited for an answer, but it never came.

"Kevin, are you there?"

"Yes, it seems to be all right. I mean, on the surface it's impressive. But I, uh, do have some questions about the ID number."

"Like what?"

"Well, my wife is pretty upset about material she was handed by Bethany Assembly members while shopping in Winn Dixie this morning."

"Imagine that," replied an unimpressed Dwayne as the spirit of compromise prepared to manifest itself.

"The material states that by taking the ID number you are denying Christ and accepting Hendrick as your lord!"

"Why is that?" Dwayne asked almost sheepishly.

"Well, isn't the ID system Hendrick's plan?"

"Yeah."

"And last month when he proclaimed himself to be god, didn't he demand everyone worship him?"

"So?"

"Well, doesn't it stand to reason that if we take his ID number we are following him?"

"Incredible," replied Dwayne while looking up at the ceiling. "Yes, it's true that Wolfgang Hendrick has intervened to bring the world back from disaster with the help of some international financial geniuses. Their plan is designed to bring down the walls that have existed since the days of Nimrod and Babylon. The only reason he asked to be worshipped is to bring about a harmony of peace the World Faith Movement couldn't achieve. Some don't necessarily agree with this unusual theology, but most religious leaders have decided to be tolerant and give the World ID System a chance!"

"But, Dwayne, the material they gave my wife says that the book of Revelation . . ."

"I know, I know," interrupted Dwayne. "The book of Revelation warns believers not to take the mark of the beast. But tell me, Kevin, do you know people who have 666 as their ID number?"

"Well, no, I don't."

"Look. The handouts probably label Wolfgang Hendrick as none other than the evil antichrist, right?"

"Yeah, that's what they're feeding us."

"Let's be logical, my brother. If this were true, why would so many pastors and Bible teachers register for their ID numbers?[4] Even Gene Lloyd and Arthur Lawrence are encouraging believers not to worry but to keep looking up, for our Lord Jesus could come at any moment."

"Okay," Kevin replied, not sounding totally convinced. "When do you plan to sign up?"

"Well, I was thinking about this weekend. I don't know. We might just wait for our sign-up date. Do I need to come over and talk with your wife?"

"No, that's all right. We know this is just a scare tactic from Satan."

"Hey, the girls and I are going out for a movie. Do you want to meet us?"

"No thanks, Dwayne, we'll have to take a rain check. But we do appreciate your wise counsel and your friendship."

"No problem, buddy," said Dwayne. "What are friends for?"

CHAPTER 29

IS IT REALLY YOU, GOD?

Remember the word I said to you,
a servant is not greater than his master.
If they persecuted Me, they will also persecute you.
John 15:20

While the young teenager crossed over Vaughn Road and headed for his house, Simon never dreamed his life could become so complicated. Growing up, Simon couldn't remember a time when he had a real father-son talk. He had always reasoned that his dad was a very busy man, and the members of his church deserved his help. Being a pastor's kid, he was brought up to believe whatever his dad taught. Right is right; wrong is wrong. If he asked a question about anything, his father would give him the answer and instruct him on how to say it, where to say it, when to say it, and why he should say it. Throughout his childhood, the young boy never questioned his father's teaching or counsel. When faced with friends who disagreed, Simon would often lash out without really knowing how to handle the situation. But it was clear to him now. He had never really understood what he believed. Like a sponge, he had soaked up thousands of sermons his dad had preached. But Simon had never really known whether the messages were true or not. He had met a lot of pastors' kids while growing up, but most of them were not really happy as far as he could see. But then he met Joshua Hirsh at a Christian summer camp. Joshua, the son of Pastor Benjamin Hirsh, was really unique in Simon's eyes. It didn't take long for the kid from the west side of town to break through the walls Simon had built up over the years to protect himself. It didn't seem to matter how much Simon tried to hide or how many mind games he played, by the end of the two-week camp, the two had become good friends.

Joshua had taught Simon that consistent obedience to the leading of the Holy Spirit was the only way to keep one's relationship with God on track. He knew what he believed, and his goal in life was to obey God.

As Simon entered the back door of his house, he stumbled slightly over several cardboard boxes that were scattered throughout the kitchen.

"Hey, what's all this?" yelled Simon.

"Son, is that you?"

"Yeah, Mom, what's going on?"

Looking a bit anxious, Allen and Mary Colson entered the kitchen.

Mary asked, "Where have you been? We've been so worried about you."

Before he could answer, his father added, "Have a seat, Simon. We need to talk."

Wondering what he might have done wrong, Simon took a seat at the kitchen table. His mother sat across from him as his father started to pace nervously with his arms folded tightly together.

"As you already know, son, we've had a lot of changes in the past four years. We moved, and you had to switch schools and make new friends. Our new church was just completed this past year, and you know how busy that kept us. Of course, your mother had to have a lot of rest in order to recover from the virus she caught during Christmas."

"Yeah, I know, Dad, so what are you trying to say?"

"Well, son, there's just no easy way to say this. Your mother and I have been fasting and praying over this New World ID System, and we feel that it is closely involved with the newly proclaimed world leader, Wolfgang Hendrick."

"Really?" Simon slowly replied while nervously shifting in his seat.

"Yes, and I'm afraid this is going to sound pretty extreme to you."

"After what I've gone through the last few months, I guess I'm pretty much up for anything," said Simon.

"Do you remember back a couple of years ago the night the evangelist Steven Corbin from California came and preached on the Lord's coming?"

"Sure, Dad. I remember. I was seated with my friends right behind the seminar committee. Boy, were they hot with that preacher!"

"What do you think of his interpretation on the timing of our Lord's return?" asked Allen.

Simon thought for a moment and then answered, "At first, I didn't quite get the part about Jesus not coming back until certain events happen. Some of the kids at the Bible Club started studying and really got into it until their parents found out. Then it died out, at least for most of them."

"Well, your mother and I have been studying the passages that were given out that night, and we believe that this view has some real merit."

"That so?" replied a stunned Simon.

"Yes. We also feel Pastor Mark Bishop's messages on the tribulation period are scriptural and are real warnings to believers not to be deceived."

"Who's going to deceive us?" asked Simon as he got up and leaned against the refrigerator.

"The antichrist," replied Mary.

These were the very words Simon did not want to hear. "That can't be right!" snapped the confused teenager. "Dad, you have taught me over and over again that before the antichrist can come and before the tribulation period can begin, the body of Christ must be raptured! Remember? We are looking for Jesus, our blessed hope, not the antichrist!"

"The fact of the matter, son, is that my teaching about how Jesus could come at any moment was wrong," his father quietly confessed.

"Wrong? After all these years of studying and believing, now you just say, 'Oops, I was wrong?' And I suppose you think that the ID number is the mark of the beast and that if we take it we will lose our salvation, right?" asked Simon sarcastically.

"This isn't easy for us either, son. But your mother and I now believe that Wolfgang Hendrick is the antichrist and that by stepping into the Jerusalem Temple and proclaiming himself to be god, he literally fulfilled the prophecy of II Thessalonians 2:4!"

A sudden rush of fear gripped the young boy as he desperately tried to understand the words coming out of his father's mouth.

"Your father and I have prayed, and we have decided that we are not going to register for our ID. What I mean is . . . that your father and I will never register!"

"But, Mom, what about the Thompsons, the Garcias, and the Werners? Aren't they going to register for their IDs?"

"Families will have to decide for themselves whether to register or not," replied Allen. "We have left a note explaining our decision to our church administrator. He will read it to our congregation this Sunday morning."

"Where will we be?" asked Simon suspiciously.

"We will be gone, son," answered an emotionally exhausted Mary. "Our packing is almost done. No one knows we are leaving or where we are going."

Mary could sense the war of emotions raging within her only child.

"Don't you see, honey? It seems easy now, but before long, the mark will become mandatory. They will first begin by targeting all those who have not registered. Eventually, those who refuse the mark will be killed by NWC agents!"[1]

"Okay, Mom," replied the young teenager, who looked totally disoriented.

"I'm glad you understand, son," replied his relieved father. "Now let's all finish packing so that we can be on the road before dark."

Simon followed his parents upstairs. While his mother gathered articles from the bathroom and his father disappeared into their walk-in closet, the young boy raced to his bedroom. It would only take a few minutes to pack everything he needed. Sitting down at his desk, he pulled out the middle drawer and flipped it over. Pulling off an envelope of money that was taped to the inside of the drawer, he stuffed it in his pocket. Then he grabbed a piece of paper and started to write.

Dear Mom and Dad,

I don't want you to worry about me. I need to find the truth about Jesus, and I have asked God to lead me. I love you very much, and I know your decision to leave the church took a lot of courage. I want you to know that no matter what happens you will always be close to my heart.

Till Jesus Comes,
Simon

Simon cracked open the door to his room and listened intently. Sounds of packing gave him a green light to sneak out of his room and move quickly down the stairs. He stopped just long enough at the kitchen table to prop his note up against a vase filled with wilted flowers.

Slipping out the back door, he whispered, "I'm sorry, Mom and Dad."

The ministries of Gene Lloyd, Arthur Lawrence, and J. R. Greer were completely overwhelmed by the sheer volume of the telephone calls. Believers from all over the country were begging for some sort of direction on what to do. Most callers would have six months to decide whether or not to register for their ID. Those with names beginning with A through C would be the first to face mandatory registration. Some were frantically seeking answers.

The prince of darkness continued to have a field day as many believers embraced a spirit of rationalization. Those deceived would follow whatever direction the majority was taking. Indeed, the antichrist had made his big move to deceive millions of unsuspecting souls. Who would even dare come against the propaganda machine of Hendrick now?

The news hit the Christian community like a bolt of lightening. Gene Lloyd Ministries was preempting normal TV on channel six to present a prepared statement concerning the World ID System.

"My fellow Christians, I come to you tonight with news that every believer in America needs to hear. After reviewing events of the past few months, I must say I have become a little perplexed. I have studied eschatology thousands of hours over the last thirty years. I feel God has given me a sound grasp of the events that will take place before our Lord's return for His saints. But with the way things currently are, uh, what I'm trying to say is, uh, well, there is a chance that my teaching on the pre-tribulation rapture position needs to be revised. We must all pray and allow God to speak to us concerning this World ID System. I don't want to cause any alarm, but if believers decide to resist this new financial system, there could be some serious consequences."

Gene paused, wiped his wrinkled forehead with a handkerchief, and took a deep breath.

"I've been receiving a lot of calls and letters asking about the NWC law to worship Wolfgang Hendrick. I want to make one thing perfectly clear. Wolfgang Hendrick is not really a god. He is only a representative, an advocate for the many religious faiths of this world."

Gene Lloyd laid his paper down and stared into the camera with troubled eyes.

"Each believer needs to seek God for direction concerning the future as new events unfold daily. That's all I can tell you now. God bless you all."

The reaction to the newscast was one of confusion, which quickly spread fear throughout the Christian community. Listeners throughout America and around the world wanted to know what exactly Gene Lloyd meant by his recent announcement.

"Next please," announced the ID agent as the line continued to move forward at a steady pace.

Simon could see the people ahead of him slipping their right hand into the ID machine. "It's no big deal," he thought. Some of his friends were already bragging about their own personal IDs that they would have for life. Because they couldn't actually see the eighteen-digit number, most had already memorized it. As he inched forward, Simon wondered if Joshua and his family would be registering this week. Then he recalled something Joshua had told him at summer camp.

"Remember, Simon, if we are all here to see the antichrist and the false prophet, don't be deceived into taking the mark of the beast. It's a one-way ticket to hell!"

It seemed as if everything that Joshua had taught Simon on the end times was the very opposite of what his father had always preached.

"Who knows," muttered a confused Simon under his breath.

"Name and Social Security number, please," said the bored ID agent.

"Simon Colson. My Social Security number is 931-24-2150."

After the agent checked her records, she looked up at Simon and said, "The ID files show me that you are sixteen, Simon."

"That's right, ma'am."

"Is your family with you today?"

While purposely avoiding eye contact, Simon answered, "No, I've come alone."

"Are you aware that you must be nineteen in order to apply for a personal ID?"

"I thought so."

"Simon, before you can receive your ID number, you must be accompanied by one of your parents or have written permission from one of them."

"I didn't really know that, ma'am."

"Why aren't your parents with you?"

"They said they were going to wait until the lines get shorter," replied Simon, whose head was spinning so fast that he could barely maintain himself. "What I really mean is, uh, I think they might not register because it is against their religious beliefs."

"Young man, are you aware that this is a mandatory law, and every citizen of this country is required to register?"

"Yes, ma'am."

"For the safety of your family, you need to report here tomorrow morning at ten o'clock, and I will personally register each of you. How does that sound?" asked the agent smiling.

"Real good, ma'am," replied an uneasy Simon. Feeling unexpectedly relieved, the young boy dropped out of line. As he reached the sidewalk, the agent called out, "Oh, by the way, Simon, what are your parents' names?"

Without even thinking, he automatically answered, "Allen and Mary."

"Thanks so much," said the agent.

As he turned to leave, Simon saw the agent remove a red file from the top drawer of her desk and begin writing in it.

Heading towards Main Street, Simon tried to shake off the feeling of doom that was sweeping over him. While waiting for the light to change, the Lord brought Joshua's cheerful smile to his mind. He could see his friend so clearly.

"What am I going to do now?" Simon asked himself, wishing he could talk to Joshua.

The walk downtown seemed to last forever. The loneliness of the moment gave Simon a yearning to know God better. Then it hit him right between the eyes. He had to find Joshua! His good friend would have the answers Simon so desperately needed. Immediately, the young teenager picked up his pace toward the west side of town, toward the home of Joshua Hirsh.

CHAPTER 30

A WITNESS FOR THE TRUTH

Let not your heart be troubled;
you believe in God, believe also in Me.
John 14:1

By the time Simon finally reached Joshua's house, he was utterly exhausted. The Hirshes had switched to an unlisted phone number nearly three months ago. Since then, Joshua and Simon had not seen very much of each other. As the sun dropped behind the Alabama hills, Simon stepped up to the Hirsh's front porch, cupped his hands above his eyes, and looked through the front window.

"My God!" gasped Simon. "They're gone too!"

Tired and hungry, the young boy slipped across the front porch and sat on their small wooden swing.

"Oh, Lord, where are the Hirshes?"

After about twenty minutes, the answer came to Simon as he drifted off to sleep: The Hirshes had become watchmen.

Driving down Main Street, Matt and Sam realized that the friendly atmosphere of their cozy little town had disappeared. The busy crowds at the newly erected NWC stations and the constant supervision by ID agents had replaced the once peaceful summer days.

"Seems like everything is right on schedule, huh, Sam?" Matt opened his Bible and read, "Then they will deliver you up to tribulation and kill you, and you will be hated by all nations for my name's sake. See I have told you beforehand."[1]

Over the past few years, the sons' beliefs concerning the events that will precede the Lord's coming were totally rejected by their father. Even so, the heated debates had really inspired Ashley, their mother, to search the Scriptures for herself. Pulling into the driveway, the young men fervently prayed for the Holy Spirit to supernaturally reveal the truth to their father concerning the antichrist and his evil plan to deceive the world.

"Hey, folks, we're home!" the sons said as they received hugs from their parents. "Matt and I are ready for a little R and R, and Mom has some serious laundry work ahead of her," kidded Sam.

The young men immediately joined their parents for a home-cooked meal of meatloaf, black-eyed peas, and mashed potatoes. Compared to dorm food, this was a real treat.

Their father spoke first, "Ya'll won't believe this, but I've got some great news. This past Tuesday we, as a family, received an early sign-up date from the local ID office."

"Really, Dad?" asked a tense Sam.

"It's kind of a privilege they've granted to the members of the Bethany Ministers Association. By signing up immediately, we'll miss the heavy lines the ID officials are anticipating," explained a thankful Tom. "So, since you're home for summer break, I thought we could go as a family this Saturday and register for our IDs. What do you say?" asked Tom while pouring gravy over his mashed potatoes.

Matt slowly put down his fork, his eyes focusing on Sam and then on his mother, Ashley.

"Dad, after much prayer, Sam and I have decided not to register for our personal IDs."

"Well, that's your choice. If you want to register yourselves, you're certainly of age."

"No, Dad, I'm afraid you don't quite understand," Matt carefully replied. "We believe taking the ID is a form of worshipping Wolfgang Hendrick as god. We believe he is the antichrist!"

As he continued, his father attempted to interrupt, but Matt would not allow it.

"No, Dad, this time you need to listen to what we have to say. After much prayer and study, we've decided that we will never register for the mark of the beast or worship his image!"

The young men knew what they believed. They had thoroughly thought out their future and the decisions that they would be forced to make.

"Sam and I have both withdrawn from school. After we get you and Mom settled in one of the Watchman Camps, we plan to enlist in the resistance movement and become watchmen!"

Matt didn't need to go any further; the damage had been done.

"Have you both lost your minds?" shouted Tom. "If you want to give up everything we have worked for, the calling that God has placed on your lives, the respect of family and ministry friends, your reputation within our denomination, your security for your future, to follow this watchman cult, go ahead, but leave your mother and me out of it!" Tom slid his chair back and quickly turned to leave the room.

"Wait, Tom!" insisted Ashley, who had prayed for boldness to stand firm. "The boys are right. The World ID System is clearly a form of worship that our Lord Jesus wants none of us to be a part of."

Quickly turning toward Ashley in anger, Tom was immediately blocked by the presence of his two sons.

"That's right, Tom, I won't be registering either."

"Do you all realize what you're doing?" yelled Tom, while pointing an accusing finger in their faces. "Without a personal ID, you will eventually be treated like common criminals. Just refusing to register opens you up to arrest. Sooner or later the ID force will track you down like animals because you refuse to obey the law. How can you willingly break the commandments of God by choosing to follow this cult?"

The stress of the moment was almost too much for Tom's high blood pressure. Ashley stepped around her boys and embraced him as tears began to fall down each of their faces. "God will be with us, Tom. He will take care of us just like He always has."

The experienced preacher was so upset; he was unable to discern the power of God radiating from Ashley's face.

"Well, I need some time to pray over my decision," replied a tired Tom.

As their father retired to his study, Matt and Sam cleared the table while Ashley washed the dishes.

Tom sat motionless in his dimly lit study. It was here that he met with God to write his sermons. Kneeling to pray, it seemed as if his whole ministry was on trial.

"It's a test!" Tom whispered to himself. "That's it. This is a test from God!"

After Ashley served Matt and Sam some homemade peanut butter cookies and French vanilla shakes, she slowly made her way up the backstairs to Tom's study.

While opening his study door, Ashley softly asked, "Tom, would you like to have some cookies with the boys in the family room?"

"What's taking Mom so long?" asked Sam, downing the rest of his milkshake.

Suddenly Matt felt a prompting from the Holy Spirit. Something was wrong.

"Hey, Mom!" he yelled out, while bounding up the backstairs to Tom's study.

Stepping through the doorway, a shocked Matt could hear his mother sobbing almost uncontrollably, as she lay prostrate across the floor. Leaning down to comfort his mother, he saw a small note slip from her fingers.

"What's wrong, Mom?" whispered Matt.

"He's gone, son! You'd better hurry. Your father has gone to take the mark of the beast!"

Matt froze, unable to breathe. The words from his mother felt like a painful slap across his face. It would take less than a minute to make it to his car.

By the time he reached the bottom of the stairs, Matt yelled, "Let's go, Sam!"

The two watchmen had just received their first assignment, their own father.

As Matt and Sam drove past the last ID station in Bethany, their hearts were pierced with the realization that their father had taken the deceiver's mark. After completing another lap around the eastside ID station, a nervous Matt confessed, "I don't see him, Sam."

The moon was bright as the town celebrated its annual Summer Rodeo. It was family night, which always featured the popular chili cook-off. The cotton candy machine was working over-time, while kids under ten lined up to see if they could hit Cowboy Clyde with a banana cream pie. A recently married couple had just arrived to claim a raffle prize of an all-expense paid vacation to Hilton Head, South Carolina.

As the boys drove by, Matt slowly uttered, "For as the days before the flood, they were eating and drinking, marrying and giving in marriage, until the day that Noah entered the ark, and did not know until the flood came and took them all away, so also will the coming of the Son of Man be."[2]

Turning left on the next street, Sam saw a figure of a man slumped down on an old park bench.

"It's Dad!" Sam screamed.

After Matt hit the brakes, Sam jumped out of the car and sprinted toward the old park bench. Reaching his dad, an indescribable fear filled his heart.

"Did you register, Dad?" he asked, his heart beating furiously.

"No, son, I just couldn't do it."

Matt arrived just in time to hear his father's words. Tears of relief filled both boys' eyes.

"Dad, now more than ever we've got to take a stand," challenged Matt. "Jesus is calling each of us to stand firm until He comes back for us."

"Praise you, Lord," uttered the relieved preacher.

"Dad, remember when I was a young boy, and you were pastoring at Christ Cathedral?" asked Sam.

Tom nodded.

"Well, one day I came home after an argument with one of my class-mates. It was about something in the Bible that really scared me. So I asked you if everything you taught was true. Deep down, I knew that my dad would always tell me the truth."

Sam and Matt both smiled.

"Well, you really surprised me that day when you said, 'No, son, the only person who is one hundred percent right is God.'"

"Yes, Sam, I remember it like it was yesterday," said Tom.

"Well, that's what the Holy Spirit is saying to you right now, Dad! Just because you taught a pre-tribulation rapture doesn't mean that everything you taught was wrong. Some of the greatest ministers that ever preached were wrong on certain points of theology. I mean, what about Charles Spurgeon? Isn't he one of your favorite preachers? Look at how many lives he touched with his ministry, yet he taught that a Christian could never deny the Lord!"

"You know what, Sam? You're absolutely right. These past few hours I've been more transparent with God than in my entire life. I truly believe that the Holy Spirit was waiting for me to humble myself and repent so that He could show me the truth."

"What do you mean?" asked Matt while each son took a seat atop the park bench.

"I believe some call it the Messiah complex," replied a reflective Tom. "You see, when God opens a door of ministry for you, you can sense His anointing to accomplish that specific goal. It's very exciting at first. Gradually, before I realized it, instead of relying on God, I began to live off the experiences of the past. Eventually, the need for God's anointing became secondary. By going through the motions, I could still see believers growing, but God was not being glorified because the control was in my hands. When people sought God for answers, I believed that God had called me to be his spokesman, so I would be the one with all the answers. Actually, it seemed so easy at times that I became blinded by my pride and by the constant compliments from those to whom I ministered."

"The approval of man can really be a trap, can't it, Dad?" asked a curious Sam.

"Well, to be honest, when I first arrived at the ID station, I just sat in the car for a long, long time." Shaking his head in disgust, Tom softly confessed, "You see, I was shocked because I finally realized I would rather register than have to admit I was wrong."

There was a sober realization of how close Tom Bray had come to separation from God and his family for eternity.

His voice cracking with emotion, he slowly uttered, "Just imagine how many believers don't even believe in the mark of the beast due to what I've taught. I owe a lot to each of you for your willingness to stand up to my threats. You stood for Jesus no matter what I threw at you. Your mother was even willing to risk our marriage for what she knew to be right." Ashamed of his actions, Tom quietly acknowledged, "She was far more courageous than I ever was."

"C'mon, Dad," encouraged a smiling Sam, "let's go tell, Mom!"

As Tom and his sons rushed by the ID station to get to their cars, they noticed that the lines to register stretched all the way around the block. A man in line whispered to one of his friends, "Isn't that Tom Bray, the famous prophecy teacher?"

"It sure is," replied his friend. "He must've come to register with his two sons. You know, our church has been blessed so much by his teaching on the end times. Remember when the churches were having so much fuss over the timing of the rapture?"

"Sure do. I so much appreciate Pastor Brown for having Reverend Bray come and teach his three-day prophecy seminar. God's plan for the end times became so clear to me. Even my twelve-year-old niece could understand it."

"You can say that again. We are so blessed to have Bible teachers like Tom Bray who are willing to speak the truth no matter what the consequences."

"Next please. May I have your name and . . ."

While lying prostrate across the Oriental rug in Tom's study, Ashley prayed from the depths of her heart.

"There are so many things I want to confess to you, Lord. I now see that I've learned to go through the motions. Everything always seemed so easy as we moved from one assignment to the next. You have always provided for us, protected us, and led us, but we took it all for granted. Oh, Lord, please forgive me for my pride."

As she prayed, Ashley could barely confess her sins that she knew were very real and very evil. The approval of man had always been a top priority in the Bray household. The competition even among their peers created walls that prevented men of God and their families from building each other up with God's love. The depth of her sobbing was anchored in the reality that she would never be able to go back and make it right. Bowing to pray, Ashley could see flash backs, situations in which she could have made a difference for the Kingdom of God but chose to let it pass.

"Oh, Father, I commit my loving husband into your arms of protection. For all the times that my disobedience and selfishness grieved You, I ask your forgiveness. From now on, I put my faith and my life in You and Your Word alone. I have played games for way too long, and now the eternal destiny of my husband is being weighed in the balance. Jesus, I beg you; please don't let Tom take the mark. Please, Lord, intervene before it's too late."

Almost immediately, Ashley could feel God's forgiveness, followed by an overwhelming peace. The words from the Lord came to her mind ever so softly, "Let not your heart be troubled; you believe in God, believe also in Me."[3]

"Mom, Mom, we're home!" yelled Sam.

Jumping up, a strengthened Ashley ran down the backstairs to the kitchen door. While looking out anxiously, Tom quietly slipped through the front door and caught her waist from behind. As he turned her around in his arms, she knew deep inside of her heart that God had answered her prayers.

"Thomas Nelson Bray, you are a mess!" exclaimed the preacher's wife, weeping with joy.

As Matt and Sam looked on smiling, Tom clutched his beautiful wife close to his heart and whispered, "Oh, thank you so much, Lord, for opening my eyes to Your truth."

Chapter 31

Jake's Dilemma

And I will pray to the Father,
and He will give you another Helper,
that He may abide with you forever.
John 14:16

"How many times do I have to tell you, Jessie?"

The frustration between Jessie and her parents was just about ready to explode into a major fight.

"But Daddy, my friends believe . . ."

"Hold it right there, young lady. Your mother and I have had enough of this religious propaganda your so-called friends are feeding you. What do you want from us anyway? You know we do not believe in these right-wing interpretations of the end of the world! Don't you see, little one, that no one really knows what the future will bring us?"

"It's a crazy world, Jess," interjected her mother as she lit a cigarette. "Your father and I thought the sixties was a rough time. Families were fighting over long hair, drugs, sex, and rock music. But things today are even more confusing than they were back then."

"Don't forget the college riots we used to get caught in the middle of," added Jessie's father with a smile on his face.

"Are you kidding? I could never forget that, darling. After all, that's where you and I first met."

"Really, Mom?" You actually met Daddy at a college riot?"

"Jess, do you mean your daddy and I have never shared with you how we first got hooked up?"

"No, Mom. There are a lot of memories we as a family have never taken the time to share."

"Well, your father and I lived pretty sheltered lives until we arrived on the University of Alabama campus for our freshman year. It was like stepping into an exciting new world with no rules or regulations. We had the freedom to embrace new ideas. Our eyes were opened to see the injustices being promoted by those in power. We witnessed leaders who didn't care about the people but only about the furthering of their own agendas. Those injustices gave us a cause, a purpose in life that was worth fighting for."

"It's amazing, Jess," said her dad. "After all this time, I still remember seeing your mother standing on a street corner in the middle of a riot across from the ROTC building. She had absolutely no fear on her face."

"I was scared to death, dear," laughed Jessie's mother.

"Well, I couldn't tell. Anyway, I was really attracted to your mother. What a brave woman. She wasn't afraid to stand up for what she believed in, even when the police shot tear gas at us. A lot of people just ran away, but your mother stood her ground."

"Sounds like you both were willing to sacrifice for what you believed in," Jessie quietly said.

"That was many years ago, Jess. Times have changed."

"And how is that, Mom?"

"Well, to be perfectly honest, we were a very small minority trying to convince a huge majority to open their eyes to the truth. We thought we could influence our country, but in reality, most of our pleas just fell on deaf ears. I imagine that to a lot of people many of the things that we did looked pretty fanatical. In hindsight, who knows if we made any difference at all?"

"You know what, Mom? That's just the point I'm trying to make. It doesn't matter what the majority believes. What matters is whether or not your convictions and beliefs are the truth."

"Yeah, and your truth may not be my truth," added her father with absolutely no emotion.[1]

"But, Daddy, what about the mark of the . . ."

"Oh, no! Here she goes again on this wild conspiracy about the evil antichrist and his one-world government. Give it a rest, Jessie. That story has gotten pretty old, and I for one am extremely tired of hearing about it. I'm sorry, honey. What you really need to learn is to stop pushing your beliefs on others. Honestly, some things are just not worth fighting for."

"He's right, Jess. Besides, by this time next year, everyone will be subject to the NWC financial system, and everything will be perfect. No more wars. No more famines. A peaceful world where everyone is safe to be his or her own person! Who could ask for anything better than that?"

"It's a new world, Jess, and the best is yet to come," her father cheerfully predicted.

Jessie grimaced, more confused than ever. After a long pause, she bowed her head and whispered, "I hope you're right."

✳

"Jake! Jake! Can you hear me?"

"I'm out here, Mom," he yelled from the back of the garage, where he kept his weights. "I just started my bench press routine."

"Your father will be home in approximately twenty minutes. We need to be ready to go downtown as soon as he changes into his civilian clothes."

"But Mom, Jessie and I were planning to go to our first Bible study tonight."

"Sorry, son, your father advised us over two weeks ago that we would be registering for our ID numbers tonight. You know how he is. If we try to change plans on him now, you know what'll happen."

Jake knew she was right. As he ran up the stairs to change clothes, the demonic spirit of compromise arrived through the window over Jake's bed.

Opening the door to his bedroom, Jake could feel something super-natural touch his heart. The Spirit of God had come in response to someone's prayer. As he paced back and forth in his room, trying to figure out what was going on, the two voices spoke to him subtly but clearly.

"You don't want to disappoint your father now, do you, Jake?" asked the evil spirit. "Besides, you're young, and this is a new world. Your whole life is ahead of you. Tonight is just the first step for you to be on your own!"

The voice of the demon was pushing him, tugging on him with a kind of manipulation that could be felt but not seen.

"What should I do?" Jake muttered to himself.

Suddenly the encouraging words of Luke, Jake's good friend, came to mind, "Therefore, if anyone is in Christ, he is a new creation; old things have passed away; behold, all things have become new."[2]

The Holy Spirit began to gently speak to his heart, "Fear not, Jake. The Lord will lead you and guide you as you follow Him. He will take away your fears and doubts. Today is your day for salvation."

"Be careful, Jake, you don't want your family and friends to think that you're some fanatic, do you?" whispered the spirit of compromise. "Think of all the good times you're going to have to give up if you refuse to take your ID number. Hey, what's so wrong with obeying the law anyway? Look at all the people who have registered. They're all doing just fine."

"Jake, 'if you love Jesus, you will keep His commandments. Jesus will pray to the Father, and He will give you another Helper, that he may abide with you forever.'"[3]

"Your dad is coming up the stairs; you'd better hurry," prompted the spirit of compromise.

"Jake, are you ready yet?"

"Come on in, Dad. I'd like to talk with you for a second."

"What's wrong, son?" asked his father, taking a seat on the floor with his back leaning against Jake's bed.

Jake sat at his desk and tried to collect his thoughts.

"Dad, all my life you have taught me that if I applied myself and lived by a proper set of rules, I could achieve anything I wanted to do."

"That's correct, son."

"Well, this past year I've made some really great friends at Lakeview. Now, I know I gave you and Mom a hard time when we first arrived here. I want you to know that I'm really sorry about the way I acted."

His dad smiled and said, "You forget that I was an army brat too. Believe me, son, I understand how you felt. Besides, you grew from the challenge of reaching out and making new friends."

"That's just the point, Dad. Most of them are gone."

The look on Jake's face was one of deep pain, like someone who had just lost hope.

"Jake, that's life. People move for many reasons. Look at us as an example. We've been forced to move five times in nine years."

"No, Dad, I'm not talking about moving to another city, another state. I'm trying to tell you they've all vanished."

"I'm afraid I'm not getting your point, son?" replied his suspicious father.

"Dad, listen to me. Luke, Hope, Whitney, Ned, Drew—they all just disappeared right when the New World Coalition took over. You know, when everyone started to register for their ID numbers."

"Do you mean to tell me your friends are part of this right-wing conspiracy cult hiding people in the hills of Alabama? How ridiculous!"

"That's just it, Dad. They're taking a stand for what they believe in. Just like you taught me to do!"

"Son, I don't want to talk about this anymore. These people have nothing to do with us. Their parents are irresponsible lawbreakers. I don't want you to have anything to do with kids that are so deceived. Is that clear, son? Besides, I doubt that any of them will ever be heard of again."

Sergeant Jamison stood to his feet and faced his son. His eyes looked stern. Jake groaned inwardly. He could tell by his father's stance that he was about to receive another lecture on personal responsibility.

"Jake, a soldier is sworn to uphold the Constitution of the United States of America and to obey the orders of his superiors. The Congress, with the approval of our president, the commander in chief of the Armed Forces, has agreed to become a member of the New World Coalition. Last week on national television our president shared that sometimes you have to implement desperate measures in order to achieve one's goals. I support the United States and the president. And what I support, I expect my whole family to support. Is that understood?"

"But Dad . . ."

"Son, I'm sorry, but that's the way it is. You should have never gotten involved with this religious click at school. Your mother and I know how convincing they can sound. But it's all conjecture. Even the pastors from the Bethany Ministers Association stated that a person's individual ID number has nothing to do with Bible prophecy. I read about it yesterday in the *Bethany Herald*."

"So, you've heard about some of it?" asked an excited Jake.

"Why, of course. Our company commander is worried sick about his son. Seems that Brock went AWOL about five months ago. From what our captain said, Brock refused to register with his family. The whole scenario is pretty sad. And just think, it all could have been avoided if his family had gone by the rules."

"What rules, Dad?"

"They should have briefed their son on the responsibility of every American supporting our president. If you break the rules, you suffer the consequences. It's that simple. Are you ready to go, son?"

"I guess, Dad," replied a reluctant Jake.

"Okay, then. I'll meet you and your mother out back. Let's first register, and then we'll go to Max's for some barbecue ribs."

The sergeant looked very pleased that his talk with his son had gone so well. Five minutes later, as they were backing out of the driveway, Jake could hear the phone ringing in his bedroom.

"C'mon, Jake, pick up the phone," said Jessie.

"What's wrong, Jess? Isn't he home?"

"I guess not, Mom. That's strange. We were supposed to go to Bible study tonight. Funny, it's not like Jake to forget something he was looking forward to. Hey, Mom?"

"Yes, dear?"

"Would you be mad at me if I passed on dinner tonight? I promised to give Jake a ride to the Bible study."

"Can't it wait, Jess? Dinner will be ready in ten minutes. Besides, I thought you said he wasn't there."

"I guess so," replied a disappointed Jessie. "But maybe he is there. Maybe he just couldn't get to the phone for some reason."

"Tell you what. Why don't you take your father's car over there and see? If he's there, bring him back for dinner."

"That sounds great, Mom," said the tall brunette as she grabbed the car keys and headed out the backdoor. "I'll just be a few minutes, I promise."

Jessie's mom just smiled and said to herself, "Yeah, I've heard that before."

The ID station that the Jamison's picked was jammed with college students who were home for Thanksgiving break. After his dad pulled into the last available parking space, Jake suddenly remembered that he had forgotten to call Jessie to tell her he wouldn't be able to make the Bible study.

"Hey, Dad, since there's going to be a wait, do you think I could use the phone across the street? I need to talk with Jessie."

"Okay, son, but make it quick. We don't want to lose our place in line."

"That's strange," thought Jessie, ringing the doorbell for the fifth time. The Jamison home was dark, and the car was gone. "Didn't Jake ask me for a ride to the Bible study?" Jessie thought to herself. Pulling out of the driveway, she sensed that her good friend was in danger.

✳

Jessie's mom had just removed the roast from the oven when the phone rang.

"Yes, Jake, how are you doing? Did Jess catch you? Are you coming over for dinner?"

"I'm afraid not, Mrs. Hyatt. Is Jessie there?"

"Sorry, Jake, she left about ten minutes ago for your house. You must have just missed her."

"Well, thanks for the invite, Mrs. Hyatt, but my family has decided to register tonight," Jake replied rather nervously.

"Well, good for you, Jake!"

"Thanks Mrs. Hyatt. Uh-oh, I can hear my mom calling. Can you tell Jessie I'll call her when I get home?" Not waiting for an answer, Jake hung up and made his way back to his place in line.

"Did you get her, Jake?"

"No, it looks like we're playing phone tag."

"I'm sorry, son, but we all agreed we would register tonight."

"Yeah, I know, Dad. Everything's cool."

"Hey, Mom, I'm home," yelled Jessie.

"Dinner's ready," her mom replied while taking the roast out of the oven. "Why don't you wash up," she added without bothering to look up. "Oh, Jake called while you were out and said he can't make it tonight."

"Did he happen to say why?" asked a concerned Jessie.

"What do you think, Jess? Do you think we should use the neat candles you bought for me at last week's garage sale?"

"Mom, please."

"Sorry, dear. What did you say?"

"I said, did Jake say why he wasn't coming?"

"Uh, yes. Yes, he did. He said that his family was registering tonight. Come to think of it, your father and I also think that signing up early is a good idea. Now, our official sign-up date doesn't come till . . ."

Jessie spun and bolted for the door.

"Jessie! What's wrong?"

Reaching the car, she knew it would take at least five minutes for her to reach the nearest ID station.

"Oh, please, God, let it be the right station," prayed Jessie. Turning the corner on to Vaughn road, she whispered, "Please warn Jake, God."

Pulling up in front of the station, she frantically scanned the crowd. "Where is he?" she wondered. Then she spotted the Jamison family stepping up to register. They were next in line! Rolling the window down on the passenger's side, a desperate Jessie yelled out, "Jake! Jake! Hey, Jake! Come here for a minute. We need to talk!"

Immediately, the young man could sense the urgency in his best friend's voice.

"Dad, hold on a second. I need to talk to Jessie."

"Sorry, son, she'll have to wait. We are next up."

"But, Dad, it'll only take a second, okay?"

"Jake . . ."

"Look, Dad, I'm really having some doubts about . . ."

"Doubts about what?" snapped his father. "Don't you remember you gave me your word?"

"Besides," whispered the spirit of compromise into Jake's ear, "it will only take a second to register."

"Next please. May I have your name and social security number?"

Stepping up to the main desk, Jake's father turned towards his son, "Jake, do you want to go first so that you can talk with Jessie?"

The young man wanted to do what was right, but not for his country, his family, or even for Jessie. He wanted to do it for himself.

"Jake, your father asked you a question."

Jessie knew that it was now or never; she pulled up in front of the station and frantically honked the horn. Without any warning, Jake bolted for the car.

Before Jake's father could even react, he felt his wife grip his hand. She whispered, "Let him go, honey. He needs to find his own path."

Jake's father took a deep breath, held it, and then said, "My wife and I will be registering today. My son wants to do it later this week with his friends."

As the car disappeared out of sight, the demon of compromise seethed with anger.

"Oh, so close," cursed the evil spirit.

✳

As Jessie pulled up in front of the Jamison house, she turned and looked at her best friend.

"What are we going to do now, Jake?"

"I have no idea."

"If your folks registered, then that means the ID agents will be paying you a visit."

"I know. I know. Everything is happening so fast."

"So, what are we going to do?"

"Well, before we can make any more moves, we need to have some answers."

"Who are you going to ask, Jake? Everyone who believes that the ID system is evil has disappeared."

"Not everyone," said Jake.

"Who do you have in mind?"

"Well, I don't know if it's true, but I heard a rumor at school that Lance and Lee Ryan are secretly part of the underground resistance movement."

"Well, okay," said Jessie. "But it's gonna take a little time for me to get my stuff together. Avoiding my parents isn't going to be easy either. Tell you what, I'll meet you behind Max's in two hours."

"Sounds like a plan," replied Jake.

CHAPTER 32

THEY CALLED HIM THE MOLE

By this all will know that you are My disciples,
if you have love for one another.
John 13:35

Lydia, Jason Wylie's secretary, calmly locked the front door to the office and placed a closed sign in the window. As Jason closed the blinds, Lydia lifted the phone and punched in a number. Jason then took the phone and punched in one of his own. Neither knew the number the other used. As he hit the last digit, the wall to the left of the lawyer's desk silently slid open, revealing several THX computers. He went to one and set it up to receive encrypted data. Lydia sat down in front of another, which had a webcam on the top of it. She stared at the camera as she brought it out of standby. Once it acknowledged her, Lydia opened a folder and began to enter names of believers into the special database. These believers would be eventually routed to Watchmen Camps all over the Southeast. Jason, whose code name was the Mole, had been anxiously waiting for this moment. He and Lydia would be receiving top-secret information concerning the resistance movement for the southeastern section of the United States.

For many believers in the South, the man they affectionately called the Mole had almost become a legend. There were so many stories about Jason's narrow escapes that it had become pretty difficult to determine whether they were fact or fiction. One time he calmly directed three ID agents to another part of town while he hid twenty-three overcomers in his office. As a defense attorney, he once represented several underage resisters. After the case was presented, Jason persuaded the judge to give them another chance to register for their ID numbers. When the judge released them to the nearest ID station, they, of course, made an escape and safely reached the Pensacola Watchman Camp. But the story that really earned the respect of the saints was the one in which Jason risked his own life by interrupting the physical beating of three underage resisters by two drunken ID agents. The one they called the Mole stood up to the agents and convinced them to let the children go back to their families.[1]

Soon after mandatory registration went into affect, the persecution of believers skyrocketed. Bible prophecy was being fulfilled almost daily as God continued to reveal his end-time sequence of events. For Jason and other watchmen, the handwriting was on the wall.

After receiving their official sign-up date, Kevin Collins and his wife each decided to take the day off and register at the nearby Eastside ID Station. Pulling into the parking lot, the couple quickly noticed that the lines were shorter than usual.

"Hello Pastor Brown, Mrs. Brown," greeted a smiling Kevin from the back of the line. "You see, dear," he whispered as he softly nudged his wife. She quickly turned and smiled, noticing several friends from church in line to register. Reverend Elmer Dyer was also in line but didn't look too happy about it.

At the first window, people were required to identify themselves by producing a social security number and a picture ID. After a positive identification, each person would then move to the second window and take an oath of allegiance to Wolfgang Hendrick and his New World Coalition. As soon as the oath was completed, the World ID Number would be applied to people's right hand or forehead, depending upon their preference. Anyone under the age of nineteen was required to have written approval from a parent or guardian.

Kevin watched closely as Pastor Brown and Pastor Dyer calmly received their NWC ID number on their right hands. Very subtly, a false peace seemed to come over Kevin. He could hear Pastor Dyer laughing nervously over a funny story that Pastor Brown had just shared. "Look at them," reflected the former Bethany Assembly deacon. "These pastors love God. They are faithful to their families, and they've helped so many believers over the years." Stepping forward to the first window, Kevin wondered why he had ever had any doubts about such a simple, painless procedure. It would take less than two minutes.

As he extended his hand into the ID machine, a young man in an old yellow Chevy drove by the ID station and yelled, "Don't take the ID number. It's the mark of the beast!"

Before the agents could react, the young man sped away.

"Thank you very much for your cooperation, Mr. and Mrs. Collins," said the agent.

It had happened so quickly that Kevin and his wife hadn't even noticed.

"I'm telling you, honey. They're tracking our every move."

"So when you answered the phone, there was no reply?"

"Not a peep!" answered a nervous Lee.

In his heart, Lance knew that he and Lee were definitely at risk. While most of their Christian friends had secretly made their way to the Watchman Camps over the past six months, the Ryans elected to stay in order to save as many as possible. It hadn't been an easy decision for Lance. Lee was the love of his life. Nevertheless, when the youth pastor prayed, all he could see were faces of young kids searching for the truth. After much prayer and fasting together, the young couple finally grasped the calling God had placed upon their lives. The Holy Spirit would lead them to children whose parents were just about to take the mark of the beast. Lance and Lee would literally snatch young ones from the jaws of damnation. They didn't have any children of their own, but in the coming months, they would become the spiritual parents of hundreds of children.

CHAPTER 33

LIGHT VERSUS DARKNESS

Here is the patience of the saints;
here are those who keep the commandments of God
and the faith of Jesus.
Revelation 14:12

Watchman prayer groups continued to cry out for the conviction of the Holy Spirit to fall on those who were in line to register. A family that had just arrived at a Watchman Camp in Jackson, Mississippi, joined other prayer warriors in interceding for children who were on the run from ID agents.

Warren knew that the Lord had supernaturally led his family to this specific camp. The Watchman Camp near Birmingham had received way too much traffic. It would have created a risk that could have been disastrous. Even so, his heart was breaking with remorse over the mix up that had left their young daughter behind.

"Oh, Lord, how could we have ever lost her?" cried Joyce, her mother.

Suddenly, as Warren was praying, he could sense a cloud of oppression coming against his daughter.

"In the name of Jesus, I rebuke the spirits of compromise and lying away from my precious one," he called out in a loud voice. "Wherever she is, Lord, I know You are faithful to protect her from the evil one's lies!"

At that very moment, Dwayne and Gloria Pressley and their two daughters were driving in their new silver Land Rover near the corner of Vaughn and Cherry. Their destination was the ID station on the east side of town. The NWC ID stations were set up in every city in America. For the convenience of the citizens, all stations were now open twenty-four hours a day. The chairman of the NWC ID system in America had just announced that families of four or more could receive a two-hundred-dollar bonus for registering before the end of the month.

"Just think, honey. With this bonus, we can refinish that old chair that was given to us by your grandmother last summer," said Dwayne beaming.

Stepping to the back of the line, Dwaynes' daughters spotted friends from Lakeview High School.

"Hey, there's Cindy Johnson. Now that's weird."

"What's weird, Rachel?" asked a curious Dwayne.

"She's alone. I guess her parents signed up already and just gave her a permission slip. Hey, Cindy!" Rachel yelled over the crowd.

Cindy didn't move a muscle. With tears running down her already red cheeks, she pretended to look forward, her shoulders beginning to shake ever so slightly.

An older lady standing behind the Pressleys leaned over and spoke to Rachel.

"Young lady, I don't believe you've heard the recent news report out of Washington DC. Last night Congress voted in favor of dropping the nineteen-year-old age requirement."

"Really," replied Rachel. "When does it take affect?"

"Immediately," answered the grandmother.

Cindy's tears began to subside as she got closer to the front. For some, the first impression of the ID stations seemed very scary, like a scene out of a *Brave New World* novel.

"Good morning, may I have your name and social security number, please?" asked the ID agent.

"My name is Cindy Johnson, and my social security number is 901-74-2303."

"Miss Johnson, our records show that you are sixteen. Is that correct?"

"Yes, ma'am."

"You have a father and a mother. Is that correct?" the agent suspiciously asked while reviewing her current computer update.

"Yes, ma'am."

"Our ID files have no record of your parents. Do they have a legitimate reason for not registering?"

"I don't think, uh, I don't believe they will," replied the cheerleader while almost choking on her words.

Lowering her reading glasses, the agent asked, "And the reason?"

"They plan to refuse on the grounds that they believe the ID number is the mark of the beast," replied the young teenager, who immediately felt better after telling the truth.

"Is this some sort of joke?" the agent blurted out. "Young lady, do you know that this is a mandatory law, strictly enforced by our New World Coalition Security Force?"

"Yes, ma'am."

"Do your parents still reside at 449 Fulton Road?"

Suddenly an invisible demonic cloud seemed to engulf Cindy as she fought to keep her composure.

"No, I believe they live somewhere else now."

"In order to register you, I must have your parent's current address and phone number, Miss Johnson."

After a long pause, someone in line yelled out, "Can we move a little faster? I have to pick up my nephew for his baseball game."

"Miss Johnson, are you okay?" asked the agent.

"Yes, I'm all right, thank you," she responded as she wiped away her tears.

Before Cindy could reply to the agent's question, the Spirit of God fell on her, and the demons of compromise and lying departed.

"I've got their new address in my car. Can you give me a minute to go and get it?"

"Well, make it quick," ordered the agent.

Cindy stepped out of line, crossed over Vaughn Road, and unlocked the front door to her parent's car.

"Hey, Cindy, it's me, Rachel! What are you doing after you . . ."

Cindy wasn't listening. She had other plans. Jumping into the front seat of her folk's Chevy Blazer, she started the engine and tore out of the temporary parking lot.

The head agent, who immediately spotted her, hit the button to the sirens. With sirens blaring, two agents on motorcycle took off after the under-age resister.

"Daddy! What's going on?" screamed Rachel.

Because registration had become mandatory the week before, newly installed sirens were added to warn agents of those who refused to register. The loudness, which hurt the ears of anyone within twenty yards, also acted as a scare tactic to keep the people in line.

"It's okay, girls; everything's all right," assured Dwayne, hugging both Rachel and Anna at the same time.

"Next, please. May we have your name . . ."

"It's okay, Rachel; we're almost there."

"But, Daddy, why did Cindy run away, and why did those agents chase after her?"

Dwayne motioned for his wife and two daughters to form a small circle.

"To be perfectly blunt, I don't know the Johnson family very well. I know they are faithful Christians, and that's about it.[1] I guess Cindy is unsure about Hendrick and his plan for the world. But I'm sure his plan has nothing to do with the Bible. I think it has everything to do with keeping our country, as well as the entire world, from going belly up. We cannot afford to panic! I'm not prepared to lose my job, my reputation, and everything we've worked for as a family over what some religious fanatics call the mark of the beast. Let's not be deceived. Doesn't the Bible say that Jesus will rescue His own before the tribulation period? Before the antichrist appears?"

"Next please," said an agent while motioning for the Pressley family to step up.

"My name is Dwayne Pressley, and my social security number is 545-31-1302."

"Thank you, Mr. Pressley. Is this your family?"

"Yes, this is my wife and my two daughters. We have come tonight to sign up for the two-hundred-dollar family bonus, please."

"Of course, sir. May I please have your family's names and social security numbers?"

It was only five minutes later that Dwayne turned the Land Rover out of the parking lot. Rachel blurted out, "I want to go home!"

"Sure, honey. I just need to drop by the bank to cash this check. There's nothing worse than being stiffed by the government!" joked the relieved father.

"Momma, I don't feel good. I feel . . . empty."

Reaching over to comfort her daughter, Gloria knew that something was very wrong. "What do you mean, Rachel?"

"I feel exactly the same way I felt when I was thirteen," she quietly replied.[1] "You know, Momma, before I became a Christian!"

The silence in the car seemed to last forever. As Dwayne turned the corner of Vaughn and Cherry, he could hear the loudspeaker blaring in the background.

"Next please, may I have your name and social security number, please?"

CHAPTER 34

THE FIFTH SEAL: SOULS UNDER THE ALTAR

When He opened the fifth seal,
I saw under the altar
the souls of those who had been slain
for the word of God
and for the testimony they held.
Revelation 6:9

The seven-sealed scroll lay before the Father and His Son. The first four seals had been broken. Standing to the right of the throne, the Lamb of God broke the fifth seal. The angels present were filled with sadness when the next event was proclaimed. The altar in heaven would soon be filled with souls of those who would be killed for their testimony of Jesus Christ. When the number of saints that were to be killed was complete, then the end would come.[1]

The shock of it was almost too much to bear. Family members wept as the ID agents dragged the young rebel away. Within the hour, the dramatic news had reached the ears and eyes of the world.

"This is *CNN World News*, and I'm Gerhard Wimmer, reporting live from Munich, Germany. We have just received word that a nineteen-year-old university student named Eric Bahman was arrested earlier in the day for not having a World ID Number. He was taken to a Munich ID station by authorities, where he still refused to register. The spokesman for the NWC reported that Bahman was repeatedly warned of the outcome should he continue to refuse. At 1:02 p.m., the head of the German ID force ordered the young man's execution. After it was carried out, the NWC announced that no refusals to register would be tolerated. In the future, anyone who refuses to register, regardless of age, race, or religious preference, will be executed on the spot!"

Watching the live broadcast on TV, Wolfgang asked one of his aides, "Was Bahman a follower of the One in Heaven?"

"Yes, my lord. I believe they reported that he was studying to be a minister."

"So, he was a follower," said Hendrick. "Excellent! He will make a perfect example for others who dare resist my plan. When the media announces his execution, followers all over the world will run like scared rabbits." The evil dictator erupted in mock laughter. "Yes, they will run, mind you, right to my ID stations!"

The antichrist made his way down the hall to meet with news reporters, thankful the evil spirits of this world had done their jobs.

"Now Satan, my lord, will speak through me to stop what the One from above has prophesied will come to pass," the evil leader whispered to himself. "That's right," he snickered. "If enough followers deny their God, then the world will remain in the hands of my master."

✳

The president of the United States and his advisors had badly misjudged the reaction of the American people. As news of the execution traveled the airways, the nation's capital was buried under a deluge of phone calls, e-mails, and faxes from the outraged public. In utter disbelief, the world was given the opportunity to watch a taped relay of the execution. Within hours, demonstrations erupted throughout the world.

"Mr. President, is this what you're going to do with our boys?" shouted an angry eighty-eight-year-old grandmother during a street protest in Albany, New York.

Demonstrators on American college campuses protested in support of their fellow student. The president's advisors knew this was a very volatile situation. The commander in chief needed to be compassionate yet firm in his speech to the nation. Technicians from all the major networks were already setting up for the White House press conference. In less than an hour, the president would attempt to convince the American people that the New

World Coalition's system was absolutely necessary for the financial stability of the world.

"My fellow Americans," announced the composed president, "this afternoon, at 1:02 p.m. European time, a young college student was executed in Munich, Germany, for refusing to register for his World ID Number. We grieve at this loss of life, and our prayers go out to the family of this young man. We have unfortunately received accurate reports from the German ID Security Force that Eric Bahman honestly believed that our new registration system is a weapon of evil. The NWC report shows that several agents had to physically restrain this resister in order to keep him from possibly hurting himself and others. To be perfectly honest, I'm afraid Eric Bahman was actually mentally disturbed!"

Pausing, the president knew the future of the NWC could be at stake.

"This is why Americans for a New World Coalition has produced a video that is being run hourly on CNN. This valuable presentation explains the reasons our world must come together as one. As your commander in chief, in no way do I condone the killing of innocent lives. But we cannot jeopardize the future of our children by allowing individuals to choose what laws they will obey. My fellow Americans, this ID plan is crucial for the safety of our country. This financial system is so critical to our national security that Congress has enacted a new law, which makes refusing to cooperate with this system a treasonable offense. For college students who are planning to resist, I beg you to rethink your position. The future of our country depends on a united front."

The leader of the free world raised his right hand to display his ID number, which had been rendered temporarily visible in order to reassure those watching the broadcast. "Trust me, my fellow Americans, there is really nothing to it."

The pressure of the moment seemed to fade away as a false peace permeated the Oval Office. The spirit of compromise seemed pleased while perched upon the right shoulder of the smiling American president.

"Good night, everyone," concluded the president, "and God bless you all!"

CHAPTER 35

DON'T YOU REMEMBER?

He who has my commandments and keeps them, it is he who loves Me.
And he who loves Me will be loved by My Father,
and I will love him and manifest Myself to him.
John 14:21

It had been over a month since Jake's parents registered for the mark of the beast. After several failed attempts of trying to reach the Ryans, the two teenagers realized the consequences of not having an ID number.

Jake and Jessie slipped further into the bushes behind the shed. They moved to where they could see the house without being seen themselves. Two NWC agents were still sitting in their car about a half block away, watching the Ryan's home. They had not moved in over four hours. Jake and Jessie both knew that the Ryans were in deep trouble.

"We have to warn them."

"It's too dangerous," whispered Jessie. "How about phoning them from Flips?"

"No way, Jess! The phone was probably the first thing they bugged. Somehow we need to get a message to them without being observed."

"Well, it's too risky right now. Let's spilt before the agents see us."

"Wait, Jess! Look!" Jake pointed excitedly.

The NWC squad car was slowly pulling away. They waited until the car was completely out of sight.

"Ok, let's go," motioned an anxious Jessie.

Jake grabbed Jessie's arm and pulled her back abruptly.

"Look over there," he said, pointing to an unmarked truck.

"What about it?"

"Why would the agents suddenly leave unless they had some kind of backup? That truck arrived about ten minutes ago, and no one has left it."

Jessie nodded in agreement. Carefully, they both slipped from behind the shed in the backyard of the house facing the Ryans. Just as they reached the curb, the driver of a '57 yellow Chevy slowed down and offered them a ride.

The New World Coalition Committee, headed by Father John, had just arrived in Geneva, Switzerland, to evaluate how the world was adapting to Hendrick's leadership.

"But, Father John, look at the tremendous expense it has already cost us in setting up Lord Hendrick's image around the world," pleaded a committee member from Kenya.

"I must agree," replied the Mexican representative. "We must be . . ."

"Gentlemen, please," interrupted Father John. "Need I remind you that the alternative to this plan is to return to the days when your young men died in worthless wars and your children went to bed hungry? To ensure the success of this plan, we must enforce the mandatory acceptance of Lord Hendrick's system. If we do not, life as we know it will most certainly cease to exist. Do I make myself clear?"

The whispers from the committee members were more out of fear than respect.

"Gentlemen, countries will be responsible for setting up images throughout their cities, airports, schools, movie theaters, sports arenas, even their homes. In addition, Lord Hendrick has established some new rules for the Internet. All commercial, organizational, and educational sites are being modified so that only those who have a valid ID can use them. That means, gentlemen, that a person must have an NWC ID in order to access the Internet. Because most businesses rely heavily on the Internet, we foresee no problems. Within thirty days, not one person in the world will be able to use the Internet without first acknowledging Wolfgang Hendrick as god of this world."

The committee sat in stony silence as the evil priest calmly explained the penalty of those who resist. For some, the silence of the committee would have been a little suspicious, but to Father John, it was meaningless.

"You may all leave," dismissed the priest, who barely acknowledged their departure.

✳

As Lee was preparing dinner, Lance heard a faint knock come from the backdoor. When he reached to open it, he heard muffled voices from the other side. He lifted a blind and then opened the door.

"Jake, Jessie, come on in," Lance whispered, waving them inside. "What's up?"

Before they could answer, the youth pastor motioned for silence and pointed toward the living room. After settling down on the couches, Lance reached over and turned up the stereo really loud.

"Hey, Jessie, it's so good to see you," greeted an excited Lee as she entered the living room.

"Do you know you're being watched?" asked Jessie.

"It goes with the territory if you know what I mean," said Lee.

"Have you seen the agent stakeouts that have been coming and going?"

"Sure have."

"Why haven't they arrested you?" asked a suspicious Jake.

"That's a good question," replied a solemn Lance.

"I'm scared, Lee. Jake's parents decided to register, and I've heard through the grapevine that mine have too."

"Well, Jess, everybody was warned that this wasn't going to be fun and games. You know, it's for eternity," responded a firm Lee.

"If you don't mind, we have some questions," Jake asked in a hesitant voice.

After feeding their hungry guests and listening to their questions, the Ryans explained how Satan introduced the NWC to the world through his two pawns, the antichrist and the false prophet. Lance pointed out the deceptiveness of the one-world religion, the Babylonian Harlot, and how the antichrist used this religious system to gain power.

"So you see, guys, when Hendrick forced the nations to register for his mark, the great tribulation of Christians quickly spread throughout the world. At the same time, God raised up a Christian resistance movement in order to help believers overcome."

Jessie sat staring ahead, tears dropping from her eyes.

Jake openly confessed, "If what you just explained is true, then a majority of people in our world are deceived, and they're going straight to hell!"

Placing her arm around Jessie, Lee replied, "Guys, the bottom line is this: either you choose to believe in the evil propaganda this world is dishing out or you place yourself in the hands of a loving God."

"What Lee is trying to say is that there is no gray area when it comes to being an overcomer for Jesus," added Lance.

"Yeah, yeah, it's real easy to say, but it's hard to do when your family and friends aren't buying it," said Jake.

"You're right," Lance replied as he opened the curtain slightly to see if any surveillance units were watching. "Jesus never said it would be easy. Our Lord said, 'If anyone loves Me, he will keep My Word and My Father will love him'[1] In fact, Jesus said, 'Narrow is the gate and difficult is the way which leads to life, and there are few who find it.'"[2]

"Let's go, Jessie, I need some time to think."

"Before you go, we need to ask you something."

"What's that, Pastor?"

"Jessie, Jake, if you died tonight, would you go to heaven or would you go to hell?"

"If you're asking us if we've become Christians, the answer is not yet," replied a confused Jake. "It's a big step."

"We can pray with you right now," encouraged Lance. "In fact, we can help you get to a place of safety where you don't have to be on the run."

"Look," interjected Jessie. "I just don't want to be a hypocrite. At school, it seemed like a lot of Christians were the first in line to register!"

"Jessie, if everyone who lives on your block were a hypocrite, that still wouldn't make Jesus any less real," challenged Lee.

As they got up to leave, Jessie turned and said, "You know, that's what Luke used to say."

CHAPTER 36

IN THAT HOUR

But whatever is given you in that hour, speak that;
for it is not you who speak, but the Holy Spirit.
Mark 13:11

Stephen Corbin arrived at Lakeview High around lunch time. As he entered the side door to the gym, he could hear voices coming from the bleachers. The uneasiness of the students was not a good sign. From here on out, the watchman knew he needed to be extra careful. The Spirit of God must lead and guide his every action. Stephen would often meditate on Jesus' exhortation to His disciples: "But when they arrest you and deliver you up, do not worry beforehand, or premeditate what you will speak. But whatever is given you in that hour, speak that; for it is not you who speak, but the Holy Spirit."[1]

The watchman had come in response to God's leading. A subtle nudge in Stephen's heart prompted him to change his plans for the afternoon. He quietly took a seat off to the left side of the bleachers. A young man named David Cowley, wearing a Michigan State sweatshirt and a Chicago Bulls hat, was sharing the Gospel with about thirty students. Stephen had heard about him from Pastor Mark but had never met him.

David was thirty and had been a youth evangelist for close to seven years. After graduating from Bible college, the young preacher had been ready to walk through any door of ministry God would open. His first position as a youth pastor began in a Pentecostal fellowship in Yuma, Arizona. For some, the hot summers would have been too much, but not for David. This was his opportunity to disciple young people and turn them into prayer warriors.

After just three weeks of ministry, the senior pastor had called David into his office and exhorted him to tone down the intensity of the youth meetings.

"You see, David, this is the Southwest, and we don't want our kids being labeled fanatics," warned the angry pastor.

The rebukes from leadership became weekly occurrences, until God closed the door and moved David to Chicago to become a full-time youth evangelist. The kids loved David's style of preaching. Often, his no-nonsense messages would appear harsh to some, but to David, they were like life preservers being thrown to kids who were dying. The young evangelist desperately desired to see the power of God transform the lives of his young people. They needed to experience the presence of God, not just emotional orchestrated songs or well thought-out programs that looked good but produced nothing. Yes, there was a fire in David's belly, and he was committed to sharing it with anyone who would listen.

"Listen up! I've answered your questions the best I can; it doesn't matter how well you think you've understood what I said. The bottom line is that without Jesus as your Savior and without the Holy Spirit guiding you, you will not make it! When the fourth seal was opened, the two beasts of Revelation, Wolfgang Hendrick and Father John, were given power to kill all those who refuse to worship Hendrick or his image or take his mark. If you do any of these three things, you will spend eternity in hell!"[2]

Several students got up to leave as soon as the word *hell* was used.

"The choice before you is really quite simple. We, as watchmen, call it the Test. For those of you who have not yet been confronted by the New World Coalition Agents, it's only a matter of time. If you refuse the mark and take a stand for Jesus, you might physically die, but you will receive eternal life."

"Might die? Yeah, right!" yelled a blonde surfer-type in the third row. "What about the dude in Germany who refused? They sure wasted him! I ain't going like that."

"Go ahead, register then," yelled a voice from the back of the bleachers. "Most have anyway!"

"That's right," yelled another student. "Hey, has anyone seen Jessie or Jake lately? I overheard an ID agent asking questions about them at last month's pep rally."

"And what ever happened to Cindy Johnson?" interrupted one of the cheerleaders from the right side of the bleachers. "The *Bethany Herald* reported last summer that she refused to take her ID number and took off in her parent's Chevy Blazer."

"Yeah, I heard that two ID agents tried to catch her, but she got away."

"Some say she and her family are Christian resisters."

"Oh, that's so bogus," yelled one of Cindy's neighbors. "Cindy would never have the guts to do anything like that!"

Several students who knew Cindy looked down and shook their heads in agreement.

"How do you know?"

"I grew up with her. She wouldn't do something that stupid."

"Yeah, pretty stupid all right," interrupted another student. "Without an ID number, your life is pretty much gone. No family, no parties, no graduation, no future! Why would anyone want to throw all that away?"

Rachel couldn't take it any longer. "Wait a minute!" she yelled, waving her right hand to get everyone's attention. "I was there when Cindy refused to register. It's true! She took off from the ID station in her parent's car. She refused to take the mark and . . ."

The memory of that day produced a sense of disgust that Rachel had never experienced before. Gasping, she slumped down, buried her face in her hands, and began sobbing uncontrollably.

"Hey, everybody, listen up!" pleaded David. "I've already given you the verses on the Lord's coming. Jesus said, 'When you see these things happening, know that it is near—at the doors!'"[3]

"What are these things Jesus is talking about?" asked one of the students.

Simon Colson stood to his feet and asked to speak. "Jesus is talking about the first five seals in the book of Revelation: the antichrist, wars, famines, persecution, and martyrdom. In the past four and a half years, we have all watched as each seal has unfolded right before our eyes. The next event we will all see is the sixth seal, the cosmic disturbances! Any Christian who sees the universe go black will actually see the Son of Man coming!"

The ID agents had come in response to a tip that a watchman had been seen on the grounds of Lakeview High. The dragnet had already covered the main building and the teachers' offices. As the agents passed by the gym, a faint cheer could be heard coming from the bleachers inside the building. When the doors burst open, sunlight flooded the dark gym, and the three ID agents yelled, "Freeze!"

Kids ran away in all directions. Most ran for the hallway exits, and others jumped through the open first-floor windows. A few of the boys ran to the top of the bleachers and escaped through the windows leading to the roof over the auto shop. Through the commotion, David stood quietly praying.

The armed agents cautiously approached the speaker.

"Are you David Cowley?"

"Yes, I am."

"We have a warrant for your arrest for teaching propaganda to under-age children."

Without any hesitation, the agents surrounded the preacher, hand-cuffed him, taped his mouth, and led him away. Stephen Corbin sat nearby motionless, quietly interceding. After a minute or so, a young boy slipped through the slats between the first and second rows of the old bleachers. He had planned to use the window in the bathroom for his exit. Suddenly, he stopped dead in his tracks.

"It can't be," whispered Simon to himself. "But it is; it's the watch-man! God must have supernaturally protected him during the arrest. But what about David?" thought Simon. "Why didn't God protect him?

As the young teenager walked toward the watchman, he prayed, "Lord, if it be your will, allow this man of God to help me find Josh."

"Brother Corbin! Is that you?" asked the frightened boy.

"Yes, I'm Stephen Corbin. Are you okay?"

"Man, am I glad to see you! What's up with all these agents? Where are they going to take David?"

"Probably to the main ID security station."

Pausing to check out several students who were still escaping, Stephen asked, "What's your name, son?"

"My name is Simon Colson."

"Nice to meet you, Simon."

"My dad used to pastor Calvary Community down on Vaughn Road. Do you know it?"

"Sure do."

"Last year I tried to register for my ID number, but I was turned away for being underage," stated a matter-of-fact Simon.

"Praise the Lord!" said the relieved watchman.

"Yeah, this was after I found my parents packing. Some of my friends were really having problems with their parents, but this was something I was not ready for. They told me that a pre-tribulation rapture is a myth, that the antichrist is Wolfgang Hendrick, and that the NWC ID Number is the mark of the beast," Simon fired off in rapid succession while keeping a watchful eye out for trouble.

"Must have been pretty hard to swallow," reflected Stephen.

"You can say that again!"

"So what do you believe now, Simon? You know you're going to have to take a stand for Jesus if you're going to make it. Most of your friends have already taken the mark. Do you know Ricky Jackson, the star running back on the football team?"

"Sure do, everybody knows Ricky!"

"Well, what you don't know is that Ricky is a committed watchman and has been evading ID agents for the past year. Several weeks ago, after being threatened by ID agents, Ricky's father revealed where his son was hiding."

"No way!" blurted out a shocked Simon.

"Simon, Jesus said, 'You will be betrayed even by parents and brothers, relatives and friends; and they will put some of you to death. And you will be hated by all for My name's sake. . . . By your patience possess your souls.'"[4]

"For sure, I know this passage, but I never thought it would happen in my lifetime."

"Simon, do you know Jesus as your Lord and Savior?"

"Yes sir! I love the Lord with all my heart, Brother Corbin. During this past year of hiding out and searching for the truth, He's become so real to me. I've lost so much that used to be important to me: my friends, my home, my church, and my school. I can still remember dozing on the Hirsh's front porch swing when the Holy Spirit laid on my heart that the Hirshes had just become watchmen in the Christian resistance movement!"

"How do you know the Hirshes?" asked Stephen.

"Oh, Joshua and I met at Bible camp. Do you know them?"

"Sure do," said Stephen. "The Hirshes are part of a watchman camp up North. Are your parents Allen and Mary Colson?"

"Yes sir!"

"Well, your folks have been living in the same camp where the Hirshes are for almost a year!"

"Yesssss, Jesus! Thank you, Jesus!" hollered a relieved Simon.

The pressure of the moment was almost too much for the popular prophecy expert. Arthur Lawrence had sold millions of books on the end times. His TV prophecy programs were produced in over thirty languages. He had always enjoyed the spotlight by walking on the edge of controversy. But today was different. The incessant phone calls from the public,demanding answers had taken a heavy toll on him and his staff.

"That's right, Sylvia, hold all my calls 'till I can relax enough to think. What do these people want from me anyway?" said Arthur. "Can't they pray and find God's will for their own lives!"

"Reverend Lawrence, you have a call from . . ."

"Sylvia, didn't I just tell you to hold my calls?"

"Of course, Reverend Lawrence, but I thought you might want to talk with your good friend, Reverend Thomas Bray."

Without hesitating, the preacher grabbed his phone.

"Well, it's about time I heard that strong baritone voice," joked a smiling Arthur Lawrence. "How has my favorite prophecy teacher been?"

"I really do appreciate your taking my call, Arthur. I know your schedule for the last few months has been really hectic. Actually, I've been praying for you and your family," replied a relieved Tom.

"No problem, my friend. I've always got time for you. By the way, how are Matt and Sam doing with their studies?"

"Funny you should ask, Arthur," said a nervous Tom.

"What do you mean? They haven't dropped out, have they?"

"Well, Arthur, the Lord seems to have given them a new direction for their lives."

"Don't tell me, Tom. It's got to be politics, right? I always knew this would happen."

"To be perfectly honest, my brother, both Matt and Sam have withdrawn from school, forfeited their scholarships, and become watchmen in the underground Christian resistance movement. As we speak, they are rescuing underage resisters!"

After at least ten seconds of silence, Tom asked, "Are you still there?"

"Is this some sort of joke?" snapped Arthur. "Because if it is, it's in extremely poor taste. Do you realize how much pressure my family and I have been under this past year? It's been a nightmare. Maybe you should just spell it out for me, Tom." The conversation had definitely taken a turn for the worst.

"They are good boys, Arthur. You and I could learn a lot from their biblical studies on the Second Coming."

"I'm sure. Get to the point. I'm a busy man."

"The point is the mark of the beast, my friend!"

"So, that's it. Your two boys have convinced their old man that the World ID Number is the mark of the beast and that Wolfgang Hendrick is the evil antichrist, am I right?" asked the sarcastic preacher.

"Right on," Tom replied. "And after praying, I don't think I have to even try to convince you, Arthur. Deep down, you know we have entered the great tribulation."

As the seconds ticked by, the sheer silence seemed like an eternity to Tom.

"Because you have been up front with me, Tom, I'll be honest with you. Yes, I've been having some doubts about our biblical interpretation of the Lord's return. So what? Lots of ministers are searching for the truth concerning the Lord's coming. We are all in the same boat. The problem is that we all need to be on the same page concerning the end times."

"That's why I called, Arthur. It all began last summer when Ashley and I had an encounter with the Spirit of God. It was like my life, my motives, and my false teachings were lit up like fireworks. In an instant, Ashley and I could see clearly with spiritual eyes."

"Hold it, Tom. What's gotten into you? False teaching? Spiritual eyes? You're not sounding very rational."

"You know as well as I do, Arthur, that the only way to understand the sequence of events that must precede His coming is by the Holy Spirit's supernatural revelation. The reason the traditions of men have deceived millions of believers is that the Holy Spirit has been ignored!"

"Well, I'm not ready to go that far, but I'm willing to begin a new book on how we've not been consistent in interpreting events in the book of Revelation. Now if we . . ."

"Arthur! You don't have the time to write another book. Look out your office window. They are taking the mark of the breast as we speak!"

"What are you suggesting, Tom?"

"You need to invite Gene Lloyd and J. R. Greer to your studio for a taping. The four of us need to come together and warn Christians throughout the world that if they submit to Hendrick and his mark, they will be denying Jesus Christ as their Lord and Savior!"

"Out of the question!" Arthur shouted. "Besides, I don't believe Gene or J. R. would make such a hasty judgment. Surely you know we would all be arrested for treason! Don't you think a meeting to study and compare notes is more in order?"

"You've got to be kidding, Art! We were wrong in teaching the pre-trib myth. We were wrong about the apostasy of Christians in Matthew 24! Don't you see what is happening? It's the mark, Art, the mark of the beast! Tell me, have you registered for your ID number?"

"Uh . . . no, not yet," he faintly replied.

"What are you waiting for, Art? It's just a silly number, isn't it? Just an ID number the antichrist wants to put on you for eternity!"

"Now hear me, and hear me good, Tom. I'm not ready to risk my reputation, my ministry, and all my years of teaching just because you feel we have entered the great tribulation! Do you understand me, Mr. Big Shot Orator!" yelled the heated preacher.

After a few seconds, Tom replied, "Yeah, I understand you and your fellow prophets all too well. I guess what it comes down to is the approval of man. The problem is the end doesn't justify the means, now does it, Arthur?"

"Tom, you are making it look a lot worse than it really is."

"No, my friend, I am afraid I'm seeing clearly for the first time in years. By the way, I'd like to read a scripture the Holy Spirit has just laid on my heart for you. The Apostle Paul warned, 'Let no one deceive himself. If anyone among you seems to be wise in this age, let him become a fool that he may become wise.'"[5]

"What's that supposed to mean?" interrupted Arthur.

"It means that I always thought the false teachers that would deceive millions of believers in the end times would be New Agers, Satanists, deceptive cults, and false prophets. I never dreamed that professing Christian ministers could also be so deceived. Ashley, Matt, Sam, and I have decided to stand for Jesus against the spirit of the antichrist. Our advice to you is to do the same. Good bye, Arthur."

Arthur Lawrence, the well-known celebrity, fell to the floor and began to weep over his spirit of rebellion. He knew, deep within his heart, that he had no intention of repenting from his pre-tribulation message.

"We just all need to be ready," he rationalized. "Somehow it'll all pan out."[6]

CHAPTER 37

BE NOT ASHAMED

I am not ashamed of the gospel of Christ,
for it is the power of God to salvation for everyone who believes.
Romans 1:16

Throughout the world, more and more watchmen were being martyred for their testimony. Everyone knew the risks for openly sharing the Gospel of Jesus Christ. But it just didn't matter to Carl Russell. He would share the Gospel at Little League games, malls, family picnics, and rock concerts, anywhere people would gather. The previous Saturday afternoon the local symphony orchestra had been warming up for an outdoor concert at George Wallace Park when Carl stepped up, unannounced, in front of the six-foot stage.

With his megaphone turned all the way up, he got the crowd's attention when he declared, "Jesus said, 'Therefore whoever confesses Me before men, him I will also confess before My Father who is in heaven. But whoever denies Me before men, him I will also deny before my Father who is in heaven. Do not think that I came to bring peace on earth. I did not come to bring peace but a sword. For I have come to set a man against his father. . . . A man's enemies will be those of his own household.'[1]

"My dear friends, these words apply directly to our lives. Over a year ago, we all witnessed the evil deception of Wolfgang Hendrick. As a believer in Jesus Christ, I challenge those of you who have not yet registered to reject the lie of this deceiver. Deep down in your soul, you know the words of Jesus are the truth."

Carl knew he had been reported the moment he mentioned the name of Jesus Christ. ID agents would be arriving at any moment. But there had to be someone in the crowd who had not yet taken the mark or worshiped Hendrick's image.

"How do you know this to be true, son?" asked a retired minister seated in the second row. "You're too narrow minded. Your type of Christianity might be right for you, but not for others."

The crowd applauded for the lie the spirit of the antichrist had spread throughout the world.

"Is there anyone here today who hasn't registered for an ID number yet?"

"Who do you think you are?" someone from the crowd yelled.

"He's a messenger from god!" sneered another. "Tell us, Mr. Prophet, when will the world end?"

The crowd roared with cruel laughter.

Tragically, the vast majority had already made their choice, which had left their hearts mean-spirited and resentful.

Carl could see the flashing blue lights from the agents' cars as they made their way around to the front of the gazebo. With one quick move, he dropped to the ground and ducked under the platform.

"Never go in a place without an escape route," he thought to himself. He couldn't recall where he had heard it. But in the past year, it had become his watchword. He made his way under the platform, through the pine trees, and over the wall separating the park from the new shopping mall. There would be another day for Carl Russell to share the Gospel, but a watchman from Washington DC would not be as fortunate.

Munching cheap hot dogs and cold fries while pretending to watch a little league baseball game, Jake and Jessie talked quietly.

"Jake, do you think the Ryans are for real?"

"I don't know, Jess. I think they're really nice people. And they certainly believe what they teach. But as far as believing this whole end-time scenario, I . . . I just don't know."

"That's our whole problem, isn't it? Who can we trust to tell us the truth?"

"I trusted Luke."

"Yeah, for sure, but no one seems to know where he is."

"I've heard a rumor that Luke made it to a Watchman Camp somewhere in Alabama."

"Ok, even if it's true, do you think the Ryans know how we can find this camp?"

"I don't know, Jess. It's been months since we have seen them. Do you think they've made it to one of the camps?"

"Who knows?"

"Each day, more and more arrests are being made. Sooner or later, we are going to get caught. There's got to be a way, Jess!"

"That's for sure. But maybe if we ask around or get back to the Ryans, we can catch a ride to one of these camps."

"We can try. But talk about long-shots," said Jake with a sigh.

"Hey, who knows?" said Jessie grinning. "Maybe someone is praying for us."

"Okay, Frank, everyone's accounted for. You can go ahead and shut down the outside power."

The Bethany Watchman Camp, deep within the caverns just outside of Birmingham, had become a haven for Christians seeking protection. Many were full time watchmen while others tended to the details of feeding and housing the continually growing numbers. The portion of the caverns blocked off from the public for safety reasons was almost completely full. Campers without critical skills were shown how to dig and shore up tunnels needed for emergency escapes from ID agents. They had two shifts working and were beginning to make progress. Most believers in the camp had lost part or all of their family. Nevertheless, they were all warriors for Christ, driven by a purpose worth dying for.

Each night was set aside for praying, teaching, and fellowship. It would all begin as soon as the tunnelers returned from their second shift.

Pastor Mark started it all off. "Tonight, we've decided to study Matthew 24:45-51. This story is about the coming of our Lord and the choices believers will make before he returns. Go for it, Ned."

Ned stood with his Bible open and read, "Who then is a faithful and wise servant, whom his master made ruler over his household, to give them food in due season? Blessed is that servant whom his master, when he comes, will find so doing."[2]

"Okay, because of the natural break in the story, let's stop here," announced Mark. "Now, before we examine who the faithful servant represents, let's check out what Jesus said right before this story. Any takers?" asked the pastor.

Luke stood to his feet and shared, "Jesus tells believers to keep watch because we don't know the exact day or hour our Lord will come. Pastor

Mark, this verse doesn't make any sense if the elect are taken out of this world before the tribulation period begins. Don't the events of Matthew 24 take place within the tribulation period? How can the saints watch for specific events during the tribulation if we're raptured before the seven-year tribulation begins?"

"Excellent point, Luke. Go on."

"Jesus said, 'If the master of the house had known what hour the thief would come, he would have watched and not allowed his house to be broken into.'[3] In other words, we can be ready when Jesus comes by watching for the persecution that will precede His return!"

"Very good. Does everyone understand the truth Luke has just pointed out?" asked the pastor, scanning the excited crowd. A chorus of amens could be heard throughout the cave.

"Okay. Now, who does the faithful servant represent?" asked Mark.

"A believer in Jesus, born again by the blood of the Lamb!" yelled Whitney.

"That's right, Whit. Jesus told us that if this servant remains faithful in helping those he's been given, his Master will reward him. Now, someone read the rest of the story."

Diana stood up, smiling shyly, and began to read, "But if that evil servant says in his heart, my master is delaying his coming, and begins to beat his fellow servants, and to eat and drink with drunkards, the master of that servant will come on a day when he is not looking for him and at an hour that he is not aware of, and will cut him in two and appoint him his portion with the hypocrites. There shall be weeping and gnashing of teeth."[4] After reading the passage, Diana took a seat with her friends.

Luke stood again and replied, "Jesus showed us a faithful believer who decides to sin against his Lord. The servant thinks his master won't be back any time soon, so he begins to take advantage of those in his care and does anything he wants. While the servant is committing his habitual sin against his fellow servants, his master returns on a day the servant is not aware of. Since the servant, who was once faithful, refused to continually follow the Lord, he was assigned a place in hell where there is weeping and gnashing of teeth."

"Excellent interpretation of the story, Luke. Does anyone have any comments?" asked Mark.

"I know this might sound a little strange to most of you," shared Alice, "but all my life I've been taught this story represents two servants. The faithful servant is a believer, and the evil servant is a person who had an opportunity to get saved but rejected it."

"Okay, Alice," Pastor Mark slowly replied, not wanting to embarrass her. "Has hearing Luke's interpretation made you think any differently?"

"Well, it's pretty clear to me now that there is only one servant in the story. He was faithful for a while but began to rebel and actually hurt those in his care. When Jesus returns, the servant has backslid to the point that he rejects his salvation, and he is assigned a place where there is eternal weeping and gnashing of teeth!"

"Pretty scary stuff, saints," reflected the pastor. "For someone like Alice, even the suggestion a Christian can fall away from God due to habitual sin is unthinkable."

"Hey, Alice, what made you change your mind?" yelled someone from the back of the crowd.

Before the pastor could intervene, Alice replied, "It's all right, Pastor Mark. I want to give an answer." The brave teenager slowly stood to her feet and faced the massive crowd. "When the mark of the beast was first introduced to the United Nations, my whole family got together. Each of us shared what we believed concerning the end times and the rapture. It was at this time that God sent Hope Bishop into my life. She explained to me the truth about the timing of the rapture, but even more important, she explained the truth concerning my salvation!"

Intercessors had already begun to pray as tears began to fall from her blue-green eyes. Many within the camp knew what Alice was going to say because they too had suffered the same nightmare.

"Even though I disagreed with my folks and my two brothers that night, I . . . I never dreamed they would each take the mark." Several of her closest friends immediately circled the perky redhead as she broke down and wept.

"Pastor, could I share my testimony?"

"Sure, Tracy. Okay, everybody, listen up!"

"I would like to thank the Lord for opening my eyes. I was in my own little world, living a sinful lifestyle that Apostle Paul warned believers not to live. The Holy Spirit was convicting me to repent and turn away from my life of sin, but I refused even though the Word of God clearly warns that those who live in sexual fornication will not inherit the kingdom of God!"[5] Only those closest to Tracy knew how much courage it took for her to publicly testify. "I stand before you today as a former backslider who turned away from my habitual sin against God. By God's grace, I have repented, and now I am free," proclaimed a jubilant Tracy. The applause was electrifying.

"Even though my family chose out of their own free will to follow the deceiver, I give my Lord praise and glory for being so faithful to His Word!"

"Awesome, Tracy," affirmed Mark. "Saints, we have an incredible responsibility that has been laid before us by our Lord. Our time is short! We must pray while there is still time. Very soon the sixth seal will be opened. The sun will go black, the moon will turn red, and the stars will give up their light. When the world is plunged into darkness, then and only then will we see the glory of God flash across the black heavenlies from the east to the west! It is at this time that our Jesus will come to rescue his own and pour His wrath on those who have rejected His truth."

The pastor dropped to his knees, bowed his head, and led the camp of overcomers in fervent intercession for the salvation of souls. At that very moment, watchmen the world over were risking their lives in order to fulfill the great commission. They were devoted believers, willing to die for their Savior, the only begotten Son of the Father.[6]

Sara Cassie Whitaker grew up in a tiny suburb outside of Alexandria, Virginia. The thirty-one-year-old was single and still remained very close with her family. Just recently she was appointed to a high security position at the Pentagon. It had always been her dream, even as a young girl, to serve her country within the confines of the nation's capital. God had led every step of the way.

The rush hour traffic inched along very slowly as a light mist of rain fell on her windshield. Her Pentagon ID had always gotten her by the local checkpoints before, but tonight would be different. As she approached the bright blue lights, the Holy Spirit spoke to her spirit, cautioning her that her escape plan was in jeopardy. Many of her Christian friends had warned her not to wait too long before going to the Watchman Camp outside of Washington DC. If Sara had stayed in closer contact with her underground sources, she would have known about the planned roadblocks of all major highways leaving the capitol. The security was becoming tighter in order to reduce the number of resisters escaping. Now she was trapped on a major highway with a checkpoint coming up. Sara composed herself and tried to hide her concern.

"Good evening, ma'am. May I have your ID number, please," said the agent as he clicked on his hand-held scanner.

"I'm afraid I haven't signed up yet. My schedule at the Pentagon has been crazy. But I do have my Pentagon ID that . . ."

The agent cut her off abruptly.

"Please step out of the car and put your hands on the hood. According to the NWC ID policy you are under arrest for failing to register for your personal identification number." Sara got out, still trying to show her Pentagon badge. The agent brushed it aside and handcuffed her wrists behind her back. "You will be taken to the nearest detention center, where you will be formally charged. If you want to have these charges dropped, you can register there and pay a one-thousand-dollar fine."

Later that night, the agents at the Washington DC Regional Detention Center were beginning to lose their patience with the uncooperative resister.

"I told you over and over again. My name is Sara Cassie Whitaker. I work at the Pentagon, and my social security number is 721-84-1023."

"You don't seem to understand, Ms. Whitaker," growled the ID agent. "Your position at the Pentagon and your social security number have no bearing on this situation at all! You must register for your World ID in order to be recognized by the NWC."

As Sara prayed silently, the peace of God began to flow within her soul. She stopped arguing and just smiled at the agents.

"Do you have anything to add to what you have already told us?"

"I'm afraid I'm going to have to report you to my . . ."

"You shut your mouth!" screamed the ID agent in charge. "We know you are playing games with us. In fact, we have just received evidence that you are a member of the Christian underground. But we are willing to make a deal with you. Tonight, if you will lead us to the Watchman Camp you were going to, we will let you go. It's that simple."

"That is something that I will never do," said Sara with a smile.

"That's it!" screamed the interrogator. "We just got the green light from the captain. Make an example of her!"

The agents immediately removed the Christian resister from the interrogation room by dragging her outside in full view of the other people being detained. She made no effort to resist as the agents pushed her up against a reinforced brick wall. There they secured her wrists to two iron rings.

"Is your name Sara Cassie Whitaker?" asked the agent.

"Yes, it is."

It was obvious to all watching that the young woman possessed a peace that the agents despised.

"Are you a resident of Alexandria, Virginia?

"Yes, I am."

"Under Article 21B of the New World Coalition ID agreement, each citizen of the United States must be in possession of an NWC ID Number. Do you have such a number?"

"No, I do not."

"Are you willing to register at this time?"

"No, I am not."

Sara knew what was coming and had spiritually prepared herself. Her countenance was peaceful, even angelic.

"Under what grounds do you refuse to register for your ID number?"

"I am a believer in Jesus Christ, the Son of God. He alone is my Lord and Savior. I will not worship or bow down to any other." Turning to the people watching, Sarah cried out, "Listen to me! Do not register for your ID. It is the mark of . . ."

It was over. Those watching recoiled in horror as blood splattered her white blouse. Screams from the crowd subsided into heavy weeping. As the people shielded their eyes from the atrocity, the agent still holding the gun shouted, "This is what happens if you refuse to register." It only took an hour of minutes for a majority of the people detained to register and be released.

Within minutes of her death, *CNN Nightly News* informed the nation that Sara Cassie Whitaker had been executed for refusing to register for her NWC ID Number. The officer in charge of the detention center where the execution took place described Ms. Whitaker as abusive, even delusional, after repeatedly refusing to comply.

The CNN reporter on the scene solemnly added, "Sara Cassie Whitaker has joined an ever increasing number of resistors within the United States, who have willfully challenged the national security of our country. She was executed for the capital offense of treason for refusing to comply with New World Coalition ID law."

Chapter 38

Who Really Cares?

What do you think?
If a man has a hundred sheep,
and one of them goes astray,
does he not leave the ninety-nine
and go to the mountains
to seek the one that is straying?
Matthew 18:12

"There's another one," reported Michelle.

"Which one?" asked Stephen.

"The white sedan, two cars back."

"Can you tell if they are agents?"

"No, but it's been there for the last three turns."

"We had better pull in somewhere, just to be safe," cautioned Stephen.

The watchman made several random turns before pulling into a twenty-four hour Quik Mart. Simon got out and pretended to fill the tank.

"They're pulling in!" whispered Michelle.

Simon tensed, ready to drop the nozzle and make a run for it.

"Hey look!" Stephen called out.

Simon turned and grinned in relief as a father and his two grown-up sons got out, talking all at once, and went inside. Sliding into the backseat, he let out a big sigh.

"Another false alarm," whispered Michelle. "Sorry, guys."

"Don't be sorry. You've spotted two for sure, and I'd rather dodge ten false ones than miss the real one."

Michelle smiled and softly said, "Thanks, honey."

"I don't know about you, but that one scared me so bad that I've got to go," announced Simon.

Stephen laughed. "Good idea. I'm up for a pit stop. But let's hurry; we're almost there."

It had been a nerve-racking journey so far, consisting of unmarked turns and constant back tracking designed to lose anyone who might be following them. Any time Michelle reported a car that lingered too long behind them, Stephen would veer from the planned route, making random turns and stops until they were clear again. Camp lookouts, unknown to the believers escaping along the route, reported their progress to the camp.

As they climbed back into the car, Stephen cautioned, "Michelle, Simon, from here on out I'd like us to be even more cautious. If you feel the least bit suspicious about a car, let me know at once."

As Stephen pulled back on the highway, all three of them watched with anxious eyes.

Jason Wylie, the Mole, stepped outside his Bethany law office for a quick breather. Every day more and more families looking for protection were seeking him out. His job was to coordinate a scheduled departure-arrival date with the camp they were going to. It was critical that each family leave precisely on time. This procedure would prevent a mass exodus like the two that exposed the location of camps in New York and Illinois.

More important, Jason had to be sure that each camper didn't have the mark. The mini ID scanners he obtained on the black market were extremely expensive, as well as very dangerous. Anyone caught with one would be arrested immediately. The security within the Alabama camps was extremely tight because NWC agents had just infiltrated several camps in Mississippi and Georgia. Jason and the watchmen leadership knew Bethany ID surveillance teams were searching the countryside for resister camps.

The camps' first objective was to provide protection for those who refused to take the mark, especially children and senior saints. The second objective was to enlist intercessors around the clock to pray for unbelievers to repent and obey the warning of the Gospel angel, Glory.[1]

"You got the license plate, Joe?" asked Frank as he checked his schedule sheet.

"Sure do. It's GOJ 316."

"That's the watchman's car, all right. Check to see if the Colson boy is with them."

As the Corbins cruised through the final checkpoint, a loud cheer erupted throughout the camp. Leading the cheers were Allen and Mary

Colson, who had never given up hope that they would see their son again. Before the car could come to a complete stop, Simon opened the passenger door and ran into their arms.

"Oh, Simon, how are you?" Mary sobbed, holding him tightly.

"I'm a watchman, Mom. Jesus took care of me every inch of the way."

"We're so proud of you, son," added Allen as he reached over and gave his boy the biggest hug he had ever received.

In seeming disbelief, Simon asked, "You mean you're not mad at me, dad, for what I did?"

"No, son. You turned to the Lord, and the Holy Spirit led you here. That's all that really matters."

"It's crazy out there, Dad. Most of the kids at Lakeview High have taken the mark. Do you know Pastor Brown and Pastor Dyer?"

"Yes, we know them," replied his father as he shot a fearful glance in Mary's direction.

"Well, they registered all right. Yeah, and it didn't take long for their congregations to follow their example. The deception of the antichrist and the delusion sent by God is much greater than anybody ever thought it would be!"[2]

"You're right, son. The watchmen leadership in South America, Europe, and Africa have all reported large numbers of believers being deceived."

After sharing a few moments with his family, Simon was suddenly engulfed with campers eager to hear any news from the outside. A long line of overcomers quickly formed, asking if Simon had seen or heard from any of their unsaved loved ones. The Hirshes waited patiently in line while other parents described what their missing children looked like. When Simon turned and saw Benjamin and Ruth Hirsh, he burst into tears, the emotion of the moment completely overwhelming the young boy.

"Pastor Hirsh, Mrs. Hirsh, it is true! You made it safely! You won't believe this, but God used Joshua to save my life. It's a long story, but I really need to see Josh." Anxiously looking around, he asked, "Where is he?"

As Ruth abruptly turned away, Mary Colson took her hand in order to comfort her. Ben put his arm around Simon's shoulder and led him and his father a short distance from the women.

"Josh is hiding, isn't he?" asked Simon smiling.

Ben was silent, searching for the right words. "Joshua is not here any-more."

"Where is he?" asked a confused Simon.

"When we first arrived at the camp, we sat down with your parents, and they told us what had happened to you. The afternoon you left, they went searching for you. They already had a scheduled departure time, so they tried to contact the Mole and have it changed. Unfortunately, ID agents somehow learned that your parents were not going to register because of their religious beliefs. It didn't take long before they issued a warrant for their arrest. When your mom and dad found the Mole, he told them about the agents and insisted they leave immediately. No one knows how the agents got the information."

"That's right, Simon. Your mother and I prayed, and the Holy Spirit gave us Psalm 34:7-8. It says, 'The angel of the Lord encamps around those who fear Him, and He delivers them.' We just knew God would take care of you."

"But, Dad, you don't understand. I was the one who told them you weren't going to register. I was confused and angry." Hanging his head in shame, he mumbled, "It all happened so fast."

During Simon's confession, both Ruth and Mary joined them.

"It's okay, Simon," replied Ben in a relieved voice. "We now know it wasn't an informant."

"So, where is Josh?"

Ruth quietly explained, "Simon, when Joshua found out from your parents that you were searching for the truth, he hid in a delivery truck that was leaving our camp."

"But why would he do that?"

"He went looking for you, Simon."

"Why?"

"His note said he was willing to risk his life for you. That's how much you mean to him," Ruth replied as she began to weep.

"No, no, this can't be right!" screamed Simon. "God would not allow this to happen! Would He, Dad?"

Allen had always provided easy answers for Simon's life, but this time the Holy Spirit was in control. "I've been doing a lot of soul searching, son. I'm afraid I haven't been the kind of father you deserved. Instead of allowing you the time and space to learn how to be guided by the Holy Spirit, I pushed my own ideas and beliefs on you. Your mother and I can now see how God has stretched you, teaching you lessons we never allowed you to learn. I think that you already know the answer to your question, Simon. But I'll answer it anyway. Yes, God will allow painful consequences to come into believers' lives as a result of their own decisions. Joshua knew the risks he was taking when he left to find you. We are all praying that a watchman will pick him up before the ID agents do."

"Listen to me, Dad," pleaded Simon. "The agents are not as concerned with underage resisters as they are with the adults. I just know God will lead me to Joshua if you let me go after him."

"I'm sorry, son. No campers are ever allowed to leave the camp once they enter. Watchman Camp rules."

"There are exceptions," interjected Stephen Corbin as he walked towards them.

"There are?" asked a puzzled Allen.

"As watchman commander, I'm required to re-enter Bethany for emergencies that could affect the security of the camp."

"You mean we need to rescue Joshua because if they catch him, he could be a security risk?" asked an anxious Simon.

"Precisely," replied Stephen.

"But why do you need my son?"

"Being the same age, Simon would have better contacts as we search for Joshua. He would also know the ins and outs of where Joshua might hide better than I do."

"How about it, Dad?" asked a hopeful Simon. "Can you trust the Holy Spirit to lead us to Joshua?"

Allen was already pacing back and forth. This was new territory for the pastor. The spirit of control had always attacked him at his weakest moments. Looking up, he could see the Hirshes praying. "How hard this must be for them," he thought. "Yes, Lord, just as hard as it was for me when my son was lost." Bowing his head again, Allen thought about the risks involved and about how very much he loved his son.

Softly the Holy Spirit spoke to him, "Remember the ninety-nine sheep Jesus left in order to recover the one. You can do no less."[3]

Allen could feel his heart beating. The struggle within his spirit was raging. How could he give up his only son?

"Dear Father, help me to hear the heart's cry of my son. We have no idea where Joshua is, but You know, Lord. I pray that You will guide Stephen and Simon to Joshua's side. Give me the faith and courage to let go and trust You. In Jesus' name, amen."

A grateful Ruth Hirsh reached over and hugged her good friend Mary Colson.

"God bless you, Allen," encouraged Ben. "Our Jesus will bring our boys back."

Cheers could be heard throughout the picnic area. The news traveled fast as intercessors began to lift up the names of Joshua Hirsh, Stephen Corbin, and Simon Colson.

"This is so awesome, Stephen. When are we going to leave?" asked a pumped up Simon.

"As soon as we get clearance from the Mole, we can be on our way. I suggest you spiritually prepare yourself, Simon, with some fervent prayer before we leave."

Simon rushed to his mom and dad for a group hug.

"Don't worry, Mom. If we stand for the truth, God will always be on our side."

Stephen and Michelle each smiled as they looked on, wondering if the young watchman was really up for the task God had just assigned him. Only time would tell.

Chapter 39

Are You a Watchman?

Everyone . . . competes for the prize. . . .
Now they do it to obtain a perishable crown,
but we for an imperishable crown.
I Corinthians 9:25

"He's not here," Simon muttered, slipping into the passenger's side of Stephen's white van. "We've been to his high school, old man Jenkin's deserted farm, the river crossing, on top of the Go-Cart Center, and our secret tree house at George Wallace Park, and still there's no sign of him. It's so strange. No one has seen him in months. It's like he just disappeared."

A concerned Stephen knew Simon was beginning to struggle with the lies of the enemy. Glancing over at the young overcomer, he grinned and said, "C'mon, Josh, hang on buddy. We are going to find you."

Driving by the Eastside ID Station, both watchmen instinctively stiffened, looking straight ahead without making any eye contact.

"Could I ask you a question, Stephen?"

"Sure, Simon. What's on your mind?"

"Is it all worth it? I mean, when you follow God's calling for your life. Is it really possible to fail?"

Looking away, Simon wished he could have used a better choice of words.

"When God calls a believer to a specific calling, He will always empower him or her to fulfill His purpose. Simon, although you have seen many believers judge and second-guess your father's decisions as a pastor over the years, it is only God who will be the real judge of what was really successful. For example, in the book of Hebrews, God commended Enoch, Noah, and Abraham for their faith, yet none of them received what had been promised.[1] In other words, my friend, obedience to the leading of the Holy Spirit doesn't always bring immediate results."

"So you're saying it's not always a picnic?"

"What I am saying is that there is a cost that comes from obeying God and allowing Him to truly be Lord of your life. Is it worth it? Absolutely. But sadly, for many professing Christians, their stubborn refusal to deny their sin nature keeps them from fulfilling God's will for their lives."

"Yeah, I can relate to that," replied Simon. "But how do you know when God is calling you?" he asked as he continued to check out the faces of those walking down Main street.

"Speaking for myself, I couldn't imagine doing anything other than teaching and preaching God's word. The desire to serve the Lord is a gift, Simon, a gift from God." The watchman couldn't help but glance over at the young boy who was slowly becoming a man of God.

"Yeah, but look what I've done," admitted a frustrated Simon. Slumping down in the front seat of the van with his arms crossed and head down, he freely admitted, "God has rebuked me so many times."

"Simon, the Apostle Paul wrote, 'My son, do not despise the chastening of the Lord, nor be discouraged when you are rebuked by Him; for whom the Lord loves He chastens, and scourges every son whom He receives.'[2] Let's remember, my friend, that God desires a relationship with us that is holy but not so perfect that we never sin. John the Apostle wrote, 'If we say that we have not sinned, we make Him a liar, and His word is not in us.'[3] In other words, we all sin and fall short of God's perfection. John also wrote, 'Whoever abides in Him does not sin. Whoever sins has neither seen Him nor known Him.'[4]

"Gee, Stephen, these verses seem to contradict one another. What is God really telling us?"

"Relationship, my brother. Yes, we all sin and fall short, but we do not habitually sin against our Lord. Those who continually sin, with no repentance, cannot abide in God's grace."

"So God will empower us to live holy lives as we continue to follow Him?" asked Simon.

"You got it, bro! The Lord exhorts us never to give up but to strive to become overcomers in Him!"

Turning left off Main street, a young man in a yellow Chevy signaled to Stephen to meet him next to Sluman's Garage. The watchman slowly maneuvered between two cars and pulled up alongside the garage.

"Good to see you again, Stephen," said Carl Russell with a smile.

After exchanging code names and information, the younger watchman informed Stephen of a resistance meeting being held at the closed-down Bethany Assembly Church.

After receiving an up-to-date list of new resistors from Stephen, Carl replied, "It's really the Lord that we got to meet like this."

While calmly watching two ID agents walking down the other side of the street, the watchman said, "Carl, we're looking for a seventeen-year-old boy named Joshua Hirsh. He's about five-ten, weighs close to 150, and has dark blue eyes with dark curly hair."

"Yeah, that sounds like Ben Hirsh's boy. I remember a report we got from one of our contacts last year about a teenager fitting Joshua's description. He was spotted over at Lakeview High. We checked it out, and it came up bogus. My guess is that Joshua's been arrested. It's getting ugly, Stephen. Christian families are really scared. They are turning each other in to avoid any confrontation with the authorities. Pretty much dog eat dog, if you ask me." The pain of so many submitting to the antichrist had become an emotional roller coaster for the young man.

"What is the Lord leading you to do, Carl?" asked Simon.

"My calling is Proverbs 11:30: 'The fruit of the righteous is a tree of life, and he who wins souls is wise.'"

"Have you thought about coming out to the camp?"

"I would like that, Simon," replied an appreciative Carl. "Heard you have twenty-four hour intercession going on that's very anointed. Thanks anyway, but my place is among the sinners until Jesus comes for us."

"Praise the Lord, Carl," encouraged Stephen. "May the Lord be with you," he added as he slowly steered the van away from the curb.

Their next stop would be Bethany Assembly. At the stoplight, Simon looked in his rearview mirror and saw two ID agents approaching Carl from his blind side.

"Stephen, isn't there a good chance that Carl will finally get caught?" asked a nervous Simon.

"Definitely."

"But we were taught that God promised to protect the saints during the great tribulation!" the confused teenager blurted out.[5]

"Simon, have you ever heard of Chernobyl, located near the border of Russia?"

"Sure, we studied it in world history. Wasn't that the city where a nuclear reactor blew up in the '80s, and several countries were exposed with radiation?"

"That's right. Several years ago Michelle and I had the opportunity to preach in the Ukraine. We were invited to come to a nearby city called

Chernigov. After visiting with the minister of health, Igor Kiroff, I found out that most of the kids in the city had either cancer or anemia. A large majority under the age of ten would die within five years."

"What happened?"

"Well, I was given the opportunity to visit some churches in America in order to recruit some teams to come to Chernigov and share the Gospel. In one Spirit-filled church in Arizona, an officer from the United States Army interrupted me during my presentation. He told the church that the damage someone would suffer by visiting Chernigov for more than a month would be equal to receiving one thousand x-rays from the dentist. When I told him that was correct, he asked why would I want to send anybody into such a mess."

"Why would you?" asked a shocked Simon.

"The answer was Axanna. She was nine, had red hair and freckles, and lived in an orphanage with two hundred other children. When I first visited with her, she asked Jesus to be her Savior. I can still remember her excitement after she received the Holy Spirit. The little redhead asked me all sorts of questions about heaven. Then she asked if her friends Galina, Sasha, and Tanya would also go to heaven."

"That's pretty cool, Stephen. Did you get a chance to pray with her friends?"

"No, Simon, I didn't. They had all died within the past six months."

"Oh, how sad," whispered the young boy.

"I promised to come back and give Axanna a doll. As we were leaving, she took my hand in hers and asked me, 'Can Jesus take away the pain that's in my stomach?' You see, Simon, Axanna had cancer. She wasn't able to sleep at night due to the constant pain."

"What happened to her, Stephen?"

"Four months later, I arrived at the orphanage with a beautiful Barbie wrapped in a big red bow. Ivan, the administrator, asked me if we could go for a walk on the grounds. As we walked among the children playing in the yard, he expressed how much Axanna loved me. Ivan's eyes filled with tears as he shared how the little red head with freckles had died in her sleep just three days earlier." Stopping at the light, Stephen looked over at Simon and said, "Only the Spirit of God can reveal the cost of a single soul for eternity."

With his eyes on the road, Simon nodded in agreement. He could not believe how his life had changed in such a short amount of time. There was no turning back. He was now willing to give his life for his best friend, Joshua Hirsh.

Pulling to a stop on a side street several blocks from the Bethany Assembly parking lot, both watchmen approached cautiously on foot. As they neared the church, they were stunned by the dramatic changes. It was hard to believe how deserted the church looked. There were no cars in the parking lot. The brown grass was choked with weeds. The building itself boasted no less than seven broken windows. Bethany Assembly's beautiful redwood church sign was painted with the words, "Beware of False Prophets."

Stephen stepped up to the side entrance and knocked lightly. He could hear movement inside. When the door swung open, there stood a smiling Jason Wylie.

"Stephen, what are you doing here?" asked the Mole as he slapped his friend on the shoulder and welcomed him inside.

As soon as the door was secured, the two friends greeted each other with a big hug.

"We've got to talk, Stephen. The ID force in Bethany has doubled since the increase of underage resisters. And they are looking even harder for you. Seriously, my friend, they plan to make an example of you and Pastor Mark in order to divide the resistance movement!"

"Thank you, my brother." The warning from Jason's eyes seemed to have no affect on the evangelist. "I'll try to be careful. The reason Simon and I are here today is to find a seventeen-year-old named Joshua Hirsh."

"A watchman on the east side of town may have spotted him in a truck that was traveling down Vaughn Street sometime last year," replied Jason.

"Has he been arrested?"

"Our contacts within the NWC have no record of him. No one seems to know where he is, but that would be my guess."

"Please tell all remaining watchmen that we need to find this boy as soon as possible! He's been to the Bethany Watchman Camp. It's top priority, Jason!"

"You got it, Stephen."

Entering the church's Activity Center, both men could see the intercessors quietly seeking the Lord in prayer.

"I've already briefed them concerning the camp," shared Jason. "I was just going to give them their departure times. You know it's no accident that you're here today. Do you think you could give them a message of encouragement? Would you?"

Only the Mole knew how scared this group really was.

"It would be an honor, Jason. Good afternoon, everybody," greeted the smiling watchman as he shook hands with all seventeen believers. "My name is Stephen Corbin, and I greet you in the glorious name of our Lord and Savior Jesus Christ."

A young lady named Esther asked, "Are you the watchman whom God has sent to our city?"

"I'm one of many watchmen God has called to take a stand against the false theology that has deceived a large portion of the body of Christ. For example, how many of you still believed in a pre-tribulation rapture when the antichrist proclaimed himself to be god in the Jewish temple in Jerusalem?"

All seventeen hands went up.

"Don't you see? God has supernaturally opened your eyes to the truth of Christ's Second Coming. Even though deceived teachers tried to manipulate you into submitting to their pre-trib teaching, the Holy Spirit eventually became your teacher and showed you . . ." Suddenly, Stephen sensed that something was wrong. "Quiet everybody! Jason, hide in the basement."

"But I . . ."

"Move it, bro. You know what's at stake." Within seconds the Mole disappeared. "Quickly, everyone move to . . ." Before the overcomers could respond, the doors flew open, and several ID agents stormed through the side entrance with their weapons drawn. The watchman motioned to the believers not to run but to stay in their seats. As Stephen was being handcuffed, Simon slipped unnoticed under a table near the water cooler.

"My name is Harvey Clay, and I'm the regional commander for the Bethany ID Security Force." He paused, taking the time to look at each resister. "Now listen to me," snarled the agent as the presence of demons filled the room. "Your two sentries who were stationed across the street are dead. Whether or not you live is entirely up to you. We are looking for a man whom the resistance movement calls the watchman. We have reason to believe he is in this room. The person who identifies him will be allowed to go free."

The overcomers sat motionless. The angry commander, having made a number of such raids before, had anticipated their reaction. He drew his 9mm from his holster and cocked it. Then he stepped forward and grabbed a young lady seated in the first row. He pulled her to her feet and placed the barrel of the gun to her temple.

"I'm going to count to five, and if no one says what I want to hear, then this little lady gets to see if Jesus really is real," said the commander laughing. "1 . . . 2 . . ."

"No need for that, Commander, I'm the watchman," confessed Joey Hipp, standing to his feet.

"Not true, I'm the watchman!" yelled Sonny Swann.

Within seconds, the commander was faced with seven men claiming to be the watchman. As he conferred with his agents, the spirit of death arrived and positioned itself next to Simon. At that moment, Simon got a quick glimpse of Stephen's face. When their eyes met, the watchman smiled. The young boy, who expected to see fear on Stephen's face, could only see peace.

Immediately the Spirit of God spoke, "Simon, Simon! Indeed, Satan has asked for you, that he may sift you as wheat. But I have prayed for you, that your faith should not fail; and when you have returned to Me, strengthen your brethren."[6]

After receiving a thumbs-up sign from Stephen, the young boy relaxed. "Everything is going to be all right," he thought.

A seething commander turned to face the group.

"If the real watchman gives himself up, we will let everyone else go. If he doesn't, then we will execute each of you, one by one! Now, what's your answer?" demanded the commander while motioning his agents to prepare themselves.

The overcomers could see the flashing blue lights from the agents' cars reflecting off the broken stained glass windows of the church. The young children present began to cry, pressing closer to their mothers.

"I'm your man," admitted the evangelist, stepping forward.

"Prove it," demanded the suspicious commander.

"There's no need for that, Commander," interrupted his lieutenant. "It's Corbin all right."

"Well, boys, we have finally got the watchman himself!" smiled the commander. "Under the jurisdiction of the New World Coalition ID System, I am required to ask you why you have not registered for your ID Number." His grin grew wider as he contemplated the probable answer.

"I'm a Christian. Jesus Christ is my Lord and Savior. I hereby refuse to worship anything other than the only true God: the Father, the Son, and the Holy Spirit!"

The overcomers began to cheer for their leader.

"Silence!" shrieked the commander.

As Harvey stepped away, the agent closest to Stephen cocked the trigger to his handgun and placed it to the watchman's head.

"Well then, Mr. Corbin, I must ask you to reconsider your decision not to register under the penalty of death."

Stephen smiled. The agents could hear him praising God for the honor of being a watchman. At that very moment, Simon remembered Stephen, the first martyr of the early church.[7] This courageous disciple gave his life for speaking the truth about the Father's Son, Jesus Christ. "Not much has changed," Simon whispered to himself.

The Spirit of God strengthened Stephen Corbin's soul as he continued to worship the Father. It would be his last act on earth and his first in heaven. Closing his eyes and lifting his handcuffed hands in an act of worship, the watchman whispered, "Forgive them, Lord. Reveal your love to those who have not yet received the mark of the beast." Opening his eyes, he lifted them heavenward. "Praise you Lord, for taking care of my lovely Michelle."

Bang! It only took one shot. The overcomers recoiled in shock. The watchman was dead!

"Shut up!" barked the commander. "This is what will happen to you and your children if you continue to resist the law. We know who you are, and we are granting you a twenty-four hour grace period to register. Do you understand me?"

Several of the overcomers nodded numbly.

"Remember this: If you do not register during this time period, we will be paying you a visit."

The commander turned and led his men out. Within the hour, the local news agency announced the execution of a resister named Stephen Lawrence Corbin from Santa Barbara, California.

"Hello, this is the Ryan's. May we help you?"

"Hey, Lee. This is Damien. How are ya'll doing?"

"We're doing all right, Damien. What's up?"

"Well, uh, I need to talk with Lance. Is he in?"

Damien's voice seemed nervous, almost halting to Lee. She knew something wasn't right. "Lance should be home any time now. Can I help you, Damien?"

"Boy, do I ever need some help," replied the troubled teenager. "I've been doing some heavy thinking lately, and I know something is wrong with me."

The silence that followed was a sure tip off to Lee that Damien was under the attack of the enemy.

"I'm working late tonight. Could you and Lance meet me behind the Industrial Arts Building at Lakeview High around ten o'clock?"

"Sure, Damien. Why don't you invite Jessie and Jake to meet us there too?" asked Lee.

"No, I can't, uh, I mean I haven't seen them in a long time. Besides, it would be better for me if I come alone. I'd be embarrassed if anyone else was around listening to what I had to say."

"But Damien, it would . . ."

Without any warning, the phone went dead.

Simon heard several believers sobbing out of control in the hallway of the church and realized that he had to get out of there. Slipping out the side door of the Activity's Center, he headed for Main street.

"Why now, Lord?" pleaded the distraught teenager as he thought about Stephen's death. "So many people depended on him, and now he's gone! And what about Michelle! Oh, Lord, this is too much!" With tears streaming down Simon's face, the voice of God seemed strangely silent. "But Lord, time is running out, and even if I find Joshua, how are we going to make it back to the camp?" The streets of Bethany had never looked so lonely. While making his way down Main street, he prayed out loud, "Please, God, I need someone to help me find Josh."

As the teenager paused to let a car go by, the Holy Spirit spoke to his heart, "Simon, do you not know that those who run in a race all run, but one receives the prize? Run in such a way that you may obtain it. And everyone who competes for the prize is temperate in all things. Now they do it to obtain a perishable crown, but we for an imperishable crown."[8]

With tears still running down his cheeks, the young overcomer answered, "Yes, Lord, I will never give up. Fear, discouragement, self-pity—none of it is going to disqualify me. Even though I can't see it yet, You will make a way for me if I continue to follow your leading and not mine."

After crossing over the intersection next to Max's BBQ, Simon continued his search, totally unaware that a warrior angel named Mordecai was walking several feet behind him.

At that very moment, back at the Bethany Camp, Simon's parents were crying out for their son.

"Oh, Allen, do you really believe God will send an angel to protect our Simon?" asked a worried Mary.

"Yes, I do, honey. Remember the verse the Holy Spirit comforted us with this morning during our prayer time? Jesus said, 'For He shall give His angels charge over you, to keep you in all your ways. In their hands they shall bear you up, lest you dash your foot against a stone.'"[9]

Chapter 40

The Signs That Follow a Believer

And these signs will follow those who believe.
Mark 16:17

After some much-needed sleep, Cindy Johnson slipped out of the back seat of an abandoned Lincoln Town Car. It had been several months since the young cheerleader had made her escape from the Eastside ID Station. Life before the New World Coalition takeover seemed like just a distant memory. After some more narrow escapes, Cindy had met Ray, Jay, and Faye, who were hiding out in a vacant boxcar over by the old train station.

Ray Largent and Jay Wilson were both freshmen at Lakeview High School when they refused to register for their ID numbers. They had briefly met during fall orientation but never traveled in the same circle of friends. Faye Braun was a junior at Cornwall Jackson High School, Lakeview's cross-town rival. She had first met the two boys while hiding out in a closed-down church on the west side of town. Ray and Jay finally managed to talk her into leaving just moments before ID agents crashed the scene.

They never really talked much about their families or how they all ended up together. But tonight was cold and foggy. Huddling next to each other in dirty blankets, they began to reminisce.

"So, Cindy, what's your story?" asked a curious Ray.

"You mean why I'm here?"

"Yeah, like, where's your family?"

"I don't know where they are. We were supposed to meet at Max's and then make our way to the Watchman Camp outside of Birmingham."

"What happened?"

"When I arrived at Max's, two ID agents were on duty, just waiting for something to happen. I couldn't put my folks at risk, so I hid out for a while. I came back later, but they were gone."

"Then what?"

"It's a long story. I wasn't spiritually ready for the persecution. It got so bad that one time Satan's lies almost got to me. My mom and dad were gone. My friends who registered seemed to be doing okay. The voice tormenting me told me it would go away if I would just register."

"He's a filthy liar," replied Ray.

"Yeah, it was Satan all right. I was just about to take the oath to Hendrick when the Lord supernaturally opened my eyes. I've been on the run ever since."

It was not hard to spot an underage resister. The circles under their eyes, the sweaty wrinkles on their forehead, and the shaking of their hands from the constant fear of being caught were telltale signs. The pressure of not knowing where their family was caused many to give up.

"How about you, Ray?"

"Well, my old man really flipped out when I told him that God was calling me to join the Christian resistance movement."

"He was pretty mad, huh?" asked Cindy.

"You could say that," said Ray smiling. "He really blew me away. I mean my family had gone to church every Sunday for over thirty years. The problem is that my dad thinks the world of J. W. Brown, the pastor of Bethany Presbyterian over on Winston road."

Cindy lit up. "My parents know the Browns! Are they okay? I've been praying they would make it to the Watchman Camp safely."

Ray just glanced over at Jay and Faye and then looked down at his breakfast, consisting of red kidney beans on wheat bread spread with Miracle Whip.

"Man, oh man," muttered Ray, searching for the right words.

"Ray, you have to tell her," whispered Faye. "She deserves to know the truth."

"What's wrong? Did something happen to them?" Cindy asked fearfully. Faye knew that the young boy from the east side was clearly in over his head.

The tall blonde was the only believer in her family too. After becoming a Christian, she got involved with the Jews for Jesus church on the west side of town. The pastors, Ben and Ruth Hirsh, gradually became Faye's spiritual parents. Joshua, their teenage son, played a major role in her discipleship. In fact, it was Joshua who practically begged Faye to come with them to the Bethany Watchman Camp. After praying and fasting, Faye was led by the Holy Spirit to wait for another time. Even though no one could see it, God was calling this young lady of God to help rescue believers during the persecution of the antichrist.

"What Ray is trying to tell you," Faye calmly shared, "is that Pastor Brown, his wife, and most of his congregation registered for the mark during the six-month voluntary period!"

"How can that be?" Cindy cried in horror. "Didn't they realize Hendrick proclaimed himself to be god?"

"It all seems like such a big blur now, doesn't it?" Faye said. "I can still remember when my family got their sign up dates."

"Must have been pretty intense, huh, Faye?" asked a bewildered Cindy, who was beginning to feel the pain of her three new friends.

"It sure was. My mom started accusing my pastor of brainwashing me. Of course, my dad was convinced that I was a member of a cult.

"Yeah, Faye's dad refused to lie to ID agents investigating her disappearance because he considered himself to be a believer. In his dreams. It sure didn't take him very long to report her now, did it?" Sitting on old tomato crates across from Cindy, Jay sadly shook his head. He and his friends knew the popular cheerleader was still struggling to grasp what had gone so wrong.

Jay Wilson had been a Christian since he was seven years old. At the age of twelve, he became the number-one backstroke swimmer in his age group in America. It was at this time that he developed severe asthma and had to give up his goal of someday swimming for his country in the Olympics. Most of his Christian friends knew that swimming had become Jay's god, and his relationship with the Lord had become, at best, lukewarm. With his idol of swimming cast away, Jay began a new life with new dreams. At one of the youth meetings at school, several of Jay's friends prayed for him to receive the baptism of the Holy Spirit. When he began to speak out in his new prayer language, Jay was instantly healed of his asthma. The power to witness became like a fire within him. It didn't matter where he was; Jay would always share his testimony with anybody who would listen.

"It's really pretty simple," replied Jay, leaning up against the wall of the boxcar.

"Simple!" Cindy blurted out. "There's nothing simple about it! There are wonderful Christian people being deceived, millions of them, with no chance of repentance once they take the mark of the beast!" cried the exhausted overcomer.

"What I mean, Cindy, is that Satan's strategy to deceive the elect in the end times is pretty simple to see. A few years back I loved studying about the end times and the coming of the Lord for His saints. The more I studied, the more opportunities I had to tell people that Jesus could return for his bride at any moment."

"Yeah, he shared so much," said Ray laughing, "that they started calling him Rapture Man."

"For sure," said Jay chuckling. "I memorized so many verses on the pre-tribulation rapture position that hardly anyone could debate me."

"Let's not forget Joshua," said Faye. "Right, Rapture Man?"

"You got that right," replied an appreciative Jay. "I still remember the first time I met Joshua Hirsh. It didn't take long before we were discussing the Lord's coming."

The tired cheerleader had stopped crying and was really listening. "Could you tell me about it?"

"Well, we first met at a citywide Bible Quiz competition. I looked up to Joshua because of his strong witness for Jesus. But what really bothered me was Joshua's belief that Christians would face the persecution of the antichrist. I asked him, 'But, Joshua, why does your church believe the rapture occurs in Revelation chapter 7, and my church believes it happens in chapter 4?[1] You see, for the first time in my life," Jay admitted, "I was beginning to have serious doubts about a secret rapture taking place before the seven-year tribulation."

"What did Joshua say?" asked Cindy.

"He said the Holy Spirit will reveal the truth concerning the coming of the Lord to any person who is open to hear."

"I've heard that one before," added a smiling Faye.

"Yeah, my pastor, Elmer Dyer, used to say that about believers who didn't believe in a pre-trib rapture."

"So, Jay, what verses did Joshua use to prove his point?"

"He really surprised me, Cindy. Instead of trying to prove his belief on the timing of the Lord's coming, he brought up the signs that Jesus said would accompany those who believe."

"You mean where Jesus said that believers will cast out devils, speak with new tongues, and lay hands on the sick."[2]

"That's right," answered Jay.

"So was your church open to the Holy Spirit in speaking in tongues, healing, and deliverance?" asked Cindy.

"No, not a chance. When I received the gift of tongues, most of the deacons just laughed it off and said it was not for today."

"What did your pastor say when God healed you of your asthma?"

"Now that's a good question," said Jay.

"What he means," interjected Ray, "is that Pastor Dyer said there was no way you could know for sure that Jay's healing was from God."

"So your pastor's problem was unbelief," replied Cindy.

"You got that right," affirmed Jay. "Josh was saying that if someone is open to the Holy Spirit in the signs that follow a believer, then the timing of Christ's coming and the events that precede it should be perfectly simple to see."

"But so many . . ."

"You're right, Cindy. The deception is pretty widespread. You see the devil knows exactly what he's doing."

"What do you mean, Jay?"

"Well, if you were the devil and you knew your time to deceive the body of Christ was almost up, what type of deceptions would you use?"

"I'd trick the most well-known Christian leaders into teaching that the body of Christ will be raptured before the antichrist appears."

"There it is!" added Ray.

"How about tricking Christians into taking a mark that denies the only true God?" asked Faye.

"Yep," agreed Jay. "A pretty smooth move Satan will use to eventually deceive millions. Put these two teachings together, and you pretty much have the deception of believers in the latter days."

"So, Jay," asked Cindy, "what made you change what you believed for so long?"

"It took the anointing of the Holy Spirit and a good friend who was willing to stand for the truth, to show me how wrong I was. Actually, it came down to deciding who I was going to believe—my pastor or the words of Jesus?"[3]

"You're so right, Jay," agreed Cindy. "The Spirit of God will guide those who really seek the truth."

Jay paused for a moment and replied, "Sadly, in the end, every person who rejects Jesus will be without excuse."[4]

After receiving permission, Luke took a walk into the hills sitting atop the well-hidden caverns. Thoughts of regret seemed to plague the young man. Continual flashbacks of what could have been were a tactic of the enemy that every overcomer had to defeat. For some it would require hours of warfare praying. For Luke, it had become one of the greatest challenges of his life.

"Oh Lord, so many lost, so many wasted opportunities. Yet You saved my whole family, my friends, and so many throughout the world who have just recently accepted You!"

With fervent prayers being lifted to heaven continually, the attacks of the enemy within the Bethany Camp were certainly limited. Nevertheless, the spirit of doubt had come with strict orders to stop Luke Appleby from praying.

"That's right, my son," whispered the evil spirit. You did everything you could. Trust me, you need to rest."

Suddenly the burden of intercession gripped Luke's spirit with deep conviction.

"Yes, Lord, but who do you want me to pray for?" asked Luke.

Instantly, the Spirit of God brought back the memory of Luke's last birthday party. All his friends were there: Ned, Drew, Hope, Jake, and Jessie.

"That's it, Lord. You're saying Jake and Jessie are under attack from the enemy!" The prayer warrior immediately shifted into prayer for the salvation and protection of his two friends.

"You're too late, Luke," said the foul spirit of doubt. "They both took the mark of the beast last week. And where were you when they really needed your help? You could have done so much more. Think of it, they will be burning in hell while you're enjoying heaven!"

"In the name of Jesus, I rebuke you, Doubt! Be gone!"

"Lord, I lift up Jake and Jessie and commit them into your loving arms of grace. May you save their souls for eternity. I pray for a divine appointment for them, an appointment no demon in hell can stop!"

"Hey, honey, I'm home!" called out Lance as he hung up his Georgia Bulldog hat on the closet doorknob.

"I'm in the kitchen," Lee yelled back.

She was just putting the finishing touches on Lance's favorite dinner: roast pork with applesauce and sweet peas. Entering the kitchen, Lance sensed that Lee was very troubled. He walked over and put his arms around her.

"Oh, Lance," Lee sighed softly, laying her head on his shoulder.

"What's up, honey? Are you okay?"

"Damien called earlier today and asked if he could meet with us tonight at ten o'clock. He said his life is really messed up. But . . ."

"That's awesome, Lee," interrupted an excited Lance, "another answer to prayer."

"No, wait, Lance. Something is really wrong with this whole thing. I can feel it. I don't think you should go tonight."

"Talk to me."

"Damien's voice sounded really funny, as if he was nervous about something. Who knows, Lance, maybe he was loaded. I don't know why; it just feels wrong."

"You know our rules, Lee. We don't witness to anyone who is high on booze or drugs. I'll call him back, and we'll set up a time for tomorrow. Let's say three o'clock, right after school lets out. We'll meet him behind the closed-down factory on Cherry Street."

Lee looked relieved. "Okay. I've got his work number. I'll call him right now." As she went to the kitchen to use the phone, Lance turned on his favorite Christian praise music and spread out on the couch in the living room.

A minute later, Lee re-entered the living room with a puzzled look on her face.

"So, did Damien understand our rules?" asked Lance.

"I'm afraid not. He wasn't there."

"He wasn't? I thought you said he didn't get off work until ten o'clock."

"I just talked with the manager. He said he fired Damien over three weeks ago. He thinks the boy was stealing from the store, but he couldn't prove it. I'm telling you, honey; something's wrong."

"Sounds like he's in trouble, Lee. If he is, we can't just ignore him. We have to help him if we can. You know that."

"But, Lance, do you . . ."

"I'll tell you what. After we spend some time in prayer, I'll go over and check out the high school ahead of time, just to make sure that everything is cool. Okay?"

"All right, honey, but what if it's a set up? Who knows what type of kids Damien's been hanging out with lately? Please, can you take another watchman with you?"

Lance smiled, reached over, and gave her a hug. "Sweetheart, if it will make you feel better, I'll take Lamar with me. I promise you; I won't go alone. Everything will be fine. God will be with us."

CHAPTER 41

THE BETRAYAL OF A FRIEND

What are you willing to give me if I deliver Him to you?
And they counted out to him thirty pieces of silver.
Matthew 26:15

"What do you think, Lamar?" Lance whispered while checking to see if anyone was following them.

The hill above the football field provided a perfect lookout of the Industrial Arts building.

"I don't see anyone, Lance, but it's still a little early," Lamar replied.

Lamar Minnich and Lance Ryan grew up together as best friends in a small town in southern Georgia. Both accepted the Lord at a youth summer camp when they were in junior high. Once they entered high school, Lance responded to God's call on his life while Lamar took a one-eighty and backslid. As the years flew by, Lamar's rebellion came close to the blasphemy of the Holy Spirit. He was at a party one night, high on speed, when the fear of God gripped him for the final time. The next morning when he woke up, Lamar immediately felt led to call his old buddy Lance Ryan. Before the day was over, Lamar was crying out for forgiveness on the living room floor of Lance and Lee Ryan's home in Bethany, Alabama.

"Wait a second. There he is, Lance," whispered Lamar.

They watched as the muscular teenager took a seat on top of a lunch table behind the Industrial Arts building.

"Is there anyone with him?"

"No, Lance, he's all alone," replied Lamar. "But . . ."

It was crunch time, and Lamar didn't like it. To him, it was just too risky. The funny thing was that his buddy didn't seem to care. That really made Larmar nervous.

"Lance, maybe I should go down with . . ."

"He's only expecting Lee and me. You stand watch. If anything goes wrong, give me a signal with your flashlight. I'll meet you as quickly as I can in the alley next to the tennis courts. You got it, bro?"

"I don't like it, Lance. What if this fog gets stronger? If you ask me, it's just too risky. Why can't you meet with him in the daytime?"

"Knowing Damien, tomorrow might be too late. He is reaching out for our help, Lamar. Don't worry. God will be with us."

Just after the mark of the beast was introduced, Lamar had become a Watchman for the Lord. It didn't take long for Lance to invite his best friend to move to Bethany and team up together in rescuing underage resisters. The bond between these two young men was like the one between David and Jonathan in the Bible. Either one would risk his life for the other.

Damien sat on one of the tables behind the Industrial Arts building, staring into the darkness. His hand shook as he lit another cigarette. It was 10:20, and the young man was beginning to think that the Ryans were going to be no-shows. Suddenly, the outside lights to the entrance of the football stadium automatically went on. There was a circle of fog surrounding a full moon, and the smell from the smoke of barbecue was in the air. As he rose from the table to leave, he heard some footsteps coming from the direction of the football field.

"You can do this," Damien whispered to himself as he flicked away his lit cigarette.

"Hey, Damien, how are you?" greeted a smiling Lance.

"What's up, Pastor," he replied rather uneasily.

"Got your message from Lee," said Lance as he took a seat atop a table, facing Lamar's direction, across from Damien. "Sounds like you need some help?"

"Well, lately it's been pretty rough."

"Okay, let's talk. You know the Lord can make things right."

"Isn't Lee coming?" Damien asked while nervously glancing over his shoulder.

"I'm afraid she's not going to make it tonight. I have to tell you though; Lee really has a burden for you. To be honest, Damien, we just don't get it. Some of your closest friends have accepted Jesus, and you've seen their lives totally transformed by the power of God. What has kept you from believing in Jesus as your Savior?"

Damien began to shake, conviction gripping his soul. The anger and bitterness bottled up within him began to pour out in heavy sobs. Knowing how bad the bondage within the boy was, Lance moved over and joined Damien with his back to Lamar.

"What's up with that?" Lamar muttered to himself, wiping away tiny beads of sweat from his forehead. Suddenly, he froze. Several dark figures were making their way toward the Industrial Arts building. Lamar began flicking the flashlight on and off repeatedly. "He's not seeing it. He's not seeing it! Lance, what are you doing? Turn around! Turn around!" Lamar couldn't wait any longer. It would take him at least a full minute at top speed to make it to the benches. As he started to run, he prayed for a miracle.

"Hold up!" Lance interrupted a rambling Damien. "Do you know what a word of knowledge is?"

Puzzled by the sudden shift, Damien just shook his head no.

"It's when the Holy Spirit tells you something you would have no other way of knowing. And the Holy Spirit just told me that you're not being completely honest with me. You're hiding something, aren't you? What is it, Damien?"

"Huh! What do you mean?" replied the shocked teenager.

"You can fool a lot of people, my friend, but you can't fool God. He sees right through your lies and says, 'Come unto Me, and I will give you Living Water.'"[1] As the strangers turned the corner, Lance heard a muffled cry coming from the direction of the football field.

"It's a trap, Lance. It's a trap!" screamed Lamar.

Without any warning, Damien jumped off the bench and moved away from Lance.

"Hey, what's going . . ."

"Hold it right there, Ryan," commanded the ID agent. "You're under arrest for refusing to register for your ID number and for promoting unlawful resistance among underage children."

Lance turned and stared at Damien. Lance's eyes of hurt seemed to burn a hole in the young boy's heart. The agents quickly handcuffed the pastor and taped his mouth. It only took a few more seconds for Lamar to turn the corner of the building.

"Freeze!" yelled two agents at the same time.

"He's packing!" shouted another.

As Lamar skidded to a stop, shots rang out. His body then lay motionless as the agents cautiously approached another dead resister. Lance and Damien stared in shock. Tears of sorrow trickled down Lance's face as Damien yelled, "That's not a gun! The dude had a flashlight. A flashlight, you idiots!"

The agents ignored the snitch as they frisked the body.

"Well, did he have an ID?" asked the agent in charge.

"No, sir, no ID. He was a resister, all right. I'll get the truck so that we can bring them both in."

The smiling head agent turned to Damien. "Okay, ace, you can go now. You can pick up your reward money tomorrow at the usual drop-off spot. And by the way, hotshot, don't forget that the reward was for a couple. If you want top dollar, you need to deliver Ryan's wife within twenty-four hours," snapped the agent, turning away in disgust. He hated hired informants. As necessary as they were at times, he had no use for traitors on either side.

As they took Lance away, one of the agents could see the hurt from being betrayed in his eyes. "What's the matter, Pastor? Don't you know that the name Damien really means devil?" asked the agent laughing.

As the ID agents drove away in their truck, Damien slumped down against the concrete wall. Immediately, the evil spirit of condemnation whispered, "You are a Judas, Damien. Just think of it, for thirty pieces of silver you destroyed Lance's life."[2] The foul spirit began to perfectly weave his web of deception. Within the hour, the demon of darkness would attempt to indwell his victim for eternity. Getting up to leave, Damien could not get the image of a weeping Lee out of his mind.

"Oh God, please, help her," he sobbed.

Several United States senators, led by Eugene McKnight, took their assigned seats as Wolfgang Hendrick and Father John made their entrance into the Grand Ballroom. The meeting was a mere formality because the outcome had already been decided.

"I greet you all in the name of peace and welcome you to Jerusalem," announced the official world ruler, Wolfgang Hendrick. "We express our appreciation for each of you for taking time out of your busy schedules in order to meet with us at this crucial time. Of course, since becoming a one-world government, we have been able to recognize the inherent needs of specific countries. Whenever special requests are received, we do our best to answer them with the utmost expediency. Today you will help millions of people who desperately need someone to care. Father John, please, come," said Hendrick as he handed the microphone to his prophet and took a seat that looked out over his guests.

"We have prepared a list of specific topics that we plan to discuss with you today." The priest motioned to his aides to begin to pass out the detailed agenda. "Please, let me remind you not to introduce any topics that are not on the list. Only those on the list will be addressed."

Senator Eugene McKnight raised his hand, and the priest acknowledged his right to speak. "As leader of this fact-finding mission from the United States, I want to congratulate the leadership of the NWC. Their overall vision nearly encompasses every country of our world. The unity we have managed to achieve is a direct result of the outstanding global vision of Lord Wolfgang Hendrick." All the guests in the room stood to their feet and applauded the man who had proclaimed himself to be god.

As the applause died down, the senator continued, "The peaceful coexistence of hostile countries is truly a miracle. While it took several world leaders a little more time to come around to our way of thinking, it was well worth the wait. Many countries have cut back on their military arsenals in order to strengthen the NWC's economy. We, as members of the NWC family, can now proclaim peace and safety for our world!"[3] Suddenly, the senator's voice changed from enthusiastic to quietly cautious. "Nevertheless, I am very troubled by the reports I've been receiving from our friends from Israel."

Hendrick's smiling lips froze and dissolved into a thin line of anger.

The Senator bravely swallowed and said, "Israeli intelligence has reported the build up of military forces along their borders by several neighboring countries. We have come to ask . . ."

"Enough!" yelled Father John, jumping to his feet. "Senator McKnight, you're completely out of order. You have deliberately broken the established laws of the NWC."

"But, Father John, we have come peacefully to ask if . . ."

"Silence!" the priest frantically yelled.

After a simple nod from Hendrick, security moved in and escorted the frightened senator from the room. As soon as the rebel was removed, all eyes turned toward their leader.

"Listen, my friends, the vision of the NWC was established in order to benefit you and your countries. The rebellious display you have just witnessed is unacceptable. Do I make myself clear? The deployment of troops in specific Middle East countries, mainly Syria, Jordan, Iraq, Sudan, and Egypt, is to help us maintain security over resisters who continue to defy our ID system." Hendrick slowly rose to his feet, paused, and then smiled. "If there was ever a time when we needed to trust one another, now is the time!"

✳

After his arrest, David Cowley was fingerprinted and assigned a bed in cell block C at the county jail. The entire cell block was filled with Christians who were arrested for trying to purchase bar-coded goods without having a personal ID, except David's cellmate. David wasn't too sure about him. The man kept to himself and hardly ever talked. The youth evangelist did notice that the quiet stranger in the top bunk would definitely perk up when anyone would begin to pray. As he lay on his lower bunk, David's mind began to reflect back to his days at Bible college. Everyone was so excited the morning of graduation. The scenes from that weekend seemed like only yesterday.

"Oh, David, we just know God has great things for your life," one of his teachers had praised him.

"She's right, honey," David's mom had gushed. "Just imagine, someday you will be a respected leader of your denomination."

"Remember that, son," said his proud father. "You make the right decisions, and someday you will wind up in some pretty big shoes."

The filthy smell of his cell brought David back to the harsh reality of what he was now facing. He had preached in prisons all over Illinois, so he was familiar with the odors and emotions of being incarcerated. But for most, it was a terrifying experience. Adding to their fears, was the harshness the guards showed toward anyone who professed Christ.

The fifth seal had been broken, which meant the martyrdom of believers worldwide. The Holy Spirit had already showed David that Eric Bahman, the first Christian martyr under the NWC, was purposefully singled out because he was a watchman. Within months of this death, millions lost their lives for their Savior. It was only a matter of time before everyone arrested would be facing an execution squad.

Bowing his head to pray, David whispered, "Dear Lord, strengthen the overcomers who are on the verge of caving in to the threats of the devil. Grant them the spiritual discernment not to entertain the lies of the enemy."

The young watchman was amazed to see so many believers who were willing to give their life for their Savior. Many of those who were arrested attended churches that did not train their members in spiritual warfare. Who would have ever thought that such anemic Christians would be called upon to do warfare in the final generation before Christ's Second Coming? Righteous anger welled up in David as he recalled the zeal of the pre-tribulation teachers, confidently teaching the saints that they would never face the persecution of the antichrist.

"Many ministers looked good in their Sunday morning clothes," thought David, "but their blatant disregard of Jesus' warnings to the elect living in the end times will eventually send a multitude to eternal hell."

"Now, no one really believes that," whispered the spirit of compromise.

"It's only when they see the fires of Hades that they realize they are doomed for eternity," said the spirit of death laughing.

"Lights out!" yelled a guard, hitting the main power switch.

The demons of fear and lying loved the darkness. They used it to weave their deceptions against the believers who didn't know how to defeat them. "The key to tormenting followers," bragged the spirit of fear, "is to find a weakness and then wait to attack when they are the most vulnerable."

"Just think of how many followers in America struggle with our voices and threats," said the demon of lying. "And their lack of knowledge of Scripture completely cripples any chance they might have for deliverance."

"I love the fight over the control of the human spirit," bragged the spirit of compromise. "The most thrilling part is when they surrender their will to resist."

"Yeah, it's amazing to see how ignorant humans really are," mocked the spirit of religion. "Most continue to think they can free themselves from our attacks through their own intellect and inner strength. They don't have a clue."

Throughout the night, David could hear the quiet weeping, the result of nightmares. At any moment, believers would be making a decision that would determine their destiny for eternity.

"Remember, son, you make the right decisions, and someday you will wind up in some pretty big shoes," mocked the spirit of pride. "Look at all those who believed in you, David! You could have really made a difference in so many lives that desperately needed your help. And now look at you—just another burned-out preacher whom no one will listen to. You might as well give up; you're not going anywhere," cursed the foul spirit.

David welcomed the five o'clock breakfast call. While the prisoners were marched in and seated, those on kitchen duty started dishing out the food. Today was a special day for the prisoners in cell block C. Right after breakfast they would get to exercise in the main yard for sixty minutes. It was one of the few times a prisoner could talk without the fear of being heard.

As the prisoners lined up, the normally hostile guards seemed almost friend-ly. David immediately sensed an evil presence and prayed, "Dear Lord, please help me to discern the enemy's plans so that by your grace we can overcome." As soon as the last man in cell block C passed through the metal detector into the yard, the answer to his prayer arrived from a most unexpected source.

"Oh, Brother David," said one of the guards sarcastically, "have you heard the latest news about the resistance movement?"

David knew this particular guard very well. He was an avowed atheist and was bad news to all those who openly professed Christ. "No, I haven't, but I guess you're going to tell me anyway."

"You betcha. They got him!"

"Got who?"

"Stephen Corbin." The guard paused for a second to enjoy the pain evident on David's face. "That's right, Davey. The watchman is dead!"

David's heart froze. "Where did they take him?" he asked sheepishly, acting like he didn't care.

"In a body bag, Cowley, in a body bag," said the guard laughing. "They wasted him right in front of a group of resisters."

David nodded to the guard and walked out into the middle of the courtyard. Instantly, he sensed the spirit of fear attacking the prisoners on the grounds. The prison crowd had heard every word.

An elderly prisoner approached David and whispered, "They're going to destroy the resistance movement, aren't they?"

David motioned to a small crowd of prisoners that had gathered around him. "We must hold on to God, do you understand me? The next seal, the sixth, is the sign of the end of the age. It's late in the game, guys. Don't believe the voices that come into your mind, especially when they threaten your children's lives. Remember that God will never leave us nor forsake us."[4]

"God would not allow my children to be hurt, would he, David?" asked a frightened father.

"In the first century when the Romans fed the Christians to the lions, men, women, and children lost their lives. They refused to deny their Savior by bowing to Caesar, another evil leader who claimed to be god. Jesus said, 'Therefore whoever confesses Me before men, him I will also confess before My Father who is in heaven. But whoever denies Me before men, him I will also deny before My Father who is in heaven.'[5] If we aren't willing to count the cost, should it even mean the lives of our children, Jesus will stand before His Father and deny knowing us!" Looking into their worried faces, David's heart ached. "When you signed up for this ride, you knew the cost. You knew there was a possibility that your own children might be sacrificed in an attempt to make you deny Christ."

One of the younger guards overheard David's message to the men and quietly approached the watchman from behind. "Hey, Cowley, you give a great speech! But when they put a gun to your head, you'll worship Hendrick just like everybody else. Wait and see. You're no different than the rest of your buddies."

Suddenly, David's cell mate ran toward the guard and tackled him from behind. Holding the guard's face down in the dirt, David's cell mate whispered, "I have a message for your stinking Hendrick. Tell him that I spit on him and on all of his plans."

As the cell mate lifted the guard up, another guard struck him from behind. He fell to the ground unconscious.

"Give him a week in the hole!" yelled the officer in charge. "That'll teach him never to touch a guard."

As they dragged his cellmate away, David committed to fasting and praying for him for the full seven days.

The *Bethany Herald* headlines announced that the NWC ID security force executed a criminal named Lance Christopher Ryan at 2:37 a.m. By refusing to register, the twenty-seven-year-old broke the NWC ID Law of Unification. Ryan, according to reports from the security force, was a leader in the underground youth resistance movement. The rebellious resister showed no remorse before his execution.

"Hello, is this Jason Wylie?"

"Yes, it is. May I help you?"

"How have you been, Jason? This is Lee Ryan."

Jason froze. "Lee, are you all right?"

"The Lord is faithful, Jason. Is there somewhere we can meet?"

"Of course, how about the spot where Lance and I used to get together."

"Perfect."

"Give me one hour. I'll have to clear my calendar."

"Thank you, my friend."

Lee went back to her corner table at Bertha's Coffee Shop. She knew she was being watched. It was just a matter of time before an ID agent would be standing at her table. Just after the waitress served her lunch, she discretely got up to use the restroom in the back of the Café and never returned.

CHAPTER 42

THE TWO WITNESSES

*And I will give power to my two witnesses,
and they will prophesy 1,260 days, clothed in sackcloth.*
Revelation 11:3

Hendrick met a small delegation from the United Nations that had just arrived at his coalition headquarters in Jerusalem. After seeing to the placement of the NWC security agents, Father John joined his lord in escorting the delegates outside to the terrace overlooking the magnificent grounds. Off to their left were rows and rows of Hendrick's beautiful rose gardens, his most prized possession. As they approached the center of the gardens, the two witnesses were waiting. The antichrist and his evil prophet stopped dead in their tracks. The delegation stood motionless. One aide whispered to another, "They have come just like the Bible said they would."

Hendrick turned toward his aides seething with anger. "Don't ever mention that book in my presence!"

The false prophet immediately ordered the removal of the intruders.

"No!" interrupted Hendrick, ordering the agents to put away their weapons. "Let these two beautifully dressed prophets enlighten us with their wisdom," he added sarcastically.

"We know who you are, Hendrick," announced Elijah, his words burning with righteous indignation. "We are aware of the lie with which you've deceived the people of this world!"

"And what is this lie you say the people have no knowledge of?" replied Hendrick while winking at his delegation.

"A lie that proclaims you, Hendrick, as god," Moses boldly declared. "There is only one true God: the Father, the Son, and the Holy Spirit," announced the prophet as he deliberately approached the deceiver. The closer Moses got, the more panicked Hendrick became. "The ruler of this world has created an unholy trinity consisting of himself, Hendrick, and Father John.[1] Your counterfeit signs and miracles have deceived millions into trusting in your promises, but your demise is coming!"

The visiting delegation was flabbergasted! No one had ever challenged Hendrick with such a total lack of fear.

Moses stopped and faced the delegates. "Listen to us, men of authority. Salvation is found in no one else but Jesus Christ. There is no other name under heaven given among men by which you can be saved.[2] If you confess with your mouth that Jesus is Lord and believe in your heart that God raised him from the dead, you will be saved. Everyone who calls on the name of the Lord will be saved."[3] The glory of God immediately burst forth from Moses' face, prompting the delegation to shield their eyes. Hendrick was forced to look away as Moses moved within three feet of the deceiver. "Let those who have ears to hear and eyes to see know that these two beasts standing before you have been given power to rule only until our God in heaven has accomplished his Word."[4]

The antichrist and the false prophet quickly turned and made a hasty retreat back to their headquarters. The two witnesses wasted no time in proclaiming judgment on all who had worshipped the beast's image or taken his mark!

During one of the breaks at the final checkpoint, Billy B. was asked by some of the teenagers to teach about the Day of the Lord. The word spread quickly, and soon a group of more than three hundred teenage overcomers surrounded the former trucker.

Luke stood and asked, "Hey Billy B., can you show us what events must still take place before the Day of the Lord can happen?"

"Sure, Luke," he answered while motioning for quiet. "Well, we know from God's Word that there are three major wars connected with the seven-year tribulation period. First there will be the Jerusalem war, then the Jehoshaphat war, and later the Battle of Armageddon. Jesus warned us of the Jerusalem war in Luke 21:20. This took place when the antichrist surrounded the Temple Mount and broke the Jerusalem Peace Accord he signed with Israel. How many remember the day Hendrick and his armies attacked Jerusalem?"

Every hand went up. It was an event still fresh in everyone's mind. An evil massacre of an unsuspecting people the world would never forget.

"The next war will take place in the Valley of Jehoshaphat, which is located near Bethlehem.[5] The gentile nations, which surround Israel, will again brutally attack the Jewish people just before the Day of the Lord."[6]

"Gee, Billy B., if the Jehoshaphat war takes place before the Day of the Lord, then when does the Battle of Armageddon take place?" asked a youth leader from Montgomery.

"The Battle of Armageddon is the last event of the Day of the Lord, immediately following the seventh bowl judgment. Whereas Armageddon takes place after the seven-year tribulation period has ended, the Jehoshaphat attack will begin sometime in the second half of the tribulation period."

"I get it!" yelled Drew. "Before the cosmic disturbances can occur, which signal the Day of the Lord, the surrounding Arab countries will come against Israel in the Valley of Jehoshaphat. Wow! That means the Jehoshaphat war must take place before we are caught up to be with our Lord!"

"That's correct," replied the smiling trucker. "The return of Christ will become imminent when the gentile armies of the antichrist attack the Jewish people in the Valley of Jehoshaphat. We must all seek the Lord, for the time is coming when . . ."

Even as Billy B. spoke, Arab armored units were aggressively advancing toward the Valley of Jehoshaphat. For years, Israel had friends who would stand with them against their powerful neighbors. That day was long gone. The United States, Israel's most valued ally, remained silent as the neighboring Arab countries positioned themselves for another all-out attack upon the Jewish people.

"Yes, Pastor Brown, they arrived about ten minutes ago. They're waiting for you in the fellowship hall," the church secretary nervously shared. "I'm afraid so, Pastor," replied the secretary, who had no clue on how to describe the utter fear and confusion of the parishioners who were waiting. As the pastor entered the side entrance to the fellowship hall, he could hear the murmuring among the parents. Every eye followed his uneasy stride as he stepped up to the podium.

"For those who have come this morning for answers, let me assure you that I too have been seeking the Lord. We all need His wisdom to help us overcome the confusion and division that has affected so many Christian families in our city." The experienced preacher could sense the urgency of those standing before him. He knew that this meeting could easily get out of hand.

"Pastor, what should I tell my wife and children concerning my son's disappearance? When Ray first told us he was going to join the underground resistance movement, we just couldn't believe it! Pastor, you know my son. He was only fourteen when his sign-up date expired. We haven't seen him in over a year, and my wife blames me for his disappearance."

"Yes, I know, Mr. Largent," Pastor Brown calmly replied without any emotion. "It is very unfortunate that young people all over our city seem to have accepted the false teachings of this resistance cult. In view of this tragedy, I have produced a doctrinal guide that will help our members stay faithful to the biblical truths that I have taught for over thirty years."

"What do you mean by biblical truths?" asked Ray's worried father.

"I'm afraid many of our young people have been deceived by these false teachers because they were not grounded enough in the doctrines of the Bible," replied the pastor.

"Are you saying that my Ray will lose his salvation if he believes in the teachings of this cult?"

The anger within the pastor could not be discerned with the human eye. Nothing was more important to J. W. Brown than the biblical dogma of his family. It was a legacy his great-grandfather had passed on to the Brown family. It was a belief system that his grandfather preached to thousands and the only standard of theology that his father taught him when he was a young boy. Nothing was more important to J. W. than the biblical legacy of the Brown family. He knew that sooner or later he would be forced to expose the resistance cult's evil perversion of God's Word.

"Now listen to me," said the pastor as he waited until he had everyone's attention. "The lie that you can lose your salvation through disobedience to God has been sowed by the devil for thousands of years. Jesus said, 'Not everyone who says to me, "Lord, Lord," shall enter the kingdom of heaven, but he who does the will of my Father in heaven.'"[7]

"So how do we do the will of the Father, Pastor?" asked a fearful mother.

"You simply profess Jesus as your Savior through baptism." Looking into the fearful eyes of his members, it was hard for the pastor to remember exactly how many times he had taught on this passage. "Jesus went on to say, 'Many will say to Me in that day, "Lord, Lord, have we not prophesied in Your name, cast out demons in Your name, and done many wonders in Your name?" And then I will declare to them, "I never knew you; depart from Me, you who practice lawlessness!" ' "[8]

"What is he trying to say?" whispered a grandmother who had just lost two nephews to the underground resistance movement.

"Don't you see the connection between the warning of this passage by our Lord and this watchman cult?" While the pastor paused for a response, the spirit of the antichrist moved off the podium toward a couple sitting in the first row. The demons could move about freely because these followers did not even believe in spiritual warfare. The foul spirits knew from experience that this particular pastor never discerned their presence. "Trust me, my friends. The prophecies of these self-proclaimed watchmen are false. They openly teach that demons can control the actions of a believer. Add that to their so-called miracles of healing, and you come up with a perfect picture of false teachers that Jesus warned us of in the end times!"

"Pastor, are you saying my son, Ray, was never a Christian because he was deceived by these teachers?"

"Mr. Largent, God chose who would be saved before the foundation of the world. He predestined those who were chosen for salvation and condemned those who were not. Nothing can change that. The blood of Jesus will atone for the sins of only those God has chosen. Jesus said He will not lose one of his own. Salvation is not about measuring up to God's standards. It's about believing in the death, burial, and resurrection of Jesus Christ. I can assure you that if your son truly is a believer, God will never allow him to be deceived. Let's remember that salvation is by grace alone!"

Hands of desperate parents went up all over the fellowship hall. The irritated minister knew he would never be able to answer all of their questions. "Listen up, everybody," he said, raising his arms and motioning for their attention. "To protect our families, we must expose the manipulations of this rapture cult. Are you aware that they are targeting children all over our city? These watchmen are encouraging underage children to disobey their parents and reject the biblical teachings their families have always believed in. Believe me, predestination and the imminent return of Jesus Christ are and will always be the cornerstone of our belief system!"

To J. W. Brown, this was just another attempt to put out a fire spread by the false teaching of this evil cult.

"Yes, Mrs. Samuelson," acknowledged the nervous pastor while wiping his sweaty brow with his handkerchief.

"Pastor, I have heard both Pastor Bishop and Evangelist Corbin teach, and I don't believe they are . . ."

"Excuse me, Mrs. Samuelson," interrupted the pastor as the spirit of control manifested itself at just the right time. "I do believe I have some very damaging evidence concerning these false teachers. Our own Thomas Bray and Gerald Pierce have come before our Bethany Ministers Association and have produced evidence that these so-called evangelical ministers are actually leading a cult."

"But, Pastor, I seriously doubt . . ."

"Excuse me, please," Pastor Brown interrupted again. "If you desire to defend the teachings of these two men, please, do it after our meeting. For those of you who have not been able to find your children, I'm afraid you have no choice but to report them to the NWC branch here in Bethany. I'm painfully aware of how agonizing this must be for you, but the fact remains that we cannot change our doctrines of belief just because those we love have been deceived. Let us remember that our Lord Jesus died for those who were chosen for salvation before they were born. The grace given to God's chosen is irresistible; in other words, every believer picked by God will persevere and be saved. God's word can be trusted, no matter what happens to your children!"

Stepping off the platform, the weary pastor headed for his office. After a short prayer, the associate pastor dismissed the fearful parents, totally unaware that they were leaving just as confused as when they arrived.

"Oh, Lord, where is he?"

The abandoned church building was a strange sight to the youth pastor's widow. Lee had so many wonderful memories of this sanctuary. She had never dreamed that her life would take such a cruel turn. "Lord Jesus, please, give me your strength, or I'll never make it."

"Do you love me, Lee?"

"You know I do, Lord."

"Do you trust me?"

"Yes, Lord, I trust you with my life."

"Will you obey me?"

"Yes, Lord, I know obedience to You will further the kingdom of God."

"Then peace be with you, my child, as you forgive Damien for his betrayal of your beloved Lance."

The release of anger came deep from within her soul as tears of repentance soaked the carpet floor. Lee knelt before God, asking forgiveness for her bitterness against the teenage Judas who was responsible for her husband's death. "Wherever you are, Damien, I forgive you!" Lee cried. "Lord, if it is still possible, I ask that you save his soul from eternal hell fire."

Outside the church, two ID agents were engaged in a conversation with Jason Wylie, the town's most respected lawyer. The agents had orders to check all churches that had been closed down in order to capture any resisters who were hiding out. Both agents personally knew Jason from his trial cases over at the courthouse.

"So tell me, how is your work going at the new ID security station?" asked the lawyer.

"It's getting a lot easier, Jason," replied the heavyset agent named Doyle. "For a while there, we were losing a lot of children. But now it looks as if the ID system will pretty much be assimilated throughout the country by the end of the year. It'll only be a matter of time before we crush the resistance movement for good," the agent proudly announced.

As Jason continued to stall the agents, a truck rolled quietly to a stop on the other side of the church. Its driver got out and moved quickly to a sanctuary window that was slightly ajar. He pushed it open far enough to slide inside. Lee heard a sound and looked up. She carefully watched as a stranger slipped through the open window and cautiously dropped to the sanctuary floor. With no hesitation, she moved from under the piano to behind the large podium near the front of the sanctuary. Outside, Doyle waved goodbye as he and the other agent began to move toward the church.

"Sorry, Jason, but we've got to be going. We have to check four more churches before dark."

The lawyer was talking as loud as he could as he bid the agents goodbye.

"Please, Lord, warn Lee of the danger coming her way," Jason softly prayed under his breath as he hurried back to his van.

The stranger got up and started walking toward the front of the sanctuary.

"Is anyone there?" he whispered.

Lee gasped. "Damien!"

"Is that you, Lee?"

"What are you doing here?"

"The Lord sent me. I was praying, and I felt led by the Holy Spirit to come to this church. Lee, are you aware that there are two ID agents in the church parking lot talking with Jason Wylie?"

Stepping over to the window, Lee could see two agents within thirty feet of the entrance.

"We've got to be going, Lee," whispered Damien.

"Why should I trust you?" she asked as she turned away and folded her arms.

"Please, forgive me, Lee. I was lost in bondage to the devil when I sold Lance out. But because of you, Lance, Lamar, and Carl, I asked God to forgive me and to save me." Bowing his head in shame, the young man uttered, "There are no words to express how sorry I am."

Opening the door to the Activity's Center, the agents could immediately hear talking inside the sanctuary.

"Looks like we got some visitors, Doyle," whispered the other agent as they drew their revolvers and began to run. Bursting through the double doors leading to the sanctuary, Doyle pointed his gun at the back of a man climbing through an open window.

"Hold it right there!" yelled the heavyset agent.

"Come on, Damien, just a little more and you got it!" whispered Lee.

"Hey, you! Did you hear me?" yelled Doyle. "Get down right now!"

Suddenly, a dark green van came tearing across the lawn of the church. As it slid to a halt, the side door of the van flew open.

"It's Jason!" Lee whispered. "C'mon, you can make it!"

"You go. They've already got me."

Grabbing Damien's arm, Lee urgently replied, "Not without you!"

With one last thrust, the young man raised himself up, only to be struck with four bullets in the span of two seconds. Tumbling from the ledge of the window, Damien's back hit the floor of the sanctuary with a mighty thud.

"It's time, Lee!" yelled Jason, glancing up to make sure his most effective escape route was clear. After the fall, Lee whirled and jumped into the waiting van. "Hang on, Lee!" yelled Jason as he accelerated away, exploding down Vaughn Road before making a quick left onto Hillsborough Avenue.

Doyle dropped down from the ledge of the window. He did not look pleased. This was not the first time that these two agents had stood staring over the dead body of an underage resister.

"What do you think, Doyle?"

"Well, whoever was with the kid got away in a green van identical to the one Jason Wylie was driving five minutes ago."

"You don't think the lawyer is mixed up with the resistance, do you?"

"Let me ask you. Have you ever scanned Wylie for his ID number?"

"No, I don't believe I have. But somebody must have checked his registration file."

"Yeah, I know that," growled the irritated agent. "I personally checked his file during last December's inspection."

"So, was everything in order? Did he have an ID number?"

"Yeah, he had a number, all right," replied a suspicious Doyle. "Let me ask you another question. Have you ever found any evidence of resisters attempting to falsify registration files?"

"Of course, Doyle. That's one of the main objectives of the resistance movement nationwide. You know that."

"What about here in Bethany? Has anyone ever been caught trying to falsify an ID number?"

"Well, there was that case last month when we picked up those three sisters who refused to register."

"So, refresh my memory."

"It was during a shift change. Day shift had a hard time punching up the girls' files and turned the problem over to the swing shift. Swing shift checked again, and the computers showed all three girls as having valid ID numbers. So they let them go."

"Did they scan them to be sure?"

"Nope."

"What a bunch of idiots!"

"You got that right! A total screw up. Our security commander, Harvey, almost had a heart attack. It took us a while, but we finally discovered the resisters' computer hideout on the west side of town. This was the genius who created the girls' IDs."

"So, what'd you do to this computer hack?"

"We wasted the punk right on the spot," said the agent smiling. "Even though his older brother got away, he never got a chance to escape."

"I just wonder," thought Doyle out loud. "You know what? I think it's about time we pay Mr. Big Shot Jason Wylie a little visit!" said the evil agent snickering.

"You know, this geek looks mighty familiar," said the other agent, reaching down and scanning the right hand of the dead body. "That's what I thought, no ID!"

"Who was he?" asked a curious Doyle.

"I believe his name was Damien Haley. He used to be one of our best informants. The commander ain't going to like this. No, no, no." The agent cursed under his breath.

Doyle began to fill out the death report of the underage resistor while his partner phoned the morgue for an immediate pickup. Through it all, no one seemed to care that the blood of another martyr had stained the carpet of Bethany Assembly.

It was several minutes before either spoke.

"Are you okay, Lee?" Jason asked.

"Yes, I suppose so. What happens now, Jason?"

"In about an hour, there will be a group of overcomers leaving for our Watchman Camp near the Florida Caverns State Park. I think it would be good for you to join them."

"Did you see the young man in the window that I was trying to help?"

"Yes, I believe it was Damien Haley."

"How did you know?"

"I know this might be difficult for you to grasp, Lee, but Damien was picked up by a watchmen named Carl Russell just hours after Lance's arrest. The Holy Spirit led Carl to the west side of town. He found Damien hiding in an old burned-out warehouse. It's really amazing how God protected the boy. When the ID agents used him as an informant, they purposely did not register him. Don't you see, Lee? The believers never would have trusted Damien if he had taken the mark!"

Staring out the window, she whispered, "Why wasn't I told?"

"It was for your own protection," responded a concerned Jason.

The vivid memory of Lance saying his final goodbye was still lingering in the back of Lee's mind. "Damien told me that the Holy Spirit led him to come to the church. As soon as I saw his face in the sanctuary, I knew he had become a believer. Just moments before, the Lord had convicted me of my bitterness and asked me to forgive him," said Lee with a sigh. "You know, after Lance died, I thought that the hardest thing in the world would be to forgive Damien. But when it came right down to it, it wasn't that hard at all."

"And how is that?"

"There isn't anyone I can't forgive after what Jesus has done for me," said Lee.[9]

"Glory to God," replied a smiling Jason.

The families were preparing to leave when the dark green van arrived at the BP gas station. The Mole stepped out of the van, discreetly signaling the leader of the three families. Just as she reached the group, Lee could barely make out the leader's reply. "Sure, Jason, we got room."

"Okay, Lee, you're all set. You will be inside the Florida Camp before midnight," shared a relieved Jason.

Reaching out for a final hug, tears running down her face, Lee had lots to say but the words just wouldn't come out. "Thank you, Jason. Thank you for everything!" With her head resting upon his massive chest, the Mole could feel her pain.

Bowing his head, he whispered, "It will be all over very soon, my dear friend."

As the two unmarked vans pulled out of the parking lot, Lee and the three families waved good-bye. She would never forget Jason. His love for the body of Christ was truly a gift from above. Softly the Spirit of God spoke to Lee's heart: "Greater love has no one than this, than to lay down one's life for his friends."[10]

CHAPTER 43

THE SIXTH SEAL:
COSMIC DISTURBANCES

I looked when He opened the sixth seal,
and behold, there was a great earthquake;
and the sun became black as sackcloth of hair,
the moon became like blood.
Revelation 6:12

The angelic host knew the opening of the sixth seal would produce different reactions from the children of light than from the children of darkness. The sun would turn black, the moon red, and the stars from heaven would refuse to shine. Mountains and islands throughout the world would suffer massive earthquakes. Many would hide themselves in caves in anticipation of God's wrath, which would soon break forth.

The face of the Lamb was majestic as He stepped before the throne. Reaching over, He picked up the scroll and broke the sixth seal with the touch of His right hand. The cheers from the heavenly host assembled before the Father were glorious. The time had come for the cosmic disturbances from above, the sign of the end of the age.

The periodic rumblings in the ground and the looks of fear and confusion upon the faces of the guards needed no explanation for the believers in cell block C. Since one o'clock in the afternoon, the bottom rim of the sun had begun to turn black. Norman, a good friend of David Cowley, who was in the next cell over, began to read: "I looked when He opened the sixth seal, and behold, there was a great earthquake; and the sun became black as sackcloth of hair, and the moon became like blood. And the stars of heaven fell to the earth, as a fig tree drops its late figs when it is shaken by a mighty wind."[1] Within minutes, the demons of doubt, fear, and death created an atmosphere of total panic within cell blocks A and B. The prisoners were cursing and demanding the guards set them free.

In cell block B, a nineteen-year-old boy convicted of selling crack started screaming, "I'm too young to die. Let me out of here!"

One of the overcomers called out to him, "Listen, my friend, Jesus can set you free right now. Pray these words . . ."

Before he could finish, the overcomers were pelted with anything the prisoners could get through the bars. The profanity and evil spewing forth was a harsh reflection of the demonic bondage within their spirits. The guard that was on duty deserted his post immediately after the first earthquake.

"Everybody ready?" yelled the worried producer. "C'mon, guys, it's now or never. 5 . . . 4 . . . 3 . . . 2 . . . 1 . . ."

"Good afternoon, everyone, this is Michael Dupree, reporting from the CNN International News Office in New York City. *CNN News* has interrupted all live TV coverage to announce that close to ten minutes ago hundreds of earthquakes began to erupt throughout the world. Unofficially, the death toll could easily reach into the millions. Immediately following the initial earthquakes, several European nations reported that the moon began to turn red on its outer edges. This has been verified by news agencies in Munich, Rome, and London. We are now switching to Ross Griffith in our Washington DC bureau for a more detailed update."

"Thank you, Michael. As the moon was turning red on one side of the globe, we can report that almost simultaneously the sun began an eclipse, with its outer edges becoming pitch black. Astronomers have been unable to explain these eclipses that commenced several minutes ago," announced the animated Griffith. "Scientists are at a loss to explain such a rare phenomenon. They do want to stress that this type of cosmic disturbance does not pose any immediate danger."

"Ross, we have just received news from the White House that the president and his advisors are, at this very moment, discussing the implementation of the New World Coalition Emergency System."

"Excuse me, Michael, would you please tell our listeners exactly how this emergency system will affect us if it is implemented?"

"Certainly. Our NWC leader, Wolfgang Hendrick, is the only person who has the power to activate the Worldwide Emergency System. This means that all member countries will have to abide by any decisions set forth by the NWC. Then the United States will . . ."

"Sorry, Michael," interrupted Ross, "We just have received a news update from the U.S. Seismological Bureau reporting a considerable shift in the earth's core. This appears to be the cause of the massive earthquakes that are occurring throughout the world. Several experts on earthquakes have assured us that this scenario was going to happen sooner rather than later. We expect to have updated reports every five minutes along with a complete evaluation of the cosmic eruptions. Please stay tuned."

As people huddled in their homes anxiously awaiting some sort of news, Carl continued to make his rounds in his old yellow Chevy. He had just received his final report of all underage resisters still at large. Most of these kids had been on the run for a long time. "Not a pretty sight to see, parents submitting to the antichrist and then turning in their own children," reflected Carl.

Store owners on Main Street were at first making jokes about the eclipse while they talked with customers outside their shops. But once the earthquakes began, "That's all she wrote," said Carl. The young watchman quietly observed employers deserting their businesses, not even taking the time to lock up, even though they knew looters would be appearing shortly. Carl shook his head in sadness as he turned right at Sluman's Garage. Movement out of the corner of his eye pulled his head around as a teenager ducked behind two parked cars.

Simon didn't get a good look at the car but sensed he had been spotted. He jumped up and started to run. His only thought was to get far enough away to prevent the agent from identifying him. Carl hit the gas, cutting through Sluman's in pursuit. There was something familiar about the boy, but Carl couldn't quite place him. "Hey, wait!" yelled the watchman.

Simon continued to run as fast as he could until the Spirit of God spoke to his heart. "Trust me, my child. There's nothing to fear." Slowing down, the young boy turned and faced the yellow Chevy. Immediately, Simon's eyes lit up as he recognized his pursuer.

"Carl, Carl, it's me, Simon Colson!"

"Well, I'll be a monkey's uncle!" squealed Carl as he stopped the car and got out. As the two brothers in the Lord began to laugh, joyfully slapping each other on the back, the devastating earthquakes of the sixth seal continued to pound the earth. Who would have ever imagined that in the very near future, after the opening of the seventh seal, the entire planet would be engulfed with the fire of God's wrath?

The office of Wylie and Wesson had provided a perfect front for the Mole. Jason had done an excellent job directing resisters to camps all over the Southeast. He had just finished contacting every watchman still within the boundaries of Bethany with detailed instructions. A new update reported two underage resisters being rescued right out of the ID agent's car. Sadly, this event only escalated the conflict. Within the past hour, all Bethany NWC agents were given permission to shoot anyone who had not officially registered. Suddenly the Holy Spirit spoke to Jason's heart. "Mayday, Mayday, you must go! Now!"

"Lord, please save their souls," prayed Jason as he quickly locked the front door to his office and slipped out the back entrance.

Like all the other watchmen, the Mole would make one final search before making his way to the Bethany Watchman Camp. Pulling his dark green van into a small dark alley, the lawyer knew the risk he was taking for just one more look. It only took a minute for several squad cars to converge on Jason Wylie's law office.

Wasting no time, Doyle ordered the office surrounded. "Remove the door!" he barked. After one of the agents attached a small device, the front door was blown to pieces in just a matter of seconds.

"Here we go, sir," yelled one of the agents.

"So, what have we got?" snarled Doyle.

"That's strange," uttered the agent. "He disconnected the surveillance equipment but left his computer on standby."

"So the little coward must have fled the coop when he heard us coming," said Doyle. "He didn't even take the time to dispose of his evidence. Punch up the screen, and let's see how much Mr. Wylie really knows about the Christian resistance movement." It only took a second for the agent to touch a key. After a short pause, there was a puff of smoke coming from the back of the computer. "Turn it off. Turn it off!" screamed Doyle. It's a set up, you idiot!" Within seconds the computer completely melted from within. "He must have known we were coming. That does it!" yelled Doyle. "He must have been tipped off. But who is the rat?"

"Do you want us to issue an APB?" asked one of the agents.

"Top priority, guys. If I'm not mistaken, I think we got a top soldier in the resistance movement right under our noses."

"Hey, boss," hollered an agent manning one of the squad cars. "Looks like we got a positive ID on Wylie's green van. Our dispatcher has tracked his vehicle to the east side of town, close to Lakeview High."

"Let's move it! Wylie has slipped through our hands for the last time! I'm going to personally waste him just like I did his buddy Corbin," said Doyle with a smile.

By three o'clock in the afternoon, a quarter of the sun was blacked out. Mountains all over the world were trembling. No nation was untouched. The devastation, especially in the major cities, brought mass panic. The mourning for the dead and those missing could be heard around the globe. A frightened and hysterical world looked to its god and leader, Wolfgang Hendrick, for some sort of miracle!

The bodies of Jews lay scattered throughout the Jehoshaphat Valley. The picture of death had invaded Israel's borders a second time. When the first earthquake hit the Jehoshaphat Valley in Israel, tanks from the neighboring countries sputtered to a halt. Immediately, thousands of Arab soldiers began to withdraw. The nation of Israel began to shout with joy.

"Our God has answered our prayers for deliverance! He will fight for us because we are his children!" proclaimed an overjoyed rabbi.

Unlike the rest of the world, the Jewish people began to proclaim victory. But the nation of Israel had forgotten the prophet Joel and his frightening end-time prophecy. The prophet had proclaimed, "Let the nations be awakened, and come up to the Valley of Jehoshaphat; for there I will sit to judge all the surrounding nations. Put in the sickle, for the harvest is ripe. . . . Multitudes, multitudes in the valley of decision! For the Day of the Lord is near in the valley of decision. The sun and moon will grow dark, and the stars will diminish their brightness."²

As the Jewish people pretended to pray to a God whom they had mostly abandoned, stars started to go out all across the sky. The lights of the universe were being systematically turned off.

Ray and Jay took turns keeping watch throughout the night. The boys knew that it was only a matter of time before the NWC agents searched the boxcars. During their night watch, they would pray and continue to ask God for His leading. It was just before dawn when Jay sensed the Holy Spirit's warning them of danger. As soon as the sun came up, Jay shared with the others what God had laid on his heart. After weighing out their options and seeking the Lord in prayer, the foursome decided to make their move, unaware that the sun had just begun to turn black.

Winding their way through the train yard and down to the beginning of the town square, Ray and Cindy got a quick glimpse of a small group of agents scanning people on Main street. Crouched behind two trucks from the *Bethany Herald*, Ray asked, "Hey, Rapture Man, are you sure that God is leading us to do this? I mean the box car is looking a lot better all of a sudden," whispered his close friend.

"They are coming our way, so we had better decide something and fast!" whispered Cindy.

Just then, a driver rushed out of the newspaper distribution center and jumped into the front seat of one of the trucks. After starting the engine, he slowly pulled away from the curb.

"So where are they?" yelled one of the ID agents.

"That's strange," muttered the other agent as the newspaper truck passed them by. "I thought for sure I saw at least four of them."

The guards stationed at the county jail froze as the ground rolled and heaved. Large cracks appeared in the exercise yard and between the buildings. They watched, unable to move, as the ground spilt under the power poles along the road. One moment they were standing, and the next it was if they never existed. The yelling and screaming from the cell blocks increased when jagged cracks started to appear in the walls. To hear the deep-seated rebellion spewing out of the mouths of those who had rejected Jesus was a hellish nightmare. The prisoners began to mock the overcomers who were on their knees praying to the Father in Jesus' name.

Suddenly, a section of the roof covering cell block A caved in on several prisoners. With the sixty-year-old facility disintegrating around them, the guards hastily decided to free the prisoners. In cell block B, the metal doors were twisted out of place. Those who were trapped were clawing at their doors seeking escape. The guards rushed in, screaming at them to get back so that they could attempt to unlock the main gate. One guard removed his revolver and started shooting into the air. At first, his shots didn't even faze the crazed prisoners.

"Get back! Get back! We can't unlock your cells unless you stop pushing and step back!" screamed the head guard.

Miraculously, the prisoners pulled away as smoke from the generator room started to seep into the cell blocks. It would take only a few minutes for the prisoners to be engulfed with heavy, black smoke. After punching in an emergency code, only the doors of cell blocks A and B opened. The prisoners surged forward, sweeping the guards with them. Outside the jail stood two guards who decided to get out before it was too late. One guard grabbed his friend and yelled, "My God, they're not going to make it!"

The ground under cell blocks A and B was opening. Suddenly, a jagged chasm appeared across the front of the cell blocks, creating a huge hole. The guards on the outside could hear the screams of sheer terror. The hole was widening as it slowly swallowed cell blocks A and B. Prisoners who were still trapped inside their cells cried out to God for help just before plummeting to their death. Cellblock C was relatively unharmed. The prisoners who had mocked the overcomers were dead!

With NWC sirens erupting all over the city, it would only be a short time before the National Guard would be called in to maintain security. Many of the ID agents had gone AWOL in order to search for their families amidst the chaos. The schools were closed, the shops were boarded up, and looters could be seen emptying the gas pumps at Sluman's Garage. Suddenly, the door to the security booth swung open. In ran the guard who was tackled by David's cell mate. He wasted no time in opening every cell that held resisters. "You're all free to go," yelled the guard, "but once you get outside, you're on your own. I'm warning you that the National Guard has been called in to help

ID agents arrest and execute anyone refusing to register. It's a war zone, guys. I pray your God will be with you."

The last cell to be opened was David's. As the guard turned the key and the bolts slid back, David asked, "Why did you come back and do this for us?"

"Aw, I was just showing off when I tried to intimidate you. Something inside me just kept telling me to harass you. To be honest, I've never taken the mark of the beast or worshipped Hendrick. I guess no one ever seemed to bother me because of my loud talking," confessed Donnie King for the first time. "The other day when you were out in the yard, I saw you lead a prisoner in a prayer for salvation."

"That's right, Donnie. Jerome gave his heart to Jesus and repented of his sins. Have you seen the awesome change in his life?"

"Sure have. It looks like weights have fallen off his shoulders. But you had better get going before they catch you."

"Only if you let me pray for you first."

As the resisters fled, the watchman bowed and prayed with the young guard. For the first time in Donnie's life, he believed in the death, burial, and resurrection of Jesus Christ. By the time they finished their prayer, Jesus Christ had become Donnie's Savior, with the Holy Spirit indwelling his human spirit.

"Wow! What a wonderful peace!"

"Let's go, my brother."

As they approached the front door to the jail, both could hear the guards running up the steps to the entrance.

"Now what?" asked Donnie.

"God will provide."

"Well, my brother, He'd better hurry."

They quickly turned and made their way back to the cell block. Hiding behind a broken down wall, David silently prayed, "Not our will but yours, Lord. If there is a way, I pray that You will show it to us."

The guards coming through the front door stopped as the ground shifted again. Made cautious by what happened to cell blocks A and B, they hesitated before entering cellblock C. The building began to shake, and more cracks appeared. The sound of stone grating on stone pierced the air. As soon as things quieted down, the guards rushed from the building. David and Donnie got up from where they had been thrown by the shifting ground.

"Are you all right, Donnie?"

"Yeah, I'm okay. I, uh, wow, God sure works fast, doesn't He?"

David turned to see what Donnie was referring to. There in the rear wall was a crack big enough for them to fit through. David grinned at Donnie as he slipped through the giant hole. The ex-jail guard quickly followed, praising the Lord for His faithfulness as they reached the street adjacent to the jail.

"Hold it right there; you're not going anywhere!" yelled a young agent. His right hand began to shake as he cocked his 9mm revolver. He was just a boy really, trying to do a man's job.

"We haven't done anything wrong," replied David, slowly moving toward the young ID agent.

"Let's see your ID numbers," the agent replied as he produced a mini scanner that was attached to his belt.

In the time it took to turn the scanner on, Donnie stepped in front of David and began to walk towards the agent. "You're no killer," Donnie insisted, continuing to move toward the pointed gun.

"Stop right there, or I'll shoot!" the nervous rookie screamed.

"No, I don't think so," replied the former jail guard. Slowly, Donnie reached over and removed the gun from the agent's trembling right hand.

"No, wait!" yelled David as the young agent took off running. Racing across the street, David and Donnie made a vain attempt to catch him. Slipping behind some large bushes, they decided to wait and watch. A short time later, a familiar truck appeared, prompting David to jump up and flag it down.

"Hey, David!" yelled Norman as he pulled up in his black Ford truck. "It's time to be going, my brother. Do you hear me? Over fifty percent of the sun is black, and all hell is breaking loose on Main street."

"Sorry, bro, but I've still got some unfinished business to take care of."

"Are you crazy? The ID agents have just been given permission to shoot any resister on sight! They all know your face, David. It's downright suicide. We've got to get out of Bethany right now!"

The faces of Eric Bahman, Sara Whitaker, and Stephen Corbin came to David's mind as he silently asked the Lord, "What would You do?"

"Hey, David!" yelled Norman while adjusting his CB radio. "Listen to this. "The National Guard has just executed three underage resisters on the east side of Bethany near Lakeview High."

"Did they give any details?"

"Wait a second. Yeah! Two boys and a girl," he shouted back.

"Any names?"

"Here it is. The boys were Tanner Harrison and Reggie Lincoln! The girl's name, uh, was, uh, Phillips! Amy Phillips! Did you hear that?"

"Yeah, I got it," uttered the brokenhearted watchman.

Norman, lowering his voice, asked, "Did you know these kids?"

"Yeah, Norm, just babes in Christ."

"What are you thinking, David?" pleaded his friend. "C'mon, get in!"

Amidst all the looting of the stores, the agents' shooting, and the utter pandemonium that had overwhelmed the downtown, a quiet still small voice spoke to the David's heart. "There is another babe in Christ that needs someone to care." The believers inside the truck refused to interfere. They patiently continued to pray for God's perfect will.

"God bless you, my brothers. Be safe in Jesus," exhorted David as he waved for them to move on. The watchman knew their next stop would be the safe confines of the Bethany Watchman Camp. Both David and Donnie waited until they could no longer see Norman's truck. "Let's go, Donnie." Running toward the jail, they rushed up the stairs, opened the heavy front door, and disappeared into the dark, smoky cell blocks.

After finishing his drive through downtown Bethany, Jason felt relieved as he turned onto I-65 North to Birmingham. "Praise you, Jesus! Thank you for making it possible for my wife and son to make it safely to the Watchman Camp. Through the entire great tribulation, You have protected me with countless miracles. And now You have made it possible for me to share the rapture with those I love." The Mole set the cruise control at sixty-five and leaned back, turning on the radio to listen to the news.

But something wasn't right. The peace of God, something that Jason had always relied on, was strangely absent. While pulling the van off the highway and coming to a stop on an access road, the Spirit of God spoke to him. "I want you to go back. There are four young people who need your help."

Jason began to struggle with what the Holy Spirit was asking him to do. God wanted the young lawyer to reflect back on instances when he was supernaturally protected. There were many times when he had trusted the Lord, even when it meant that his clients could end up behind bars for many years if he were wrong. Jason smiled, remembering a special Friday night prayer meeting when the Holy Spirit had given him a unique word of knowledge. A small group of Christian law students had been praying for over two hours for God to open the hearts of Muslim people to receive Jesus as their Savior. The powerful anointing at the meeting was a result of heartfelt intercession for a people the students had never visited.

"Oh, Lord, I can't interfere when there is such a mighty presence of your peace," the young law student had replied, not totally convinced the word in his mind was from God. After two more promptings to speak God's message to the group, Jason decided not to speak. Within seconds of his third refusal, the Holy Spirit prompted the student standing behind him to sing the exact word that he was supposed to speak. As the students rejoiced over the word of encouragement, Jason fell to his knees at the altar and asked God to forgive him for his stubborn self will.

The young law student vividly remembered God's words in response to his prayer for forgiveness. "My son, I am not angry with you. I will just use somebody else who is willing."

Jason suddenly realized the decision he would now make depended upon how much he really trusted God. In other words, if Jason had not learned obedience to the leading of the Holy Spirit within the last few years, he would not obey what the Holy Spirit was asking him to do at this very moment. After turning the van around and heading back to Bethany, Jason knew God was speaking to him.

The commitment he made that night in a little chapel in Columbia, South Carolina, had changed his life forever. That was a night when God visited Jason in a supernatural way; it was a point in time when the Spirit of God guided him in the right direction—God's will for his life!

Pulling onto Main street, the alert lawyer could hear the loud gunshots. Up ahead, four teenagers were running from ID agents, the looters not even bothering to look.

Very softly, the Holy Spirit spoke to his spirit, "Go to Vaughn Road." Accelerating, his tires squealed as he took a shortcut through the parking lot of Max's BBQ. He hit Vaughn Road just in time to see four kids rounding the corner. Skidding to a stop, Jason leaned over and threw open the side door.

He yelled at them, "My code name is . . ."

"Who needs a code name!" screamed Ray as the four of them piled into the van on top of each other.

Hitting the gas, the van lunged forward. As the kids struggled to untangle themselves, Jason curved onto a side street. Bullets slammed into the van, prompting everyone to hug the floor. One bullet struck the speaker in the backseat; another struck the driver door, narrowly missing Jason's leg. Gunning the engine, Jason jerked the wheel and exited down a narrow alley. No shots followed.

A relieved Jason sighed, "Praise God, we've lost them."

The Mole glanced back over his right shoulder at the four exhausted teenagers. He smiled after recognizing Cindy from the Bible studies at the high school.

"Hey, Jason! What's up?" greeted a joyful Cindy.

"Nice of you to drop in," said Jason laughing. "Want to introduce me to your friends?"

"Sure. This is Ray Largent, Jay Wilson, and Faye Braun," she said as everyone began to crack up.

"Excellent! You're all on our final list of overcomers at large."

As Jason turned onto I-65 North toward Birmingham, he began dodging the large cracks that had just appeared on the highway. The trip to the camp would not be easy. The intensity of the earthquakes seemed to be increasing by the second.

"I know this sounds crazy," said Ray, "but I've heard rumors about a leader within the watchman movement that is called the Mole."

"Me too, but no one really knows who he is," added Jay while keeping watch out the rear window.

Before the Mole could answer, Cindy interrupted and asked, "I don't suppose you have my parents on your list of those who are at the Bethany Watchman Camp, do you?"

Jason reached for his camp list updates and began to thumb through the J's.

"I'm very sorry, Cindy. According to our files, your parents never checked in at the Bethany Camp."

After bowing her head, Cindy whispered, "Oh, Father, I come to you with a thankful heart for all the miracles you have performed for us. I give you my folks and place them in your loving arms." Then she began to weep quietly.

After finding another printout, a smiling Jason replied, "Hey, wait a minute. If your parents are Warren and Joyce Johnson, they checked into a camp in Mississippi over a year ago!"

"They sure are!" squealed Cindy, who received a big hug from Fay while Ray and Jay gave each other high five's.

CHAPTER 44

OVERCOMERS FOR JESUS

Fear not, for I am with you;
be not dismayed, for I am your God.
I will strengthen you, yes, I will help you,
I will uphold you with My righteous right hand.
Isaiah 41:10

"How about Lakeview High?"

"It's too dangerous, my man," insisted Carl while pausing to see if Simon had any fight left in him.

"What do you think our chances of getting caught are?"

"Pretty high, I guess," replied Carl, leaning up against his car and calmly clipping his fingernails.

"We've looked everywhere!" yelled the frustrated PK. "Where could Josh be?"

Lowering his nail clipper, Carl suggested, "Maybe we should look in a place where he would never go."

"Are you saying that Joshua is hiding in a place where we would never look for him?"

"Yep!" said Carl.

Simon grinned back. At the same time, they both said, "The Main ID Security Office!"

"Do you think he's okay?" asked David.

"Only time will tell," answered Donnie as they moved past the back of cell block C.

They could still hear the guards inside moving about. Entering the solitary confinement building brought an eerie silence. Just inside the door was an empty guard post.

"Must have spilt during all the shaking," muttered Donnie.

As the new convert searched the key cabinet, David moved down the row of cells that had broken the spirits of many prisoners. The four padded concrete cells were six by six and had no windows. David's cell mate had been in solitary confinement for more than five days.

"Got the key!" yelled Donnie. He paused as he reached the door. "David, you had better brace yourself. Your cell mate may be dead." Donnie inserted the key into the lock, activating the door release. Slowly, the heavy metal door swung open and flooded the concrete hole with light.

The prisoner immediately shielded his eyes with his left hand and whispered, "Praise the Lord."

While lifting the prisoner out of the hole, the floors of the prison began to shake.

"How do you feel?"

"Sorry, David," Donnie interrupted, "but we don't have much time."

Grabbing hold of the weakened man, Donnie slung the prisoner over his shoulder. "Run!" he yelled as the rumbling grew louder. When they reached the front door, David cautiously opened it and peaked out. Several National Guard soldiers had set up a temporary headquarters on the front steps of the jail. "Let's try the backdoor," Donnie suggested as the ground rolled beneath their feet. After locking the front door from the inside, they quickly moved toward the back of the prison. Suddenly the former guard realized that the backdoor was wired for security and locked tighter than a drum.

"Did you hear that? They are trying to get in through the front door. What's our next move?" asked David. Donnie was not used to this type of spiritual warfare and was beginning to blank out. The spirit of confusion had just arrived and was hitting the new convert with a barrage of evil thoughts. "In Jesus' name, I bind you, foul spirit, and rebuke you away from us!" commanded David.

"Here we go!" Donnie cried out, opening the door that led to the underground parking lot. As they rushed down the stairs, they could hear voices of agents coming from cell block C. The underground garage housed a half dozen police cars, two swat vehicles, and one armored truck. Donnie had the keys to his squad car, so they jumped in and positioned his car about thirty feet from the entrance. Just as the agents burst through the door leading to the garage, Donnie hit the button in his car for the entrance door to lift up.

"How long will it take?" whispered David.

"Everybody stay down. It's going to take at least eight seconds."

The agents hit the basement floor running. Two agents veered toward Donnie's squad car but acted as if they didn't see anybody.

"Hang on," whispered Donnie. "4 . . . 3 . . . 2 . . . 1."

The souped-up squad car took off like a rocket, prompting the agents to spray bullets as they drove by. Hitting the ramp, they leapfrogged onto the main road leading away from the jail. Donnie knew Bethany like the back of his hand, so the chances of their escaping were looking pretty good.

"The quickest route would be to drive by the Main ID Security Station."

"That's crazy, Donnie. There's got to be another way!"

"Think about it, David. If we don't take the east route, then they can easily trap us at the river before we can get to the interstate. Besides, I think the Holy Spirit wants us to go by the station!"

Driving toward the Main ID Security Station, Carl slowly explained to Simon their three options in rescuing Joshua. "We could try to position ourselves at a high lookout and see if Joshua is hiding close to the station."

"What's the second option?"

"We can drive right up and check to see if they got our boy. If not, then at least we got a chance to get away with our wheels still under us."

The young PK was finally realizing that Carl was not the everyday, normal Christian.

After taking a big gulp, Simon asked, "What's the third option?"

"We could ditch the car behind Amos' Barber Shop, and we can search for Joshua on foot."

Glancing out the car window, Simon could see that the sun was already three-fourths black. Softly the Spirit of Christ whispered, "Fear not, Simon, for I am with you; be not dismayed, for I am your God. I will strengthen you, Yes, I will help you!"[1]

"Yes, Lord," said Simon, "I choose your will and not mine." Everything in his life had changed so quickly. Nothing else mattered anymore—fun times, his friends' approval, even getting married someday. All Simon wanted now was to please Jesus. He knew that in the very near future, he would stand before God and would have to give an account of his life. "Okay, Carl, whatever the Lord gives you, I'm up for it."

"You are?" replied a flabbergasted Carl while slowing his yellow Chevy down to ten mph.

"Amen, bro! Let's just do it for our Jesus."

"Okay, check it out. The first option will take too much time. The third option is not the best, since they are scanning everybody on the streets."

"So what's left?" responded an uneasy Simon, who was wondering what really was going on in Carl's mind.

"I say we drive up to the security office, go in, and ask if they know where Joshua is."

"Say what?" asked Simon, who sort of lost it for a few seconds.

"It's perfect. They'll never suspect a watchman from the resistance movement walking into the Main ID Security Station and asking for another watchman. Believe me, it's a lock!"

Simon had never met a Christian who didn't fear anybody or anything. Carl had learned to trust the Lord, no matter what the situation. As they moved into position, the Holy Spirit spoke a word of knowledge to Simon.

"Carl, I think Joshua is just inside the main lobby. In fact, in just a little while, he will be sitting handcuffed in a chair right behind the main counter!"

"Praise the Lord, Simon. God is leading us. Okay, we'll park close by, and I will go up and . . ."

"No, the Lord wants me to be the one to get Joshua."

After a long pause, Carl softly replied, "Look, Simon, I understand that Josh risked his life for you. But, my man, we are facing some pretty high stakes, if you know what I mean. It's one thing to miss giving a word of knowledge in church on Sunday morning. It's quite another when three lives depend on it being from the Holy Spirit."

"I know, Carl," responded the young boy as he glanced toward the almost black sun. "This is all pretty new to me, but I can sense that God is leading me to do it."

"How?"

"I think the Holy Spirit is going to provide a diversion when I ask for Joshua," replied a drained Simon.

Across the street, the angel Mordecai smiled while facing off to fight the spirits of fear and lying, who had just arrived.

"You have no right to interfere, Mordecai," hissed the spirit of lying. "We have permission to . . ."

Suddenly Mordecai delivered two blows that sent each demon spirit reeling backward.

"How about it, you lying little imps?" challenged the warrior angel. "Do you want some more?"

Realizing that they were no match for the angelic warrior from heaven, the demons departed for a more opportune time.

As Carl slowly drove by the ID station, Simon tried to get a good look inside the front lobby.

"Remember, bro, you need to grab Josh and go for the back door, which would make it a whole lot easier for me during the getaway."

"But, Carl, what if I'm wrong? What if Joshua isn't there?"

"He will be," said Carl. "This isn't about you, my man; it's about trusting God!"

"I'm ready, bro."

Turning right, Carl parked the car on the left side of the building. Simon got out and walked evenly for about thirty feet, turned left, and headed for the main entrance to the station. His heart seemed to be pounding nails as he stepped through the open front door and approached the receptionist.

"Good afternoon, young man. May I help you?" asked the smiling receptionist, who seemed a bit relieved to see anybody out and about.

"Yes, thank you. I'm looking for my brother, Joshua Hirsh," said Simon while trying to look as grown up as possible.

The smile on the receptionist's face quickly disappeared. As she eyed Simon suspiciously, the door to the interrogation room swung open, and two ID agents came out leading a handcuffed Joshua Hirsh. The hope of seeing their parents was suddenly rekindled when the watchman from the west side signaled to the watchman from the east side that he was okay.

As Donnie gunned the accelerator, the car took a sharp turn, almost climbing the curb. The ID agents from the jail had been busy on their radios. An all-station alert had been called in, and alarms in every ID station in Bethany were blaring. The agents in the main office were moving so fast that Simon barely had time to get out of the way. They hastily pushed Joshua back in the room, shut the door, and ran outside. Every available agent poured out of the station into the street. With the Lord leading him, Donnie waited until the last possible turnoff before the ID station, as bullets began to rain down on his dark brown squad car.

With the receptionist on her knees, hiding under the counter in the lobby, Simon bolted for the interrogation room. It was locked. He scanned the room looking for anything to break open the door. Spotting nothing of use, he hung over the edge of the counter and yelled, "How do I get this door open?" The frightened receptionist reached over and pushed a button under the counter, which automatically opened the door. "Come on, Josh, let's go!" Both boys sprinted toward the rear entrance. Looking through the small bulletproof Plexiglas window in the back door, they could see Carl poised and ready to roll.

"It's locked!" Josh cried out. Immediately they turned and made a hasty retreat for the front door.

"No, wait! God is going to help us," exhorted Simon, stopping dead in his tracks. "Yes, Lord, I do trust you," whispered the PK. They could hear the sound of running feet coming closer. Simon grabbed Joshua and pulled him into a storeroom.

As precious seconds ticked by, Joshua turned and asked his good friend, "How did you find me?"

"The Lord," he whispered back.

After a few more seconds, Joshua asked, "Are you sure God is speaking to you, Simon?"

"Okay, Josh, here's what we'll do. Whoever comes through the door, you take them high, and I'll go low. Then let's try for the front door." Joshua nodded in agreement as the footsteps halted outside their hiding place. The boys tensed up as they waited for their pursuer to make his move. When the door opened, Simon lunged forward. The long-legged receptionist shrieked and jumped back, one shoe in hand.

"Boy, these heels are killers," griped the receptionist, pulling a set of keys from her purse. "Here it is!" she cried, triumphantly holding up a key, her smile reaching from ear to ear. She quickly led them to the back door and unlocked it. After taking a look outside, she motioned for them to go.

While Joshua made his escape, Simon paused and asked, "But why would you help us? Do we know each other?"

"Get going, kid. And if you see my little brother, tell him I love him. His name is . . ."

As the agents struggled to get back in, the warrior angel Mordecai just smiled, while holding the front door shut. Jeri calmly closed the double-plated reinforced backdoor, securing both the top and bottom locks. Stuffing the keys back in her purse, she turned to face one of the agents running down the hall.

"Hey! What do you think you're doing down here, Jeri?"

"I thought I heard something. And since none of you were around, I thought I'd check it out," replied the slender blonde. "Actually, I think it was the best thing I've done in a long time." She began to weep.

By the time the agents could get to their cars, the old yellow Chevy was long gone.

"Hey, Frank, we got a signal coming in!" yelled Billy B.

"Well, glory be to God! It looks like the Mole's van. We thought we might have lost him!"

"It's Jason, all right," confirmed Billy B., "and it looks like he has a few overcomers with him."

"Incoming," announced Frank over the camp loudspeaker.

As the four teenagers poured out of the van, parents in the camp who still had a missing child on the streets held their breath.

"Great to see you, Cindy," said Hope Bishop as she reached out to hug her classmate from Lakeview High. "We've got great news from your parents. They want you to know that they love you and that they are super proud of you."

"God bless you, Hope, for being such a powerful witness for Jesus. Your obedience to the Holy Spirit played an important part in my being here today!"

They hugged again, and then Cindy turned to the waiting crowd. "Hey, everybody, I want you to meet some kids who saved my life. This is Ray, Jay, and Faye. I thank the Lord for answering my prayers. Without them, I never would have made it!"

One of the mothers couldn't help but ask about the safety of their parents. There was an awkward silence for a few seconds until Ray volunteered to speak. "Thank you for your concern, but my whole family took the mark of the beast over a year ago."

Jay could relate. He shared with the crowd how his folks assured him that they were Christians, but when the agents visited their home, they caved in to the pressure and decided to register. Deep within cavern two, Ben and

Ruth Hirsh were counseling kids who were completely overwhelmed with the pain of losing their families. Only the power of prayer, under the guidance of the Holy Spirit, could deal with such pain.

"Hey, Ben, have you heard about the four teenagers who have just entered the camp?" asked one of the checkpoint guards.

"Oh, Ben!" cried Ruth.

"Did you catch their names?"

"Two boys, named Ray and Jay, and two girls, Cindy and Faye, I think."

"Faye!" Ruth blurted out. "Was her last name Braun?"

"I don't recall her giving her last name," replied the guard.

The eyes of the campers slowly turned to Faye Braun, who was not handling it as well as the boys. When Faye had become a believer at the age of ten, she thought for sure her whole family would become Christians within a year. She bought everyone in her family small leather New Testaments to celebrate her first Christmas as a believer. Her older brother had sarcastically complained, "Oh goody, look what Jesus is bringing each of us for being such good little boys and girls." That didn't stop Faye. As the years went by, she would see whole families put their trust in Jesus Christ as their Savior. The loving teenager would write testimony letters to her family about how great it was to be a Christian. From time to time, she would give them CDs, hoping that their hearts would be touched through Christian music. She just knew that someday Jesus would save her family.

"Thank you so much for your love and concern for my family," shared the exhausted overcomer. "I'll always love my parents for having me and for praying with me to receive Jesus when I was a little girl." Fighting back the tears, she struggled to continue. "I believe it was one year, one month, and six days ago that my father, mother, and two brothers each took the mark of Hendrick," she sobbed, collapsing into the arms of the woman who had asked about her family.

Standing silently among the crowd, Pastor Mark Bishop watched the heartbreaking scene before him. The utter sacrifice that these four young people had made in order to remain faithful to their Savior was sobering. They had risked everything they had, even their families, to be with Jesus. It was frightening to know there would be many more. The children of generation Y, the most criticized youth America had ever had, in the end produced a vast multitude of Christian warriors, a vast army of young people who refused to bow to the antichrist.

The sheer possibility of seeing their precious Faye seemed to ignite the Hirshs' faith. After reaching the entrance to the cavern, Ben and Ruth could see the massive crowd surrounding the new arrivals. As they ran with all of their might, it seemed like a dream where everything was in slow motion.

"Faye, Faye!" Ruth called out as she reached her exhausted friend.

"Ruth, Pastor Ben, it's a miracle!" cried Faye. As the exhausted blonde slipped into the loving arms of her spiritual parents, prayers of thanks could be heard from the lips of parents throughout the crowd.

"God is so faithful, Faye," said Ben beaming.

"It's so great to be with ya'll," wept Faye. "Hey, where's my Josh? Boy, do I have some stories to share with him."

CHAPTER 45

TILL THE END OF THE AGE

Lo, I am with you always,
even to the end of the age.
Matthew 28:20

Word of David Cowley's capture spread quickly through the camp. In honor of the man of God who risked his life for so many young people, a prayer vigil was held that night in place of the evening service. A large group of kids who were personally rescued by the watchman formed an inner circle to pray for him, not knowing whether he was dead or alive. They vowed his death would never be in vain. In their hearts, he would never be forgotten.

The bullet-riddled squad car slowed at the final checkpoint. The men on duty took a quick look inside and then hastily waved them through. As they pulled into the parking area, believers came running from caverns one, two, and three.

"He's alive, I tell you!" yelled a jubilant youth leader. "David's alive!"

For many of the youth at the camp, it was too hard to believe. Most had accepted the fact that they would never see David Cowley alive again. Slowly the evangelist stepped out of the police car and received a big hug from Pastor Mark. "Glory be to God! You made it, David! It's a miracle," proclaimed Mark.

"We heard so many rumors that we didn't know what to believe," added a relieved Julie as she joined her husband in hugging the committed watchman.

David turned back to the car, raised his hands, and announced, "Look, we've got a man here in pretty bad shape. Can we get some help?"

Mark quickly grabbed one arm of the frail-looking man. "Okay, David, I'll get this side and you . . ." The pastor froze for a brief moment. Mark could hardly recognize the man who had just spent six straight days in the black hole. "It can't be! Is that you?"

"Yep! It's me, all right. Other than that, I don't know how I feel."

Many could relate as laughter erupted throughout the crowd.

Mark joyfully announced, "Hey, everybody, welcome Jimmy Curtis from Sluman's Garage!" The pastor could hardly believe his eyes. "So, Jimmy, you finally asked Jesus to be your Savior?"

"Well, the way I look at it, when you're all alone and have nothing left to hang onto, the hand of the Lord looks mighty inviting," confessed the skinny mechanic.

"Hang on, my brother," said Mark.

Two infirmary workers moved up and quickly took charge of the weak overcomer.

"Brothers and sisters," announced David, "I want you to meet Donnie King. God used Donnie to set free more than sixty overcomers who were facing execution at the county jail!"

"You're an answer to prayer, sonny boy," praised an eighty-two-year-old grandmother, who laid a kiss on Donnie's forehead.

"Thank you all very much. To see you all here, I now know that God is a miracle-working God," replied the grateful ex-guard.

Prompted by the Holy Spirit, Pastor Mark stepped forward to speak. "Jesus said, 'I am the vine, you are the branches, if a man remains in me and I in him, he will bear much fruit. Apart from me you can do nothing. If anyone does not remain in me, he is like a branch that is thrown away and withers. Such branches are picked up, thrown into the fire and burned. If you remain in me and my words remain in you, ask whatever you wish and it will be given you. This is to my father's glory that you bear much fruit, showing yourselves to be my disciples.'[1] We give you glory, Jesus, that by remaining in You, we will bear much fruit."

After several cheers of praise, Donnie waved toward the bullet-ridden squad car and shouted, "I think we should also thank the Bethany Police Department for providing us with such well-ventilated transportation!"

Amidst all the celebrating, Jason motioned to Mark that the final call had been made. Within the hour, all watchmen in the surrounding cities would be reporting to their perspective camps. The coming of the Son of Man was right at the door.

While the massive crowd moved toward the safety of the caverns, Mark walked over to Jimmy, who was lying a on stretcher. "So, have you heard from your sister, Jeri?"

"I'm afraid not, Pastor. Because she works at the Main ID Security Office, she really didn't think she had much of a choice. I believe she took the mark of the beast the first month it was out," replied the choked-up little brother. "You know, Pastor, it's strange the way things worked out. When we were kids and got into trouble, Jeri would always be the one to do the right thing, even when it really hurt." Jimmy hesitated and then glanced skyward, barely noticing the almost full red moon beginning to rise. "Wherever you are, Sis, I will always love you with all of my heart."

As the overcomers moved deeper into their sanctuary, the main topic was David's miraculous escape from jail. Nearing the entrance to the cavern, David motioned to Mark to meet him for a little walk. "Is it true about the watchman?" asked David.

"You mean Stephen?"

"Yeah. I heard in jail that he gave his life so others could go free."

"That's right. Stephen fulfilled his calling as a disciple of Jesus Christ!"

Over to his left, David could see Michelle Corbin walking alone among the families who were hugging and greeting one another.

"What about Michelle? How did she take it?"

"Well, Julie and I were with her when she was told of Stephen's death. After a long cry, she shared about her wedding day. Stephen told her that he wanted their lives to count for something. For him, it was not enough to go to college, get a job, buy a house before thirty, get married, have some children, and then wait to die at eighty. The man of God she married wanted more out of life. He always prayed to be in God's will, to be about the Father's business."

Many could be seen saying their final good-byes while others began to pray their final words before going to be with their Lord. Over near the entrance, the watchman's wife, Michelle, was on her knees praying to the God she so dearly loved. "Praise you, Father, for your divine love and grace that you have bestowed upon us all. You are so faithful! And to my precious Jesus, who died in my place, that I might have eternal life, forgive me, Lord, for the times I doubted your love for me. And to the Comforter, the Spirit of God, who indwells us, words cannot express how grateful Stephen and I are to You, for leading us through this evil world. All praise and honor and glory to the only true God: the Father, the Son, and the Holy Spirit!" Whispering a final prayer, Michelle smiled and said, "I love you Stephen, and I will be with you very soon."

"Hey, Mole man, how you doing?" yelled David as both watchmen tackled each other, each going for a pin.

"Some things never change," said Julie laughing.

A small crowd of youth thoroughly enjoyed watching the two characters roll around in the dirt. The overcomers had truly come to love and appreciate those who were called to be watchmen. After getting up and dusting themselves off, Jason asked David if he had had any contact with any other watchmen in the last eight hours. The evangelist was having a hard time remembering; the exhaustion from the last few days was beginning to kick in.

"No, I don't think so," replied David, with Donnie nodding in agreement. "We might have been the last ones to make it out."

Standing close by were Ben and Ruth Hirsh and Allen and Mary Colson. David's answer brought a piercing to their hearts. Both couples had prayed that no matter what trials their sons would face each boy would remain faithful to God. "But I felt so sure that God would bring them back," wept Ruth while turning to Mary for comfort. "While praying this morning, the Holy Spirit spoke this verse to me, 'See, I have set before you an open door, and no one can shut it; for you have a little strength, have kept My word and have not denied My name.'² This promise was for Joshua and Simon," confessed Ruth. "God promised He would open a door for them to come back to us, a door no man or demon can shut."

"What do you think, Ben?" asked Allen. "What are their chances out there?"

"Our surveillance reports have always been pretty accurate. As of last week there was still no evidence of either boy being executed. While reaching over to hug his wife, the choked-up father added, "I refuse to believe that our sons will take the mark." After a long thought, Ben yelled over to the Mole, "Hey, Jason, is everyone accounted for? I mean, the specific watchmen assigned to Bethany?" asked the hopeful father.

"I'm afraid so, Pastor Hirsh. The only watchman left in Bethany is Carl Russell, and we've had no contact with him since the National Guard started shooting anyone who didn't have the mark. I'm so sorry, Ben, but if I know Carl, he's with the Lord." The one they called the Mole quickly moved through the crowd and joined his wife and son.

"Jason, you made it!" yelled Matt Bray, hugging the young lawyer from behind with all of his might.

"Praise the Lord, Matt."

The emotion and love from so many people was almost too much for the exhausted lawyer.

"C'mon, I want you to meet my parents. Dad, Mom, this is Jason Wylie, the Mole."

Tom Bray shook Jason's hand warmly. "We can't thank you enough for what you've done. You have saved the lives of countless others by your willingness to put your life on the line."

"I praise God for making it all happen, Brother Tom. You know, I really want to thank you for the opportunity to work side by side with Matt and Sam. Your sons rescued over 250 underage resisters who never would have made it without their sacrifice."

"We are deeply grateful to our Lord," Ashley replied while hugging Jason's wife, Jackie.

Picking up his four-year-old son, Noah, Jason added, "Oh, by the way, I received a note from the three sisters Sam gave his life for. The sisters said that after Jesus their hero is Samuel Hosea Bray!"

As everyone praised the Lord, Matt looked upward and whispered, "You beat us there, little bro, but we will be joining you before the throne real soon!"

Speaking to the whole camp, Pastor Mark gratefully declared, "Brothers and sisters in Christ, we can all give praise to the only true God for allowing us all to come together to witness the events that precede His coming. Apostle Paul warned us that the catching up of the saints and the Day of the Lord would come like a thief in the night to a world blinded by the prince of darkness. But we, as overcomers, are not in darkness so that this day should surprise us like a thief. We are sons of the light and sons of the day. We don't belong to the night or to the darkness. So, my dear saints, let us be found spotless, blameless, and at peace with the Lord, for surely, He can now come at any moment."

"Hey, someone's coming!" yelled Billy B.

"Is the checkpoint manned?" asked Frank.

"No, they've all gone inside," answered the trucker, stepping into the lookout tower.

"Besides, there are no more scheduled arrivals. Any idea whose car it is?" asked Jason.

Billy B. cautiously moved toward the final checkpoint as the old yellow Chevy struggled up the hill. "It's Carl! It's Carl!"

Jason, turned and ran back yelling, "It's Carl Russell! It's Carl Russell!"

Within seconds of stopping, the old yellow Chevy was engulfed with believers. Sticking his head out the driver's window, Carl yelled, "I guess you could say I'm here to make a special delivery!" The backdoors opened, and Simon and Joshua jumped out.

"Hey, everybody!" screamed Simon. "Look who the Lord finally found!" Joshua's words were lost over the noise as Ruth grabbed her son's handcuffed hands and gave him a loving hug.

"God's never late! You made it just in time for the big snatch!" yelled the official Rapture Man, Jay Wilson.

"Joshua, we know you went to find Simon. So what happened?" asked his delirious mother.

"Well, as you know, or may have guessed, I hitched a ride in the back of one of the supply trucks," answered a weary Joshua. "When the truck arrived in Bethany, I decided to start looking for Simon. When the driver stopped at the light facing Main street, I jumped off."

"Then what happened?" asked his relieved father.

"You won't believe this, Dad, but two ID agents were eating burgers and fries on a park bench near the corner where I landed. They immediately scanned me, and the rest of the story is history. I was handcuffed and taken downtown to the Main ID Security Station."

"How come they didn't execute you like they did the rest of the overcomers?" asked Jason.

"There were times they were going to shoot me, but something always happened to distract them! It was like there was somebody working behind the scenes protecting me."

Mordecai just smiled, his assignment finally coming to an end. As he lifted off, he relished the idea of being created in the image and likeness of God. Within seconds, he joined the heavenly host as they lined up behind the Son of God. With all eyes focused upon the Father, it was almost time!

"But how did they rescue you out of the security station?" asked Ruth.

"Well, when Simon walked into the ID station and asked for me . . ."

"Simon did what?" interrupted a shocked Allen.

"That's right, Dad! The Lord led us to be bold and not to lean on our own understanding. Carl, Josh, and I are here today because of all of you who took the time to petition the Lord for the safety of our lives. Believe me, there were times when my faith was almost gone."

"What helped you keep going, son?"

Looking over at the Bishop family, Simon smiled and said, "I once heard a believer at my high school comfort someone with something her dad taught her. It goes like this: 'If you stand for the truth, God will always be on your side.' Right, Hope?"

"Amen, Simon. Amen," answered a smiling Hope Bishop.

CHAPTER 46

THE COMING OF THE LORD

Then the sign of the Son of Man will appear in heaven,
and then all the tribes of the earth will mourn,
and they will see the Son of Man coming on the clouds of heaven
with power and great glory.
Matthew 24:3

As the red moon appeared high above the Alabama hills, the over-comers began to praise the Lord for the faithfulness of His eternal Word. Pastor Mark opened his Bible and read, "And there will be signs in the sun, in the moon, and in the stars; with perplexity, the sea and the waves roaring; men's hearts failing them from fear and the expectation of those things which are coming on the earth, for the powers of the heavens will be shaken. At that time, then they will see the Son of Man coming in a cloud with power and great glory. Now when these things begin to happen, look up and lift up your heads, because your redemption draws near."[1]

The eruption of praise was electrifying. God's Word had become a guiding light to those who would believe and trust in Him. "Listen up, saints," Pastor Mark continued. "'When you see these things happening, know that the kingdom of God is near. Assuredly, I say to you, this generation will by no means pass away till all things take place. Watch, therefore, and pray always that you may be counted worthy to escape all these things that will come to pass, and to stand before the Son of Man.'"[2]

"Look, everybody!" yelled Lindsey Bishop, who was standing at the entrance to cavern two. "The Little Dipper just went out!" She pointed to the famous Milky Way star system, which would soon lose all its light!

Campers poured out of the caverns into the massive picnic area in order to get a glance at the stars. Truly, God's Word was coming to pass right before their eyes.

✳

The inhabitants of the earth who had been deceived by the dragon began to curse God and those who followed Him. As the world was plunged into darkness and earthquakes rocked every nation, the miraculous signs and wonders of the antichrist and the false prophet didn't seem to matter much anymore. Those living in Jerusalem, Munich, Rome, and Moscow would wake up to a morning of darkness, to a sun totally blacked out. Billions of people would be groping in the dark, refusing to believe what a Holy God had decreed.

Those living on the other side of the world would see a blood red moon surrounded by stars that would soon lose their light. As the sky became darker, the final prayers of the elect were lifted up to heaven for the lost. A multitude of souls throughout the earth who had not yet worshipped the beast or taken his mark dropped to their knees and received Jesus as their Lord and Savior.

In the midst of total darkness, with the nations paralyzed with fear, a faint light could be seen far off into space. All the people covered their eyes as a flash of lightening covered the whole earth, sweeping across the sky from the east to the west.[3] The Son of Man could be seen coming on the clouds with the power and glory of His Father. Millions upon millions of gleaming angels, girded with golden bands around their chests, were at His command.[4]

The world cried out in anguish as the shout from heaven was given, prompting the heavenly host to encircle the entire earth. With the sounding of the trumpet call of God, in the twinkling of an eye, the dead in Christ, both Old Testament and New Testament saints, received their resurrection bodies.[5] Almost instantaneously, the heavenly host of angels gathered together His elect from the face of the earth. In an instant, those who had previously died in Christ and a multitude from every nation, tribe, people, and tongue were joined as one before the glorious throne of the Father.[6] The radiant smile of the Father greeted His Son, the Lamb of God, as the saints of God bowed in reverence.

It was over!

Those left behind, who witnessed Jesus coming for his saints, felt His words pressing down upon their hearts like a heavy weight. "Behold, He is coming with the clouds, and every eye will see him, even they who pierced

Him. And all the tribes of the earth will mourn because of Him. Even so, Amen."[7]

For others in the world, the appearance of Jesus was very similar to the mysterious appearance of Mary. Many thought, "So what if millions of Christians suddenly disappeared?"

The antichrist immediately began to create a positive spin, denying the very truth of the Lord's return. "We must persevere for the sake of our families and our world," declared Wolfgang Hendrick. In spite of his lies, millions of people who once professed Christ wallowed in their shame. The words of John the Apostle could not be denied. He wrote of Christ's return for His children, "And now, little children, abide in Him, that when He appears, we may have confidence and not be ashamed before Him at His coming."[8]

A deep sense of shame overwhelmed those who had denied Christ by taking the mark of the beast. Jesus had warned all who had ears to hear: "But whoever denies Me before men, him I will also deny before My Father who is in heaven."[9]

"Salvation belongs to our God who sits on the throne, and to the Lamb," roared the multitude from every nation, tribe, people, and tongue. The Bride of Christ stood before the throne, worshipping the Father and the Lamb. All believers, those who anticipated the sacrificial death of their future Messiah and all who believed in Jesus after His death at Calvary, worshipped side by side.

The prophet Isaiah had written of the resurrection of Old Testament believers: "Your dead shall live. . . . Awake and sing, you who dwell in dust. . . . And the earth shall cast out the dead."[10]

For the believers who were alive at Christ's coming, they would never hunger or thirst again. Their blessed hope had delivered them out of the great tribulation. "For the Lamb who is in the midst of the throne will shepherd them and lead them to living fountains of waters. And God will wipe away every tear from their eyes."[11]

Immediately after the catching away of the saints, an angel coming from the east having the seal of the living God arrived in Jerusalem. He instructed the four angels not to harm the land, the sea, or the trees until they put a seal of protection on the foreheads of the servants of God.[12] When the Lord came in the clouds of glory, the 144,000 wept over the One their fore-fathers had pierced.[13]

Mark and Julie turned to marvel at the believers kneeling at the base of the Father's throne. They couldn't stop smiling as they soaked up the powerful radiance of His glory.

"Just think, Julie, of all the people born since Adam, only a few actually made it before his throne," reflected Mark. "Jesus said, 'Enter by the narrow gate; for wide is the gate and broad is the way that leads to destruction, and there are many who go in by it. Because narrow is the gate and difficult is the way which leads to life, and there are few who find it. Strive to enter through the narrow gate, for many, I say to you, will seek to enter and will not be able!'"[14]

As the saints continued to worship, the angels of the Most High looked on in utter admiration. "The Father sent his Son so that every human that we see here today might have everlasting life," declared a gleaming Mordecai.

"It's the plan of the ages!" rejoiced Amad.

"Yes, I see many of our assignments," affirmed Ian. "What a sight to behold!"

"Ian, how did you feel when so many humans rejected your message and took the mark of the beast?" asked a curious Mordecai.

"I could only think of one thing."

"And what was that?"

Ian slowly turned, facing his fellow angels, and solemnly declared, "That God the Father desired every human creation to spend eternity with Him. His desire was that none perish but all should come to repentence.[15] Think of it," reflected Ian, "to be created in the image and likeness of God and then allow habitual sin to rob you of everlasting life!"[16]

Sadness struck Mordecai as he wondered aloud, "What could be so important to humans that would make them reject the everlasting love of the Father?"[17]

CHAPTER 47

THE SEVENTH SEAL: GOD'S WRATH

When He opened the seventh seal,
there was silence in heaven
for about half an hour.
Revelation 8:1

Not one sound could be heard throughout all of heaven. No one moved. Even the seven angels carrying the trumpets of God's wrath stood motionless. The Lamb of God broke the seventh seal, and the large scroll before the throne slowly began to open![1] Soon an angel from heaven would take a censer from the alter, fill it with fire, and hurl it to earth.[2] After the fire of the seven trumpet judgments completely immersed the earth, those who were still alive would brace themselves for the final judgment of God's wrath, the seven bowls![3]

The Apostle Peter's warning to the people of the earth that was hardly heeded would now become a reality. "But the day of the Lord will come as a thief in the night, in which the heavens will pass away with a great noise, and the elements will melt with fervent heat; both the earth and the works that are in it will be burned up. Therefore since all these things will be dissolved, what manner of persons ought you to be in holy conduct and godliness, looking for and hastening the coming of the day of God, because of which the heavens will be dissolved, being on fire, and the elements will melt with fervent heat. Nevertheless we, according to His promise, look for new heavens and a new earth in which righteousness dwells. Therefore, beloved, looking forward to these things, be diligent to be found by Him in peace, without spot and blameless."[4]

It was a surreal setting as former members returned to the abandoned church on Vaughn Road. "Listen to me," pleaded Jolene, a former Bethany

Assembly choir member. "Jesus said, 'Then the sign of the Son of Man will appear in heaven, and then all the tribes of the earth will mourn, and they will see the Son of Man coming on the clouds of heaven with power and great glory. And He will send His angels with the great sound of a trumpet, and they will gather together His elect from the four winds, from one end of heaven to the other.'[5] Don't you see how clear it is?" she cried, burying her face in her hands. "Believers all over the world are gone! Jesus has gathered His elect! We've missed the rapture!"

"It happened so quickly. How do we really know what really took place?" scoffed Harriett Jones, the former Sunday school teacher. Crossing her arms in stubborn rebellion, she challenged, "No one really knows!"

"I'm afraid we will all know in a very short time."

"What are you babbling about, old man?" mocked one of the teenagers seated across from the frightened pastor.

Glancing downward, his eyes filled with tears, he shared, "Jesus taught that His elect would be taken by His angels to heaven, and on that same day, God's wrath will be poured out on those left behind, just like when Lot was rescued from the fire of Sodom and Gomorrah."[6]

"The Bible doesn't say that," interrupted Harriett.

The dazed pastor slowly shook his head. "When the seventh seal is opened, there will be thirty minutes of silence in heaven. Then seven angels will sound the seven trumpets in successive order. When they have finished, the earth will be burned by the fire of God's wrath!"

No one moved.

"The first trumpet will burn one-third of all the trees of the earth," the pastor quietly explained to the small crowd of former members. "The second trumpet will turn one-third of the sea into blood and kill one-third of its living creatures. The third trumpet contains a giant star that will fall . . ."[7]

"No, no, no! This can't be happening! It's like we're all trapped in some evil nightmare," cried Jolene as she ran out of the sanctuary.

"Why are you here, Pastor?" asked Harriett snickering. "Why aren't you over at your church trying to help explain this mystery to your congregation? Shouldn't they be preparing for these so called trumpet judgments?"

"I've already been to my church, and I've talked with most of the members. Their response to the Lord's coming was a lot like yours, one of denial and disbelief!" Getting up to leave, he muttered, "Please, excuse me as I continue my search."

"What are you talking about, Pastor? Who are you searching for?" asked one the teenagers laughing.

He suddenly stopped with his back facing the people. Without moving, he replied, "I'm searching for anyone who has not taken the mark of the beast or worshiped the image of Hendrick." Not waiting for a reply, the pastor left.

"Oh, he's a fool!" mocked Harriett. "I'm sick and tired of hearing all this gloom and doom preaching. If you ask me, I think we're going to be just fine. To interpret the book of Revelation literally is just guesswork. Look at how many of these famous Bible teachers have been wrong! It seems like everyone has their own interpretation of the end times, for God's sake!"

"You're so right," whispered the spirit of religion.

While the former members emptied out of the church, the evil spirit continued to speak through the Sunday school teacher to anyone who would listen.

Several members of Bethany Presbyterian Church could hear the sobbing of their pastor, J. W. Brown, as they entered the side entrance to the sanctuary.

"Hey, Pastor Brown, are you okay?" asked Rhonda as the others took seats around their respected leader.

"No, I'm afraid I'm not," he replied, his bottom lip beginning to quiver. "The recent visitation by our Lord could not have been more devastating!"

"What does it all mean, Pastor?" demanded Mr. Largent, Ray's father.

"How many of you saw Jesus coming in the clouds?"

A few hands went up, but most just sat motionless. The shock of it all had emptied them of any strength that they might have had.

"I just don't understand," whispered a shocked Rhonda. "I've been a good Christian all my life. I haven't hurt anybody. My faithfulness to my church, my family, even my job has been excellent. So why have I been left behind?" she asked as she subconsciously rubbed her right wrist.

"The reason we are mourning the coming of the Lord is that we have been deceived by Hendrick, the antichrist!" the pastor openly confessed.

"Deceived?" the associate pastor blurted out. "That's impossible! Once people are saved, they can never be deceived, even if they make the mistake of registering for an ID number. Salvation is a gift; nothing can change that!"

"Believe me, there are no words to express how wrong I've been!" cried the pastor, who couldn't bear to look anyone in the eye.

"What do you mean by wrong?" asked Ray's father.

"The reason we have been left behind is that we have denied our Lord," admitted the stunned pastor. "I can now see the critical flaws in the biblical foundation of the pre-tribulation doctrine."

"Flaws, what flaws?" yelled an angry youth leader.

"I taught for over thirty years that the seven-year tribulation period was God's wrath. Why didn't I see the truth?" he screamed, pounding his fists upon his lecture notes.

After a few seconds, the anger within a member of the worship team suddenly erupted. In a fit of rage, the young man started to curse the pastor and throw hymnals at the altar. This immediately ignited a wave of frustration among the bewildered members.

"I trusted you, Pastor!" shouted a farmer named Otis. "My family and I came to you for counsel, and you told us that without a doubt Wolfgang Hendrick wasn't the antichrist. You told us our ID numbers had nothing to do with the mark of the beast!"

"Yes, I know, and I'm very sorry about . . ."

"In fact," interrupted a board member, "you labeled Mark Bishop and Stephen Corbin as instruments of the devil, and they were teachers who tried to warn us of this very evil! Remember, Pastor, you taught that Jesus would never allow His bride to be persecuted by the antichrist! You stinking liar! You're the deceiver, and now we are all doomed to hell!"

"I know, I know!"

"We placed our lives in your knowledge of the Bible, and you deceived us!" hollered a hysterical mother of three. "My daughters are anxiously waiting for me to come home and assure them everything is okay. What am I going to tell them? You're just a wolf in sheep's clothing, and we fell for it!"

"But I don't get it," moaned a confused deacon. "Pastor, you taught almost thirty Sundays a year that nothing could change our relationship with God. You convinced us that God was speaking through you. What fools we were to trust you and not God's Word!"

With deep remorse, he slid back his chair and said, "I'm very sorry."

It took only a few moments before he slipped out the side entrance, never to be seen again.

Immediately following the catching up of the saints by the angels of God, several students from Lakeview High met by the lunch tables behind the Industrial Arts building.

"What's up, Jessie?" asked Nicki. "This is such a trip! People disappearing! You know several friends of mine are saying . . ."

The tall brunette nodded her head vaguely and turned towards her best friend.

"I'm scared, Jake! It's all happening just the way Luke said it would."

"I know. Last night I had a creepy nightmare about Ned and Drew. They were crying out to me to cross over this enormous ravine that separated us. I kept trying to find a way to cross over, but I wasn't able to. Then I heard a voice say to me, 'You will never be allowed to cross over . . . for eternity.'"

"Oh Jake, what are we going to do?"

After a long silence, Jake heard loud laughing and looked up to see Rachel and Anna Pressley coming their way.

"Hey, J and J, how ya doing?" greeted a giddy Rachel.

"Did you see Jesus' face when he rose above the clouds just before he gave the command?" asked a shocked Jake.

"Yeah. It was so awesome," said Rachel laughing. "Just after the sun started blacking out, Annie and I met some of our friends at one of the abandoned houses on our block. Wow, did we party!" Her eyes looking bright red, she bragged, "Boy, we smoked some awesome weed!"

"What's up with that, Rachel?" asked a surprised Jessie. "You've never partied before?"

"Hey, we don't know what type of pills they were passing out, but they sure do take away your problems," interrupted an almost out-of-control Anna.

"Cool it, girls!" declared Jessie. "We are all in very serious trouble. Now is not the time to be loaded. We need to seek the truth about what has just happened. Do you understand me? We need some answers!"

"Answers? For what? You don't get it, do you?" asked Rachel.

"Get what?" asked Jessie.

"Well, let me spell it out for you. No, better yet, let me name some names: Cindy Johnson, Ricky Jackson, Amy Phillips, Luke Appleby, Hope Bishop. Where are they, Jessica?" challenged Rachel as she rolled her eyes. "Well? Can you tell me where a single one of them are?"

"I think that most of them went to a Watchman Camp somewhere in Alabama," replied a sad Jessie. "They didn't tell anybody where they . . ."

"Oh, give me a break!" shrieked Rachel. "You couldn't possibly be that stupid, could you? Cindy Johnson ran like hell when they tried to give her the mark of the beast. Ricky Jackson has been convincing kids from the east side for over a year not to register. They were all resisters, Jessie! Every last one of them were believers in Jesus Christ who would have rather died than register!"

"Yeah, we heard about the resistance movement, but we never could find anyone to take us to one of their camps."

"A lot of good that will do you now," said Rachel.

"What do you mean?" asked a worried Jessie.

"Hello! Is anyone there?" squealed Rachel as she turned and looked away.

"Jessie, have you ever read the book of Revelation?" asked Anna.

"I've read a little about the end times."

"Oh, that's sweet, really sweet," mocked Rachel, whose tears covered the top of her blouse. "Well, I hate to break it to you, but the black sun, the red moon, the earthquakes all over the world, and the people freaking out since one o'clock this afternoon, that was the sixth seal of the book of Revelation. As good ole Luke used to say, the sign of the end of the age!"

"You mean when Jesus came a little while ago . . ."

"You got it, sister! Remember the lightening coming from the east to the west? That was the sign of His coming. Back to back signs of back-to-back events. C'mon, don't you remember Ned and Drew preaching their stupid end-time show at lunch time," asked Rachel, who looked pretty much out of it.

"Okay, so we all missed the rapture!" snapped Jessie. "What do we do now?"

"Do? There's absolutely nothing we can do. The Day of the Lord is coming, my friend. And when the seventh seal is broken, we'll all be seeing some pretty heavy-duty fireworks!"

"What are you saying, Rachel? You're not making any sense."

"Fire, Jessie! God's wrath is going to be poured out on this earth, and there's nothing you can do to stop it."

"Oh, my God, what are we going to do?"

After she glanced at her watch, Rachel whispered under her breath, "I'm afraid that question is a little too late."

The priest cautiously entered Hendrick's inner chamber within his Jerusalem headquarters. An atmosphere of depression completely engulfed the room. The recent visitation by the One from heaven had completely paralyzed the antichrist.[8]

"Yes, Lord Hendrick, I have seen the recent reports concerning the disturbance," replied Father John. "Absolutely, my lord, we will eliminate as many Jewish resisters as possible. Yes, that is correct; there are just over two million still living in the nation of Israel," answered the false prophet. "Yes, I understand the powerful impact that the two witnesses have had on the Jewish people. The problem with trying to kill them, my lord, is that we have suffered major casualties. Our NWC Committee feels that deceiving the people through the press and TV would be a far more effective way of controlling the two witnesses than just killing them."

The beleaguered leader slowly turned away from the window and removed a picture from the top drawer of his gold-plated desk. Handing it to Father John, the evil prophet could see that it was a collage of several pictures depicting the glorious day when Hendrick's gentile armies overwhelmed Jerusalem. To the two beasts, the literal slaughter of millions of Jews stood as a monument of glory to the prince of darkness. The evil priest knew that the stakes were high. The battles of Jerusalem and Jehoshaphat had destroyed many of their enemies. The crisis they now faced was by far the most critical. For the dragon to prevent Jesus from taking back physical control of earth at the Battle of Armageddon, his two pawns would attempt to inflict an all-out genocide on the Jewish nation!

"Excellent image of our enemies being destroyed, my lord," said the false prophet. "Think of it, Lord Hendrick. Before you are done, you will have killed more Jews than the Holocaust did." Both the antichrist and the false prophet rejoiced at such an achievement. Who would have ever dreamed it could happen again?

"I understand, my lord. The preparation for Armageddon has already begun," replied Father John while double-checking his orders. "The victory is in our hands."

Suddenly, in a fit of paranoia, the man of sin dismissed his evil prophet like he would a hired servant.

✳

With his wife sobbing in their bedroom, Pastor John Ryals sat listless in the darkened den. The lights were turned off, the blinds drawn; updated reports coming from the radio could be heard faintly in the background. A bottle of pills lay open on the coffee table, next to a spilled glass of water. The constant flashback of memories continued to torment the bewildered shepherd. He'd left a recorded message at his church. What could he say to them?

A lonely figure used the side gate as he entered the backyard. He wasn't even sure they were there. Even so, it was worth a chance. A sudden pounding on the kitchen door seemed to awaken the pastor out of his depressed stupor. Slowly rising from His favorite chair, he walked over to the blinds and peeked out. "Go away!" he yelled. "I have nothing to say."

"Pastor Ryals, I've got to talk with you."

"Why? What could I say that would have any meaning whatsoever?"

"I'm begging you; please, let me in!"

Reluctantly, the shell of a man unlocked the door, turned, and walked back to his chair. His listless stare and a tone of sadness in his words proved that it would only be a matter of time before total despondency took control.

"Pastor, are you okay?" asked the visitor while taking a seat on the sofa.

"What do you think?" he scoffed.

"It's pretty crazy out there. You won't believe what's happening downtown at the old WFM office. Some religious fanatics tried to . . ."

"So, Dwayne, where's your family?" muttered the pastor.

"I don't know. Rachel and Anna are out somewhere with their friends. Gloria is visiting her parents who live over on . . ."

Interrupting again, the pastor asked, "So, what's your story?"

"A lot of people are hurting, Pastor. I've been seeking the Lord in prayer in order to . . ."

"Pray for what?" squawked the preacher. "That's funny, I don't remember you ever praying."

The deacon sat back and smiled. The pastor had seen his evil smile before.

"You know a lot of people are ready to give up, but not me," sneered Dwayne. "I must have been a fool to come to you for counsel. What I want to know is when you're going to talk with the members of our church. Remember, you're our pastor?"

"Don't you know that . . ."

"Know what?" shouted the spirit of control through the deacon. "Listen up, old man! Stop all this nonsense. There are a lot of people looking to you for guidance."

"Is that so?" the pastor replied as he got up and walked over to the kitchen.

"I'm afraid there's going to be some real trouble," shot back an anxious Dwayne. "Now what are you going to do?"

Returning from the kitchen with a cloth, the weary pastor knelt down and started to wipe up the spilled water off his new coffee table.

The throne radiated with the glory of the Father. He was seated before the vast multitude of saints from every nation, tribe, people, and tongue. The Lamb of God stood to the right of His Father's throne, facing those for whom He died. After scanning all of heaven, God the Father glanced to His right, looking into the eyes of His beloved Son. It was time! Turning toward the angel holding the first trumpet judgment, He signaled with His right hand.

The magnificent messenger spread his wings and shot high above the Father's throne, arcing downward as he began his journey toward a Christ-rejecting world. Surely, the Day of the Lord was near.

After their friends left to party, the quietness of the moment seemed to help Jake and Jessie collect their thoughts.

"Jess, we've got to do something before it is too late," pleaded Jake.

"You mean ask Jesus to forgive us of our sins?"

"Yeah. I haven't told anybody, but I've been hearing voices in my mind. One keeps telling me that God will never forgive me."

"That sounds familiar," confirmed Jessie.

"The other voice is peaceful and always points me to Jesus."

"That's strange. I always thought . . ."

As the two teenagers continued their talk, a mysterious figure could be seen approaching the lunch tables from the lighted football stadium. "Hello, do you mind if I join you?" asked the slim man in his late fifties.

"Sure, why not," replied Jake. "I don't know what you believe, mister, but my friend Jessie and I have been discussing how Satan has been playing with our minds."

"You mean spiritual warfare?" asked the stranger.

Jessie and Jake paused and stared at this man they had never met. "That's what Hope used to call it," said Jessie with a sigh.

"Do you mean Hope Bishop?" asked the smiling stranger.

"Why, yes, did you know her?"

"Sort of. Actually, I knew her father."

"It's so strange to think we'll never see them again."

"Oh, I wouldn't say that."

Up until now, their emotions and doubts raging, Jessie and Jake hadn't really been listening to their new friend. His words suddenly brought their full attention.

"What do you mean?" Jake asked.

"What I mean is that even though you missed the Lord's gathering of His saints, the Holy Spirit is still saving those who have not taken the mark of the beast or worshipped Hendrick as god."

"Who are you?" asked Jake.

"What really matters now, my friend, is not the messenger but the message. You don't have much time. Have either of you registered for your ID number yet?"

"No sir, they tried to make us, but we escaped," answered Jake.

"Praise God, that's great to hear," said the stranger. For the next ten minutes he calmly shared the plan of salvation in such a way that even a seven-year-old could understand. "Jessie, Jake, both of you are going to have to decide whom you're going to trust. God is going to judge the people of this earth very soon, and you need to be ready to face Him."

"Sir, I want to trust Jesus with all of my heart," declared Jessie.

"Me, too!" added Jake. "We want to be forgiven of our sins so we can be with Jesus for eternity."[9]

The conviction of the Holy Spirit drew both teenagers to their knees as they fervently prayed to God to save their souls. Afterward, Jessie whispered, "I can just feel God's forgiveness."

"It's like feeling really clean all over," said Jake.

"God bless you, my friends. I must go now and continue my search."

Before they could answer him, the lonely stranger turned to leave.

"Wait, sir!" yelled Jake. "We can't thank you enough for sharing the Gospel with us."

"Could you please tell us your name?" called out a radiant Jessie.

Not missing a step, the stranger yelled back, "My name is Elmer . . . Elmer Dyer."

"God bless you, Elmer." With tears streaming down her face, Jessie cried, "We will never forget you!"

"That's right, Elmer!" shouted a smiling Jake. "We will see you in heaven someday!"

Tears of regret filled the pastor's eyes as he walked away. Glancing down at the mark on his right hand, he knew that day would never come.

THE END

SCRIPTURE REFERENCES

Chapter 1
1. Daniel 7:7-8
2. Revelation 17:3-6
3. Revelation 5:1
4. Revelation 5:2
5. Revelation 1:14-15
6. Revelation 6:2
7. Revelation 17:7-8, Daniel 2:40-43
8. Zechariah 13:8
9. Matthew 24:4-5

Chapter 2
1. Matthew 24:36
2. Revelation 3:22
3. Matthew 20:18-19
4. Matthew 24:3
5. Matthew 24:4
6. Ezekiel 3:17-21
7. Mark 16:17-18
8. II Timothy 3:5

Chapter 3
1. Hebrews 13:6
2. Revelation 11:15, 19:11-21
3. Daniel 9:27
4. Revelation 5:1
5. Daniel 9:27, Luke 21:20
6. Matthew 24:3-29, Revelation 6:1-17
7. Revelation 3:3
8. Matthew 24:6, Revelation 6:4
9. Matthew 24:7, Revelation 6:5
10. Revelation 6:8
11. Revelation 8:1
12. Revelation 14:12
13. Revelation 13:15-17
14. II Thessalonians 2:9
15. Matthew 24:24
16. Matthew 24:15, Matthew 24:30-31

Chapter 4
1. Titus 2:13
2. Galatians 1:10
3. I Thessalonians 5:4
4. Luke 17:26-27,30
5. II Thessalonians 2:1-3
6. Matthew 24:15, Matthew 24:9-12

Chapter 5
1. Matthew 24:30, I Thessalonians 4:15, II Thessalonians 2:1
2. Matthew 24:40-41
3. Acts 4:12
4. Titus 2:13-14

Chapter 6
1. Luke 17:28-30
2. Luke 17:35-36
3. Matthew 24:8
4. Matthew 24:21-22
5. Matthew 24:10
6. Matthew 24:13
7. Matthew 24:12
8. Matthew 24:15
9. Matthew 24:33
10. Matthew 24:29
11. Matthew 24:27
12. Matthew 24:30-31
13. Matthew 13:38-40
14. I Thessalonians 5:9
15. Revelation 12:12
16. Revelation 6:15-17
17. Revelation 7:14
18. Matthew 24:15, II Thessalonians 2:3-4
19. II Thessalonians 2:3
20. Matthew 9:37-38
21. John 12:44-46

Chapter 7

1. Revelation 13:1, Matthew 24:15,
   II Thessalonians 2:3, 8
2. Revelation 13:3
3. I Timothy 4:1
4. Matthew 24:13
5. II Timothy 3:1-5
6. Hebrews 3:17
7. Matthew 5:28
8. James 5:16
9. John 14:30

Chapter 8

1. Revelation 6:4
2. Matthew 24:6-7
3. Revelation 2:1-3:22
4. Revelation 3:14-19
5. Luke 21:36
6. I Timothy 4:1-2
7. Matthew 24:24
8. Matthew 24:2

Chapter 9

1. I Corinthians 15:51-52
2. I Thessalonians 4:16-18
3. Revelation 6:1, 8:1, 15:1
4. Ephesians 2:8
5. Galatians 1:10
6. Matthew 24:3
7. Matthew 24:9
8. Revelation 10:1
9. Matthew 24:22
10. Revelation 17:4
11. Revelation 17:5
12. Revelation 17:9
13. Revelation 17:16

Chapter 10

1. Revelation 13:11-12
2. Revelation 17:1-16
3. Revelation 17:6
4. Matthew 5:10-12
5. Genesis 11:1-9
6. Ezekiel 8:14-15
7. Jeremiah 7:18
8. Revelation 17:9, 18
9. II Corinthians 11:13-15
10. Revelation 10:7, 11:15
11. Revelation 13:7
12. Revelation 13:4

Chapter 11

1. Revelation 17:1-3
2. Luke 14:26-33
3. Romans 8:31
4. Genesis 26:3-5

Chapter 12

1. Jeremiah 44:17-25
2. Exodus 20:4-5
3. Revelation 17:3
4. Luke 14:27
5. Revelation 7:14, Matthew 24:30-31
6. Matthew 24:34
7. Matthew 24:6
8. Matthew 24:24
9. Matthew 24:11
10. Ephesians 6:11-13
11. II Timothy 1:7
12. Revelation 3:3, 3:21-22
13. I Corinthians 12:8-10
14. Hebrews 13:2
15. I Timothy 4:1-2
16. II Timothy 3:13-15
17. II Timothy 3:16
18. Matthew 12:30-31

Chapter 13
1. Revelation 6:5
2. Mark 13:7-8
3. Revelation 13:4
4. Revelation 13:7
5. Revelation 14:12
6. Revelation 13:16-18
7. Daniel 12:4, 12:9-10
8. John 15:9-11

Chapter 14
1. Revelation 3:19
2. I Corinthians 6:9
3. Jude 1:4
4. Romans 3:23
5. Matthew 24:29, Revelation 7:14
6. Joel 2:30-31, Matthew 24:29,
   Revelation 6:12-14
7. Luke 21:28
8. II Timothy 3:12
9. 1 Peter 4:17-19
10. John 16:33
11. Revelation 12:12
12. Galatians 5:19-21

Chapter 15
1. Revelation 13:16-18
2. Daniel 11:31-32
3. Daniel 11:30-32
4. II Peter 2:20
5. Daniel 9:27
6. Revelation 13:16-17
7. Revelation 13:18
8. II Peter 2:17-22
9. Hebrews 10:26
10. Hebrews 10:29
11. Jude 1:1
12. John 6:37
13. John 8:31
14. II Thessalonians 2:11-12
15. Revelation 17:8
16. Acts 13:52
17. Ephesians 2:8

Chapter 16
1. Revelation 3:5
2. I John 2:16
3. Revelation 13:15
4. Revelation 3:5
5. Revelation 6:9-11
6. Matthew 24:15
7. John 9:4
8. I Timothy 4:1
9. John 14:6
10. II John 1:9
11. John 14:21, 15:23
12. I Timothy 4:16

Chapter 17
1. John 3:16
2. John 14:2-3
3. Revelation 1:7
4. Revelation 19:13
5. Revelation 13:8
6. Revelation 4:1
7. Isaiah 2:7
8. II Timothy 4:3-4

Chapter 18
1. Ephesians 6:12
2. II Timothy 3:1-5
3. II Timothy 2:11-12
4. Matthew 24:29, Matthew 24:27
5. Mark 13:14
6. Revelation 11:15
7. Revelation 13:14

Chapter 19
Colossians 1:13

Chapter 20

1. Daniel 12:11
2. Revelation 6:7-8
3. Revelation 6:9-11
4. Revelation 14:10
5. Joel 2:28-32
6. Joel 3:14-15, Isaiah 13:6-13
7. Revelation 12:12
8. Matthew 24:36
9. John 10:27-29
10. Matthew 24:10
11. Revelation 3:5
12. Ezekiel 3:20-21
13. Matthew 7:15
14. Revelation 14:11

Chapter 21

1. Galatians 4:16
2. Revelation 17:16
3. Revelation 14:6-7
4. Matthew 24:14
5. John 14:6
6. II Corinthians 5:17
7. Matthew 24:21-22

Chapter 22

1. I Thessalonians 4:15
2. Revelation 3:10-11
3. Revelation 8:1
4. Samuel 4:21
5. Mark 16:17-18
6. II Thessalonians 2:1-4
7. Luke 21:20
8. II Thessalonians 2:7
9. I John 2:28, Matthew 10:32-33
10. Revelation 12:11

Chapter 23

1. Ephesians 6:10-18
2. II Timothy 1:7
3. II Thessalonians 3:3
4. I John 4:4
5. II Corinthians 7:1
6. II Peter 3:4

Chapter 24

1. Revelation 13:2
2. Revelation 13:1, 17:7
3. Revelation 17:10
4. Revelation 13:3-4
5. Revelation 9:20
6. Revelation 19:20, 20:10
7. Revelation 12:7-14
8. Matthew 10:37-39
9. John 3:16

Chapter 25

1. Titus 2:11-13
2. I John 4:20

Chapter 26

1. Revelation 12:7-12
2. Revelation 14:6-7
3. Revelation 14:8
4. Revelation 14:9-10
5. Revelation 10:1-3
6. Revelation 11:15
7. Daniel 12:1-4
8. Luke 21:20
9. II Thessalonians 2:4, Matthew 24:15
10. II Thessalonians 2:9-12
11. Revelation 11:6
12. Revelation 11:10-11
13. Revelation 6:7-8
14. Isaiah 55:6-7
15. Isaiah 55:8-9, 11
16. Matthew 24:14
17. II Corinthians 4:4
18. Matthew 24:16-18
19. Zechariah 13:8
20. Revelation 6:7-8
21. Revelation 7:4-8
22. Ezekiel 20:34-35, 37

Chapter 27
1. II Thessalonians 2:4
2. Revelation 13:6-7
3. II Thessalonians 2:9-12
4. Matthew 5:6, 10-12
5. Revelation 11:3
6. Isaiah 55:11
7. Malachi 4:1, 5
8. Matthew 17:2-3
9. Revelation 11:5
10. Revelation 14:9-11
11. Revelation 9:20
12. Revelation 14:8
13. Luke 21:20

Chapter 28
1. Revelation 14:9-10
2. Revelation 3:16, 22:18-19
3. Galatians 5:7-8

Chapter 29
John 15:20

Chapter 30
1. Matthew 24:9, 25
2. Matthew 24:38-39
3. John 14:1

Chapter 31
1. John 17:17-21
2. II Corinthians 5:17
3. John 14:15-16

Chapter 32
1. John 13:35

Chapter 33
1. Revelation 14:12

Chapter 34
1. Revelation 6:9-11

Chapter 35
1. John 14:21, 23
2. Matthew 7:14

Chapter 36
1. Mark 13:11
2. Revelation 14:9-11
3. Matthew 24:33
4. Luke 21:16-17, 19
5. I Corinthians 3:18
6. Matthew 23:27-28

Chapter 37
1. Matthew 10:32-36
2. Matthew 24:45-46
3. Matthew 24:43
4. Matthew 24:48-51
5. Galatians 5:19-21
6. Romans 1:16

Chapter 38
1. Revelation 14:6
2. II Thessalonians 2:9, 11
3. Matthew 18:12

Chapter 39
1. Hebrews 11:5-13
2. Hebrews 12:5-6
3. I John 1:10
4. I John 3:6
5. Revelation 3:10
6. Luke 22:31-32
7. Acts 6:8, 7:1-59
8. I Corinthians 9:24-25
9. Psalm 91:11-12

Chapter 40
1. Revelation 7:14, 4:1
2. Mark 16:17-18
3. John 2:26-27
4. Romans 1:20

Chapter 41
1. John 4:10-14
2. Matthew 26:15
3. I Thessalonians 5:2-3
4. Hebrews 13:5
5. Matthew 10:32-33

Chapter 42

1. Revelation 16:13
2. Acts 4:12
3. Romans 10:9
4. Revelation 17:7
5. Joel 3:12-15, 2:28-32
6. Zechariah 14:2
7. Matthew 7:21
8. Matthew 7:22-23
9. Mark 11:25
10. John 15:13

Chapter 43

1. Revelation 6:12-13
2. Joel 3:12-13

Chapter 44

1. Isaiah 41:10

Chapter 45

1. John 15:5-8
2. Revelation 3:8

Chapter 46

1. Luke 21:25-28
2. Luke 21:31, 32, 36
3. Matthew 24:27
4. Matthew 24:31
5. I Corinthians 15:52
6. Revelation 7:14
7. Revelation 1:7
8. I John 2:28
9. Matthew 10:33
10. Isaiah 26:19
11. Revelation 7:16-17
12. Revelation 7:2-3
13. Revelation 7:4
14. Matthew 7:13-14, Luke 13:24
15. II Peter 3:9
16. Galatians 5:19-21
17. I Samuel 3:11-14

Chapter 47

1. Revelation 8:2
2. Revelation 8:5
3. Revelation 15:7
4. II Peter 3:10-14
5. Matthew 24:30-31
6. Luke 17:29-30
7. Revelation 8:10
8. II Thessalonians 2:8
9. I John 1:9

About the Author

Paul Bortolazzo is the founder and director of 7th Seal Ministries, a nonprofit ministry devoted to teaching God's truth concerning the Second Coming of Christ. A former pastor, missionary, and Bible teacher, Paul now teaches prophecy seminars throughout America and abroad. He is a graduate of the Assemblies of God Theological Seminary and has a Masters degree in biblical literature. Paul and his wife, Jenny, reside in Montgomery, Alabama.

7th Seal Ministries offers a variety of outreaches, including prophecy seminars, Bible conferences, and college and youth presentations. If you would like more information about this prophetic ministry or would like to schedule a seminar, please contact us. It would be a privilege to work with you by helping bring an end-times presentation to your church or area.

7th Seal Ministries
PO Box 241915
Montgomery, Alabama 36124-1915

bortjenny@juno.com
www.7thsealministries.org